IGNITE

Also by C. S. Doraga

RISE OF THE EMPRESS
Defy
Shatter

IGNITE

Book Three in the Rise of the Empress Series

C. S. Doraga

Dragon's Nest Books

To the many English teachers it took to persuade me to giving writing a try, because this book simply wouldn't exist without all of you.
Thank you!

The Mount
Imperial Capital
Hidden Gems
Agicae Mountains
The Diablo's Fangs
Diablo's Maw
The Diablo
The Diablo's Jaw
Poli
ERIDIAN EMPIRE

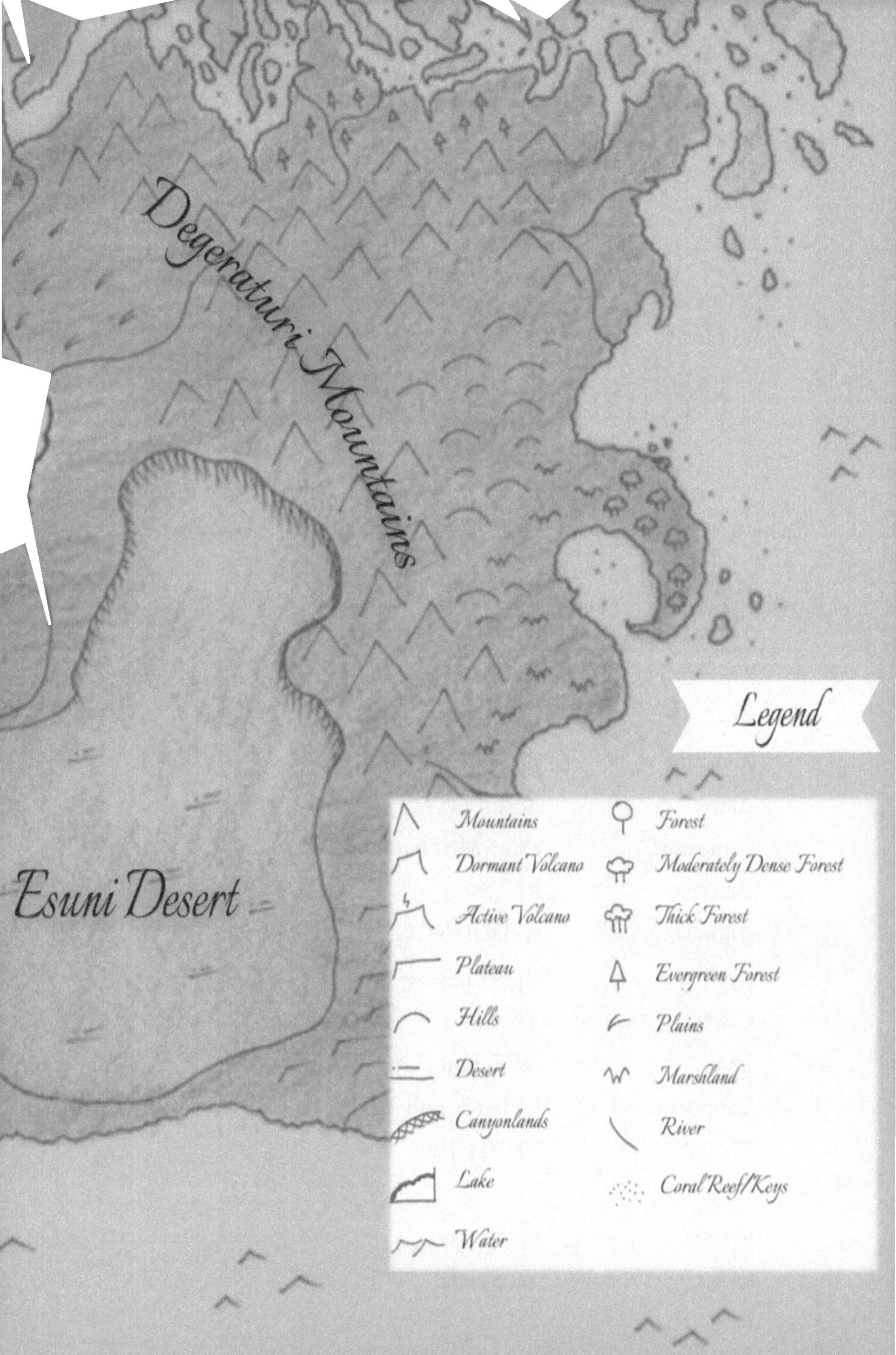

Degeraturi Mountains
Esuni Desert
Legend
Mountains
Dormant Volcano
Active Volcano
Plateau
Hills
Desert
Canyonlands
Lake
Water
Forest
Moderately Dense Forest
Thick Forest
Evergreen Forest
Plains
Marshland
River
Coral Reef/Keys

Pronunciation Guide

Cast:

Redrinna:	REH-dree-nah
Timothon:	ti-MUH-thawn
Tak:	tahk
Kyvo:	KEE-voh
Xandrin:	ZAN-drin
Astra:	A-shtrah
Chumani:	choo-MAH-nee
River:	RI-ver
Adonis:	ay-DOHN-is
Aretha:	ah-REE-thah
Calix:	KA-liks
Dion:	DEE-ohn
Leonora:	LEE-oh-noh-rah
Thala:	THAH-lah
Will:	wil
Matte:	MUH-tay
Osiris:	oh-SY-ris

Tehl:	tel
Athanasios:	ah-thah-NAH-see-ohs
Reyna:	RAY-nah
Andor:	AN-dohr
Cael:	kayl
Leon:	LEE-ohn
Kelvair:	KEL-vayr
Brion:	BREE-awn
Indigo:	IN-di-goh
Gaylon:	GAY-lohn
Sofronio:	soh-FRAH-nee-oh
Vivar:	VI-vahr
Takota:	dah-KOH-dah
Leander:	lee-AN-der
Cybill:	SI-bil
Nadeja:	nah-DAY-hah
Mato:	mah-DOH

Places:

Póli:	POH-lee
Manon:	MAN-ahn
Esuni:	eh-SOO-nee
Oriana:	oh-REE-ah-nah
Agicae:	A-ji-kay
Eridia:	eh-RI-dee-uh

Other:

| Kitsune: | ki-TSOO-neh |

Torijin:	TOH-ree-jin
Boyar:	BOI-yahr
Peplos:	PEHP-lohs
Pastitsio:	pas-STEE-see-oh
Souvlaki:	soo-VLAH-kee
Choriatiki:	hor-YAH-tee-kee
Kleftiko:	klehf-TEE-koh
Tiropita:	TI-roh-pi-tah
Bougatsa:	boo-GAHT-sah
Esunian:	eh-SOO-nee-ahn
Pelikyra:	peh-LEE-kaee-rah
Zamfir:	ZAM-feer
Gogola:	goh-GOH-lah
Hikarijin:	hee-KAH-ree-jin
Ioana:	ai-oh-AH-nah
Vasilica:	va-SIL-lee-kah
Luminiţa:	loo-mee-NEE-tah
Ardeleanu:	ahr-deh-LEH-noo
Eridian:	eh-RI-dee-an
Lykaios:	laee-KAEE-ohs

The Story Thus Far...

After being thrust from the only life she'd ever known, Imperial Princess Redrinna learned from the ghost of Timothon, her uncle and a past member of the Dragon Kin—a group of humans and dragons sworn to protect their homes—who told her the truth about the sinister creation of the Eridian Empire: it was orchestrated by Osiris—a man who sold his soul to a demon for power. He destroyed the first Dragon Kin and waged war after war to create the Empire for reasons known only to himself.

Redrinna's struggle to claim a Dragon Gem of her own and forge the Dragon Kin anew led her on a desperate mission to the destroyed Imperial City, which resulted in a confrontation with a weakened Osiris. Her triumph resulted in her becoming the first new member of the Dragon Kin.

Soon after, Redrinna was plagued by nightmares and sleepless nights, and she vowed she'd do anything to keep her friends from getting hurt regardless of the cost to herself. Tak, with a Dragon Gem calling for him, struggled to believe he was worthy of becoming a member. Both left the Mount with Xandrin to find a new dragon, harboring the hope that their adventure would be quiet and brief.

The dragon wasn't where the notes gifted to Redrinna from her father claimed it should be, so the trio began combing the forest. Tak discovered the dragon, but she dredged up painful memories and he kept it secret. While searching, they met Kyvo, a kistune once saved by

Redrinna, before happening across a circle of blood eerily similar to the one they'd discovered in the Imperial City. They were then beset by a mudslide before—when Tak set his feelings aside to save the new dragon, Astra—being attacked by Reyna, who, in attempt to kill Astra, severely injured Tak instead.

They fled to Astra's friends for help, a tribe of Torijin—winged humans—whose ancestors were the victims of a horrific genocide. As a result, Redrinna was shunned from the village, only being tolerated because of Tak's injuries.

When a demon that craved human flesh attempted to steal a child from the village, Redrinna intervened, earning her some of the village's respect in return. However, because of her success, a spirit then came to Redrinna to ask her to help rid the village of the beast.

Later, when examining her injuries, the healers of the village determined there was something supernatural about Redrinna—she possessed a strange healing ability, causing her wounds to heal at an accelerated rate.

The demon soon managed to snatch Redrinna and her friend, Chumani, which sent Tak into a wild frenzy. He was stopped by the dragons and Takota, but Reyna was the one who saved Redrinna from the demon's clutches. In desperation, Redrinna ran from the village to save Chumani before it would be too late. Tak attempted to stop her, only to be spurned by her anger.

With help from Kyvo and Takota, Tak set his fears and anxieties aside and, they too, went after Redrinna and Chumani.

When Redrinna returned to the demon's lair, she was stopped by Reyna, who trapped her and left. She was saved by Kyvo and Tak, who helped her realize the pain she was putting her friends and herself through. Together, with others from the Toriijin village and the dragons, they defeated demon and drove Reyna away.

After the fight, the spirit gifted Redrinna a sun-shaped mark on her hand but failed to explain what the mark was or what it was for. It simply said it would be something she needed.

In secret, Tak used his magic—which he'd once hated—to heal Kyvo's injuries. He and Redrinna promised each other that they would find a hobby to help them both deal with the pain of their pasts, and when they were mostly recovered, they returned to the Mount with their new friends in tow. They both vowed not to shut out their friends again...

Chapter One

A debt, even one that didn't count against you, was difficult to re-pay, especially when the person or creature you were indebted to was disinterested in compensation.

That was what Redrinna realized while staring at the pan of sea-soned eggs she cooked under Timothon's watchful eye. The flames beneath the pan glowed a bright red, the heat licking at Redrinna's hands, but she hardly noticed.

It'd been nearly two weeks since her time in the forest with their Torijin friends; nearly two weeks since her friends had saved her from herself. The one time she'd worked up the courage to ask Tak and Kyvo—the two who'd helped her at the most critical moment—what they wanted in return, they'd both said they were fine. They didn't want anything. They would be happy if she was happy, etc. She was grateful, but even still, she couldn't get rid of the urgent need to do or give them something.

She couldn't take their goodness and give them nothing in return.

Redrinna was so absorbed in her thoughts that she didn't notice a couple eggs fly out of the pan as she flipped a few, and a part of her mind registered her hope that she wasn't spacing out so much she'd burn the eggs again. They couldn't find things like eggs often, so they were a delicacy.

"Hey," Timothon said, picking up the bits of egg and dropping them back in the pan.

"Those are hot," she said absentmindedly.

Timothon stared at her for a second before touching his finger to the side of the hot pan. "I'm aware, but ghosts can't feel things like that, you know."

"Oh," was all she could think to say.

He studied her for a minute, and it looked like he was trying not to smile. "Is your head bugging you again?"

"No," she said, shaking her pain-free head. She'd gotten a concussion during their last adventure, but due to her newly realized healing powers, it was already pretty much gone. "I was just thinking."

"A dangerous way to spend your time, especially if there are eggs nearby."

That almost made her smile.

Once she decided the eggs were done and lifted them from the stove, her thoughts wandered back to her debt. So far, she'd been subtly sneaking Tak and Kyvo more of their favorite foods. It didn't feel like it made a dent in the debt that seemed to exist solely in her mind, but it was better than doing nothing.

While Timothon studied the eggs (he took her cooking instruction very seriously), Redrinna considered her two friends. So far, she'd discovered Kyvo seemed to adore berries—though he seemed to enjoy eating just about anything—and Tak seemed to enjoy bread the most. At the very least, it was one of the few things he'd consistently taken another helping of when they had it. Well, she also knew he loved fish, but Timothon hadn't let her cook any of that yet, and she wasn't sure she was ready to force it down. However, if it would be for the sake of her friends, the idea wasn't without its temptation.

"Well, they don't look half bad," Timothon said, cutting through the curtain of her thoughts.

Redrinna glanced at her eggs. She wasn't a great cook yet—she was just scratching the surface of the art, she'd realized—but they looked appetizing, at least. Especially considering this was only the second time she'd ever cooked eggs.

Timothon hefted their plate of bread and picked up the bowl of remaining berries. "You bring those," he pointed at the eggs with the berry bowl, "and then you guys can eat."

Redrinna nodded, carefully picking up the plate of steaming eggs before following Timothon out of the kitchen to the dining hall. The others were already there. Green-haired Tak watched Kyvo break up one of Xandrin and Astra's arguments, an amused smile lighting up his green eyes.

"Hey, enough of that. It's time to eat," Timothon called, getting everyone's attention.

Kyvo sprinted forward and vaulted onto the table, his face lighting up when he spotted Redrinna's plate of eggs. "Yay, more eggs!"

"You can't have them all," Tak said, a hint of a smile still playing at the corners of his mouth.

Kyvo's tail dropped a little, but he quickly said, "I-I know. I wasn't going to hog them all!"

Tak raised an eyebrow.

"This time," Kyvo added, ears lowered.

Even still, Redrinna and Timothon both set the food down closer to Tak than Kyvo.

Redrinna waited until the others had their food before grabbing some for herself, warmth bubbling up in her chest as her friends chatted and ate. How she'd ever thought pushing her friends away was what would make her happy was a mystery to her. Being here, being with them and all their craziness—that was what made her happy. It chased away the bad memories and regrets and stupid fears; it chased away the things she simply didn't want to think about, and that was how she liked it best. Though it did make her more aware of that sensation of owing each of them for what she'd put them through.

The food vanished in what seemed like minutes, and once Redrinna and Tak finished, they made their way to the training room. It felt like it'd been an age since Redrinna had been inside, and for a moment, she recalled her early days in here, training with Timothon. Back then, she'd barely been able to hold a sword but could now wield one with some level of comfort. That said, her skill paled in comparison to Tak's, and, because of his natural talent, it probably always would.

It almost made her smile to think that a few months ago, that had bugged her.

"So, what should we practice today?" Tak asked, his gaze traveling over the rack of wooden practice weapons.

Stepping up beside him, she frowned at the weapons. "It's been a while since we've done anything with lances," she said after a minute.

He nodded, and they both selected one from the rack. Then they stepped into the open center of the room and faced each other. The spear Redrinna had chosen felt nice in her hand, and if she was honest, she liked the feel of a lance far more than a sword.

Quickly, she shook that thought away as Tak lunged towards her, beginning the fight. With their spears, they jabbed and dodged, waiting for an opening. After a few stabs, Tak lunged at her again, missing her side by only inches. Taking advantage of that, Redrinna hooked her lance under his spearhead and jerked, not giving him a chance to adapt (because he could and would). His lance flew out of his hands, and she managed to catch it.

Grinning, she said, "I win!"

Tak frowned, but a smile tugged on the corners of his mouth after a moment. "Good job."

She tossed his lance back to him, and they started again. This time, within a matter of seconds, Tak somehow hooked the bottom of her lance and launched it out of her hands. She stared at him wide-eyed, and he stared at her lance with a similar expression.

"How did you do that?" she asked.

Cheeks going a bit red, he shrugged. "I-I don't know."

They spent the next few minutes trying to figure out what he'd done, and eventually they were able to replicate it. They practiced it a few times, adapting to it. Redrinna didn't honestly think they would ever need a technique like this, but it was kind of fun to figure out.

At some point, Kyvo had wandered in without either of them noticing, and all at once, he barked out, "You guys are doing this again?"

They both jumped, Tak having to scramble to keep hold of his lance.

"Hey, Kyvo," Redrinna said, doing her best not to laugh. "What are you up to?"

"Timothon's busy in the kitchen, Xandrin's napping, and Astra went out on one of her 'missions' again, so I'm bored," the kitsune huffed from where he sat near the door. Redrinna wasn't completely sure, but during the couple weeks they'd been cooped up in the Mount, she would've sworn he'd grown a couple inches. "So you guys have been training?"

She nodded. "Now that our headaches are gone, we can."

Hopping to his feet and padding over, Kyvo said, "Can I join?"

She paused, unease creeping into her chest. Right after that came that sharp prick that she owed him. "You...want to learn how to fight?"

He hesitated. "Well...not really, but last time we got in trouble, there wasn't anything I could do to help you guys without getting hurt. Since we're going to keep getting in trouble, I want to do my part."

"I don't know, Kyvo," she said despite knowing he made a good point. Even still, the idea of him plunging into danger gave her chills. He didn't have armor like them or the dragons, and she didn't know how to find or make any for him either. It would be so much harder to protect him in a fight, and even if he was better prepared, he would still be pretty vulnerable compared to the rest of them. "It'll be dangerous for you to try and fight like we do."

"Please?" he begged, staring at her with his massive, brown eyes. "I just want to help."

"You already are helpful, though," Tak put in. "You help me gather berries, and you're talented at finding us game and fish."

"Yeah, I know, but everyone else helps with the food plus extra too—even Timothon. All I do is help with food." Kyvo stamped his front paws, his tail swishing from side to side.

"You help with more than just the food," Redrinna added, almost smiling. "You help me and Tak with our studies too. Neither the dragons nor Timothon do that."

He frowned, not seeming convinced. "I guess."

Tak glanced at Redrinna, his green eyes almost sparkling in the Mount's light. "It wouldn't be a terrible thing to at least teach him how to protect himself, would it?"

A part of her acknowledged that, but at the same time, she couldn't help remembering Xandrin and Tak both getting seriously hurt while fighting. If Kyvo had been in either of their places, he would have died. While it might have satisfied that part of her that felt indebted to him, that wasn't a risk she was desperate enough to take.

However, she knew from the determination on Kyvo's face that he wasn't going to take no for an answer. But telling him no outright would crush him.

"Look Kyvo," she began slowly, "I'd rather you didn't have to fight at all, but...I'll think about it." That was fair, and knowing herself, she would think about it. A lot.

Kyvo's ears perked up even though it wasn't a yes, and Redrinna couldn't deny the guilt that bit at her. He raced out of the room and, from the sound of it, went to harass Timothon.

After a minute, Tak turned to her. "Do you not want Kyvo to fight that bad?"

Fear and shame waltzed through her chest, and she didn't turn to face him until she had them under control. "The kind of people we're fighting nearly managed to kill Xandrin and seriously wounded you, Tak. How do you think Kyvo is going to fare against people like that?"

He didn't answer right away, staring at her for a moment before lowering his gaze. "Not good."

She nodded.

Without warning, Tak lifted his gaze. "Especially if he doesn't know how to protect himself."

Speechless, she stared back, a little stunned. Ever since their misadventures in the forest, Tak had become more...open, in a way. But it was in moments like this, moments when he was brave enough to say what he thought, that Redrinna wasn't sure how to respond. It made her happy he was comfortable enough to speak his mind. At the same time, sometimes, he said things that struck like an arrow.

Her discomfort wasn't his fault; she knew that. However, as she glanced at the lance in her hand, it reminded her how much she hated this. She hated the fact they had to fight at all, that her friends had to keep putting their lives on the line, and that she couldn't do anything to stop it.

Even though sparring with Tak was fun, all at once, she wasn't in the mood for it anymore.

"Thanks for practicing with me," she said, returning her lance to the rack.

Tak didn't say anything, just watching her leave instead. She wasn't sure what emotion was on his face; it wasn't his usual concern, and it wasn't annoyance or shock. It was...something she couldn't place.

Shaking those thoughts away, she headed to the Hall of the Dragon Kin, a smidgeon of relief filling her chest once she was surrounded by the rainbows from the stained-glass windows.

You're not mad at Tak, are you? her gem asked.

Frowning, Redrinna tugged the end of the ponytail that hung over her shoulder, eyeing the vivid red of her hair for a moment before tossing it aside. "No, I'm not mad."

I see.

"Is it wrong of me to not want Kyvo to fight?" she asked after a minute, gaze on the ground.

Not necessarily. That said, I could see why someone might think it was.

Sighing, Redrinna reached up and fingered the second necklace hanging from her neck, the necklace that had once been her mother's.

There was a price to fighting, one Redrinna was familiar with and one she'd already had to pay. If she let Kyvo fight... She couldn't help the terror that seized her chest at the idea that he, in all his sweet, well-intentioned innocence, would have to pay it too. She couldn't stand the idea of that happening to him; she couldn't stand the idea of failing Kyvo like that.

Pressing her hands to her chest, right above her heart, Redrinna squeezed her eyes shut. This was another reason she'd never believed she was cut out to be an empress—or any kind of leader for that matter. Leaders had to be prepared to make hard calls, maybe even harsh calls, because a nation's safety had to come before any single individual's, even if that life was the life of someone close to her. She wasn't supposed to let her heart rule—she wasn't supposed to let her fear be what guided her.

"I've never wanted to be an empress for a good reason," she whispered, more to herself than the gem. "I'm too much of a coward to do it well."

∽◉ ◉∾

It took Tak some time to find Kyvo after his and Redrinna's abrupt end to training. The kitsune had harassed Timothon for a few minutes before vanishing, and neither of the dragons had seen him since breakfast.

After a while of searching, Tak found him perched in one of the windowsills in the library, staring out at the vivid green mountains towering around them.

"Kyvo?" he said.

The kitsune glanced back, and as Tak had suspected, that downcast expression he'd tried to hide earlier was back. "What?"

Tak gave the end of Kyvo's tail a light, playful tug. "Are you okay? You seemed a bit upset earlier after what Redrinna said."

"Oh that." Kyvo turned his head back to the window, hiding that expression Tak kept noticing flickers of. "No. I was just thinking."

Tak hesitated for a second before he leaned against the windowsill. He'd been about to speak but something about the way Kyvo stared outside made him pause. Instead of speaking, he waited instead.

At length, Kyvo said, "Do you think Redrinna doesn't think I can fight good enough to help?"

"I don't think that's the reason," Tak replied, watching Kyvo as he spoke. "I think she's just scared for you and wants to protect you."

Kyvo's ears drooped a little. "But I want to be able to protect you guys too! You guys always protect me, and having to just sit by and watch is so frustrating. It makes me feel small." Kyvo's eyes flicked in Tak's direction. "Well, smaller."

The corners of Tak's mouth tugged upwards.

"I want to be big and strong—like you and Xandrin and Astra. Redrinna lets all of you fight, so why not me too?"

Tak paused, thinking before he answered. It wasn't necessarily true Redrinna let him and the dragons fight; it was more that she'd resigned herself to it because she knew she wouldn't be able to stop them. Though, while Tak wasn't sure how much truth there was in Kyvo's belief that he was physically strong, something his aunt had once told him about his uncle came back to him.

"You know, Kyvo," he began slowly, the kitsune gazing at him with big, mournful eyes, "I don't think physical strength is the best strength. Someone once told me true strength is something inside of you, a part of you that can't be broken no matter what comes your way. It's the ability to overcome anything that's thrown at you."

Kyvo just stared at him, not seeming at all swayed by his aunt's words.

"And you know, Kyvo, I think you have that kind of strength. It's quiet, so I don't think Redrinna has noticed it yet. But she will. Just...give her some time, okay?"

"Yeah." Kyvo all but sighed. Even still, his ears lifted slightly, and some of his usual light returned to his eyes as he returned his attention to the world outside.

Tak's did too as he stewed on his aunt's words. He'd thought he'd understood what she'd meant once, but now that he was older and had experienced more things, he couldn't help wondering if he really did. He thought he had, but a few months ago, he'd been on the brink of giving up on everything and had only been saved by chance. At the very least, he took that to mean he didn't have the kind of strength his aunt had been talking about.

Even still, Kyvo had a point. Tak was stronger now; thanks to Timothon's training and the fact he could eat as much as he pleased, he'd gotten a lot stronger already—at least physically.

However, back in the forest, Tak hadn't been able to protect anyone—not Redrinna, not Chumani, and not Kyvo. Despite the fact he'd become stronger, he couldn't help wondering if he would be able to protect his friends from danger. If they got into a similar situation as their last adventure, could his new strength keep things from getting out of control? He wasn't sure, but this time, he wasn't afraid.

Chapter Two

Pausing, River tugged his hood lower over his brow and adjusted his scarf. After rolling his head from side to side, he slipped out the side door and onto the streets, holding his sack close as he stalked through the town blanketed in early morning quiet. It wasn't a calm quiet; it was the quiet like a deep but fast river, the calm surface disguising the danger lurking beneath.

He turned towards the street, the sharp tang of the salty sea breeze biting his nose. He ignored it. He glanced around him, moving his head as little as possible. Once he was certain the streets were empty, he moved. His steps were swift and silent while his gaze flicked from one shadow to the next, watching for the slightest sign of movement.

There was none. So far.

Right as he thought that, he heard the scuff of a boot in the alley directly ahead. Immediately, he turned into the alley two steps back, ducking behind a heap of trash. The rancid smell from the garbage seemed to cling to everything it touched: the wall, the earthen street, even him. While he waited, he flicked away the couple flies that ventured too close to his sack.

After another minute, a pair of white attired soldiers passed, walking in sync. Despite their relaxed air, there was a tension in their shoulders, a wariness to the way their eyes darted from shadow to shadow.

Even the soldiers sensed the undercurrents.

Under his breath, River counted the paces of the soldiers, waiting until they'd turned the corner before continuing on his way. He headed towards the barren main square, the place devoid of life since the sun was just peeking its head over the mountains towering over the city, their dark, jagged outlines framing the horizon like teeth.

The square was empty due to the hour, but even still, a chill raced up his spine at the square's centerpiece—a large wooden platform with a dark stain at the front. The reality of what would happen to him if his grandfather ever found out what River was doing was always on his mind, but whenever he saw that platform, it was like the blade was already coming for his throat. Despite the resolve he had whenever he snuck out, that stand always made him hesitate.

He stopped at the short wall bordering the square and gazed at the blue gray of the ocean, the water seeming to stretch on forever. His gaze slipped downwards, to the rest of the city, hidden in deep shadow. Unlike the upper half that surrounded him, down there, the buildings crumbled, little more than decayed shacks. People lay passed out in dirty, narrow alleyways, and—unlike the upper half of the city—tired, slumped men and women were already leaving their homes for another grueling day of work at the quarry and docks.

River gritted his teeth before shaking his frustration away and hopping over the wall. He landed on the thin lip of land, keeping his right hand on the wall in case he slipped. When he had his balance and made sure one more time there were no soldiers in sight, he descended to the city below.

Despite the fact he only had three functioning limbs, River was getting faster at scaling the cliff face. While his prosthetic arm couldn't support his weight, it was useful for helping with balance, at least.

As he descended, the sea air mixed with the rancid smell of human waste and filth. Once his feet were back on the ground, he tugged his scarf over his nose to mask the smell and lessen the chance of being recognized by someone. Before he set off, his gaze slid to the other half of the city crouched on the cliff above like a hungry vulture, and that uneasiness grew a bit stronger.

Shaking that thought away, River resumed walking, continuing at a confident, steady pace. While most of the people down here kept their heads lowered, a few hopeful eyes watched him from the shadows and alleyways, eyes far too old to be in faces so young. Even still, he kept his sack close. As much as it pained him to withhold what was inside, he couldn't give it to every poor person he saw. It wouldn't go far enough, and even though it stung, the people he had to prioritize were the people he cared about most.

A few minutes later, River arrived at his destination: a dingy, run-down inn, rust and rot hiding any sign of its former glory. Its front door clung on by just one rust-caked hinge like a stubborn mule that refused to budge.

Careful to avoid bumping the door, he slipped into the building. Dust covered the floors and decaying remains of furniture while cobwebs were strung between the rafters like pearls around a wealthy woman's neck. Without sparing any of that a second glance, River slipped into the back room, scooted a large spider out of his way, popped the hatch in the far corner, and descended the steep staircase without a sound. When he pulled the hatch closed, he was left in complete darkness. After tugging his scarf off his face, River reached out and rapped two fingers against the wall three times. After a pause, two taps rung out in response. He responded with one. The wall to his left slid open, weak firelight illuminating the tiny space in which he stood.

A tall, aging man with sparse, gray hair stared at River like he was a ghost before seeming to shake himself and pull the door open enough for River to slip in.

"River," the man breathed, "what are you doing? If that man finds out you're out again, he'll—"

"I know," he replied, keeping his voice mild, almost conversational. There were some things that were easier to do if one didn't consider the consequences of things going awry.

His gaze flicked to the rest of the room, filled with tables and chairs and a crumbling kitchen. At the tables sat several men and a handful of women, all of whom bore the rough and tumble appearance of people who'd been making a living on the streets for a long time. The Noble Renegades, they liked to call themselves. River thought the play on their former status was too on the nose to be as clever as they liked to think, but even still, it was the only glimmer of their former lives that remained. So he was content to keep his thoughts to himself.

Despite how big and burly they were, River wasn't the least bit intimidated, and they simply watched him in silence for a moment before returning to their conversations. As River made his way to the furthest table, where a large man with a mane of untamed curly hair and a rough, close-cut beard sat—watching his every move like a hawk—he caught snippets of the conversations, whispers of how they could disrupt an upcoming slave sale, plans on how to reduce the crime rate in the poor sector, ideas for keeping everyone fed—the usual topics of interest in a greasy, washed-up has-been of a town like Póli.

"Kid, what are you doing?" the gruff man said, swirling the dregs in his cup. "You got a death wish?"

"Perhaps," River replied as he set his sack on the table. "But this was going to the garbage, so I figured you could try and make something of this, Adonis. Better than the rats would, at any rate."

All at once, a woman with deep black hair woven into a tight, braided crown hurried out of a back room, soot smeared over her face and hands. Aretha, Adonis' wife. Her dress was ragged, bearing deep stains that would never come free. It was still a shock to River that there were nobles—even if they were ex-nobles—who didn't care about whether or not their hands were dirty so long as work was done. Nobles who worked at all were a foreign concept to him.

"River!" the woman cried as she reached him, ignoring the sack and hugging him like he was her own son. Her grip was tight enough to make his wounds shoot fire up his back. He didn't cry out, but he exhaled sharply, sharp enough he knew Adonis and Aretha would know he'd been whipped again.

Aretha released him, a cool gleam in her critical gaze. "So the rumors were true—that beast beat you again."

River stared at the swirls in the wood table, choosing not to answer.

Adonis leaned forward. "Is it true you nearly cracked open that noble's skull when he tried to get fresh with your sister?"

River met his gaze. "It's not my fault he panicked, fell, and hit his head on the ground like an idiot."

A sardonic kind of smile tugged at Adonis' mouth.

"You stupid boy," Aretha said, though her tone was affectionate. "Always too worried about someone else to take care of yourself."

Ignoring that, River pushed the sack her way.

Her eyes widened as she opened the sack and revealed the pathetic, shriveled fruits and wilted vegetables. "River, you know we're grateful, but you shouldn't have. If he catches you again—"

"It doesn't matter. It was all bound for the garbage anyway, so I doubt he'll notice," River said. "Besides, with how many are going hungry, what I brought isn't going to make much of a difference."

With a sigh, she rested her dirt-smeared hands on his shoulders. "River, I love you, but you are the most depressing child I know." She gently rapped her knuckles against his head.

Adonis shifted, calling River's attention back to him. "By the way, River, since you're here, I thought you'd been interested to know our messengers returned."

"Calix and Dion are back?"

Adonis' shoulders stiffened, setting River on edge and priming him for bad news. "Well, not Calix. But Dion, yes."

River frowned, his heart clenching even though it had already sunk a little deeper into all-too-familiar despair. "Not Calix?"

Leaning forward, Adonis gazed at him with unnerving intensity, the weak firelight highlighting the man's tanned cheekbones. "According to Dion, they made it to the Imperial City to petition the royal family like we'd hoped, 'cept the city's destroyed. Everybody's dead."

"What?" River stared blankly at him, struggling to process that. His heart, while prepared for this kind of news, seemed to sink another inch into the mires of misery.

"Dion said Calix touched something in the city square, something that looked like it was drawn in blood. The second he did, a massive, shadowy beast came after him." Adonis lowered his voice to the barest whisper. "There wasn't anything left of him. Dion had no choice but to leave and come straight back here."

River's gaze fell, his head dropping a fraction. "So if the princess was there, she's dead."

"It's too soon to give up hope, River," Aretha said, raking him over with her stern gaze. "Dion mentioned the destruction didn't seem to reach the palace, so she might be alive yet. Or she could have gotten away. There's still a chance."

River didn't respond. After how long he'd been here, he no longer entertained such fleeting fancies of hope; more often than not, they led to disappointment. And he'd already had enough disappointment to last the rest of his life.

"We're not quitting," Adonis said. "So long as we draw breath, there's still a chance we can take Póli back from the corrupt hands that stole it."

"That's right," Aretha said, putting her hands on River's shoulders again. "My grandmother always used to say that no matter how bad things get, it's important to remember the night is darkest right before dawn. We're going to take this city back yet."

River said nothing. She wouldn't like his honest thoughts.

All at once, ringing out from the world above, bells pealed across the city, their chimes both bright and mournful. River's heart skipped a beat. The morning bells; he'd stayed too long.

As he turned to leave, Aretha caught his hand. "River, you don't have to go. We can hide you here."

"Leonora is still there, and besides," River pulled his hand away, "in a world as empty as ours, it doesn't matter where I go. Everywhere's the same."

"River!" Aretha called, but he left.

Hastily pulling his scarf back over his face, River hurried out of the hideout and into the crowds heading to work. A part of him was still numb from the news, while the rest of him was numb because that was what the news always was—there was little disappointment to be had when it was what he'd expected from the moment he'd heard the Noble Renegades had planned to get in touch with the Imperial Family personally.

All at once, as he hurried along, a shadow fell across his face, making him glance up. It took him a second to realize the shadow came from the upper hill of the city, cast by the execution stand. His insides got a little colder.

There was no hope here, not for him. He'd learned that lesson a long time ago.

☙ ❧

Thala flicked a strand of her bizarre, turquoise hair out of her face as she yanked on the spiky weed stubbornly wedged into the earth, the soil so hard from the lack of rain that it snapped off at the root. She dug around it as best she could, only managing to get a little bit more before she surrendered and moved onto the next, repeating the process over and over. It was normal for it not to rain in the summer, but summer had barely begun, and they hadn't seen a drop of moisture since winter.

Fortunately, the crops Her Highness had recommended they try growing had sprung up with surprising eagerness considering what little moisture the farmers were able to give them, meaning they might have a decent harvest come fall. Provided they could get enough water to keep the plants alive as the heat intensified.

As Thala thought about Her Highness, she wondered if Adonis' plan to tell the Imperial Family directly about what was wrong with their city would work. If it didn't, she wasn't sure how much longer the city would last before it came crashing down around their ears. More than that, she wished she could think that with some degree of panic. Instead, she felt nothing, the numbness so strong, it was like her emotions simply didn't exist.

Her thoughts wandered as she attacked the weeds as best she could, ignoring the heat as the sun rose, warming the air and chasing the early morning shade away. They'd be called from the field soon, and Thala intended to earn every leaf she'd been promised by working diligently, no matter how many beads of sweat she swiped from her eyes.

Sometime later, they were called from the fields so everyone could escape the heat. Work would resume towards sunset, which meant it was time for Thala to collect her earnings and be on her way. The farmer in charge only hired girls and women in the morning, not at night.

Thala didn't care either way. She simply joined the line with the others, and when it was her turn, she humbly accepted the meager amount the farmer was able to give her.

"Thank you for always working hard, Thala," the man murmured, pressing an extra leaf in her hand, the metal disc already warm from the heat.

For a moment, she glanced up, meeting his gaze, his eyes old and tired—not the eyes of a man who wasn't yet fifty. Then again, ever since the war had ended, and his two children who'd been abducted and forced into it hadn't returned home, his eyes had born that look.

Meekly, she dipped her head and continued on her way.

"Wait up," called a familiar voice, familiar enough to make her pause and turn back. Her cousin and friend, Will, hurried towards her as he pocketed his own meager leaf.

The sun caught on the warm olive tones of his skin, darkened from the many hours they'd spent in the sun. Thala wasn't as dark as him, but she hadn't spent anywhere near the same amount of time in the elements. His dark hair swept in front of his eyes, and he tossed it aside with a flick of his head.

Staring at him, waiting for him to catch up, Thala found herself fingering the end of her own hair, her fingers pinching the end of her braid dangling behind her back. Another mystery: once, she and Will had almost looked like siblings, but now her hair and eyes were a bizarre shade of blue, a bright blue that nearly matched the shade of the nearby lagoon.

As Will arrived, a little kid ran past them, flinging himself into the arms of a dirt-coated man who'd just come out of the fields. They were both grinning and laughing despite how tired the man appeared, and their smiles didn't fade as they joined a weary woman in the line, waiting for their meager pay.

Thala watched them for a minute, a strange sensation uncoiling inside her. It was a longing, almost, a burning desire to be able to feel whatever they were. She didn't care what the emotion was; she just wanted to be able to *feel*.

Instead, as she watched, there was only the numbness in her chest, the hollow cavity that had been left behind all those years ago.

"There's no point in lookin'," Will said, putting a hand on her shoulder and turning her around. "It's not gonna feed you."

Thala nodded and followed him down the benches of the mountainside, heading back to Póli. They took the long way, avoiding the upper half of the city entirely as they headed to the noisy and bustling docks, the salty brine thick in the air. Their leaves managed to secure them the last couple fish from that morning's catch. It wasn't much, but Aretha and the others could put it to good use.

"At least the fish seem to be eating well, eh?" Will said, glancing her way with a hint of a smile.

She studied her plump fish wrapped in waxy palm leaves. "Yeah."

All at once, a commotion in a nearby alley—a couple, gruff, almost menacing voices and a younger, quivering one, pleading for mercy—rang out. Thala stopped at the entrance to the alley, Will stopping with her, both of them staring down the narrow, dirty street. Two men with knives had a little boy cornered—pinned to the ground—and from the blood on his lip, Thala could tell he'd already been beaten.

Before either her or Will could move, the boy saw her, his face going pale as a sheet.

The two men paused before glancing over their shoulders. They went pale as well.

"The Azure Demon," they hissed.

Scrambling to sheath their knives, they ran. A few seconds later, the boy scurried away as well, though he was smart enough to vanish in a different direction.

She blinked. "At least my face is good for something."

Will snorted.

While muggings were pretty commonplace in the lower sector of the city, no one was brave enough to try it in her presence since they thought she would kill them before they could even blink. Which she could. Though, if she was honest, she never wanted to have to shed another drop of human blood ever again. In a city like this, she wasn't sure it was possible, but so far, since she'd returned, she'd been able to avoid taking another human life.

That didn't mean there hadn't been a few close calls though.

As they arrived at the hideout, Thala shook those thoughts away. The scuffles she'd gotten into paled in comparison to the lives they'd saved. Even still, despite the fact she didn't feel much—not anger, not sadness, not happiness—when she allowed herself to admit it, there was one emotion she knew: fear. A fear of the monster she'd been turned into and could become in the blink of an eye. A fear that it would rear its head and take control before she could stop it. A fear that if it came back, it would never let go again.

There was a solemn air clinging to the hideout like a stench that had been absorbed by the old wood, but Thala didn't learn anything from a sweeping glance of the room. While the Noble Renegades tolerated her, she knew many were unnerved by her presence despite the fact that if her dad had still been alive, he would've been one of them.

Even still, while crashing with them wasn't much, at least they let her eat and sleep under a roof. She was a fish out of water among them, but Will wasn't. However, she supposed it made sense; he was the son of the late boyar, the man who'd been murdered so the current boyar could be where he was. Will had grown up around the Noble Renegades before they'd become a gang, and in a way, he was one of them.

Silently, she padded after Will and added her fish to his in the makeshift kitchen. A glance in the pot hanging near the fire told her there were only a few swallows left of breakfast, and, to her surprise, a couple vegetables lingered in the broth.

Will must've noticed too. "Is River here?" he asked the room at large.

"Came and went already," someone called back.

"Will! Thala!" Aretha cried as she came out of the back room, hurrying over and hugging the two of them like they had been gone more than just a few hours. That said, this was Aretha's way, and Thala didn't entirely mind. "We managed to save some for you. It's not much, but it'll keep you going."

"Thanks," Will said with a grin.

Thala blinked at her. "River came?" It'd been nearly two weeks since the last time he'd been able to break out of his grandfather's mansion—and he'd been caught that time.

Aretha seemed to catch Thala's unasked questions. "He did, but that beast of a man gave him a sound lashing for last time. He's still in pain."

From where Adonis sat at his usual table, he said, "At this rate, I think that boy is going to die from pure misery, and the boyar is going to dance on his grave when it happens."

"Don't talk like that," Aretha snapped, but Thala could tell from her tone she believed what Adonis said too.

"Maybe I should go visit him," Will suggested casually, like breaking into the manor to see River and Leonora was akin to taking an ocean swim.

"That's asking for trouble," Adonis said, though Thala noted he didn't object, something he did quite often when it came to Will and his ideas.

"I don't want to hear about you breaking in places you shouldn't be, young man," Aretha snapped, pointing an accusing finger at Will, who leaned back an inch or two. "I remember when you used to be the sweetest little boy with no dangerous, criminal habits whatsoever."

Will grinned again, but it lacked humor. "That was back when I had parents and a house. Besides, my current habits, however dangerous, keep me alive. How else do you expect me to survive—on hopes and dreams?"

Aretha didn't say anything, her mouth pressed into a line. Even still, she ruffled Will's shaggy hair in an affectionate way.

Thala watched, staying mute, the numbness inside her more pronounced than ever.

Chapter Three

Tak parted the bushes with a long stick he'd found, hunting for berries. Kyvo pranced a little ways ahead, his nose high in the air as he searched too, while Astra trailed after, her gaze seeming to rove at random. Tak paused in his hunt to watch as Kyvo squirmed into a thick patch of brush.

"There's some in here!" the kitsune cried. "Oh, but there are bugs all over these ones. Never mind." With a great deal of tail thrashing, the kitsune squirmed back out.

After a few more minutes of searching while the sun's light gradually illuminated the woods around them, they stumbled across a tree bursting with bright, red serviceberries.

"Wow, they look so good!" Kyvo squeaked.

Astra scooped the kitsune up. "You don't get to help pick since you eat more than you help."

Kyvo's ears drooped, making Tak smile. Then he pulled out Redrinna's knife (it bothered him that he had to keep borrowing her weapons for everything) and set to work on harvesting just enough berries to last them a couple days.

By the time he finished, the sun had almost cleared the mountain peaks overhead, and Kyvo had forgotten his serviceberry sorrows by finding a patch of raspberries. Tak made sure to grab a few of those too while Astra fought to fish the kitsune out of the brambles.

When his basket was filled and Kyvo was full enough he sprawled out for a nap in a pale sunbeam slanting through the trees, Tak sat on a log.

Astra glanced at the two of them. "You'll be all right while I hunt?"

"We'll be fine," Tak said.

She nodded, hesitated a little, then nodded again and left. He smiled before pulling out his project: a little piece of wood he was determined to carve into a decent bird. When he and Redrinna had made that promise to find a hobby, it'd taken him a few days to even think of something. However, he'd recalled his uncle carving little animals out of wood for him and his aunt and had subsequently decided to give it a try.

Tak was awful at it if he was honest, but the last bird he'd taken a crack at had at least looked like a bird, unlike the first one.

Regardless, he was determined to get good enough to carve something special for Redrinna. She seemed convinced that she owed him, but as far as he was concerned, it was the other way around. She didn't think much of her kindness, but he did and wanted to do something meaningful to show his gratitude.

Woodcarving wasn't much, but it was something he could do and something that would be his. Well, if he ever got good at it.

Compared to Redrinna, Tak wasn't all that special; he knew that. She was the princess. She was the one who hadn't been handed a gem—she'd fought for it instead. She was the one who worked so hard to master the weapons put in her hands that she understood them in a way Tak did not. In the Torijin village, Redrinna had been the strong one and the one to earn the attention, and in all honesty, Tak was okay with that.

He was okay being the invisible member of the Dragon Kin, the one that lived in the shadows of the others and supported them from behind the scenes. He was okay being the unimportant one so long as he got his fair chance to show his gratitude to the person who'd altered the course of his life forever. Perhaps, if he was eventually able to do that, then he'd find that strength his aunt had talked about.

Yellow sunlight brightened the woods around Tak as he worked, his focus on the knife as he cut away little chunks of wood. The lump in his hands slowly took on the blocky shape of a bird, decent enough he could even recognize it as one. It lacked any detail, but at least it was bird-like, he supposed.

Astra returned shortly with a couple rabbits, and once they had Kyvo awake, they returned to the Mount. Tak kept his bird out of sight, embarrassed at the idea of anyone seeing it, even Astra. Perhaps he'd show someone someday, but not just yet.

⁂

Redrinna frowned as she pulled today's bread from the oven. The loaves were a little too brown again, but at least they weren't burnt this time. At least there was that.

Timothon studied her bread as she set it on the table, not saying anything until she had all of them out. "These were almost perfect this time."

She scowled at the bread a little as she closed the oven door. "Every time I think I'm getting it, I mess it up."

He shrugged. "It's only been a couple weeks, you know. Plus, bread is difficult to make. It just seems easy when I do it because I have years of experience."

She shrugged too, doing her best not to overthink it. It was just bread, after all.

"The others aren't back yet, are they?" he asked, glancing towards the kitchen door.

"I don't think so."

Turning back, Timothon met her gaze. "It's been a minute since you and I have been able to chat without distractions."

A part of Redrinna considered running away, but she restrained the urge. She didn't want to hide from her uncle and friends anymore.

"So your head really is doing okay?" he asked. "Still no headaches?"

"No headaches. I really am fine."

"Even when you're training?"

She nodded. "I haven't had them then, either."

"That's good. Since you and Tak are both getting back on your feet, you're going to be heading out again soon, right?"

"That's right." In truth, Redrinna wasn't sure if she was ready to head out again, but she couldn't shake the memory of Matte saying there wasn't much time left for them to stop Osiris. That was why the spirit had saved her.

Besides, staying in the safety of the Mount wouldn't keep bad things from happening; it would make them worse.

"Where will you be going this time?" Timothon asked.

"South," she answered. "To the coastlands there. That's where the next closest dragon is."

Nodding, he stared off to the side for a moment before he met her gaze again. "More importantly, how are you doing? Are you still having those nightmares?"

Redrinna didn't answer right away, a part of her still frustrated at how often she still bolted awake in a cold sweat. The severity of the nightmares was easing, but they were different than they'd been before. Instead of just Osiris, she saw things like Two Face or the people she cared about disappearing or dying.

"Sometimes," she said, dropping her gaze.

"You're not coming and finding me as often though, which is good. It means you're having them less?" He asked that like he was double-checking in case she'd been lying.

Which to be fair, she'd spent a good month doing exactly that.

Redrinna nodded in response to his question.

When she had nightmares now, she'd found that if she went and sat with Timothon for a while, she could eventually go back to sleep.

It made her feel childish, but at the same time, something about being with him or the others helped the nightmares go away, and she was tired enough of having sleepless nights that she didn't mind. Fortunately, neither did her friends.

Slowly, she met his gaze again. "Do they ever go away?"

Timothon almost smiled, but not quite. "Yeah."

Before either of them could say anything else, Kyvo vaulted onto the table.

"Hey!" Redrinna snatched him off before he could steal any of the bread.

For some reason, it made him grin. "Good morning!" Then he licked her face.

Recoiling, she dropped him, and he promptly proceeded to prance around her feet.

"It smells so good, so I couldn't help it!" he said, eyes sparkling. "Can I have one? Please, please, please?"

Doing her best to hold back a smile, Redrinna scrubbed at the cheek he'd slobbered. "You can when we have breakfast with everyone else."

"Well, we just got back. See?" The kitsune turned to the door right as Tak entered with a basket in his arms. The basket was the one they'd been given by their Torijin friends, and since they hadn't been able to take it back yet, they'd figured they might as well put it to good use.

Redrinna grinned at the sight of her friend with his dark green eyes and wild hair. The glowing green gem hanging from his neck accentuated his features, and she was once again struck by the realization of how much healthier he looked now compared to when they'd first met. His cheeks were no longer hollow, and there was a kind of glow to his skin. That made her happy.

Tak stared at them all staring at him before he smiled shyly and set the basket on the table. "We found some raspberries and serviceberries. It should be enough."

"Wow, you found tons," Timothon said, inspecting the bumpy red fruits and little, dark purple berries.

"Astra managed to catch a few rabbits, so she's having Xandrin cook one for us," Tak continued. With a good-natured grimace, he added, "She said she didn't want to wait for Timothon to teach Redrinna how to cook it."

Redrinna almost laughed, and even Timothon cracked a smile.

"I'm starving!" Kyvo chirped as he dashed out of the room.

Redrinna shook her head as he left before she pulled out the big plate they always used to carry bread, wondering once again where it'd come from. To be fair, there were lots of things in the Mount that Redrinna couldn't help wondering where they came from, but the gems were coy with those answers.

As she placed the still warm loaves on the platter, Tak fetched a bowl while Timothon washed a few berries. They worked in companionable silence for a couple minutes before Tak approached her, holding out the bowl of berries.

"What do you think?" he asked in his quiet voice.

Redrinna studied the berries, trying to picture the portions in her head. Since the dragons didn't like berries (Xandrin said they were so small, he couldn't taste them)... "Yes, that seems about right."

Smiling, he picked up the bowl and left the kitchen.

She scooped up her platter and followed.

Timothon fell in line with her. "He's grown a lot recently, don't you think?"

She nodded, her gaze following after Tak. Right before he disappeared into the dining room, she managed to snatch one last glance at him.

He'd grown since they'd first met, much closer to Timothon's height now than when he'd first arrived, and he'd filled out a bit. She still remembered how painfully thin he'd been before, and it was such a relief he was healthier.

Moreover, after their last adventure, there seemed to be

something else about him that had changed, something Redrinna couldn't quite place. He seemed more...confident, almost. There was a presence to him, an air that hadn't been there before, almost like he was able to be his true self. If nothing else, he was more talkative and would actually tell her what he was thinking instead of keeping it to himself—as she'd been reminded just the other day.

"There was something else I wanted to talk to you about before the others arrived," Timothon said then, his voice quieter than it'd been before. "I didn't think you'd want to talk about it in front of them, so since they're gone, I'm going to talk to you about it now."

Redrinna stopped, worry making her chest cinch tight. "That's an ominous way to start a conversation."

Timothon smiled a little before he turned to face her. "Your little group is getting bigger, and without someone in charge, it could easily fall apart. I know you're not going to like this...but I think that person should be you."

A thrill of panic raced up her spine as she turned away. "You're right, I don't like that."

"Even still, you can't just run away from things like this. It's not going to go away because you ignore it. Besides, the reason I said you should be the leader is because the others already view you as one. They already trust you, and I'm sure they'd follow you anywhere—to your credit. That's no mean feat, you know."

"I do know that, but..." Redrinna couldn't keep a grimace off her face. After all the mistakes she'd made and what she'd already put her friends through, they deserved a better leader than her. "I really... I can't do this."

"No?" he asked, tilting his head to the side. A smile tugged at one corner of his mouth. "Hey, it's not like I'm asking you to lead an entire empire again."

That almost got her to laugh.

"You don't have to do anything more than you're already doing, you know," Timothon continued. "So far, this is enough. I just wanted you to think about it and prepare yourself for the road ahead. Things are going to get worse, but there are some things you can do now that will make those things easier to handle."

Redrinna lowered her gaze, a chill racing up her spine. It wasn't the same sensation she'd gotten when she'd used to think about taking over the Empire, but it wasn't far off either.

"Hey, I know it's not fun or anything, but I believe you would be a good leader. You're smart, kind, and determined, and those things go a long way, you know."

"But leaders are the kind of people who have to make sacrifices and hard calls—and they're the ones who become the targets of blame no matter what they do. I think I'm too reckless for all of that." Redrinna didn't want to mention she was simply too scared.

"Ah yes," Timothon mused, hiding a smile, "you do tend to rush into things, don't you?"

She stared at him for a moment before sticking her tongue out at him.

He laughed. Then they were serious again.

"A good leader is supposed to act in the best interest of everyone around them, no matter what it costs," Redrinna said. "I just... I can't seem to do it. I don't want to have to choose something that's going to end up hurting my friends, and I don't want to have to make sacrifices for the 'greater good.' But if I don't, it'll make things worse, won't it?"

"I suppose that is one way of looking at it." Timothon paused, seeming to consider what she'd said. "There might very well be times where you have to make a hard decision you don't want to—the right choice won't always feel 'right.' That said, I think people who are good leaders are the kind of people who are able to create a world where those kinds of sacrifices would never have to be made—or at least, they would strive to build that kind of world."

That made her look up.

"Good leaders don't create war or leave people to die—they do everything in their power to prevent that from happening. War is a last resort in order to keep people safe—I mean, just because you don't want to fight doesn't mean your neighbors will have the same principles. That said, a good leader isn't selfish either. Instead, their first priority is to those around them, and in difficult times, they're working right alongside everybody else. Those are the kinds of people I think are good leaders. It's definitely not someone who could write off thousands of deaths and broken families as worthwhile sacrifices without so much as batting an eye."

Redrinna dropped her gaze to her bread again.

"It's been said that power corrupts, but if I'm honest with you, I think that's a stupid saying," Timothon continued. "It's like saying a sword can kill. You and I both know it isn't a sword that kills; it's whoever is wielding that sword who takes the life. Blaming the sword doesn't change that. My sister used to say that those who believe power is what corrupts people are the people who refuse to acknowledge their own faults and mistakes. They're the kind of people who blame anyone and anything but themselves. Power is like a sword—it's just a tool. What it does depends on the hands it's in. That said, if you're that scared about being a leader, then there's one thing I want you to remember: having power doesn't change you—forgetting does."

"Forgetting?"

"Forgetting how to care. Forgetting to be grateful. And forgetting what it's like to feel small and in need of help. Those are the things that twist people into heartless beasts. Not something arbitrary like having power." He shrugged a little. "I'm not trying to paint what you're going through as a good thing, but part of the reason for it is because of how compassionate you are. The suffering of others hurts you as much as your own, and that's part of the reason all of this burdens you as much as it does."

She couldn't think of anything to say in response to that.

He sighed a little. "Redrinna, you know...if you're only ever going to see yourself as a person who made a massive mistake, you're never going to become anything beyond that."

Her mouth popped open, but she still couldn't speak.

"Hey, that's all I wanted to say about it though, okay?" Timothon nudged her shoulder before turning and entering the dining room, leaving Redrinna out in the hall.

She stared after him for a minute before hesitantly following. The kind of leader Timothon described sounded like something out of a dream—no matter how hard she or anyone wished, she wasn't sure if it was even possible to be that way. It wasn't like history was bursting with people who'd managed to do so.

Even if she didn't have to make hard calls, how could Redrinna be a good leader for the Dragon Kin when she couldn't keep anyone from getting hurt? Keeping it to herself, she desperately hoped they would find someone who could do a good job at leading them soon— someone who was a true leader—so they would forget about her.

All at once, as Redrinna set down the one loaf she, Tak, and Kyvo would eat before giving the rest to the dragons, her mind went back to the day they'd left the Torijin village. The chief's words still rang in her ears: 'You are well on your way to becoming a leader I could re- spect.'

Those words still filled her with a sliver of confidence. It'd been such high praise.

However, at the same time, it made a sea of doubt flood her too. Her friends and the warriors had been the real reason things had been taken care of. If it'd been left to her, the demon would still be on the loose and the tribe still would've been in danger. If not for the others, Redrinna would've failed again, like always.

All at once, Redrinna realized Tak eyed her with that concerned expression he often wore on his face. Quickly, she busied herself with taking a portion of bread.

"Are you okay?" he whispered as she sat.

She nodded. "I was thinking about something I don't like think- ing about. I'm fine."

He seemed a bit confused but, after a moment more, turned his attention to his food.

From off to the side, Astra hissed, "Don't hog it all, red beast."

Xandrin issued a distracted growl in response, almost making Redrinna smile.

The room stayed quiet as they ate, and after a few minutes, Astra padded over. Even though her gaze was on Redrinna, she stood right behind Tak—though the young man seemed neither to notice nor mind.

"Hey, so are we leaving yet?"

Shaking her head, Redrinna said, "Not quite. In a couple days though."

"Finally! Where are we going? I know you said it was somewhere south, but where?"

Redrinna studied the earnest expression on the green dragon's face for a minute before she said, "It's a place called Diablo's Maw."

Timothon glanced up. "*The* Diablo's Maw?"

"There's only one," Tak whispered before taking a bite of his bread. "Oh, this tastes really good today."

Happiness bubbled up in Redrinna's chest at that. "My father's notes say an aquatic dragon lives in the caldera left by the Diablo, so that's where we're going."

Kyvo lifted his head out of the berry bowl. "I don't know what that place is, but it sounds kind of scary."

"It sounds scarier than it is," Timothon said. "I was just a bit surprised, is all."

"What is this maw?" Astra asked, glancing between the three of them. "If there's a giant beast we have to fight, I want to know before we get there."

"There's no beast," Redrinna said quickly, suppressing a smile. "See, a long time ago, on the southwest corner of the continent, there was an enormous, active volcano. It had frequent eruptions, so the locals who lived there at the time called it the Diablo.

"As the story goes, one day, it erupted worse than it ever had before. The eruption was so violent, it tore itself apart. To make things worse, the volcano spewed so much lava that when it collapsed, there was a massive earthquake. Then the ocean flooded the crater, making an enormous caldera, which is why it's called the Diablo's Maw."

"Are you serious?" Xandrin asked, eyes wide as he paused mid-bite.

"There was a little country there too," Timothon said with a solemn nod. "But the volcano destroyed it in a single night. No one survived."

The red dragon turned to Redrinna in alarm. "So we're going there?!"

She nearly laughed. "Don't worry. The Diablo's last eruption rendered the volcano dormant. It hasn't done anything volcanic in a long time."

"Even when I was alive, it was considered a long, long time ago," Timothon added.

"But volcanoes can stay quiet for centuries before erupting again, right?" Astra asked, her brow twisting in concern. Her claws tightened on the back of Tak's chair, making him jump. "So it could erupt again."

Where had the dragon learned that Redrinna wondered? Then again, Astra had spent a considerable amount of time in the Torijin village, so she could've picked up all kinds of things there.

"It could, but it won't erupt like it did that one time," Redrinna said. "Not without giving some kind of sign."

The worry furrowing the dragon's snout seemed to worsen.

Kyvo turned back to his berries with a flick of his tail. "I don't know why you dragons are so worried. You can just fly away from it, you know."

Tak snorted.

Both the dragons stared at Kyvo with unamused expressions.

Once she'd finished her portion of bread and berries, Redrinna rose from the table. To her alarm, every set of eyes in the room flicked to her. The conversation she and Timothon had had in the hall echoed through her mind, but she forced it away.

Flashing a quick smile at everyone and explaining where she was going, she left for the library. She wasn't up to training yet, so she wanted to tackle a new book she'd found. Granted, most of the material—it involved a lot of magical theory—went over her head, but the more she studied it, the closer she got to figuring it out.

Redrinna went to the table under the window, where she'd left the book last night. It was open to where she'd been still. Quickly she sat, trying to immerse herself in it.

However, her mind seemed determined to wander, returning once again to what Timothon, the village chief, and the new spirit she'd met while in the forest had all said.

As she thought about that, she glanced at her right palm. Since she'd taken her gauntlets off when cooking and had forgotten to put them back on, the mark the spirit in the forest had given her stood out, almost pricking at her attention. The sun, shining in her palm.

She'd attempted to study it but hadn't found a single thing in the library that even mentioned something similar to this. She appreciated the spirit's gift—or at least, she tried to—but she wished it would've explained what in the world this thing was. Or why it had given it to her. Or what she was supposed to do with it.

Anything would have been helpful, but it'd vanished the moment it'd given it to her.

With any luck, she would figure it out sooner rather than later, especially since the spirit had said she would need it.

Frowning, Redrinna rested her head in her hand, trying to get her attention back on her book.

Who knew what she would need in the days ahead, or how many days they had? Redrinna had the distinct impression she would need a lot of things, and she needed to be prepared for anything. There wasn't room for anything less.

Otherwise, she'd fail again, and this time, the consequences could be disastrous. The people she would let down wouldn't be strangers or nameless faces this time; if she failed, it was her friends who stood in harm's way.

Chapter Four

River got ready for the inane banquet his grandfather had prepared as slowly as he could. He took a bath slowly—mindful to keep his left arm out of the water—and got dressed. Slowly. However, going so slow did have unforeseen consequences. It gave him more time to stare at his left arm.

Well, it wasn't an actual arm; just metal twisted into the shape of one and attached to his shoulder. It moved like one, but that was where the similarities ended—it couldn't feel, it had no real strength, and it was cold.

This arm was all he needed to remember his greatest failure, the one that filled him with such deep shame and despair, he did everything in his power not to think about it.

Eventually, he managed to subvert the thoughts and finish getting ready. His grandfather had insisted on traditional fashion, so he wore a long-sleeved green and gold tunic, trousers that ended just past his knees, and sandals. Then, he added his gloves, effectually hiding his prosthesis from sight—his grandfather would make his life even more of a nightmare if anyone learned about it.

He ventured over to the cracked mirror in the corner and dragged his damp hair into a semblance of control, a portion of it falling across his face. It was long and unruly now, but the look had grown on him.

At the very least, it might keep others' attention away from him since they couldn't see his entire face.

A part of him wanted to do something—something chaotic and impulsive—even if it risked his life. However, a glance out the window—straight at the stand—made those thoughts shrivel away. If River had actually been brave, he would've stopped the banquet from happening at all—he would've given in to that impulse and risked death. That would have been a real act of defiance, but it was an act he could only dream about and imagine having the fortitude to pull off.

All at once, there came a knock at his door, making him freeze.

"River? Are you up?" Leonora called.

Relaxing at the sound of his sister's voice, he called, "I am."

The next moment, the door opened, and his sister crept into the room. Despite the fact they were siblings by blood, it was impossible to tell that at a glance. While River's hair and eyes were a dark, inky black, Leonora's were amber, almost the color of rich honey. His skin, while tanned from many hours working in the sun, had always been a tawny color. Hers was the lighter olive tone of most of the city's population. He bore their mother's almond-shaped eyes. She bore their father's round ones.

"I was worried you'd snuck out again," Leonora hissed as she smoothed his tunic. Then, with jerky movements, she adjusted her light blue and silver peplos.

He swiped at his hair one last time, but it was determined to remain in his face. "That was yesterday. I can't sneak out often or he'll catch on even more."

That made her scowl. "You're going to get yourself killed."

"Forget about me. Between the two of us, you're the one in real danger."

"Oh, I know." She smoothed her peplos again. "*He* says light blue fabrics are only good enough for peasants, not privileged captives. How dare I wear my favorite color."

He almost cracked a smile, but it died after twitching his lips.

Leonora closed her eyes. "You would've laughed at that once, you know."

"Your peplos isn't what I was talking about."

Her expression remained blank as she stared off to the side. "I'm sure we'll find a way out of it."

"I'm not going to let any of those beasts get their filthy paws on you, Leonora. I promise."

"If you keep making and fulfilling promises like those, you're going to lose all of the skin on your back."

Right as River went to answer, he heard the distant scuff of a sandal, and both of them turned towards the door in alarm. Less than a second later, the grating voice of their grandfather rang out.

"Leonora? Where are you?"

Leonora's mouth pressed into a tight line. In undertone, she said, "I hoped he wouldn't be hunting for me."

"With any luck, he'll skip this room." Even still, as River stared at the door, his heart thrummed in his chest, all traces of the rebellious thoughts he'd had vanishing from his mind.

To his disappointment, the door burst open, squealing on its hinges as it banged against the marble wall with a loud crack. River hid his gloved hands behind his back. Their sallow skinned grandfather stepped in, chin raised like he expected cheers and applause.

The man's gaze focused on Leonora. "There you are."

River fought against every urge and instinct in his body in order to remain still.

The broad and tall man—he had the sagging look of one who'd been muscular once, but all that muscle had long dissolved to fat—stalked across the floor, ignoring River as he approached Leonora. If River had been brave enough to lift his eyes, he would've seen what he did not want to: the traces of his dad and the truth that he really was related to a horrible beast of a man.

"This color again?" The man pinched Leonora's peplos with broad, flat fingers. "Leonora."

Leonora mumbled, "The others are dirty."

"I see." Though he seemed to accept that, there was still something about him that made unease diffuse through the room like smoke.

A touch of fear slipped into River's stomach. He hated this. He hated it so much. As much as he wanted to leave, this was why he couldn't. How could they? They'd tried to run away before, and here they were again. Where could they possibly go that he wouldn't be able to find them?

River's thoughts turned back to Adonis and the others, and the way they seemed able to believe if they kept trying things would change. That it was possible for someone from the Imperial Family to come and change this place. If Her Highness, the Imperial Princess, could come—if she could work her magic again—things would change.

She was clever; her proposals to invest in crops more suited to harsh, dry climates and ways to harness what remained of the land's natural resources to cope with the severe drought were working. It appeared they would have a harvest this year, unlike the last. Beyond all that, all those years ago, she'd done something no one else had been able to, something that had changed the city forever. Something not even River could forget.

He wanted to be like the others and believe that if she came, this nightmare would end, but he just couldn't.

"And you," his grandfather rounded on him, his face taking on a red tinge, "don't you dare cause an ounce of trouble or else."

River kept his head lowered in response. With an impatient swipe, his grandfather tried to rake River's hair out of his face. It didn't work, but it did hurt.

As River begrudgingly followed Leonora out of his room and to the front courtyard, he vowed not to let anyone near his sister. It didn't matter what his grandfather did to him, so long as Leonora would be okay. Their grandfather may have called it a party, but both River and Leonora knew it was more like an auction.

The moment they arrived in the open courtyard full of sun, food, and people, River slipped into Leonora's shadow. His gaze flicked to each noble's face as he picked out the threats and noted which ones he could dismiss. Unfortunately, because of the nature of what this was, most everyone was a threat.

Once their grandfather had finished announcing Leonora to the crowd, she shot to the shaded edges, keeping herself near a corner. River leaned against the wall beside her, placing himself between her and the rest of their noisy guests.

"They're all staring at me," she hissed, tugging on her peplos so it covered her neck and shoulder more.

River nodded, keeping his gaze on one young fellow in particular, a fellow who gawked at Leonora like she was a piece of meat. River knew this guy's type.

Come over here, I dare you, River thought with all the vehemence he could muster.

Almost as though he'd sensed River's challenge, the guy strode over, an exaggerated smile plastered on his face.

"Lady Leonora," he said, bowing low enough the end of his short cloak dragged through the dirt. "There are many ladies here, but you are by far the fairest."

Leonora's upper lip curled like she'd caught whiff of a foul smell. "Degrading others under the pretext of praise isn't a compliment."

The guy tried to initiate a conversation a few more times, but when Leonora wouldn't cooperate, he finally left. However, his attempt emboldened a few of the other young men who were desperate for a match. River was almost amused—though not surprised—that any of them believed such soft creatures who'd never worked a day in their life were a match for his sister.

Leonora's cold shoulder successfully chased them all away, and River could sense the glares coming off their grandfather, which he happily ignored. So far, River hadn't done a thing. It was obvious Leonora had no interest in being forced to marry someone who cared more about money and forcing her to have children than who she was as a person, but his grandfather wouldn't have understood that even if it'd slapped him across the face.

All at once, Leonora tugged on his sleeve. "I don't want to, but I haven't eaten all day."

River glued himself to her shadow and glared back at anyone who got brave enough to shoot him a dirty look. They all frantically turned away. At least River's ill reputation was good for something.

They reached the banquet table a minute later, and River's stomach twisted in disgust at the amount of food piled on it. Massive plates of pastitsio, souvlaki, choriatiki, kleftiko, tiropita, and bougatsa burdened the large table. Despite how many people lived off table scraps and whatever else they could find, when this event ended, their grandfather would make sure all the leftover food went into the garbage. River would salvage as much as he could—provided he got the chance—but most of it would go to waste.

As they worked their way around the table, the first young man watched with a hungry, wolfish gleam in his eye. As they made to leave and return to the safety of their corner, the fellow halted in Leonora's path, making her stop as well. River stepped up to her side, his weight already on the balls of his feet.

The fellow reached for her arm. "Lady Leonora—"

Stepping out of his reach, Leonora said, "Please don't touch me."

Regardless, the guy reached for her again.

River snatched the guy's wrist, holding him fast. "She asked you to maintain your distance. You will do as she asks or I will break your wrist."

"River!" Leonora hissed, a hint of panic in her voice.

He heard the familiar, nervous murmurs sweeping through the crowd, but he kept his attention on the guy right in front of him.

"Let go of me, you filthy half-breed," the guy hissed.

"Keep your hands to yourself."

The guy jerked his arm back, and River let him go, making him stumble a couple steps. Leonora shrank behind River, her hands trembling.

Despite River's threat, the guy reached out and grabbed Leonora's arm, jerking her forward and throwing her off-balance.

Without a second's hesitation, River snatched the guy's wrist, digging his fingers in deep where he knew a tender nerve waited. The guy cried out, his hand spasming and forcing him to let Leonora go. However, River wasn't done. In one swift motion, he wrenched the guy's wrist to the side. The bone cracked as it broke, and a few people screamed.

One of the guy's friends came charging in, so River tossed the sobbing young man into him, sending them both tumbling back. As a second guy ran at River from the side, he twisted his body and pivoted, using his momentum to smash the wrist of his left arm—his metal arm—into that assailant's nose.

There was a spray of blood, and Leonora yanked on his arm. Together, they cut through the crowd and raced back inside the mansion. Once they were in the safety of her room, she collapsed on the edge of her bed, head in her hands.

"I should be angry at you," she said, voice trembling.

He stared at her for a moment before glancing to the side. "I'm not going to let boys like that get you, no matter what. I promised Dad."

She didn't speak, just wrapping her arms around herself instead. The guilt that always lived inside him nestled a bit deeper. If it hadn't have been for him, she wouldn't be stuck in this mess.

All at once, there came a hissing crack from behind them, and River half-turned. He rolled his eyes. A man with long, unbound hair stood there, dressed in his long cloak despite the summer's heat. Tehl.

"Well, the two of you are just full of surprises, aren't you? Both submissive and yet so rebellious," Tehl said with a laugh. "And here I thought that party was going to be dull as dirt."

"What do you want?" Leonora said, irritation in her voice.

"Me? Want something from you?" He laughed. "The only thing you can give me is entertainment, which you did. Nice display downstairs, River."

River stared, wondering what the guy was after. He appeared at odd times, meddled in strange things, and dressed in strange ways—but he was the only person the boyar listened to. Unfortunately, he was as cruel as the boyar. River didn't understand him or his motivations. Tehl was just another part of the rottenness that infected Póli, the unpredictable part River couldn't peg down.

"Oh, by the way," Tehl began, pointing towards the door.

A moment later, River heard it: his grandfather storming up the hall. A distant door banged open, and after a minute, the stomping resumed. A minute later, the man arrived, purple in the face.

"You—!" his grandfather spat, so flustered, he kept repeating the word. "You—! You—!"

River stared at him, fighting to appear impassive. Even though he didn't regret what he'd done and the boyar's rage had ceased to truly scare him long ago, a numbness swept through him, almost as though it was trying to prepare him for the inevitable consequence of making his grandfather mad.

The next second, the man grabbed River by the hair, jerking his head back with enough force he stumbled. Reflex tears sprang to River's eyes, but he hastily cleared them. All he could see was the gaudy gold ceiling.

"I never should have brought scum like you here!" the man spat. "It would've been better if I'd left you to die."

A part of River agreed with that statement.

"No, don't—" Leonora cut herself off as something cool and sharp touched River's neck.

"You remember my warnings, Leonora," their grandfather hissed. "Sit."

There came the creaking of the mattress as Leonora complied.

Another source of River's shame was this, right here—if it wasn't for him, Leonora wouldn't have to sit and take this. Her life could've been completely different, but because of River, she was trapped.

He hated it. He hated it so much.

All at once, Tehl cleared his throat. "Athanasios," he said in an almost sing-song voice.

"What?" their grandfather barked.

"I'm sure this is fun, but there's something I came here to discuss with you. Now. So let's go."

The boyar hesitated, and, maybe River imagined it, his grip loosened.

"Well?" Tehl continued, his voice farther away, sounding near the door. "Or do I need to be more persuasive?"

"Fine," the boyar huffed. He tossed River aside before turning and stomping out the door.

River rubbed at his scalp, a part of him surprised he had any hair left.

Leonora stared at the door, her face pale. "I guess we got lucky this time."

He nodded, staring at the door too. Even still, when the boyar came back, River was sure things wouldn't get better.

⚜

Thala rested her head and arms on the makeshift kitchen counter after she'd returned to the hideout after another day on the farm. Because of that party-thing River and Leonora's grandfather was throwing, the fish at the seaside market hadn't been as good as usual, which meant a little less food to go around. Since she'd eaten yesterday, Thala could handle not eating today.

That said, she would have to be careful to make sure Aretha and Adonis didn't catch on to her skipping; they'd trade places with her in a heartbeat, and they worked hard enough as it was and needed to eat more often than they did. In the last few months alone, both of them had lost an alarming amount of weight.

Even still, Thala's dad had often skipped meals in the army to make sure she had enough. This wasn't going to pay him back, but in a way, she was doing something he would have done. She'd once hoped that would help heal the numbness inside her, but it hadn't yet, and she'd long since lost hope that it would.

She must've been more tired than she thought because she fell asleep and woke up sometime later with her arms numb and tingling. She sat up and stretched, not at all surprised to find everything pretty much the same as it'd been before she'd fallen asleep.

As much as Thala enjoyed living a quiet, war-free life, she had to admit that, oftentimes, it was dull. She didn't miss the fighting, but she had as little purpose now as she'd had once the war had ended. The war had been awful, but why did her life without it feel so...empty? The lack of emotions was confusing enough, so why did living in peace leave her so lost?

All at once, someone knocked at the door. One of the others rose and knocked back. The person at the door knocked again, completing the code.

A lanky young man strode through, plastered with so much dirt and general filth it took Thala a moment to realize it was Will.

"What on earth happened to you?" Adonis said, glancing up from a stack of papers on the table in front of him.

"I infiltrated the party as a stable boy. However, some of the nobles didn't think I was doing a great job, and this was how they chose to tell me. Either way, the party's over, so I left."

"Already?" one of the others asked.

"Well, I wouldn't say over so much as his honored guest left."

"Leonora left early?" Adonis raised an eyebrow.

"Yep." Will pulled a twig out of his hair. "Apparently one of the noble brats was getting handsy, so River beat him up. They escaped back into the mansion, and the boyar went after 'em, madder than a hornet."

In the kitchen, Aretha stopped what she was doing, bracing

herself against the counter like she needed it to keep herself upright. "That kid is going to get himself killed."

Thala lowered her chin onto her arms. Since River and Leonora had been brought here, she'd never seen them happy; she honestly didn't know if River even could smile. The last time she'd seen him, he'd been like a shell. In a way, it was like she'd been staring at a reflection of herself. As for Leonora, she hadn't seen her in so long, Thala struggled to remember her face. They'd used to be able to escape the mansion when they were kids, but now that they were older, it was rare when River managed it, and Leonora never could.

There were several rumors about what the boyar had in store for the two of them, and everything she'd heard made that lingering fear inside her shiver with life.

The last time River had made the boyar upset a couple weeks ago, he'd been whipped to the point of not being able to move. Now that he'd ruined the boyar's party, Thala was afraid the boyar would whip him until he was dead. Worse still, there wasn't a thing any of them could do to help him and his sister. They had to hope River could survive whatever fate was about to befall him and that his luck wouldn't run out yet.

It was enough to almost make her wish she was in the army again. At least there, she'd been able to do things instead of having to sit and watch her friends suffer alone.

⁂

Leonora sat on the edge of her bed, wishing she could hold on to the numbness River said he could find instead of wrestling with the tight, intense coils of fear and disgust squeezing her chest. Then again, River had always been better at being able to empty his head of thoughts. Leonora's mind was never quiet—and in moments like this, that fact became irritatingly obvious.

She was sure if she mentioned to River how she really felt, he'd risk his remaining limbs in order to get her out. As much as she loved him, he couldn't seem to grasp that she did so, and watching him get hurt over and over took a toll on her too. Besides, if she riled River into fighting back, she already knew what fate awaited him; the boyar knew exactly what to do in order to keep her still.

Perhaps, at the party earlier, if she'd been able to keep her fear and unease better under control, River wouldn't have snapped like he had; maybe he wouldn't be lying in his room half conscious, still bleeding from his latest whipping.

Slowly, her gaze shifted towards the head of her bed where, tucked out of sight, hid the satchel she'd packed a long time ago in the event they ever got a chance to escape. It contained nothing more than supplies that would help them survive in the wild—the bare minimum, just what they wouldn't be able to scrounge up for themselves. However, every time she thought an opportunity was about to present itself, River ended up in this state. A part of her couldn't help wondering if that was more than just simple coincidence.

Even still, as she sat there with the waning light of the sunset spilling through her window deepening the shadows of her gilded prison, she took her emotions with a firm hand and shoved them deep down out of sight. If River figured them out, it would only make their situation worse. He may have resigned himself to their present condition, but Leonora hadn't. She couldn't. River had promised to protect her, and she'd promised her parents she would protect him. This time, she wasn't going to fail.

Chapter Five

Redrinna smoothed her hand over the time-yellowed, sun-warmed paper of her book. For some reason, it made her chest ache. Her gaze turned to the world beyond the window, and she studied the miles of forest-carpeted mountains that stretched out as far as she could see in every direction.

It'd been ages since she'd been able to enjoy sitting next to a window with a good book, almost like it was from an era long past. An era where she'd been a completely different person who'd lived a life that made the one she lived now seem unreal.

She found herself fingering one of her two necklaces again, the one that had once belonged to her mother. The thought of her made the ache in Redrinna's chest dig a little deeper, the feeling burrowing into her like a tick. Her other necklace, her Dragon Gem, pulsed with warmth, helping to soothe the ache.

"Redrinna?" Tak asked from the ground below the sill, making her glance down. He lifted his book, pointing to a word. "What does this mean?"

"Verisimilitude?"

He nodded.

"Oh, it just means being believable, or having the appearance of being true," she said. Then she frowned, studying his book more closely. "What are you reading anyway?"

"It's a history book, I think," he said, showing her the cover. "If not, it's pretty boring fiction."

She laughed, and when he opened it again, she found herself reading over his shoulder. "Ah, this one's not a very detailed one."

"Huh?" Tak glanced at her, brow furrowed.

"I mean this version of that battle left out a lot," she said, setting her book aside. "This is talking about the history of the country of Manon, in its early years, right? What the book doesn't tell you is that they had a tyrant king who was jealous of his son and exiled him. When the corruption became out of control, the prince raised a rebellion by getting the entire capital to stand with him, and they were able to take the kingdom without anyone being killed. This book makes it seem like the prince took it back without any help and for no big reason."

Tak frowned at his book.

"Don't worry about it, Tak. History books never agree on how to talk about the past. And not all of them do it well, either."

At that moment, Kyvo trotted around the nearest bookshelf, tail held high. He vaulted into the windowsill and carefully sat, curling his tail over his paws.

"Hey, Kyvo," Redrinna said with a smile. "What are you doing?"

"Timothon isn't asking for us again, is he?" Tak asked, his attention already back on his book.

"Nope," Kyvo chirped. "Since we're leaving tomorrow, he said we should relax while we can. Anyway, when we do leave, we're going to find another dragon, right?"

"That's right," she said.

"Don't we need to find people too? I mean, aren't there supposed to be ten of you?"

"Yes."

"So how are we going to find anyone else?"

She and Tak shared a look before they both shrugged. "I don't know. Tak and I found each other by chance, so I don't know what to do about finding anyone else. It's not like we could pop into every village we come across and poke around."

"Especially you," Tak said. "Since a lot of people tend to recognize you on sight."

That would be a problem too, even if they didn't go into a village. Redrinna had debated bringing her cloak along, but once they left the mountains, it would feel a lot more like the summer it was, and that cloak was made for winter.

"Maybe the dragon will know someone," she said, though she didn't have high hopes of that.

"Hey, Tak and I could always go on scouting missions," Kyvo suggested, his brown eyes lighting up. "We could totally pull off a human and his pet. Nobody would suspect a thing."

The skepticism that appeared on Tak's face summed up Redrinna's thoughts on that idea.

Stifling a laugh, she said, "We'll cross that bridge if we come to it, okay?"

"Okay," Kyvo said, a bit too eagerly.

The rest of the day passed in a blur, and before Redrinna knew it, she was shutting herself in her room for the night. They were leaving tomorrow. Even though Timothon hadn't given her a weapon this time, she was as nervous as she'd been last time. She had yet to have a peaceful encounter outside of the Mount, and she had a feeling this time would be no different.

What if she messed up again? What if she did something stupid that held them up or got somebody hurt?

What is on your mind tonight? her gem said. *It doesn't seem happy.*

"Oh, I...I'm just nervous."

I see.

With almost no pressing from the gem, Redrinna found herself spilling all of the worries hounding her. "What if things go wrong? What if somebody gets hurt? What if the Dragon Slayer or Reyna find us again?"

As she paused for breath, her gem interjected, *I understand you're worried, but none of those things are under your control.*

"I know they're not, but even still..."

Take it one step at a time. Tackle each problem as it comes up instead of trying to plan for a bunch of maybes, otherwise you'll get so overwhelmed you won't be able to function.

Redrinna rubbed her head as she thought on that. The real issue, when that she allowed herself to admit it, was what if something happened and her friends needed something from her she couldn't give? What if they needed her to step into a role she wasn't capable of filling? She knew Timothon had been right about the need for a leader, but what if she tried and couldn't do it? The idea someone might be counting on her—depending on her—and she failed them terrified her beyond belief.

You're not going to let anybody down, you know. Her gem spoke so suddenly, she jumped. *You haven't yet.*

"I have too. I almost got all of them killed."

You've made mistakes, yes, but you haven't let them down. If you had, they wouldn't treat you the way they do.

Redrinna fought off a frown, unable to truly believe the gem's words. That said, the gem was right: no matter what she'd done in the past, none of her friends were mad at her for a single thing.

Just once, Redrinna wanted to be able to do something that didn't almost have disastrous consequences. Something she wouldn't have to apologize for if they all made it out alive this time. Something that wouldn't risk any of their lives.

All at once, her father's voice echoed through her mind: 'You were very brave. But today only happened because you were reckless. If you truly want to protect someone, you need to think of more than just yourself.'

Her heart ached at the memory of his voice, but after a moment's pause, she pushed that to the side.

Her father had been right. She'd been reckless as a child, and she still was as a teenager. However, knowing she had that tendency wasn't going to magically make it go away.

You should rest and prepare yourself for tomorrow.

"I know," Redrinna said with a nod. Tomorrow was a whole new world, and she would set foot in it differently than she ever had before. No more mistakes. No regrets.

She would do things right the first time.

∞ ∞

Redrinna and Tak shared a look as they stood outside of the dragon's rooms. Then they nodded. Taking a deep breath, Redrinna turned and went inside Xandrin's room.

As always, the large red dragon was asleep, curled in a ball with his snout under one set of claws. She couldn't help smiling at the sight. Even though he knew it was the day they were leaving, he still lay fast asleep. She hated waking him so early, but the sooner they left, the sooner they would be back. Hopefully.

Before she could take another step forward, Kyvo flashed past her, barreling into the dragon's side. Xandrin's head shot off the ground as his tail flailed like a fish.

After a second, he shot Redrinna a dark look.

Holding up her hands, she said, "It wasn't me, I swear."

Kyvo pounced on his head. "It was me! Wake up! Let's go!" With way too much energy, the kitsune leapt to the ground and sprinted away at top speed.

Xandrin stared after him for a minute before turning to her and blinking, his eyes struggling to stay open. "Is it really morning already?"

"I'm afraid so," she said, unable to hide a bit of a smile.

Groaning, he buried his head beneath his claws.

"Breakfast will be ready soon, okay?"

"Okay," he said with a whine.

Turning on her heel, Redrinna went back into the hall, glancing towards Astra's room.

Tak stood outside, hands on his hips. "At this rate, Astra, Xandrin's going to beat you."

A growl echoed out from the cave. Redrinna couldn't help the smile that tugged at her mouth, but she did her best to hide it.

"Don't growl at me," he said. "If you don't like that then get up."

"I'm up," Astra snapped, her head emerging from her cave as she blinked wearily. "I wouldn't be so tired if that stupid red beast could be quiet. Why does he have to breathe so loud?"

"You could always move to a different cave," Tak suggested.

Astra just stared at him blankly before she made to step past Tak, but instead, she ran into the wall with her shoulder. For a moment, she remained still. Then she backed up a few steps and tried again, this time successfully stepping out of her room.

As she stomped up the hall, Redrinna lost the battle against hiding her smile.

When the green dragon drew even with Xandrin's cave, she stopped and snapped, "I'm awake before you, red beast! That means I win." After that, she proceeded to saunter down the hall, a bit of a swagger in her step.

"I have no clue what that's about," Tak said as he stopped next to Redrinna.

She shrugged. Neither did she, but the two dragons had a...complex relationship, she'd decided.

Then, just as unexpected as Astra's snarky comment, Xandrin slinked out of his room, sneaking after the green dragon without making a sound. When he was close, he placed one clawed foot on her tail. Astra froze, turning back to him with a glare so intense, both Redrinna and Tak leaned back.

"Now we're tied," was all the red dragon said before he bolted down the hall.

"That doesn't count!" Astra roared, taking off after him.

Redrinna blinked. "At least they haven't been bored?"

Tak cocked his head to the side. "I guess. But now you and I will be the last ones to breakfast."

"Mmm," she said. Then she grinned, unable to resist. "Actually, it'll just be you."

"Huh?"

Without another word, she bolted after the dragons.

"H-hey! That's cheating!" Tak cried.

She glanced back as she rounded the corner, pleased to find him running too. Then her heart skipped a beat. Since coming to the Mount, he'd become an even faster runner.

Pushing herself as hard as she could, she barely managed to slide into the dining room seconds before him.

Panting hard, she glanced his way.

He scowled, panting too. "That was rude."

"But it was kind of fun." She grinned. "I've never done that before."

After a moment, he smiled. A little.

"All right, you guys," Timothon said as he came into the room with bread and the leftover berries from yesterday. "Keep the antics down until after you've finished eating. You won't be allowed to leave if you make a mess."

"Okay, okay," Kyvo said as he vaulted onto the table. He sat, tucking his tail beneath him expectantly.

Timothon raised an eyebrow at the kitsune before setting the bowl of berries as far away from him as possible.

Kyvo stared at it, the tip of his tail twitching.

Redrinna smiled as they all tucked into their breakfast, doing her best to ignore the nerves tightening in her chest while she ate. Despite the quiet bickering of the dragons, she couldn't help noting a faint tension in the air. She snuck a glance at Timothon, whose brow was unusually furrowed.

She supposed she wasn't the only one who worried something bad would happen.

Breakfast ended before she was ready for it to. Then, they were back in the main room, gathering the last few things they would need and preparing to leave.

As Redrinna settled Kyvo and herself behind Xandrin's head, she turned to Timothon. For a brief second, she spied the worry festering in her chest reflected on his face. Then he smiled, the worry vanishing behind the expression.

"You guys be careful, all right?" he said, glancing at everyone before his gaze returned to her. "Especially you."

"I will," she said, her voice hushed.

Xandrin nodded before turning and leaving the Mount. A minute later, they launched into the crystal blue sky. Despite herself, she turned back, watching the Mount as it shrank, becoming lost amongst the other mountain peaks.

"What is it?" Kyvo asked over the wind whipping past them.

"Nothing," she said at first. "Actually...I was wondering. Timothon is probably lonely while we're gone, isn't he?"

Kyvo didn't have an answer for her.

"I didn't think about it last time we all left, but... I wonder if he hates being left behind." After all, most of the first Dragon Kin had ended up leaving him behind, and now, even though they were all dead, for some reason, he was the only one in the Mount. "I bet it brings back a lot of bad memories."

Kyvo snuggled into her lap a bit more. "We should hurry then."

"Huh?"

"So he doesn't have to be lonely and sad for long. I mean, he's sad most of the time, but sometimes he's happy with us."

Redrinna nodded. After what Timothon had been through, he probably only had a handful of reasons to be happy at all, and there was a good chance it worsened when he was alone. Unfortunately, they couldn't stay in the Mount and he couldn't travel far from it, and, in truth, Redrinna wasn't sure how many more times they could do this leave and return. She didn't know how much time they had left before Osiris put his plan into motion, but she didn't think it was a lot.

So, even though Redrinna desperately wished for all the time in the world to spend with her uncle, she was certain they had very little.

♥♥♥

River's nose wrinkled as the hot afternoon breeze hit his face. He debated leaving the balcony railing but didn't feel like it. The only other place to go was inside the room behind him, and it was stuffier in there than outside. Sighing, he shifted his arm, making pain flare up his back from his latest whipping, but he didn't mind it so much.

He'd protected his sister and managed to stave off any marriage proposals for the time being. A few more scars to add to his collection didn't matter if it kept his sister out of the hands of men like those.

"Under house arrest again?" called a familiar voice from his other side. "This is the third time in the last two months, isn't it? Getting a little reckless, aren't we?"

River begrudgingly slid his gaze to the other end of the balcony. A lanky young man crouched on the polished marble railing with all the ease and indifference of someone on flat ground, a smirk twisting his mouth. River glanced down, eyeing the large gap between them and the ground before glancing back at the person bugging him: Will, the most annoying person River knew.

"Don't patronize me," River said, returning his gaze to the horizon.

"Adonis is pretty disappointed, you know. Aretha's livid. Though, she still sent you this, so I guess she doesn't hate you yet." The young man extended a small, roughly carved box.

River reached for it, flinching as fire poured down his back.

"So he actually flayed you this time," Will said, staring for a moment before huffing. "You're such an idiot. Do you have any idea how worried everyone's been about you? Aretha looked like she thought you were going to die this time."

River scowled at him before cracking open the small, plain box. Inside was a tiny medicine ball—clearly something Aretha had pressed together in a hurry—with instructions on how to take it. At the bottom of the note were scrawled three glaring faces. She wasn't angry; she was furious. Normally, she only drew one face.

"There are even more wild rumors about you two," Will continued. "They rival the ones about Thala."

River shot him a glare. "Unless you have something worth talking about, get off the balcony."

Will laughed. "But you'll like this one. People are saying your 'savage ferocity' comes from your mom's 'wild blood' and that you turn into a beast at night and eat children."

"At least they're starting to get creative."

His mother's blood was the furthest thing from 'wild,' but it was foreign, which for some people, apparently, was wild enough. The only reason the noble scum of Póli hated him for it was because of how much it showed through. For Leonora, whose foreign heritage was more subtly pronounced, they didn't seem able to see anything except what the boyar told them. They only saw a doll. A toy.

Will muttered something River didn't catch nor cared enough to ask him to repeat. The guy sniffed. "Oh well. That's all. Other than Thala and the others are worried about you and want you to stop being stupid. They wanted me to remind you once again that you two can hide in the hideout. Hence the name."

River ignored him, not even looking over. If they risked that and the boyar found them, Adonis and his gang were in for a worse fate than getting whipped, not to mention what the man would do to River and Leonora.

He expected the young man to leave, but for some reason, Will lingered.

"I heard the report," Will began, his voice softer now. "Do you even believe the princess is out there?"

River's grip tightened on the medicine box. There was no sense in believing someone would swoop in and save them; that was reserved for fairy tales, not real life.

"So I guess we agree on that. Besides, even if she's alive, it's not like she'd help us anyway. I mean, the last time she left her palace was what? The first of never?"

Despite himself, River shot Will a glare.

Will let out an exasperated sigh. "Don't give me that face, Mister Doom and Gloom. I know you've got that whole family connection thingy, but you've never met her, have you? You don't know what she's like."

"Neither do you," he snapped.

"You think just because she implemented a few policies that helped the crops that she cares about us? It's not like it changed anything."

"It did."

Will's eyes sparked with anger. "Yeah, it kept us all alive so we could suffer longer. She doesn't care about us; fixing problems is her *job*. If she really cared, she would've done something about the boyar and the rest of the nobles who can't live without us but want to leave us to die anyway."

As much as he wanted to, River had no response for that. He didn't know why he always seemed to spring to the defense of someone he'd never met. On the contrary, he wouldn't have been all that surprised if Will turned out to be right.

"All right, I correct myself: she supposedly took care of that one guy. But he was just *one guy*. It's not like it really changed anything here."

River looked askance at him. "On the contrary—"

"Whatever," Will spat. "I hate talking about this." Without another word, he vanished from the balcony.

River didn't bother to watch him leave, partially because he didn't care much and partially because his grandfather liked to send people to spy on him while he was in his room. Will knew how to stay out of sight, but it was all for nothing if River gave him away.

Resting against the balcony again, River stared at the little box of medicine Aretha had sent. He knew it cost her and Adonis a lot to keep patching him up—if he could stop being stupid, they wouldn't have to keep paying. However, Leonora was all he had. If he lost her, then not even being alive mattered to him anymore.

Chapter Six

Redrinna watched the setting sun vanish beneath the waves as night settled itself around them. After spending the majority of the day flying, they'd arrived on the shores of the caldera, Diablo's Maw. Tomorrow, they would begin their search for the dragon that was supposed to live somewhere nearby.

However, as she sat by Xandrin, listening to the waves breaking against the distant shore, her gaze drifted away from the sea and along the curving coastline. If she remembered correctly, there were several small villages in this area. Due to the naturally barren landscape, they depended on both the sea and the rest of the Empire for survival.

Her hands knotted into fists as she thought about them, the muscles in her jaw tightening. If anyone from those villages saw her and found out she was here, she was almost positive the reception would be worse than what she'd encountered in the Torijin village.

"You seem pretty lost in thought," Tak unexpectedly said from where he sat on the other side of her, catching her off guard. That was something new too. He was a bit bolder than he'd been before.

After a second, she turned her gaze back to the ocean. "I guess I was."

He slowly met her gaze—and she noted he could look at her now, unlike before. "If you want to talk about it, I'll listen. But if you don't, that's okay too. I won't be upset."

Redrinna hesitated, tempted to keep it to herself. At the same time, keeping things in and bottled up from those she trusted most was a sure way to ensure things ended up like they had before.

Steeling herself, she said, "I was just thinking about the villages around here. If anybody saw me, they'd probably respond worse than the Torijin did."

"Are you serious?" Xandrin asked, ear frills fanning out in irritation. "First you drag us to a dangerous volcano, and then you decide to tell us if anybody sees you, they'll try to kill you?"

"We had to come either way, and I didn't think about it until we got here," she said defensively. Truthfully, places like this were some of the things she wished she could stop thinking about.

"So it's dangerous for you here too?" Tak asked, his brow knitting in that concerned expression he often had.

"It sounds like there isn't a place on this continent where people aren't going to hate you," Astra remarked, her snout gleaming in the dying light of the sun as the last sliver rested on the horizon. Some of its light caught on the tips of the distant waves, making them shimmer.

Redrinna sighed. "That's true. You'll find people who hate me and my family all over this place."

Her friends remained quiet for a couple moments before Tak spoke again. "So why do we have to be careful of the people here?"

She didn't like thinking about it, but it was important for her friends to know. "During the last war, the Esunian War, the boyar—that's...a governor of sorts," she explained in response to the dragons' confused faces. "It's the person who's supposed to take care of the land and the people in a certain area, since my parents couldn't be everywhere."

The dragons nodded.

"The boyar and the nobles were then—" The dragons seemed even more bewildered, so Redrinna paused again. "The nobles help the boyar do their job."

"It sounds complicated," Astra remarked.

"A bit, but it makes sense and it works. Most of the time."

The dragons shared a look that made it clear they had doubts, which Redrinna chose to ignore. Most of the time, it really did work.

With the dragons seemingly satiated, Redrinna continued, "The nobles went to help in the war, and while they were gone, people came in and took their place—they stole everything from them and proclaimed themselves the new nobility. They murdered the boyar so they could instate a new boyar, one of their own. Because of the chaos of the war, my parents didn't find out about this right away.

"We weren't sure why—if they were trying to do something they thought was valuable to the Empire so my parents wouldn't kick them out or what—but for some reason, as part of their takeover, they led an operation they dubbed the Midnight Raid and created the 'dolls'. They were weapons they sent to the Esuni Desert for the war."

"Dolls?" Kyvo asked, head tilted to the side. "Aren't those some kind of toy or something?"

"Or some kind of puppet?" Tak put in.

"I suppose that was the idea, but in reality..." She still shuddered when she thought about it. "They were little kids, kidnapped from their homes in the middle of the night and forced through horrible training to strip them of their emotions and turn them into weapons that weren't afraid to die. Then they sent them to the war."

Astra grimaced. "That's disgusting."

"Your dad...condoned that?" Tak stared straight into her eyes like he was trying to find her soul.

Redrinna shook her head. "Of course not. The second he found out what was happening, he went to the Esuni Desert himself to stop it. At that point, even though the kids had only been there for a few months, most of them had already been killed. Only a few returned home alive. However, despite the fact he did everything to save those kids, many people still blamed him—all of my family—for what happened."

"So, if we happened across vengeful parents or something, you'd be in trouble," Xandrin said with the hint of a sigh.

Astra leaned forward, her gaze fixed on Redrinna. "Please tell me those awful people were punished because what they did was horrible."

Hunching her shoulders a little, Redrinna said, "They weren't."

"Why not?" the dragon snapped hard enough, Redrinna flinched.

"Easy, Astra," Tak said.

"It wasn't because we didn't want to," Redrinna said, the frustration from back then still roiling in her chest. "That boyar and those nobles he conspired with had made it impossible to trace the deeds back to them, and because of that, most of them could only be caught on lesser crimes, so their punishments were light. We knew what they'd done but couldn't prove it, so we couldn't do anything. There was only one of the men responsible we were able to prove was connected."

"Even though your dad's the emperor?" Tak asked. "His word is law."

"It is to some extent, but around the time he met my mother, he passed a decree that demanded every criminal be allowed a fair trial—they have to be proven guilty beyond a reasonable doubt. So without enough evidence, not even he could do anything against them." Redrinna wrapped her arms around herself, almost shivering. "We were able to remove the boyar and the nobles from power, but that was the best we could do. Even as a little kid, it made me so angry."

"And I bet people took that to mean they weren't willing to do anything, which led to the resentment." Tak gazed skyward. "Maybe Kyvo and I really will have to pretend to be a guy and his pet out for a walk."

"Really?" Kyvo squeaked, popping onto his feet.

The image of the two of them trying to pull that off made Redrinna smile.

"Regardless of all that, we should sleep," Xandrin said, laying his head down. "The sun will be back up before we know it."

"You're right," she said, glancing his way.

With a wave, Tak rose and returned to Astra's side. The dragon curled in a protective half-circle around him the second he was there, making Redrinna smile a little. It was funny to her how protective the dragons were over the two of them, all things considered. A part of her wondered whether or not every dragon they encountered would be this way, or if Astra and Xandrin were just oddballs.

Shaking those thoughts away, she laid next to Kyvo, curling around him a bit. She propped her head on her arm as her gaze drifted back towards the ocean, the distant sounds of the waves striking the shore seeming loud in the quiet of the night.

To be frank, Redrinna hoped they'd be able to find the dragon living there quickly. Facing the Torijin people after what had happened to their ancestors was one thing; what had happened here had happened to these people. She wasn't sure she could handle this one.

Eventually, her thoughts stopped circling and she drifted to sleep, only being bothered by strange dreams that made no sense. Fortunately, there were no nightmares tonight, and when she woke, the sun just peeked over the eastern horizon, casting its brilliant rays across the sky.

Sitting up, she stretched her arms over her head. The others were still asleep, and since she didn't want to move, Redrinna stayed where she was, absentmindedly rubbing Kyvo's head. She wasn't sure he was awake, but he did snuggle closer, a little smile on his face.

Good morning, her gem said. *Did you sleep well?*

"As well as I can on the ground."

Her gem made a chiming sound reminiscent of laughter.

"Hey, can I ask you a question?" she said after it'd stopped. She didn't know why she hadn't thought of this before.

Of course.

"Can you tell where to find the human members of the Dragon Kin? Since you and the rest of the gems are connected, and they know where the people they've chosen are, can you tell us?"

There was a long pause before the gem spoke. *I can't tell exactly because the rest of the gems are still in their weakened state, but I think I can tell if there are any close by. In fact,* another pause, *there are three near here.*

"Three?" That caught Redrinna by surprise. If they could find three people in one go, that would make the human part of the Dragon Kin halfway complete. "Where?"

I'm not sure, but I can vaguely sense that they're in…that direction.

Even though the gem couldn't point, Redrinna could tell where it meant. They were still close to the Agicae Mountain range, but ahead of them, maybe an hour's walk away, lay the crescent-shaped coast that framed the Diablo's Maw. They were near the part of the shore called Diablo's Fangs, and the gem indicated somewhere on the other side, the part known as Diablo's Jaw.

Frowning, Redrinna sat up a little more. That was closer than she'd expected, but it would still be difficult to pinpoint exactly where when she knew there were several small cities along the coastline.

I know you're hesitant to enter or even go near any of the towns here, but if there are potential members of the Dragon Kin here, you can't leave them behind.

"I know," she whispered. "But if they're from here, they might not want to come with us at all." The fact that Redrinna was a part of the Dragon Kin might turn them away, something she hadn't considered before. How would they overcome that?

Her gem didn't respond.

Redrinna sat in silence for a while longer before the others—excluding Xandrin—began to stir. While she and Kyvo worked to wake the red dragon, Astra went out and found them some breakfast. Once they were all fed and the sun had risen, they headed to the coast.

As they stood at the water's edge, Redrinna stared at it in fascination. She knew calderas were slightly different from lakes and the rest of the ocean, but even still, it surprised her that the water was so dark. The bank vanished beneath the water's surface so fast, it was almost like someone had taken a massive sword and simply sliced it away.

Something about the darkness of the water made her flesh crawl like there were bugs under her clothes, scuttling across her skin. The sensation intensified when she thought about the people and buildings buried underneath it, who knew how decayed now.

Then, Redrinna realized the others were watching her expectantly, and she shook those thoughts away.

"So, how are we going to tackle this?" Astra asked, gazing across the waters. "Oh hey. Is that the volcano?"

Redrinna looked in the direction the dragon indicated. In the center of the caldera was a large, pointed island covered in green. Even from a distance, it was huge. "Yes. That's what's left of it, at least."

Astra shivered, her wings rustling. "It looks deceptively harmless."

Lowering his head, Xandrin squinted at the water, his breath sending ripples across the surface. "So, if this is volcano water, is it even safe to be in?"

"It must be or the dragon we're searching for wouldn't live in it," Tak pointed out.

Redrinna nodded. "Calderas are safe. Fish and all kinds of creatures live in them, even when the volcano that made it is still active."

The dragons shared a skeptical glance.

Kyvo curled his tail around Redrinna's neck as he crouched lower on her shoulders. "I'm not going in there, safe or not."

She whole-heartedly agreed. There was no way, unless they were absolutely desperate, that she was getting in the water either.

"The only one of us who should go in there is me," Astra said. "I mean, unless red beast over there has a special talent we don't know about, I'm pretty sure I'm the only one who can breathe underwater."

With a snort, Xandrin said, "Even if I could breathe underwater, I wouldn't go in there with you. So I'll fly above the water and see what I can find."

"Sure," Astra quipped. "If you think that'll be helpful."

"Quit it," Redrinna said, getting them to stop. "Both of those are good ideas. Astra, you can explore under the water while Xandrin searches above for clues. Hopefully nobody from the surrounding villages will pay us much mind, if they notice at all."

"Okay then," Astra said as she dipped her claws in the water. After a moment, she stepped the rest of the way in. "We'll get started. You non-water breathing and non-flying creatures stay on the beach."

"We'll be back real soon," Xandrin said before spreading his wings and launching into the sky.

Redrinna watched them go, a frown settling on her face. She hadn't planned to stay on the beach, but she supposed she had no choice.

Kyvo gazed up at the two of them. "What now?"

"We could always train for a bit," Tak suggested.

"If we can find anything to train with," Redrinna said, glancing around the beach. There weren't a lot of trees now that they were out of the forest. It was just yellowing grass topped with pale, seed-bearing panicles until it neared the Maw and gave way to dark rock and sand.

Kyvo's ears perked up. "I'm great at finding things! I'll go look."

Redrinna nodded and the kitsune raced off, his tail streaming above the grass like a flag. Within a few minutes, he raced back with a suitable branch before hurrying and finding another. Once he'd found one, she and Tak began training. However, since Kyvo settled down to watch, her thoughts kept returning to him and what he'd asked her, and Tak ended up winning every bout.

When it was nearing mid-morning, Astra's head popped out of the water, and for a few minutes, she and Xandrin seemed to be talking about something. After a few minutes, to Redrinna's surprise, both of the dragons returned to shore.

As Xandrin landed nearby, their training was quickly forgotten and Redrinna was more than a little startled by the grim expression on the dragon's face. Astra climbed out of the water a minute later with a similar expression. Even after she'd shaken the water from her scales, her expression remained unchanged.

"What did you find?" Redrinna asked, unsure if she was ready for the answer.

The dragons shared a concerning glance before Astra said, "Your dad's notes said the dragon lived in an underwater cave near the volcano, right?"

Hesitantly, she nodded. That is what they'd said.

"I found the cave. There was only one big enough for a dragon." Astra's expression darkened. "The problem is it's empty."

"Empty?" Kyvo repeated, his ears lowering an inch.

"That's not even the worst part," Xandrin cut in.

Astra shook her head. "There's blood—dragon blood—splattered all over the place."

"What?" Redrinna's heart leapt into her throat. "Show me. Please."

Astra shook her head. "The only way in is underwater, and you'd drown before I could get you there. You're just going to have to trust me."

Panic began building in her chest.

"Was there just blood in the cave?" Tak asked as he came up on her other side.

"Huh?" She turned to him.

Astra frowned. "Yeah. There was just blood. Why?"

"If Reyna or any of their crew had gotten to it, they would've just killed the dragon and left it, knowing them. I mean, as far as we know, they only want you guys dead. So what would be the point of taking the body, especially since it would've been hidden in that cave?" Tak's brow furrowed as he thought. "I might be jumping to conclusions, but I don't think they are what happened to the dragon. If there's just some blood, it was probably taken by something or someone else, don't you think?"

Redrinna frowned. Now that he pointed that out, she agreed he had a point. As far as they knew, Osiris and his crew wanted the dragons dead, and if they'd achieved that, why on earth would they take the body? It had no value so far as she knew, not even in legends.

That said, it didn't explain why the dragon wasn't here nor who or what could've dragged it off. Or why.

"Were there any other kind of clues in the cave?" she asked.

Astra frowned before shaking her head. "I don't think so."

Closing her eyes, Redrinna shut the world out and thought.

After a few minutes, Xandrin asked, "What is it?"

"Now that Tak's pointed it out, I think it makes the most sense that something or someone abducted our dragon. Unless we find the body, I'm not going to believe it's dead. That said, we don't have any idea where or why it's been taken, and I can't just turn around and go home."

"Agreed," the rest of the group said at the same time, startling her enough she opened her eyes.

"So what are we going to do?" Kyvo asked, the tip of his tail twitching as he stared up at her.

Redrinna winced at the attention.

Then she shook herself. That wasn't what was important. Finding the dragons was, and there was only one thing she could think of to give them some kind of lead. That said, she was pretty sure none of them would like it.

"I think we need to see what the locals know."

"Locals? What are locals?" Xandrin asked, eye spikes twitching upwards.

"You want to ask the people who live around here for help?" Tak asked, that concerned expression of his appearing again.

Xandrin acquired a similar expression.

"If it makes you both feel better, I won't help and will wait outside. It's not like the dragons can go anyway," Redrinna said.

Kyvo's ears perked up. "Oh? Are we going with the human and pet plan after all?"

Astra grimaced. "I'm not trying to be rude, Kyvo, but I doubt people are going to believe Tak has a talking fox with blue markings on its face as a pet."

"Someone could try and kidnap you," Redrinna added.

"Wait, really?" Kyvo's ears lowered. "I don't want to be kid-napped."

After a moment, Tak nodded. "Yeah. It's better if you stay with Redrinna and the dragons. Sorry Kyvo."

The kitsune's tail dropped to the dirt. Redrinna couldn't help a little, sympathetic smile at that. "It's okay, Kyvo. Maybe we can try it some other time."

Then she turned to Tak. This meant he was the only one of them who could risk going into any villages or towns, and she didn't like that. However, before she could even take a breath, Astra butted in between them. Literally.

Turning accusing eyes on Tak, the dragon said, "Wait, wait, wait. So the alternative is sending you into strange, foreign villages alone? Without protection?"

He took a step back, putting a little space between him and her snout. "Don't get too excited. There's no point in going into a small village; they're too tight-knit and suspicious of outsiders. We need to try a town or city instead. Not only will there be people more willing to talk to a weird looking stranger like me, but I'll be more likely to catch wind of any rumors in a place like that without drawing attention. Well, too much of it, anyway."

Redrinna gave him a once over like she was seeing him for the first time. She never would've guessed he'd known any of that. She didn't, but then again, perhaps she should've expected this. After all, he'd grown up in a village, unlike her.

"What?" Tak asked when he caught her staring, his cheeks turn-ing a bit pink.

"Nothing, nothing," she said, smiling again. "But that was such helpful information."

His blush deepened. "Thanks, but I don't know where a town or city would be out here. So it's only so helpful."

The dragons turned to her expectantly.

It took a lot of effort to hold in a sigh as they all stared, waiting for her to make the decisions. After a minute, she managed to calmly say, "The first place we should try is Póli. Not only is it the closest big city, but it used to be the capital of the country that was here before. Plus, it's still one of the most important trade ports in the Empire, so most people wouldn't bat an eye at either one of us."

Tak and Xandrin frowned at the same time. "You're not going," they said in perfect unison.

She scowled. "I didn't say that so I could go. I was just pointing out the fact that neither one of us would be out of place!"

Astra snickered at that.

Chapter Seven

For the second day in a row, River left his room for the balcony. He drew a deep breath of morning air, wincing once again at the salty scent that intensified with the heat of the sun. He hated it here by the ocean. He much preferred the cool, dry air up north, near the Imperial City, where he and Leonora had lived before their grandfather had abducted them following their parents' death in the outbreak of the Esunian War.

He passed the time by watching the noble folk's slaves flit to and fro through the market square, picking out who belonged to which house based off the colors of their clothes. After having spent most of yesterday doing the same thing, he grew bored with it immediately.

"Again?" Leonora called from behind him, getting him to turn fast enough, pain burst across his back. "Sorry."

He waved a hand towards her. "What are you doing in here? He's gonna get mad if he finds out."

Leonora huffed, the sun catching on her amber hair that was gathered back into a low, elegant bun. "He's not going to come into your room, River. Not unless he has to."

It was then River realized she'd brought medicine and bandages. "Leonora..."

"You have to take care of it, otherwise it's going to get infected.

You know that, so don't fight me and get over here."

With a resigned sigh, River complied, removing his short cloak and tunic, exposing the welts on his back to the air, the sting of the movement making him wince.

"He didn't leave you much of a backside," Leonora whispered as he straddled the chair she'd dragged over.

River didn't reply as he rested his chin on the chair's back. There were enough scars on his back that it wasn't much of a back anymore. However, considering he'd gotten all of them protecting Leonora or sneaking food out to the others, he didn't care.

With a sigh of her own, Leonora set to work cleaning his wounds and applying medicine before wrapping the bandage all around his chest. The second she finished, he hastily pulled his clothes back on, not breathing easy until his prosthesis was hidden from sight. While his back didn't ache as much now, he'd never liked the way bandages restricted his movement. He understood why that was the case, but it didn't make him like it.

"If you don't take better care of yourself, how are you ever going to uphold the family promise?" Leonora called as he returned to the balcony.

He couldn't even look at her. "You know I can't, Leonora."

"Somebody has to. It's our family's legacy, and you're the closest in age to Her Highness. Plus, you're a much better fighter than I am. And smarter."

He glared at her.

She glared back and huffed, "You're such a pain."

Ignoring that, River returned his gaze to the blueness of the ocean and the nearby caldera. Before he could take it in, Tehl appeared on the balcony next to him without warning. River hastily side-stepped, the bandages preventing him from hurting himself too bad.

"You should be grateful to me," Tehl said, arms folded and a smug smile twisting his thin mouth. "I doubt you knew, so I thought I should tell you."

"Grateful?" River stared at the guy with a scowl.

"It's because of me you're not dead. You're welcome, by the way." Tehl tossed some of his long hair off his shoulder.

"If you hoped for some bowing, you're out of luck," River replied. It wasn't like Tehl did favors for free—there always seemed to be some kind of catch.

"Excuse me?" Tehl said, twisting a strand of hair around one finger. "After I went through the pain of placating your grandfather to ensure he didn't kill you, that's the best you can do?" He huffed. "Kids these days."

"Thank you for your sacrifice, Tehl," Leonora said as she joined them on the balcony. "But why would you care about the stuff between us and our grandfather?"

"I have my reasons," Tehl said.

He stared at the two of them, and River couldn't hold the guy's gaze for long. There was something about Tehl's eyes that always unnerved him, a deadness that warred with an overbright, feverish frenzy—both of which failed to match his personality. Staring at Tehl's eyes made River's skin crawl.

"Is that the only reason you came to see us?" Leonora asked, her words polite though her tone was frigid. She couldn't stand Tehl much more than he could, but she was a bit better at hiding it.

"Now that you mention it, there was something else." Tehl tapped his chin like he'd forgotten whatever it was.

River doubted that was the case.

"Oh, right, I recall: your grandfather has finally decided on a punishment for the two of you because of what you've done, and I can't help you out of this one without causing serious trouble. Since I hate drama, you're on your own."

River stared at Tehl, remaining mute.

"You never really help us, Tehl," Leonora said.

Tehl laughed. "No, I just don't tell you about it. I am very, very modest and humble, you know."

A chill raced down River's spine at the thought that perhaps he'd gotten away with several things because of Tehl and not because of his own skill. Just a couple days ago, after the party, Tehl had shown up just in time to save River from what very well could've turned into his death; how many times had he shown up like that before? That couldn't be a coincidence.

The empty void inside River sunk a little deeper.

"But your gramps is going to force you to get married," Tehl said, his unnerving eyes turning to Leonora. "The man is picked and the date is set."

Leonora and River both stiffened.

"It's tonight," Tehl continued, almost sounding bored, "in case you were curious. He's going to marry you off quietly and secretly. The way he talked about it made it sound like a kidnapping." Tehl laughed. Then his gaze flicked to River. "Afterwards, he's going to kill you. So if there was ever a time to bust out, now is good. Right now. This second. The old fart is out, so if you want to escape, you're going to have to go right this second."

Leonora stared, her eyes narrowed. "Why are you telling us this? I didn't think you cared about us."

"I don't—well, not beyond the occasional amusement, if that's what you mean. Just thought you oughta know." Tehl grinned, something almost conniving behind his expression.

Slowly, River turned to Leonora. She stared back, the fear in his chest mirrored on her face. When they glanced back at Tehl, he was already gone.

"Do you think he was being serious?" Leonora whispered, her voice tight.

"He's creepy, but he's never lied to us before," River said. River had long suspected an ulterior motive for the strange things Tehl did, but he was just as mystified by it now as he'd always been before. Even still, if they ignored Tehl's warning, both his and Leonora's lives were over.

Leonora's mouth pressed into a line, a determined line. "We have to go."

"What *he'll* do if he catches us is unthinkable."

"So is what's going to happen if we stay," she insisted. "We can outrun him this time."

River dropped his gaze.

"We're not little kids anymore; we can escape." Leonora's jaw was set, her hands on her hips. "I couldn't protect you before, but I will this time. As your older sister, that's my job. Be ready to leave in five minutes."

Without saying another word, she left the room.

River stared at the door for a long minute before he caved and grabbed the sack hidden under his pillow. It thumped against his back as he threw it on, but he ignored the burning waves of pain as Leonora returned with a sack of her own. Since the day they'd been brought here, they'd been waiting for this moment—they'd dreamt about it more than once. He'd never thought it would actually come; however, since it was here, there was nothing they could do but see it through. Or die trying, he guessed.

Silent now, they nodded, returned to the balcony, and checked for any of their grandfather's slaves or visiting noblemen before scaling down the sides of the mansion and creeping out of the gardens through a tight, well-disguised hole in the wall. They stole through the dirty streets, ducking out of sight of any patrolling soldiers they saw. Instead of leaving the city through either of the gates, they crept out through a musty smuggler's tunnel that was rarely used these days, though not because people didn't want to use it. Rather because all the people who'd frequented it were dead—by their grandfather's hands.

For the first time in years, River was free, except it didn't feel like it. On the contrary, he acutely aware of the oppressive weight of his grandfather's thumb, still pinning him down. The man was relentless, and what he would do if he caught them was beyond River's imagination. Despite the fact they were no longer trapped in the mansion, he still felt like there was a chain around his ankle leading back to it, and all it would take was for his grandfather to notice it and yank him and his sister back.

River was pretty sure this wasn't what freedom was like, but he honestly couldn't remember.

⁕

"Redrinna, I appreciate your concern," Tak said patiently as he pushed her proffered sword back towards her. "But I'll be fine, and better off without a weapon hanging from my waist for the entire world to see. Trust me, okay?"

She scowled. "But—"

"No buts. This is what we agreed on," he said. "You're only allowed to come after me if I'm not back by nightfall, okay?"

With a glum frown, she nodded. Even though she trusted Tak, she still didn't like this plan.

With a wave, he turned and walked towards the city snuggled at the base of the mountainside in the distance.

Restless energy flooded Redrinna's veins as Tak vanished amongst the rocky hillside, heading towards the massive port city of Póli alone. She changed her mind; she vehemently disagreed with this plan. She much preferred the plan where they'd gone to town together, but everyone else had shut her down on that one.

"Tak's going to be fine," Astra said through clenched teeth, partially standing on her hind legs in an attempt to keep an eye on him. "There's no reason to panic."

Xandrin looked askance at her before curling up on the stony ground like he was trying to make himself smaller. Or maybe he was getting ready to take a nap. "Who's the one who needs to stop panicking?"

"Zip it, red beast!" Astra whirled on him, snapping her teeth together. "You'd do the same thing if Redrinna was the one walking off on her own."

He growled in response.

Redrinna huffed and sat on a nearby rock that was partially shaded, resting her chin in her hands. Kyvo came and sat by her feet. Closing her eyes, she hoped with everything she had nothing bad would happen to Tak while he was alone, and he'd be back in a matter of hours.

⁕

The crisp sea air was strong by the time Tak made it through the gates of Póli, strong enough it almost reminded him of the village he'd grown up in. However, it was stronger than he was used to because of the heat, and he didn't much care for the smell once it mingled with the city air. Despite the sea breeze constantly blowing, there was a rankness to the air that made Tak's nose wrinkle almost without him realizing it. It took a lot of effort to keep his face straight.

His gaze roved the city around him, an uneasiness coiling around his spine the further he went. There was a general decay to the buildings around him, their weathered, stone faces marked with grooves that suggested there'd once been some kind of ornamentation there. Weeds sprang out of cracks in the cobblestone everywhere, making the ground so uneven, Tak nearly turned an ankle twice. Withered stumps lined the street, and he spied a few termites crawling in some of the cracks.

What unnerved him more than that was the lack of people. Despite being the middle of the day, the streets were empty, with only patrolling soldiers passing by on occasion. How was he supposed to hunt for any clues about the dragon if there was no one around?

After a few minutes of indecision, Tak turned a corner, heading towards the distant docks. There were people there, and perhaps he'd be able to learn something from them.

As he walked, he occasionally spied little dirt-streaked faces peeking out from the shadows of the buildings and behind decaying doors. The haunted look in their eyes unnerved him further. While he was sure the kids wouldn't pose much of a threat to him, he was glad he'd tucked his gem out of sight.

As he neared the dock, he noticed a paved path sloping up a hillside to the rest of the city, a part of the city that glowed in comparison to the rest—there were trees, no weeds cracking the cobblestone, and enormous houses glittering like they were strung with all kinds of jewels. That made him frown.

That distracted him enough he didn't notice the man who'd stopped in his path until he nearly crashed into him, only narrowly managing to avoid doing so. Tak drew up short, noting the grimy, half-starved appearances of the man in front and the four other men surrounding him, two of them flanking the man while the other two men lurked behind Tak.

For a split second, Tak regretted not agreeing to Redrinna's request to take her sword. Then he tossed that thought aside—if he'd brought it, these guys would've tried to steal it.

Hopefully, if it came to fighting, Redrinna wouldn't be mad at him for it. She'd never said it was okay to fight, but she also hadn't said it wasn't okay if something happened. On the contrary, she had tried to give him a weapon, so maybe she wouldn't freak out. No, if he told her he'd gotten ambushed, she would panic (and Astra would smother him, no doubt about that).

Well, so long as he came back all right, he wouldn't have to tell them anything too troubling.

The man directly in front of Tak pulled out a knife, and Tak just stared, noting the awkward way the man held it, almost like he wasn't used to doing so. Despite the situation, it made him a little sad.

"You've been eating good, kid," the man said, his voice raspy. "So give me all you've got on you and we won't hurt you."

Tak stared at him for a minute. "Sorry, but I don't have anything." Even though the man and his goons didn't inspire fear in him (Reyna was at least a thousand times scarier), he had to fight with all his strength against his nervous tick of stuttering when talking to people he didn't know.

The man moved his knife closer to Tak's stomach, but because of his scales, Tak wasn't all that intimidated. "Don't lie if you don't want to get hurt. You ain't starving; I can tell."

Tak glanced to the side for a second. "Well, I'm not from here, and I just got here a few minutes ago. There's plenty of food where I come from. Is that not the same here?"

"Don't lie!" the man snapped, moving closer with his knife. "Just give us what you've got and we'll leave."

Tak scowled. "I already said I don't have anything."

"Then what's this you're hiding, eh?" The man tapped against the slight bulge of the gem beneath Tak's shirt with his knife.

Tak hesitated.

It's all right, his gem said. *You can let them see me. I can protect myself from them.*

Tak hesitated another moment before relenting. If the gem said it was okay, then it was right. It knew itself a lot better than he did.

Even though it was like he was exposing himself, Tak tugged the gem free. "You mean this?"

The man's eyes went as wide as plates.

One of his lackeys murmured, "That would set us up for life."

Unease worked its way deeper into Tak's stomach.

The man lunged to grab it, making Tak instinctively take a step back. Even still, the man managed to wrap a hand around the gem, its green light sharply illuminating the filth on his hands. Immediately, the gem flared with light.

A rush of warmth zipped through Tak; however, the man clearly felt something more intense, because he cried out and dropped it.

Tell him this, his gem instructed.

"You can try and take this, but it isn't worth anything to anyone except me," Tak repeated, the words making him sound a lot more confident than he was. "So you won't get it without a fight."

The man glared at him, and barked out a word that took Tak an extra second to realize was a name. One of the men behind Tak moved in response.

As always whenever Tak entered a fight, his mind immediately cleared and everything seemed to slow. He didn't understand why this happened; it'd saved his life a few times back in the village even though he hadn't realized what was happening. The only thing he knew was it must've been tied to that gift of his Timothon had mentioned, some instinct for fighting he'd always had. And, since he'd begun training with Timothon and Redrinna, it'd gotten sharper.

Either way, when the man took his first swing, Tak was ready. He ducked. As the man's fist flew over, the sudden disappearance of his target threw him off balance. Tak rammed an elbow into his diaphragm, making the man stagger back, winded.

As Tak straightened, he heard the heavy scuff of a boot behind him. His gaze flicked back, and he leaned to the side to dodge the punch. Then he stomped a foot backwards, digging his heel into the place where the man's ankle met his foot. The man jerked forward, and Tak slammed his elbow into the guy's chin, sending him reeling back too.

The guy with the knife was suddenly wary, which made Tak feel a little strange.

All at once, from behind his three remaining attackers, someone shouted, "Oi!"

The guy with the knife glanced back and stiffened. One of his lackeys hissed, "The Azure Demon!"

In a matter of seconds, the gang vanished, hauling their injured fellows to their feet and scurrying around a corner. Tak blinked in surprise. Azure Demon? Was something worse about to attack him?

He glanced ahead, first spotting a young man with dark brown hair and eyes who carried himself in a way that reminded Tak a lot of Redrinna. He seemed to be the person who'd shouted. Then Tak's gaze shifted to the guy's companion, and his heart stuttered in his chest. It was a girl who seemed only a few years younger than either him or Redrinna, but what shocked him about her, though, was that her hair was *blue*.

A shock seemed to pass through his gem at the same second. *She's been chosen,* it said. *Not just marked, but chosen.*

Tak was too startled to move for a second.

The girl stared at him as well, her expression blank.

Her companion studied the two of them for a second before sighing and setting a thin hand on his hip. Tak realized the two of them were as skinny as the men who'd attacked him.

"Unless you've got some kind of business here, you might as well move on, stranger," the young man said. "There's not much left of this town. What's left is gonna disappear before much longer."

Tak stared at him. "I can't." He wasn't sure if this was wise, but that girl was one of the gem's chosen, and for some reason, that made him think he could take a risk. "I'm searching for a dragon."

The young man hesitated just long enough to convince Tak he knew something. "There's no dragon here."

"Not anymore, but there was," Tak said, the gem giving him the strength to stand firm and not stutter. "Right?"

The blue-haired girl nodded.

Her companion hissed, "Thala!"

"I need to find it," Tak said. "Someone took it and it's hurt."

That made the young man pause. He glanced at Thala, who stared blankly back at him, before he said, "We might...be able to help you, I suppose."

Tak didn't know if he could or should trust either of these two, but they knew about the dragon. So for now, he'd just have to tag along and see what they did. Hopefully, that would get them the information they needed before Redrinna came searching for him.

Chapter Eight

River and Leonora stuck to the mountain slopes as they walked away from Póli, the bright, burning sunlight making sweat trickle down River's back, increasing the discomfort from his bandages. Neither he nor his sister spoke as they walked.

Even though they were alone and the only sounds were the crunch of their steps, the murmur of the wind through the trees, and the occasional cry of a falcon, River couldn't shake the feeling that something followed them. A part of him was too afraid to glance over his shoulder, convinced the city would be right behind him, waiting to drag him back into its clutches. However, when he finally worked up the courage to glance back, nothing was there.

By the time it felt like they'd been walking for hours (though the position of the sun indicated it had only been little more than one), River and Leonora stopped for a break. They stepped off the path, hiding just far enough away they could see it without anyone being able to see them.

Leonora stared back the way they'd come. "This is easier than I thought it would be."

River frowned, Tehl's words ringing through his mind again. Was there a chance the reason this seemed so easy was because Tehl had done something to give them time to get away?

He didn't like the thought of that.

"Tehl might be part of the reason why," he said, voice low.

Leonora glanced at him. "So you think he was telling the truth?"

River shrugged a shoulder. He didn't want to accept that as truth, but it made sense.

"I wonder why then, if he was being honest. Why is he helping us?"

"I'm not sure I'd call it help," he said. It wasn't like Tehl had spared him from how often he'd been whipped, nor spared him or Leonora from the horrible life they'd had in any way. He'd just stopped the foulest things from happening.

Leonora seemed to concede his point, but she didn't answer. Instead, her gaze swept over the slopes that briefly evened out before vanishing into the dark, blackish blue of the caldera. "Where do we go now?"

River didn't have an answer for that question. When he looked to the future, he stood in darkness, not even the faintest spark of light illuminating the path ahead of him.

So, where they went from here? He didn't have the faintest idea.

All at once, Leonora sat a little straighter, leaning forward slightly. River stared in the same direction she was, trying to figure out what she'd seen. When he spotted it, he reacted in a similar way.

Was that a dragon?

Nestled near the base of the slopes, almost hidden from sight, appeared to be a red dragon. River couldn't be sure from this angle—he'd only ever seen a dragon once before—but the red thing below just radiated this...dragon-like quality.

"There's no way," Leonora said, her eyes lighting with wonder. She hadn't had an expression like that on her face in years.

"It's not the dragon we met before," he said, not sure why he pointed that out.

"So? If there's another dragon in the world, then that's a good thing. It means they didn't all die out in the Dragon War. Mom always wished she could see one." Leonora grabbed his arm. "Can we get a bit closer? Please?"

River stared blankly at her. "Why do you need my permission?"

"Because you always know the stupid choices from the smart ones," she said. "So if you think this is really stupid, tell me before I go down there."

Uneasy, River glanced back towards Póli. So far, it didn't seem like they were even being pursued; a part of him wondered if the boyar even knew they were gone. Turning back to his sister, he shrugged.

With the first hint of a smile he'd seen from her in what seemed like years, Leonora carefully crept down the mountain slopes with River only a few paces behind. They went slow to avoid stirring up the dirt, but because of how dry everything was, every step kicked up a little puff of dust.

Withing a few minutes, they were low enough they could almost see the red dragon in its entirety. It lay mostly in the shade, and it almost seemed to be asleep.

As he stared at it, River recalled his younger years, when his mother had told him stories about creatures like this, some of the stories from here, and some of them from her home back on the Oriana continent.

After a moment, he realized there was a second dragon, this one green, the shade of its scales blending in when it was in the shadows. The grasses were already losing their vitality despite it only being the start of summer, but in the shade, some green still clung to their blades. River nudged his sister and pointed out the second dragon.

Her eyes sparkled like stars.

Then a high-pitched voice said, "I'm so bored! Tak's going to come back soon, right?" It didn't come from either of the dragons.

"He hasn't been gone long, Kyvo." That was the red dragon, and a part of River was startled by the deepness of his voice and the fact he was awake. "I think."

"Are you sure?"

"I'm afraid he's right," said another voice, from someone he couldn't see. It wasn't the green dragon, but rather someone blocked from his sight by the trees. "It hasn't been very long at all, so we're going to have to wait a while yet."

"This is so boring!" All at once, a little white fox-like creature with peculiar blue face markings pounced into view. "We can do something, can't we?"

River blinked. A kitsune?

"Like what?" came the voice of the person he couldn't see.

"A game or something?"

"We could always swim," the green dragon suggested, lifting its head off the ground. "That'll help us cool down."

"No thanks," the mystery person said quickly. "You guys can swim if you want, but I'd rather stay right here."

That seemed to amuse the red dragon.

"How 'bout we have a bug catching contest?" the kitsune suggested.

"The only one who's going to win at that kind of a game is you, Kyvo," the green dragon said with a snort. "Red beast is so big, he'd squish them all."

"So would you," the red dragon snapped.

With a massive sigh, the kitsune—Kyvo, River supposed—threw himself down in the half-dry grass and rolled around. Then he popped back onto his feet and shook, sending bits of grass flying.

"Oh, Kyvo, there's a—" the mystery person began, getting to their feet. She stepped into River and Leonora's line of sight as she bent to remove a twig from the kitsune's coat.

River's entire world screeched to a halt.

She swept her unnatural but vivid red hair off her shoulder as she straightened, a few loose strands from her ponytail framing her face. When she glanced up, the matching red hue of her eyes became obvious. If that wasn't enough to recognize her, then the way she carried herself was a massive clue.

The Imperial Princess was right there, right below him. She was-n't dead; she was *alive*.

All at once, the princess turned, spotting him and Leonora immediately. Her eyes went wide the same second as River's.

Without warning, the little kitsune plunged up the hill. River had just enough time to stand before the kitsune launched at him, fangs bared. River dodged to the side, but the kitsune snagged his sleeve and dangled there like a snarling piranha. Unsure what to make of that, River just stared at his would-be assailant.

The red dragon leapt to his feet—his full size making a chill shoot down River's spine—a menacing growl rumbling through River's feet as the dragon slunk a couple steps closer to them.

All at once, the princess held a hand in front of the red dragon, making the growling quiet. Then she hurried forward, coming right at River. His mind went blank. A second later, he realized she was prying Kyvo off his sleeve.

"I'm sorry about him," she said quickly.

Kyvo growled at him and Leonora from her arms.

"Stop it," she hissed. "Go back to the shade before you get too hot."

She set him down and pushed him back in the direction of the trees. He went, but the second he reached the shade he whipped back around, growling with his ears flat against his skull.

"Oh, it's fine," Leonora said quickly. "We kind of...accidentally snuck up on you."

The green dragon was on its feet too, and River eyed the two creatures. Neither of them approached, but they didn't appear too friendly either. As he glanced back at the princess, he noted her watching him with slightly narrowed eyes.

"Why are you spying on us, even if it was an accident?" the princess asked, a wary light in her eyes.

"We weren't spying," Leonora said. "At least, we're not here with the intent to spy. We were...escaping."

"Escaping?"

"Yeah," Leonora said, glancing away, her cheeks turning pink. "It's not a big deal though. Anyway, we were passing by when we noticed the dragons...and we wanted to get a closer look. I'm sorry we frightened you."

"Look, red beast," the green dragon hissed. "It's all your fault."

The red dragon shot a glare at the other dragon. "She said 'dragons' not dragon. So it's your fault too."

The princess shot a glare back at the two of them before returning her attention to him and Leonora.

"We just didn't think that when we did," Leonora continued, "we'd find...you."

"Me?" the princess said slowly, almost like she didn't want to hear that.

"Your Highness?" River asked, unable to stop himself. "Is it...really you?"

A grimace appeared on her face for a split second, there and gone so fast, River almost missed it. However, she didn't deny it, so River took that to mean he was right.

Leonora took a step forward. "Your Highness, I know we've just met but if you'd—"

"No!" River said quickly, making Leonora jump a little. He met her gaze, trying to communicate a thousand things without saying them out loud. "No."

She shot him an incredulous look.

"Sorry about that," he said to Her Highness, who just stared at the two of them, looking rather nonplussed. For a second, there were so many thoughts in his brain, so many things he wanted to blurt out, he couldn't speak. At length, he managed, "What are you doing here?"

Her Highness hesitated. She glanced back at the dragons and Kyvo, hesitating before she turned back. "We're searching for a dragon. You guys...have seen it before, haven't you?"

"Hey," the green dragon hissed but Her Highness ignored her.

Leonora dropped her gaze. "We did, but it was a long time ago."

"Do you have an idea where it might be now?" Her Highness asked. "We think it was attacked and abducted. I can't tell you why, but it's important we find it as soon as possible...i-if it's still alive."

Whether River liked it or not, he had a good guess about what had happened to that dragon. "I don't know where—and I'm not sure—but I might know who."

"Who?" Her Highness and Leonora said at the same time.

With a glance at Leonora, he said, "Our tyrannical pig of a grand-father."

Her mouth popped open, but she quickly closed it and nodded. "He would do that."

However, more to River's horror, Her Highness said, "Will you take me to him?"

"No," he said immediately. What that man had done to him and Leonora was one thing, but what he'd do to the Imperial Princess was on a different level.

"Why not?"

"Your Highness," Leonora cut in, sympathy softening her features. "That man is a monster in every sense of the word. If he could figure it out, he'd own the ocean and make the fish pay him to live in it—and that's putting it mildly."

River added, "If he were to get his hands on you, he'd do just about anything to you if he thought it would get him more power."

Her Highness paused, a complicated series of emotions flickering across her face before she said, "Thank you for being so concerned about me, but finding that dragon is something I have to do, even if it means facing this tyrannical pig."

River stared at her in shock. He knew the Imperial Princess was smart; he'd seen the evidence of that with his own eyes. However, because of the nature of the rumors that tended to spread, he'd never heard a single tale of the determined courage that burned in her eyes.

For one second, a spark of something—a brief spat of light—shot through his dark depths. It didn't catch on anything, but that was the first time he'd felt something like that in so long, he hadn't been able to remember what it'd been like.

"Are you insane?" he asked before he could think about it and put it more politely.

"Without a doubt," the green dragon piped up, earning dark glowers from Kyvo and the other dragon.

"Besides that, my friend went to the city to search for information about the dragon. For the time being, we're not going anywhere." Her jaw was set. River realized almost immediately it would be pointless to argue.

"We'll help you," Leonora said.

A concerned expression appeared on Her Highness' face. "But you're in the middle of escaping. Won't helping us put you in jeopardy?"

"A bit, but we have the same enemy, Your Highness." Leonora's mouth twisted with a wry smile. "Since we escaped, he'll be expecting us to try and get far away instead of staying nearby." She glanced at River. "We can help Her Highness, can't we River?"

The determined fire burning in her eyes told him very clearly why she wanted to help, and River wasn't sure how to take that. After what he'd done, he couldn't fill that void, that unfulfilled promise between their families, in any way, no matter how badly the both of them wanted it to be.

Even still, he considered the idea. At the very least, they might find safety if they joined with a group rather than continue alone. "I suppose."

He should've known they never would have been able to get far in their escape attempt.

⁂

Tak paused in the low doorway, doubting for the hundredth time whether or not following two complete strangers around a strange city was a good idea. Now, as he stood on the threshold of a dingy, dimly lit space with several rough thug-like men inside, those doubts intensified.

The young man he'd followed here—Will, he'd gathered—shot a withering glare at him. "Hey, if you want answers, don't stand in the doorway like a lost puppy. Nobody here is going to bite you—well, they won't bite that hard, I guess. Unless you'd deserve it?"

Tak scowled, remaining where he was for a long second before venturing inside.

When Thala motioned him towards a table in the corner, where the largest and sternest man sat, Tak hesitantly followed. He did his best to ignore the people who openly stared at him with wide eyes—though he couldn't help noting they all had the thin, drawn look of those who often went hungry, a look he'd once seen every day in himself. Despite the dim light, he supposed the green of his hair shone through. If it didn't, then the dragon scales and his gem did.

"Will, since when have you been in the habit of picking up strays?" the man at the table said as the three of them approached.

"We didn't pick him up—we kept him from getting in trouble."

Tak stayed quiet, but personally, he didn't recall Will doing anything to chase off the men who'd attacked him.

"But that's not important," Will continued, sitting on the table instead of in the chair right next to him. "We came because we have a question."

The man gave Will a withering look and said, "Why do you always assume I know everything? And how many times do we have to tell you not to sit on the tables?"

Will ignored both questions. "You remember that dragon we saw that one time?"

"I recall you did a bit more than just *see* it, but yeah. Why?"

"It's missing. You heard anything about that?"

The man cocked an eyebrow. "You're sure about that?"

"I'm not, but this kid is." Will jerked a thumb in Tak's direction.

The man gave Tak a once-over. "And you are?"

Tak paused, both to steel his nerves and to decide what to say. He supposed he could partially tell the truth—so long as he didn't say anything about Redrinna, it'd be all right. "I-I'm Tak. I'm a member of the Dragon Kin."

The man's eyebrows lifted, giving him a kind of stunned expression. "*The* Dragon Kin?"

"Well, a-a new one. The one from the legend is gone, so..." Tak said quickly. "B-but that's why we need to find the dragon here. My friends and I went to where it lives, but it's empty except for the blood everywhere."

"Sounds dead," Will said in an annoying, nonchalant way.

A woman walked past, rapping Will over the head with a wooden spoon. "Mind your manners."

Will furiously rubbed his head, shooting the woman a glare. "The heck was that for, Aretha? I'm just stating the obvious."

The woman, Aretha, shot him a glare that reminded Tak enough of his aunt that he leaned back. "There is a thing in this world called 'tact,' and you need to learn it before I force it down your throat."

"But if there's blood, then it's dead!"

Tak was annoyed with Will enough after following him around for a few hours that he found himself saying, "If it was dead, why would someone make off with the body?"

Will raised an eyebrow. "Why else do people kill creatures and take the body?"

The man at the table cut in. "Will, what you don't understand or care to learn is that a dragon serves no purpose when it's dead. They're magical creatures, sure, but the magic vanishes once they die. Their meat is too tough for us to eat, and their bones become brittle. To the kind of people you're talking about, a dead dragon is worthless."

Thala stared at the man, her expression blank. Though it always seemed to be that way. "So you're saying the dragon was abducted?"

"Most likely," the man said with a nod. "The blood is probably because whoever took it had to subdue it first, and it was injured as a result."

"Okay, great. Whatever." Will huffed. "The point is this kid wants to find it, and I think the best person to ask is River. He's good at finding things."

Thala slowly looked at Will, her blank expression unreadable to Tak. Even still, she didn't seem pleased with Will's behavior.

The man at the table smirked. "I guess the boyar really is trying to keep it quiet if even you didn't hear about it."

Will and Thala both turned back to the man with alarming speed. "What's that supposed to mean?" Will asked.

The man leaned back in his chair, almost looking pleased. "River and Leonora finally did it: they ran away. They're gone."

Tak wasn't sure what that meant, but from the startled expression that appeared on Will's face, he supposed it was some kind of shock.

"They broke out?" Thala asked, something faint in her voice suggesting she couldn't believe what she'd heard.

"This morning. They're out from under that tyrant's thumb."

"Tyrant?" Tak asked before he could stop himself.

"The boyar, lad," the man explained, making Tak's blood go cold. "The Imperial Family removed the worm from power years ago, but somehow he's weaseled himself back in, and he's caused nothing but havoc since. River and Leonora are friends of ours who have the great misfortune of being that monster's grandchildren."

Tak's heartbeat thrummed in his ears, his mind whirling as he remembered what Redrinna had told them the other night.

The person her family had worked so hard to get rid of was back. The man who'd tortured children and sent them to war was here again.

He had to tell Redrinna.

But what could she do? She wasn't some kind of princess any-more—she refused to do that, though, when Tak admitted it to him-self, he didn't understand her reasoning. The events she blamed herself for weren't her fault.

But he supposed it was easier for him to see that when he was on the outside looking in.

Shaking his head, he was turning away from the others and heading towards the door before he was fully aware of doing so.

"Hey! Where're you going?" Will demanded.

Tak waved a hand, his thoughts racing too fast for him to think to speak. He didn't know what they could possibly do here; he wasn't the one who came up with plans and ideas—not good ones, anyway. However, he did know one thing with startling clarity: princess or not, Redrinna had to know. And he needed to get back to her right now.

Chapter Nine

Redrinna found herself warily eyeing their two guests, who, for the time being, had chosen to remain with them. When she'd first noticed the two of them, her gem had almost given her a shock; they were two of the people it'd told her about.

Doing her best to think about something else to escape the awkward air that had settled over them, she studied the horizon. The sun would set soon. Tak had been gone nearly all day, and while she didn't think anything bad had happened to him, that didn't stop her from worrying. She sighed, doing her best to keep the anxiety building in her chest at a manageable level.

"That's the fifth one," Astra said in monotone.

"Nope, the sixth one," Xandrin said, sounding just as bored.

"Stop counting my sighs," she said, glancing at the two beasts lying on the ground, almost in identical positions.

They both sighed in response, then glared at each other for it.

Leonora glanced back and forth between the two of them, a little smile dancing across her lips. River seemed unsure what to make of the dragons at all. And, maybe Redrinna was overthinking it, but it seemed like he was doing his best not to stare in her direction.

"I'm bored," Kyvo whined, dropping his head against Redrinna's knee. "And hot."

"Me too," she said, rubbing his head. Even though the sun no longer bore directly down on them, the air seemed hotter than it'd been all day. Their only reprieve was a bit of a breeze, but even that carried the tang of the ocean, and Redrinna didn't much enjoy it.

Kyvo's ears perked up, then he lifted his head, nose twitching as he stared in the direction Tak had gone hours earlier. She looked too, and after a minute, a relieved smile spread across her face. Finally. Astra scrambled to her feet as Xandrin raised his head. Redrinna popped off her rock and hurried to meet Tak.

However, her enthusiasm fizzled out when she noticed the expression on his face. He was grim, a sternness she'd never seen before adorning his features.

"Did something happen?" she asked once he was close.

Tak stared at the ground for a moment before meeting her gaze, fire dancing in his eyes. "I didn't learn anything about the dragon we didn't already guess at, but...Redrinna...that boyar you told us about, the one who made the dolls? He's back."

Her stomach slipped an inch. "What?"

"I don't know how, but he's back in charge, and for the most part, the city looks awful. The streets were almost deserted except for some thugs."

"Yeah," came a new voice. To Redrinna's surprise, intense exasperation spread across Tak's face. "You almost got mugged even."

Redrinna glanced behind Tak right as two people strode out of the brush—a young man and a young woman. That same shock she'd gotten from seeing River and Leonora before zinged through her gem when she saw the girl, her bright blue hair catching some of the dappled light streaming through the trees.

The young man continued, "Lucky we were there. So, you don't mind if we come and check out this Dragon Kin of yours, right? Fair is fair."

"You didn't even do anything," Tak said in a near hiss. "It was because of Thala they ran off."

"That's true," the blue-haired girl, Thala, said. "You just stood there, Will."

"Who cares?" the young man (Will, Redrinna guessed) continued. His gaze flicked in the direction of the dragons before falling on Leonora and River. His eyes went wide. "No way."

Leonora shrugged, her shoulders staying up and giving her the appearance of a turtle trying to hide. "Surprise?"

River looked about as annoyed as Tak. "What are you two doing?"

"That's rich coming from the two people who ran off without telling anybody," Will fired back, but there was a grin on his face that suggested he was more pleased than annoyed.

"What were we supposed to do: tell the entire world where we were going?" River snapped, one fist on his hip.

"That would've been stupid," Thala said, her expression still as blank as it had been before. She stared at Will, and though her expression didn't change, it was clear to Redrinna that the girl scolded Will with her eyes.

With a shrug, Will sat himself on the rock Redrinna had been using most of the day. "Whatever. The point is you guys are here, and we're here, and though I don't know what's going on, count me in."

Wary, Redrinna looked at Tak. Tak wore an expression of complete long-suffering, which did not inspire confidence in her.

"I hope you enjoy being fed to dragons," Leonora said, tugging a stray strand of hair out of her face.

"Huh?" Will asked.

"You just volunteered for you-don't-have-a-clue-what without giving it a single thought." Somehow, Leonora managed to keep a straight face. "That's what we're doing. We're going to be eaten by dragons, so welcome to the buffet."

Will hesitated. Xandrin and Astra shared alarmed looks.

Leonora snorted, unable to keep hold of her stoicism any longer. "I'm kidding! Even though it's been over a year since the last time I saw you, you still rush into anything and everything without a thought, eh? It makes me happy that you never change, Will."

"Oh be quiet," Will said, the faintest spots of pink appearing on his cheeks. "Seriously, what are we doing?"

Redrinna turned back at Tak, who met her gaze. "He's...really back?"

Tak nodded.

A moment later, she realized River, Leonora, Will, and Thala were all nodding too.

"It was only a couple years after the Esunian War," River said. "I don't know how he did it, but he got himself back in."

Her stomach clenched.

"Until River and Leonora broke out, he was holding them prisoner in his mansion. Oh, and every time River did something he didn't like, he'd whip him," Will said. "Actually, if he'll take his shirt off, you can see proof."

River shot him the most scathing glare Redrinna had ever seen.

"He always has a bunch of big feasts and parties with the other nobles, but the rest of the town is barely getting by. They're hoarding the food, I'm positive," Leonora added. "People are starving to death, Your Highness."

Redrinna stared at the two of them, her throat tight.

"Your Highness, he was going to force Leonora to get married," River said.

Redrinna glanced at Leonora. "How old are you?"

"Nineteen," the young woman said.

Arranged marriages weren't allowed to take place if either of the parties were under twenty, but even still, compared to something like the dolls, that was a minor thing. At the same time...it wasn't a minor problem at all.

"He has the stand," Thala said.

Redrinna wasn't sure what that meant, but a palpable chill swept over the others from Póli. "The stand?"

River seemed particularly uncomfortable and looked away.

Will scuffed his sandal against the ground. "The stand is where he executes the people he doesn't like."

A chill raced down Redrinna's spine.

"And he does it publicly," Will added mildly, the implication in his tone clear, which Redrinna didn't appreciate.

Leonora nodded. "It's true, Your Highness. The boyar executes people often."

Nausea poured into Redrinna's stomach.

"Executes?" Kyvo asked, looking up at Redrinna with big eyes. "That sounds bad."

She nodded, her throat tight enough she almost couldn't speak. "An execution is when someone is killed, usually for committing a crime."

Kyvo and Xandrin recoiled at the same time. "What?"

"All over the world, you'll find a common form of punishment for serious criminal offenses is public execution. A lot of the time, you're killed in a nasty way in front of your friends, family, and neighbors. People seem to believe the more humiliating and painful the death, the more it helps you regret and be forgiven for what you did."

"That's...awful," Astra said. "I thought humans killing dragons for no reason was barbaric, but maybe you humans are just barbaric in general."

Redrinna looked askance at her. "That's why my father outlawed it in the Empire. A lot of them were just horrendous forms of torture. Well, that and the fact that most of the time, it was used by figures in power to keep the people beneath them submissive, so a lot of innocent people would be killed so those leaders could stay in complete control."

Xandrin's scales went a shade paler. "So, it's illegal, but they're doing it anyway?"

Again, Redrinna nodded. "Executions aren't outlawed completely, but they're reserved for extreme circumstances, and even then, they're supposed to be done swiftly and in private."

"It still sounds worse than dragons eating people."

"Think of it this way, Xandrin. If there was a person who'd killed people, or had killed someone in a terrible, brutal way, and wasn't sorry and if they were let go, they would do it again, you'd have to do one of two things: keep them imprisoned for the rest of their life or kill them. Keeping them imprisoned is difficult, even if you have enough resources. You have to make sure they don't break out, they don't try and kill someone in prison, make sure none of the guards get hurt taking care of them—the list goes on. It's in cases like those that an execution would be used."

"That's complicated, but I still don't like it."

"You got that right," Astra snapped, her snout wrinkling. "For once."

Xandrin growled.

Redrinna shot a glare at both of them.

"Redrinna," Tak said, his voice soft but strong as he took a step closer to her. "This isn't right. We have to do something."

She couldn't pull away from his fiery gaze. Immediately, she knew what she would choose, but it was followed by a powerful rush of doubt. For the first time in a long time, she wished her parents were here. They would know what to do and be brave enough to do it.

But they weren't here. It was her.

Her stomach clenched. Even still, when she glanced at the others—at River, Leonora, Thala and Will—there was a hollow, haunted look in their eyes, a look that only a month or so ago, Redrinna had seen in her own. Even though she hardly knew any of them and she didn't know a thing about the lives they'd led, she was intimate with the feelings that carved those eyes. She couldn't just leave.

The others were watching her in anticipation, seeming to be collectively holding their breaths.

She met the gazes of the dragons, Kyvo, and Tak. "I don't know what we can do, but between this and the dragon, I'm not leaving."

They nodded, but hearing herself say that made a chill settle in the pit of her stomach.

"I can't let you do that," River said, getting them all to turn to him. "It's bad, I know, but bad things happen to everyone who attempts to defy the boyar. I understand wanting to find the dragon, but going after the boyar himself borders on insanity."

"We kind of did that by leaving," Leonora pointed out.

River met her gaze, and while neither of them spoke, Redrinna could feel the unspoken fear that zipped between them.

Redrinna turned to her friends. "As the Dragon Kin, figuring out how to help here is our duty."

Tak and the dragons nodded.

"Boyars rule over the lands they're assigned much in the same way the emperor or empress rules over the nation," Leonora said, earning a wary glance from her brother. "Their word is only a step away from being the law, and the boyar isn't going to sacrifice what he's got to a rogue group, no matter how strong."

"Leonora," River hissed.

"It's true," Will said, fixing his gaze on Redrinna. "But no matter how strong he thinks he is, there's still someone he has to bow to."

Thala and Tak both turned to her with almost expectant expressions. Redrinna looked away.

Leonora took a step closer, desperation blazing in her eyes. "Your Highness, we wouldn't ask you if it wasn't bad, but boyars have to bow to the throne. They have to bow to you, even if you're still just the Imperial Princess."

"No!" Redrinna cried, making Leonora take a step back. Terror filled Redrinna's lungs, and for a second, it was a little hard to breathe. "I'm...I'm sorry. But please, don't ask that of me."

"You've got to be kidding me," Will hissed.

Thala gave him a hard nudge in the ribs that nearly knocked him off his rock.

Kyvo shot forward, landing in front of Redrinna, his fangs bared and fur rising as he glared at Will and Leonora. "What if that crazy guy tries to kill her too? We need her, okay?"

"I won't let anyone get her," Xandrin said. "I promise."

"Yeah, the boyar would try something like that," River said, his shoulders tensing. Lowering his head, he closed his eyes for a moment before meeting her gaze. "The second he learns you're here, he'll stop at nothing to get his hands on you."

That made the others go quiet.

Redrinna's chest constricted even more, making it a little harder to breathe.

Thala approached her, head lowered. "Your Highness, I know what some people have said about you. But once, your father saved my life."

Redrinna's brow furrowed. "He...did?"

Thala nodded. "I was one of the dolls."

Her eyes widened.

"Your father saved my life. He spoke to me personally and apologized for what happened, even though I know it wasn't his fault. I've never forgotten that." Thala looked up, meeting Redrinna's gaze, a hint of an emotion flickering there, but it was so faint Redrinna couldn't tell what it was. "You saved me as well. I never met you then, but you did something I've never forgotten. Do you remember?"

A murky memory surfaced in Redrinna's mind, but she didn't want to think about it.

"You saved us again, this past year. You helped us save our crops. And ever since we've been waiting for you. We believe if you were to go there, to Póli, you could change everything. We've been waiting—not just for you to come and fight to save us, but for the chance to fight by your side. We've been waiting for the chance to repay your kindness with our own."

Redrinna turned away, fixing her gaze on the blue of the ocean. Thala referred to an event that had been more of a coincidence than something intentional on Redrinna's part, and the crops...had been mere ideas. Someone else had put them into action and fine-tuned them so they would work. While that had all been happening,

Redrinna had been busy hiding in the mountains, ready to abandon an entire country and leave everyone in it to fend for themselves.

"I know you don't understand, but I can't be your princess. I lost that right a long time ago." Slowly, Redrinna allowed herself to meet Thala's gaze, and for a second, some kind of recognition—almost a kind of acknowledgement—passed between them. "However, I will fight for your city as a member of the Dragon Kin. You have my word on that. With the help of my friends, we can change this place for good this time."

Out of the corner of her eye, Redrinna caught a flash of disappointment steal across Tak's face.

After a moment, Thala nodded. Will still seemed annoyed, but at least he stayed quiet.

"That's good enough, Your Highness," River cut in, shooting a pointed look in his sister's direction. "Even still, you should stay hidden here, away from the city. The boyar has too many eyes inside it."

Redrinna stared at him for a moment before nodding.

"Okay," Will said with a bit of an exasperated sigh. "Then what are we going to do?"

For a moment, she just thought. Then she said, "For now, you guys can tell us about the city. Running in blind is a sure way to get captured or worse."

Kyvo stared around at all of them, his ears a little low.

"What's wrong?" Redrinna asked, leaning down to him.

"I'm...hungry," he said, his ears dropping a little lower.

"I'll go find something," Astra said. "I'll have a much easier time blending in than red beast would." For half a second, she lifted her wings before she tucked them in tight and trotted away.

Xandrin rolled his eyes once she was out of sight.

Redrinna stared after her before she sat on the ground. The others sat around her, though Will stayed on his rock. Kyvo laid on the ground, resting his head on his paws. Redrinna wasn't convinced he actually was hungry, but she wasn't sure what to do about it. She hesitated for a moment before gently petting his head. He leaned into it a little, but his ears stayed low.

The others described the city for her—sometimes talking over each other so Redrinna couldn't understand what they'd said, and she'd have to ask them to repeat themselves. The more they shared, the higher the bile in Redrinna's throat climbed.

Her parents had never given her an assignment like this. Any time reports of a tyrannical boyar or something of the like came in, they'd taken care of it themselves. From time to time, she'd reviewed the cases afterwards—to learn from them, her parents had said. But she'd never managed one on her own.

By the time they finished, the sun was sinking below the watery horizon, staining the ocean waves with splashes of orange and pink. Astra returned with dinner, and since there was little to no wood around, Xandrin roasted it for them.

"So," Xandrin said as they ate. "What are we going to do about this place?"

"Well, the easiest way is to just prove he's done wrong," Leonora said between bites. She wolfed the food down like it was the first thing she'd eaten all day. "Between River, a friend of ours, and me, you have witnesses, Your Highness."

"Yes, but..." What seemed like the weight of the ocean settled on Redrinna's shoulders as the others stared at her. They had evidence, yes, but in order to use it the way Leonora implied, Redrinna would have to...

A salt-tinged breeze sailed over them, tugging on the ends of Tak's wild hair as he leaned forward. "You don't want to do something that would require you to be an empress, do you?" His voice was quiet, but there was kindness in it too.

"I'm sorry," Redrinna whispered. "It'd be so much easier if I just went in and—" Her voice hitched in her throat, making a funny, hiccup sound.

Will made an exasperated noise, and River, who'd ended up

sitting the closest to him, dug a knuckle into his foot. Will doubled over with a near wheeze. "Why'd you have to use that hand?" he cried.

That confused Redrinna, but before she could give it much thought, Astra said:

"I'm not sure it'd be a good idea anyway. If the boyar is willing to kill people in ways he shouldn't in broad daylight, he might be able to use that to make the city turn against us, and especially you." She pointed a slender claw at Redrinna.

River froze and murmured, "I hadn't thought of that."

"But he would do it if he could," Thala added.

"F-from the sound of it, the boyar won't care if you went in declaring who you were anyway," Tak said, his voice hushed. "If he can break the law so freely and keep it all hidden from your parents, he must have a lot of connections and power on his side."

"He does, you're right," Leonora abruptly said, making Tak jump. "Every noble in the city is under his thumb. Some of the thugs are too. So, even if you were to come in and rip him out, it wouldn't fix anything." Frustration swept across her face.

"It'd just make a hole people would rush to fill," River added. "Which would make the situation worse."

Astra crossed her claws over each other and said, "There could be people being forced to cooperate too. If we just went in and started taking out people who appear bad, we could attack people who are innocent or have no choice."

Redrinna took another bite out of her dinner as she thought. Those were all good points, though whether or not they set her at ease, she wasn't sure. "The best thing to do is to start by figuring out how the city works and what forces are keeping him in power. This has happened in the city before, so his connections aren't only powerful, but they must run deep as well. Whatever move we choose to make, we have to make it wisely. Otherwise we'll make things exponentially worse."

The rest of them seemed to accept that and they dwindled into silence as thousands of stars emerged in the night sky. Heart heavy, Redrinna found her gaze settling on the ocean. Here and there, she spied the reflections of the stars above in the dark waters.

This wasn't like anything she'd faced before. It wasn't like living on the run; it wasn't like facing down a demon that wanted to eat people. If they made a wrong move here—even a small one—people could die as a result of a reckless decision. They could suffer because of indirect consequences. A lot of lives were at stake, and Redrinna couldn't afford to mess up. Even still, she couldn't bring herself to walk away.

All at once, she noticed Tak watching her, that concerned expression of his out in full force. He glanced around before mouthing, 'Are you okay?'

Redrinna hesitated before shrugging a shoulder. Once, she would have said her worst nightmare lay at her feet, and while she'd had nightmares far worse than this, it didn't take the fear piercing her heart away. Something like this wasn't her worst nightmare any longer, but it wasn't far removed either.

As her thoughts turned over and over, Kyvo crawled into her lap, nudging her chin with his head. She scratched his ears like he wanted, still thinking. What did she do? How could she do it without having to risk posing as someone she wasn't and ultimately failing?

Chapter Ten

Redrinna's eyes snapped open as the ground shuddered beneath her like someone had jerked it hard. Was that a half-asleep hallucination or had she actually felt something? After a second longer, Kyvo sat up, which made her do the same.

His ears swiveled in every direction, his gaze fixed on the horizon. "Did you feel that?"

"Yes," she said, trying to figure out what he listened for.

"So I'm not crazy?" Astra said, staring their way. "I was still trying to decide whether or not I should wake one of you up."

"It's just River," Will mumbled.

River kicked Will's foot. "It wasn't me." Redrinna noted he didn't sound like he'd been sleeping.

She opened her mouth to speak but yawned instead. "What time is it?"

"Not that late," Astra said, raising her snout skyward. "I doubt it's even midnight yet."

Yawning, Redrinna stretched her arms, debating laying back down. She'd just fallen asleep before that shake had woken her.

From somewhere nearby, Leonora also yawned and said, "It's probably nothing. We get little tremors like those from time to time here."

Even still, Redrinna's gaze drifted towards the shadowy, pointed island in the middle of Diablo's Maw, the last, lingering remnant of the Diablo. There was no angry red glare of lava and, while it was hard to be sure in the dark, there weren't any hints of smoke. According to the history books she'd read, the Diablo had been full of lava before it'd erupted—that was part of the reason people dismissed the potential of it having a massive eruption. It'd always been a chaotic, violent volcano. But now, just like it had been since they'd arrived, it was quiet and dark.

Right as she made to lay down, the earth jerked again. She caught herself, barely able to keep from falling on her face. Kyvo pressed into her side, hunkering down as his ears flicked even faster.

Tak jerked upright, glancing around in a confused, half-asleep way. "What was that?"

"Dunno," Astra said.

"River," Will mumbled again.

River was on his feet, his head turning from side to side like he searched for something. "It isn't me. Get up already, just in case."

Will complied with a groan.

Kyvo let out a whine. "I think that Diablo-thingy is doing something."

Placing a hand on his shaking back, Redrinna said, "What do you mean?"

"Can't you hear it?" he asked, ears still swiveling. "It's like...something's moving."

They all went quiet, listening. Redrinna frowned. She didn't not believe Kyvo, but the night was silent. The only things she could hear were the wind as it blew past and the ocean waves making noise, though they did sound a bit agitated.

"Red beast," Astra snapped, whacking Xandrin with her tail. It took her a few pokes to get him to stir. "Hey, wake up already. We're having a crisis!"

"Crisis?" the dragon said, eyes sliding shut even as he lifted his head. One of his ear frills twitched. "Would you stop hissing at me?"

"I'm not hissing," Astra said, her snout wrinkling. "But don't tempt me."

"Something's hissing."

"Cut it out, you two," Redrinna said, struggling to hear whatever he heard. Even still, once they were quiet, she couldn't hear it.

Kyvo's ears tilted forward, in the direction of the Diablo. "Oh, I hear it too."

She stared out at the dark water, trying to hear or see anything. Before she could, the ground bucked again. She threw her hands out to catch herself before she fell. Unlike the last couple shakes, which had happened in isolation, this time, the earth didn't stop heaving. Instead, it worsened, shaking even harder. Rocks clattered against each other with loud cracks. The crashing of the ocean waves came faster and stronger.

Redrinna glanced around, heart pounding. Was this an earthquake? The last time an earthquake like this had happened here hadn't been since—

Without warning, a boom and a hiss burst from the ocean, the sound striking the mountains behind them and echoing back. Despite the darkness, Redrinna caught sight of a white, frothy plume flecked with spots of bright orange shooting out of the water near the Diablo.

As the shaking intensified, Xandrin fought to get to his feet. His wings shot out to help him stay balanced. "I thought you said it was dormant!"

Another glowing, frothy plume shot out of the water, closer to the volcano than the first had been, the resulting, ringing boom echoing off the mountains. It was so loud it reverberated in Redrinna's chest, powerful enough it was painful.

"It was!" she snapped, struggling to get to her feet. She snatched Kyvo up right before a large rock bounced past.

"We need to get in the air!" River shouted.

The next second, another boom rocked the night, the resulting plume half water and half sand as part of the beach surrounding Diablo's Maw blasted into the sky. Xandrin snatched her, Thala, Will, and Kyvo in his claws before rocketing into the sky. Astra followed with Tak, Leonora, and River seconds later. Large rocks flashed past, just missing Astra's tail. A harsh grinding filled the air as the water in Diablo's Maw pitched like it was in the middle of a raging tempest.

"Get higher!" Astra shouted.

Two seconds later, an ear-splitting boom thundered off the mountains. Redrinna flinched, ears ringing. A second later, bristling heat slapped her face, making her turn. Her eyes went wide.

A massive plume of bright orange and red lava filled the sky. A bolt of jagged lightning shot out, adding to the cacophony as the lava shot higher than they were flying before it crashed into the thrashing waters of the caldera, hissing like thousands of snakes. Redrinna winced, clapping one hand over her ear as another tower of lava erupted into the sky with a headache-inducing roar.

Volcanoes could be unpredictable; she knew that. However, for it to have this massive of an eruption without any sign—Redrinna wouldn't have believed it if the volcano hadn't been raging right in front of her eyes.

Two more plumes of lava shot up before the volcano settled, just spitting out spats of lava while the rest trickled down its slopes. It glowed a menacing red, bright despite how far away it was.

Once the rumbling below stopped, the dragons returned to the earth, landing delicately on the rocks and boulders that had buried their campsite. Aside from the distant, angry glare of the volcano, the world seemed back to normal. Regardless, Redrinna and the others remained in the safety of the dragon's claws.

"That was scary," Kyvo said, trembling from snout to tail, his ears flat against his head.

"Yeah," Astra said, shifting her weight and making some smaller rocks skitter away. "It's a good thing we can fly."

Redrinna glanced at the rocks below them before turning her gaze back to the volcano. It still wept thick streams of lava. "Xandrin, when you flew over the volcano yesterday, did you manage to see inside it?"

He cocked his head. "Kind of. I only glanced at it as I passed. Why?"

"Did you notice any lava or smoke?"

"I don't think so. All I saw was rock, I promise."

A frown twisted her mouth. For it to be spewing that much lava, wouldn't the chamber have had to be full? Granted she wasn't an expert on volcanoes, so she wasn't sure, but how could there have been next to no warning for such a massive eruption?

"What are you thinking about?" Tak asked, watching her instead of the volcano.

"This... It has to be Osiris's magic again," she said, her frown deepening. "It throws everything out of balance, and as he gets stronger, it gets worse. For such a massive eruption, there would've been some sort of sign—I'm sure of it. But in the two days we were here, there wasn't anything."

He frowned too. "Back in the forest, there was all that rain and the mudslide, and now a volcanic eruption and an earthquake."

Astra growled a little. "If it really is because of that creep and his magic, then he's getting stronger, isn't he?"

"And it's going to get worse in the future," Redrinna said.

They all went quiet, palpable tension in the air.

When Redrinna and Matte had talked about Osiris and his magic before, they'd discussed how the seasons and the weather had been out of kilter. For some reason, Redrinna had thought that would be the extent of it, even though Matte had mentioned natural disasters as well. Even still, it hadn't occurred to her that Osiris' magic had the potential to make dormant volcanoes erupt.

That fear that was never far away tightened around her chest.

"On the plus side," Xandrin put in, "at least the damage seems to have stayed in the Maw. All the villages and everything should be safe, right?"

"Unless they got buried in the rubble," Leonora said, staring pointedly at the rocks beneath them.

Redrinna's heart skipped a beat. "We need to check and make sure, just in case, okay?"

The dragons glanced at each other before shaking their heads. Xandrin said, "We will check on the villages, but you won't."

"But River said—"

"I don't care about us staying hidden at the moment," Astra said. "We're going to fly high enough most people won't be able to spot us anyway; not unless they're paying attention. Besides, it won't take long. So, on the off chance we need to fly a bit lower to get a better look, you're all going to stay here."

"Anyone who's awake will be too focused on the quake or the volcano to pay them much mind," River pointed out. "They should be all right."

Redrinna hopped to the ground. Kyvo scrambled onto her shoulders. "Fine. But you guys promise you'll be careful, all right?"

"We will," Xandrin said with the hint of a smile.

"Like we want to be stupid," Astra said before shooting a concerned glance at Tak. "If any of you gets hurt while we're gone, you're grounded."

"We won't go anywhere," Tak said. Then, in undertone to Redrinna, he added, "I'm too tired anyway."

The corner of Redrinna's mouth tugged up at that.

With a final nod, the dragons turned and launched into the night sky, quickly vanishing into the darkness.

A sigh escaped Redrinna as she sat on the nearest boulder, the panic from a few minutes ago melting away and leaving nothing but exhaustion in its wake. Kyvo abandoned her shoulders for her lap, falling back asleep almost instantly. Despite how tired she was, she didn't dare go to sleep while the dragons were gone.

A bit to her surprise—despite what he'd said—Tak didn't go back to sleep either. Instead, he came and sat next to her, his gaze fixed on the volcano. The light from the lava cast his face in an almost menacing red light.

The others didn't go back to sleep either, most of them sitting on a boulder with their gazes fixed on the volcano. Even still, they stayed quiet, but it wasn't a sleepy quiet—it was an uneasy one.

After a long minute, Tak turned to her and whispered, "Do you really think this is because of Osiris and his magic?"

"I'm not sure, since I don't know much about volcanoes, but it's...strange it would erupt like this without any warning."

"Do volcanoes usually give more warning?" Thala asked.

"It depends on the volcano," River said, his gaze still on the lava. "Steam volcanoes do tend to erupt without warning—any kind of volcano with a pocket deep underground can—but for volcanoes like this, there usually is some kind of warning. Like an increase in earthquakes or lava in the crater or smoke from in or near it—that kind of thing."

Leonora leaned forward. "Were there signs when it erupted the first time?"

Squeezing her eyes shut, Redrinna tried to remember anything she'd read about the Diablo. "I think so. It'd occasionally had small, minor eruptions, and there was lava in the cavern. A lot of it. When its big eruption got closer, there was more lava and smoke, little eruptions became more frequent. There were earthquakes too. If I remember correctly, some of the sorcerers from the nearby kingdom were convinced all those things were indicative of an impending, massive eruption and petitioned the king to evacuate the nearby cities, but he refused to listen to them. I think he might have even dismissed a lot of his court because of it—either way, the infighting became a massive problem."

"And then the volcano exploded," Tak finished, his voice quiet.

She nodded. So much destruction in such a small amount of time. When she'd learned about that as a kid, she hadn't been able to wrap her mind around an event like Diablo's eruption. However, she had a better idea now, and it made her heart ache to think of it.

"If he'd just listened to those people in his court, people who were more in tune with the world around him and the people who studied it," she began, her voice hushed too, "I wonder how many people would've been saved. Instead, thousands of people died because of him."

Leonora lowered her head.

Tak didn't speak right away. "This...is kind of why you don't want to be the next empress, isn't it?"

That caught her enough off guard that she glanced at him with wide eyes before hurriedly looking away. "One mistake is all it would take for so many lives to be ruined. That's all. I've already messed up so many times, and I don't need to make it worse."

Once again, there was a long pause before he spoke. "I get that, Redrinna. I do. But—" He stopped, closing his eyes.

Her curiosity piqued the longer he stayed quiet. "But what?"

A strong wind picked up, yanking on both of their hair. As a couple strands of hair swept in front of his eyes, he opened them and said, "I just...I wish you'd stop saying things like that about yourself. You...sell yourself short a lot, and I just..."

She cocked her head.

All at once, River shot to his feet, his gaze on the coast.

Redrinna glanced at the volcano. It still oozed lava, seeming the same as it'd been before—

Dragging itself from the water was a skeleton-like creature. It seemed vaguely human shaped though she didn't think it was human. Her eyes narrowed as she stared at it, trying to figure out what it was. She'd never read about an aquatic creature that resembled this thing. A couple more just like it crawled out of the water behind it, their pale sheen making them look an awful lot like they were made of bone.

Slowly, the things pushed themselves to their feet, their bodies clacking and clicking as they straightened. Redrinna's blood went cold. They weren't human skeleton-like; they *were* human skeletons. They were close enough she could see missing chunks of bone and reddish, tassel-like worms embedded in their ribs and legs. Barnacles clung to their heads and shoulders like armor.

The one in front stayed still for a second before opening its eyes—at least, she supposed that would've been the equivalent. Two orange orbs winked into existence in the skull's eye sockets, hauntingly similar to the eyes of the beast that had chased her in the Imperial City. Were these some of Osiris's creations?

"What is that?" Will hissed.

The skeletons' heads immediately turned towards them. They stepped forward, their boney feet silent against the sand even though their bones creaked with unnerving clacks as they grated against each other. The skeletons' gazes were fixed on them as they approached, unwavering and unblinking.

Redrinna swallowed, her mouth dry. Now was a bad time for the dragons to be gone.

Moving slow, she scooped Kyvo into her arms and slid off her rock. Keeping her steps quiet, she moved back, putting both distance and boulders between her and the skeletons. Leonora did the same, though the others willingly stood between the three of them and the skeletons.

The skeletons continued to stagger towards them in their strange, uneven walk, almost dragging their feet. When they reached the boulders from the landslide, Redrinna thought that would drastically slow them down. However, they simply put their hands down and crawled over the first few rocks like clumsy, creaky spiders. Rather than slow down, they sped up.

One fixed its gaze right on her. Picking up speed, it rushed at her, going over and around the boulders with ease, like it sprinted across flat ground. The other two charged the others.

Tak rapidly backed up, navigating through the boulders until he stood next to her. The next second, the skeleton was right in front of them. She dove to one side as Tak shot to the other. The skeleton caught itself on one of the larger rocks. Its head snapped around, eyes fixed on her even though it still clung to the rock.

Stumbling back, it took a lot of Redrinna's strength to keep herself upright when her heels bumped into rocks. Kyvo's head shot up and he sprang out of her arms, landing on one of the nearby rocks. He staggered a bit as he tried to stifle a yawn.

Redrinna took a deep breath. She focused, concentrating on the power in the earth coursing beneath her feet. As the skeleton scurried over the next closest rock, she released it. Fire burst out of the ground, consuming the skeleton.

"Yeah! You got him!" Kyvo chirped.

Relief settled in her chest for a couple seconds. Then, to her alarm, the skeleton recovered from the shock and lurched forward, impervious to the flames biting at its bones. Bad. Very bad.

"Put it out!" Tak cried.

Redrinna jerked the heat away, dousing the flames and leaving what was left of the worms dangling in charred threads. The skeleton's bones gleamed in the moonlight, highlighting its new scorch marks.

She hopped back, just managing to avoid turning her ankle on a rock. The skeleton lunged. She jumped to the side, narrowly avoiding its claw-like hands before her foot caught against a rock and sent her sprawling. The skeleton crashed against the rock that had been behind her, a nasty crunch ringing out.

"Redrinna!" Tak and Kyvo both called.

Even though she heard them, she kept her attention on the monster. It leaned back from the rock, almost seeming stunned, before it fixed its gaze on her. It'd snapped its jaw on one side when it'd crashed, making it dangle at a crooked angle and giving it a permanent expression of surprise.

A stone struck the rock as the skeleton adjusted, turning Redrinna's way again. The next second, another stone clipped the side of its head, leaving a gash. For a split second, the lights in its eye sockets flickered. It froze before turning in the direction the rock had come from.

Redrinna was positive Tak had thrown it. However, the skeleton spotted Kyvo first and rushed at him. With a high squeal of panic, Kyvo dashed for Tak.

"Go for their heads!" Redrinna shouted as she shot off the ground.

Tak had a rock ready, but it tumbled from his grasp when Kyvo vaulted into his arms. Her heart leapt into her throat.

Without warning, Thala dashed around a nearby boulder, a fist-sized rock in her hand. She reached the skeleton before it could get Tak and Kyvo and slammed her rock through its skull. It shattered, the dozens of bone shards clattering against the nearby boulders. The rest of its bones simply dropped to the ground.

Thala dashed towards the others. As River tricked one into slamming headfirst into a boulder, Thala reached him and shattered its skull too. Then River dashed across the tops of the boulders with uncanny ease. Will dragged Leonora out of the way as the third skeleton leapt for them. River reached it first, kicking its head clean off its shoulders. The skull shot back, shattering against a boulder. Its body continued forward due to its momentum. Will and Leonora dodged by mere inches. The rest of the skeleton slammed into a rock, the bones tumbling apart like blocks that had merely been stacked on top of each other.

A shudder swept down Redrinna's spine as she eyed the remains of their attackers. Between them and the volcano, she wasn't sure she was going to even bother attempting to go back to sleep tonight.

A second later, River landed right in front of her, making her take an alarmed step back. "Your Highness, are you hurt?" he asked, not even seeming winded despite the move he'd just pulled off.

She shook her head.

"What were those things?" Kyvo squeaked, voice pitched high and trembling.

Redrinna shook her head, glancing at the skeletons' remains again. "I don't have a clue. Some kind of magic had to have been involved though."

"Most likely," River said, kicking away a stray femur.

"Not something I expected to see today," Will said, leaning against the nearest rock. He squinted at Redrinna. "Are we sure you didn't bring these things with you?"

River looked askance at him the same second Leonora punched his arm.

Thala studied the skeletons for a minute before her gaze flicked back to the volcano. "That makes no sense unless Her Highness has power to control the dead."

"Which isn't a type of magic it's possible to have," River said, a frown twisting his mouth.

"Are you sure about that?" Will said, motioning to the remains around them. "Because I'm pretty sure that's exactly what caused this to happen. Or are skeletons walking around a natural thing I don't know about?"

Tak, however, met Redrinna's gaze, his expression making it clear they'd had the same thought. Together, they both said, "Osiris."

Chapter Eleven

The dragons returned near dawn, and the moment Xandrin's claws touched the ground, he stomped to Redrinna's side, not relaxing until she'd rubbed his snout. Astra did the same to Tak, but both the dragons went on the defensive the second they discovered the remains of their unexpected visitors.

With a yawn, Redrinna filled them in. Their expressions darkened.

"Were the villages okay?" she asked, looking back and forth between the two of them.

"Mostly," Xandrin said. "There was a bit of damage, but nobody seemed seriously hurt."

"There was one that got buried in a massive landslide," Astra said, her gaze dropping. "We unburied it as best we could, but we didn't find any survivors."

Redrinna's heart plummeted as she closed her eyes. There was nothing they could've done, but even still, her chest ached. If the volcano's eruption and the earthquakes really were the result of Osiris and his magic, then there were even more victims on an already massive list. How many more people had to die before this could finally end?

"You seem awfully concerned for someone who claims not to be a princess," Will said, making Redrinna pause.

She glanced at him, the glare on his face making her wary.

River shot him a scathing glare, but he either didn't notice or didn't care.

Tak glanced at Will, almost glaring at him before quietly saying, "Yeah, because someone caring about other people is weird."

Will met Tak's gaze, and even though Redrinna wasn't standing close to either of them, the tension sparking between them like lightning was still palpable.

Before she could think of something to do, Leonora stepped between the two of them, getting Will's attention. "There isn't time for nonsense like that. If you're going to be mean, Will, you can go back to Póli."

Will rolled his eyes, but he didn't say anything.

"Now that everyone is here, we should make a plan. If we're going to clean up Póli, we have to be careful and do it right." A determined expression settled on Leonora's face. "We're only going to get one shot at this."

Redrinna nodded, doing her best to shake off the unease that pricked her every time Will stared in her direction.

River frowned. "All right. We should move to a place that can hide the dragons better though. My grandfather will be determined to get me and Leonora back, and people will undoubtedly come hunting. Sitting out here in the open is imbecilic."

"There were more soldiers than usual yesterday," Thala commented, almost in a bored way, but bored wasn't quite the right word.

"Imperial soldiers," Will added, staring hard at Redrinna as he said it.

She understood his intent, but she refused to acknowledge him.

"What does that mean?" Xandrin whispered, lowering his head next to her.

Smothering a sigh, she quietly explained, "Boyars aren't allowed to have armies of their own, so all the soldiers here are Imperial ones—that means ones that belong to the Empire."

Even though she'd tried to keep her voice quiet, Will heard her anyway. "Yeah, which means if you were smart, you'd go in and order all the soldiers to do whatever you wanted."

River's glare intensified, and this time, Will purposely turned the opposite direction. "We already talked about that. I'm not going to say it wouldn't work, but if we did decide to use it, we have to use it *wisely*."

Will didn't respond to that.

"Anyway," Leonora said, "where should we go?"

Closing his eyes, River tilted his head to the side. "When you want to hide, there's two good places: far away or right under his nose."

"Under his nose is very dangerous," Thala said.

"Not if he thinks we're running," Leonora said, a hint of a smile twisting her mouth. "Especially since we have one of the best places to hide out in."

"Exactly," River said, both of them turning and staring at the mountains towering over them.

Redrinna followed their gaze, staring at the rocky crags blotting out a lot of the sky. It was difficult for her to believe these mountains were part of the Agicae Mountain range when they appeared so different from the ones in whose shadows she'd grown up. Unlike her lush, forest-covered peaks, these were harsh and barren, with little vegetation adorning their sides. These featured jagged lines instead of the smooth ones Redrinna was used to seeing.

"You want to flirt with death?" Will asked, staring at the siblings with exasperation. "People die up there, you know."

"I know," River and Leonora said at the same time. Then River continued, "That's why it's the last place that pig will expect us to be."

᪢᪢

Because they wanted to do their utmost to avoid alerting anyone in the city, particularly the boyar, River led them on a long flight over the mountain range, instructing the dragons to stay low. By the time they landed near the base of a large peak, it was past noon, though not as hot as it had been along the peninsula.

The forest on the slopes was not as lush as the forests up north; the trees were sparser and more bush-like and the ground was loose rock. Even still, they managed to find a little grove that, between it and the mountainside, would keep them out of sight.

They settled in the shade, and Redrinna found her gaze wandering to the trees. She spied some oak and pine—though they were different varieties than the ones she knew—and trees with thick, gnarled trunks and pale green leaves. Then there were thin but tall trees, their leaves a dark, lush green that reminded her of pines, but they weren't pines. They weren't like the trees back home.

"So," Will began once they were settled, the humans and Kyvo seated in a ring and the dragons crouched behind them. "What's next?"

Most everyone looked at Redrinna.

Stifling a sigh, she thought for a minute before speaking. "Well, my friends and I came here to find a dragon. It was supposed to be living in the caldera, but its cave is empty and there's blood everywhere."

"Still sounds like it's dead," Will said, fiddling with a leaf.

Leonora elbowed him in the ribs. "Knowing my grandfather, he has it, and it wouldn't be much use to him dead."

River nodded. "It's gross, but a lot of people here believe dragon blood has magical properties that'll do stuff like prevent aging or healing weird ailments. If he does have it, I'm sure he's using its blood as bribes."

Redrinna's nose wrinkled at the idea of someone willingly ingesting something's blood, and out of the corner of her eye, she caught Tak and Astra making similar expressions.

"I'll do what I can to figure out if he has it or not," River continued, a serious gleam in his eye.

"River," Leonora whispered, brow furrowing with concern.

"River is the best at spying," Thala pointed out. "It might be safer to send Will instead though. He's the second best."

The scowl that swept over Will's face made it clear he didn't think much of that idea. Or maybe it was being labeled 'second best' that bugged him.

"It would be safer to send Will, but since it's for Her Highness, I figured he'd get mad about doing it," River said, almost sounding bored. "Don't worry. That guy won't be able to catch me."

That made Will scowl even more. "Whatever. Who cares about this dragon anyway? We—"

"We do," Xandrin and Astra said in sync, both glaring at Will too much to glare at each other like they normally did.

"Why is this dragon important, Your Highness?" Leonora said, turning her attention back to Redrinna. "And that Osiris you mentioned yesterday. Does he play into this too?"

Redrinna supposed it was only fair they knew what was going on if they were going to help them out. Keeping it simple, she explained who Osiris was and who the Dragon Kin were.

"We need to find that dragon because we need to gather a new Dragon Kin," she finished. "Also, I'm worried about it. Osiris and his crew could've gotten to it, but if they haven't, we need to find it as quickly as possible." She hoped with all her being it wasn't dead. "Or they will get to it."

To her surprise, Thala leaned forward, resting her elbows on her knees. For the first time since Redrinna had met her, a hint of emotion appeared on her face: her eyes narrowed, like she was thinking. "So this Dragon Kin thing you need to find the dragon for...do you know where to find the people?"

"No," Redrinna said with a bit of a grimace. "But because of our gems—" she laid a hand on it, appreciating its reassuring warmth, "—we can get an idea of where they are. In fact, my gem says there are three people near here. That's the most we have to go on right now."

Her gem had told her she'd already met those three, but since they were right in front of her, Redrinna didn't point that out.

"And how would they know they've been chosen or marked, or however you explained it?"

Redrinna tugged some of her vibrant red strands—pulled back in a ponytail—over her shoulder. "The sudden change in the color of your hair and eyes, most likely after a big event in your life, is a sign of being marked."

Almost imperceptibly, River and Leonora both stiffened.

Thala reached up and fingered the end of her turquoise braid. "So this...this is the mark of a Dragon Gem?"

Redrinna nodded.

"Does that mean I have to join?"

"Not necessarily," Redrinna said with a shake of her head. "The gems mark more than one person, and it's from that group of people they'll choose the person they want to partner with. You'll know if you've been chosen because you'll have a dream. A specific dream."

Thala met her gaze. "A dream?"

Redrinna turned to Tak. She'd heard him describe the dream once, but she didn't remember the details.

Cheeks turning pink, Tak quietly said, "You're at the ocean and there's a voice that speaks."

"And it says...'open your eyes,' right?" Thala ventured, combing her fingers through the end of her braid.

Tak nodded.

"I...started having a dream like that almost a month ago," she continued, her gaze dropping. "But I'm not sure...I can."

"It's okay if you don't want to," Redrinna said quickly. "The gem that chose you won't force you into the Dragon Kin if you don't want to do it. You can tell it no."

At that, not just Thala frowned, but River and Leonora did too.

Will glanced at the siblings, eyeing them before he said, "That's great and all, but how is this going to help us with the city? If we can't burn the boyar out, then what are we going to do?"

Redrinna closed her eyes, racking her brain for anything they could use for inspiration. The others waited in silence.

After a few minutes, Kyvo popped up, resting his front paws on her knees, his tail wagging slightly from side to side. "So?"

"Sorry," she said, resting her head in her hands. "I'm trying to think of examples I've read about before, but everything I've come up with have been bloody coups."

"Oh," he said, dropping off her knee.

"That's all I can think of too," River said, eyes closed and the fingers of his right hand touching his forehead.

"Well, in that case, if there isn't a precedent, then we'll have to come up with one," Leonora said, a hint of a smile in her voice.

It was a moment before Redrinna could meet her gaze.

"It's not impossible; just difficult," Leonora continued, her smile fading into a thoughtful frown. "We need to figure out what we can push or manipulate that will get the boyar and the nobles to do what we want."

"What we want is for them to leave their positions of power for good." Will huffed, leaning back on his hands. "But a lot of those people used some nasty tricks to either get where they are or stay there, which means ripping them out won't be easy."

Redrinna nodded. "If we just make them run, they'll either go into hiding and eventually come back or they'll go somewhere else and set this up all over again. What we need is a way to get undeniable proof of what they've been doing and alert whoever the general of the Imperial army that's stationed here before they can catch on."

"But wouldn't the boyar be able to stop them?" Tak asked, his voice a bit quieter than usual, almost like he was nervous. Which perhaps he was. He wasn't talkative when they were around people they didn't know.

She shook her head. "No, the only thing we'd really have to worry about is who the general here is. Boyars may be governors, but the Imperial Generals aren't subject to them."

"Because they're loyal to the crown first," Will added mildly.

Leonora smacked his shoulder.

"In order to keep people in powerful positions in line," Redrinna continued, "generals have the authority—provided they have irrefutable proof—to take authority from the boyar. In which case, if we could find enough evidence to convict the corrupt nobles and the boyar, the general would be able to seize the city and punish everyone who's guilty."

"Hold on, hold on," Astra cut in. "If it's proof this general needs, wouldn't that execution stand be enough?"

That made Redrinna pause. Slowly, she said, "Well, there is always the possibility the general over this area is corrupt too. If that is the case, our plan wouldn't necessarily have to change, but we'd have to work around it. Carefully. But if they aren't, the stand in and of itself isn't proof of wrongdoing. You'd either have to have the general see an execution or have enough people testify public executions are happening. Plus, generals do have a pretty broad area assigned to them, so whoever the general of this place is might not even be in Póli most of the time. That said, surely the soldiers stationed here would know..."

As she trailed off, River leaned forward. "I've wondered for a while if maybe the boyar is threatening the soldiers in some way. They always seem tense."

"Oh yeah, they're way jumpy," Will added.

That made her look up.

"It could be some kind of corruption amongst the ranks too, among the captains or something," Leonora suggested. "Or the boyar could be threatening to harm the city in some way if they don't obey, I suppose."

"It might even be both," Thala said.

"You think he might be forcing the soldiers to keep quiet?" Redrinna asked.

"Not only is it something my grandfather would do," Leonora said, "he did it when he made the dolls all those years ago. If he wanted to do it again, he would know how."

"All right, then we need to figure out who the general over this area is and where they are right now," Redrinna said. "For the time being, we need to lay low. If the nobles or the boyar catch wind of anything, they could bolt or destroy any of the evidence we need to get our hands on."

River nodded. "Understood, Your Highness."

That almost made her cringe, but she managed to keep her face under control.

Then Thala said, "If you want inside information about the army's movements, I could get it."

Redrinna blinked. "You can?"

"Some of the soldiers still remember me," Thala explained.

Discomfort wrapped around Redrinna's spine. She was still shocked Thala had been a doll, and the idea of sending the girl back into that kind of situation increased her unease.

"I don't know," Redrinna said.

Will frowned, but it wasn't the angry one he usually had. "I kind of agree with the princess on this one, Thala. It took you years to re-cover last time, and if you go back—"

"I'll be fine." Thala got to her feet. "I can handle myself just fine; it's not like I'm going to war again. However, I'm no good at strategy, so unless you strongly object, I'm gonna go take care of my part."

Redrinna hesitated before she nodded. She barely knew Thala, and it wasn't her place to tell the girl what she could or couldn't do. On the contrary, sending Thala into the army as a spy was a pretty good idea, even if it was an uncomfortable one.

Without saying anything else, Thala left.

River stayed quiet for a minute as well before he leaned forward, almost like he was about to get up. "Should I go too?"

Redrinna thought for a minute. "It might be risky since you just escaped your grandfather, but you know him better than I do."

He hesitated before relaxing. "Maybe later would be a bit better. Us all going in together could cause problems."

If that was what he thought, then Redrinna would agree. She knew nothing about this boyar, but then again, she knew little about the inner workings of the Empire. She knew its face, but not it's heart—another reason she wasn't much cut out for leading it.

Will leapt to his feet, nabbing her attention. "Well, if we aren't going to talk anymore, I'm going to do something else." He shot a dirty look at Redrinna. "You really do look like a demon, you know that?"

Xandrin growled at the same second Leonora and River both glared at him. Without saying another word, Will left, taking the same path Thala had.

Once he was gone, Leonora grimaced and said, "I'm so sorry about him, Your Highness. He's normally not so grouchy."

"Not really," River said. "He's always irascible."

Leonora raised her eyes skyward. "Don't use words most people don't understand, River."

He blinked. "What do you mean? Irascible is a pretty common word."

"No it's not." Leonora huffed, turning to Tak and Redrinna. "Do you guys know it?"

Tak shook his head, but Redrinna said, "I do, but I grew up spending all my time reading research books and stuff like that."

Leonora turned to Kyvo and the dragons, all of whom shook their heads. She turned back to River. "See? Only Her Highness knows it. Therefore, it's not a common word."

River sighed, looking resigned.

Despite the situation, Redrinna found herself smiling a little.

Chapter Twelve

Thala made her way down the street, the people scurrying about the city's upper crust giving her a wide berth as usual, but today, she hardly noticed. She had a mission—a purpose—something she hadn't had in years. It didn't give her a spring in her step, per se, but it did give her something.

The main guard house was situated on the cusp of the upper level and main thoroughfare of the city. It was modest in its design, almost spartan. It rose above the city, slender but taller than even the boyar's mansion in the distance.

It'd been years since she'd set foot inside, but for some reason, it almost felt like home. Even still, as she stepped inside, she had the distinct impression her dad wouldn't have been happy to find her there. It came and went so fast, Thala couldn't help wondering if she'd imagined it.

The only light in the building came from the sun coming through the windows, all of which were open to let in the breeze. It was a hot breeze but it was more pleasant than stagnant air. A few men's voices trickled through one of the side rooms while Thala remained near the door, in the open space before an empty desk that stood in front of a gray stone wall. There were two open doorways on either side, and though she couldn't see anything, Thala knew that they led to the dining hall, training grounds, and sleeping quarters.

She spent a few minutes waiting, studying the grays and browns of the stone wall before she heard footsteps.

A young soldier in a crisp white uniform stepped out from behind the stone wall, jumping back when he noticed her. "The Azure Demon!" he hissed.

"Oi," someone behind him said.

The young man hurried out of the way. "Sorry, sir."

An older man Thala recognized stepped out next, giving the soldier a stern look before he turned and saw her. For a minute, he just stared. Clapping the soldier on the back of the head, he said, "Private, I'm pretty darn sure you should be apologizing to the lady, not me. What self-respecting man calls someone he doesn't know a demon?"

Rubbing his head, the young man gave her a little bow. "S-sorry, ma'am."

"It's fine," she said. Then she turned to the older soldier. "Captain Andor, sir. Can we talk?"

His eyebrow lifted a fraction, and he motioned towards one of the side rooms. "If it's you making a request, it must be important."

She went and he followed her inside and shut the door. She remained standing, habitually standing at attention as he took a seat.

"Good grief, child, you aren't in the army anymore. There's no need to stand on ceremony."

Even still, now that she was in the guard house, Thala didn't know how else to stand.

Heaving a sigh, Captain Andor got to his feet and said, "All right, Thala. It's been more than five years since I last saw you, so what do you need?"

"I need to ask you a question," she said.

That made him quirk an eyebrow again.

It occurred to her that she couldn't possibly say why she wanted to know this information without putting Her Highness in serious danger. So, thinking quickly, she said, "I've...been thinking about rejoining the army, sir, and I...wanted to know who the general here was."

It sounded weak in her ears, but perhaps it would pass in his.

Captain Andor stayed quiet for a moment more. "Thala, the last thing you need to do with your life is join the army again."

She'd never been great at lying, so instead of trying to forge a lie, she chose to say something true. "It's all I know, sir."

Even though she didn't like it, it was true. Fighting was all she knew; the army was the only thing she'd ever been able to associate with home, even if she never wanted to have to kill anyone ever again. Without it...she didn't have anything. There wasn't anything else.

"Well...if you're sure," Captain Andor began, pausing like he was trying to give her the opportunity to object. When she didn't, he continued, "I suppose it's only fair of you to wonder who the general is. A couple of the bad ones from the desert are still around, after all."

Thala lowered her head. It wasn't like she had emotions to hide, but it made her feel a little more in control, at the very least.

"It's alright, Thala. The general stationed here was appointed after the war, so he wouldn't know you. Besides that, I promise he's fair. If he could, he'd drag that—" He cut himself off with a huff, confirming in Thala's mind that the boyar had to have ears in the building or something over the guards. "Anyway, let's just say he'd love to see some big changes happen if he could. His name is Cael. General Cael."

She didn't recognize that name. "Is he here?" she asked softly.

"No. After last night's earthquake, he took a bunch of men and is touring the villages to check for damage and provide relief. He should be back within a couple weeks if you're still thinking about it."

She nodded. "Thank you, sir."

He didn't speak, just letting out one of those sighs again instead.

Giving him the proper salute, she left the guardhouse. Then, figuring it would be suspicious if she immediately turned and left the city, she wandered in the direction of the port, the stench of fish getting stronger the closer she got. When she was there, she stared at the market, thronged with slaves from the noble houses bartering for better deals before turning and heading to the docks, towards the end where no one was. Even though it was a bit hot, she sat on one of the posts, the wind tugging at the loose hairs around her face as she stared out at the blue grey ocean waters. Water lapped at the posts as seagulls cried out in the air above, circling over the docks as they hunted for scraps. Men's voices added to the din as they unloaded fishing vessels and loaded other boats.

Now that Thala didn't have a quest to keep her mind occupied, her thoughts circled back to the discussion they'd had with the princess.

Her crazy hair and eye color and that bizarre dream were because she'd been chosen to join this Dragon Kin? Despite the fact she'd killed dozens of men with her hands, she'd been chosen by a gem to fight again, but this time, against an even worse enemy. Could she do it again? If she did join, if she went to war like she had as a child, what would she lose this time? Would she be able to keep the doll part of her locked away?

"It's been a while since you came here," Will suddenly said from behind her, making her glance his way.

She shrugged a shoulder in response.

He came and leaned against the next post, his gaze on the ocean. "So, do you think she was telling the truth?"

"Why would she lie?"

He didn't respond.

Thala swung her feet, her heels tapping lightly against the hardened wood. "Why are you so mad at her anyway?" She was certain she knew the reason, but she waited to hear him speak, wanting to hear his thoughts from his own mouth.

He huffed. "I know it's stupid, but when I see her, I just get mad."

She stayed quiet, watching the light glitter on the little crests of the waves.

"The Imperial Family is the reason all that stuff happened to you," he eventually muttered, barely loud enough for her to hear. "Okay, not really, but that's what I've told myself for so long, I just..."

She'd figured that would be the case. All those years ago, during the midnight raid, River had managed to hide Will so he didn't get taken, but he hadn't been able to get to Thala in time. She was relatively okay, but she knew both of them were still upset about it. Will in particular, she knew, wished their places had been reversed.

Thala, however, would never wish what she'd been through on anyone—especially not one of her friends.

That said, she'd explained this to Will before, but it hadn't changed his feelings. That meant it was his issue to work through on his own.

She closed her eyes, thinking back to what she thought was the event that had triggered the change in her appearance. It'd been while she and her dad had been in the Esuni Desert. Every time she'd been deployed, her orders had been to kill everyone, no exceptions.

It'd started when she'd been clearing a building and found a little boy hiding amongst the devastation. She'd stared for a minute before telling him to stay put and stay quiet. Then she'd left him there. When questioned about it, she'd said the building was empty. In the next village, she'd found herself helping a woman and her infant hide. The next, a couple orphans. Her dad, who'd been her handler, had caught on to her scheme almost immediately but hadn't said a word. On the contrary, knowing him, she was sure he'd been going out of his way to keep it hushed.

She'd understood her orders had been to kill without exception and that disobeying them would mean a severe punishment if she'd been caught, but her father had told her human life was sacred. She wouldn't kill without reason.

Without a reason, she hadn't killed. Period.

However, there was one day that stood out among a span of bleak and dirty memories, one where, as she'd discovered an innocent little family hiding amongst the rubble, her commanding officer had found her and ordered her to kill. Even though she'd known it was wrong to do so, she'd refused. When the man had gone to do it instead, Thala had attacked him.

That had been her act that had led the gem to mark her, she was certain.

That said, it'd also been the reason she and her father had been sent on a suicide mission, the one that had cost her father his life. Even if he'd been killed protecting her, it wasn't a pleasant memory.

Shaking the memories away, she hopped off the post. "Will, it's okay if you're angry, so long as it's for your own sake. Don't waste it for me because I'm not angry. After all, the Imperial Family were the ones who saved me."

Leaving him to his own thoughts, Thala left. She'd stop by Adonis and Aretha's place before taking the long way back up to their mountain shelter, and with any luck, she'd arrive before nightfall.

∽✆ ✆∾

River slowly shifted his cramping leg, doing his utmost to move as silently as possible in his hiding place behind a large, ornamental vase and clusters of oleander bushes bursting with bright pink blossoms. There were sounds coming from the terrace above him, meaning the boyar's meeting would be starting soon.

There was only one bright side to having such a pompous oaf for a relative: the man was so full of himself, he never could imagine people would spy on him and subsequently held all his meetings like this out in the open. River was fairly certain it'd never once crossed his mind it was possible for someone to get away with spying on him.

After a few more minutes of River waiting in discomfort, voices began to fill the terrace, meaning the meeting was only minutes from starting. River didn't know if it would tell him anything, but it would at least give him an idea of his grandfather's mood and what steps he would need to take next.

"Gentlemen," his grandfather began in a placating voice, having to repeat himself a few times before the nobles listened. "There's no need to panic. While my wayward grandson is still on the loose, he is being routed as we speak. It will only be so long before he is corralled once more."

Yep. River was in serious danger of being apprehended.

"You've let that wild beast run amok for far too long, Athanasios," some noble barked. "I expect full reimbursement for the damage caused to my son. That beast nearly ripped his arm off."

"And for my son as well," someone else piped up. "That fiend broke his nose!"

River rolled his eyes so hard it almost hurt. They cried a lot about wounds that were miniscule in comparison to the ones they inflicted on their slaves.

"You never should have let your son marry that—that woman," the first noble continued.

"Yes," River's grandfather hissed. "You aren't the only one who hasn't forgiven Leon for eloping with a heathen. But back to the matter of payment. I suppose the usual gift of dragon's blood won't suffice?"

River perked up at that.

"I won't say no, of course. It is so useful. Regardless, because of the amount of damage inflicted on my son, it simply won't be enough. Not even the slaves would touch him until he'd bathed out of fear of contamination."

River doubted that. It was more likely they'd been ordered not to touch the spoiled boy or else. After all, slaves didn't have the luxury of choosing which orders they did or didn't obey.

"However, your granddaughter would satisfy me. After all, last night, she was supposed to be my son's."

The idea made River's blood go cold even though Leonora was safe and far away.

His grandfather released a weary sigh. "I've already explained, gentlemen, that my granddaughter has fallen ill. She could hardly attend her own wedding when she can't even get out of bed."

So that was the story the boyar was going with: Leonora was deathly ill and River had escaped. Quaint.

"Regardless, the instant she is well enough to stand, I want that wedding," the noble continued.

A pause. "Your son truly wouldn't mind having her as his wife despite her questionable lineage?"

A couple of the nobles laughed.

"I should think not. Since he only needs a woman capable of bearing heirs, who that woman is hardly matters so long as she is pleasing to the eye. Her tainted blood hardly shows through, and with my son as the sire, I doubt it would show through in any of his children."

Anger flared in River's chest, but he fought it down. As satisfying as it would be to give that noble a piece of his mind, it was a rash, brainless idea, not to mention the boyar was right there. River couldn't risk that.

As he wrestled his emotions into submission, the ground around him shuddered. Crap. That had been him this time.

After a minute's pause on the terrace above, one of the nobles huffed and said, "Just more tremors. I've had my fill of them after last night. You know, that rare heirloom vase I had broke last night because of the earthquake. Isn't there something we could do about making them stop?"

It took all of River's restraint not to laugh at the idea of people being able to command the forces of nature to stop. Far be it from River to tell them the truth about that last one. Besides, if earthquakes were that much of a pain, River couldn't help wondering why the man didn't just move somewhere they weren't as common.

The pig of a noble from before huffed and said, "Athanasios, I'll think on your offer."

Sandals slapped against stone, and after a few minutes, the terrace above him went quiet.

Even though River had had his doubts about running from the mansion, gratitude for that and—against his will—Tehl's warning rushed through him. Leonora had narrowly escaped a nasty fate.

After he'd waited a little while longer, River slipped out from his hiding place, sliding through the shadows until he reached the hole in the garden wall. As he left the city behind, he frowned.

While he'd only suspected before, now he knew for certain his grandfather had that dragon somewhere, and in order to keep harvesting its blood, it had to be kept alive. River already knew it wasn't anywhere in the manor; whenever he'd gotten the chance, he'd scoured the place from floor to ceiling in hopes of finding some kind of evidence that could get the boyar tossed out on his ear.

Because of how power hungry the man was, there was no way he'd leave the dragon in someone else's care either. That would be sharing too much of his power and leverage.

That only left one place.

River's gaze studied the mountain peaks towering over him as he walked. He hadn't wanted to hide Her Highness and her friends in the Agicae Mountains, but if you wanted to hide something big and noticeable, they were the best place. Even when people went in prepared and did everything right, many of them still died, so nearly everyone avoided them at all costs. They were the mountains of fools and thieves only.

And the Dragon Kin, he thought with a bit of morbid humor.

Regardless, if the boyar had a dragon he wanted to keep hidden, the mountains were where it would be. After all, it was where he'd hidden the dolls.

Huffing, River shook his head. All at once, he was assaulted by a memory of him and his father walking through the northern Agicae mountains during spring, when they'd been bursting with bright green foliage. The scenery in his mind stood in stark contrast to the monotonous world surrounding him now. The memories from his childhood were vivid, almost alive, unlike every memory he'd made in this place.

Shame crept through him at what he was doing. What he had already done. His father would've been so disappointed in him, but there wasn't anything River could do to change it. He'd lost the right to continue their family's legacy a long time ago.

He flinched from that thought. The idea of him pretending to be something for Her Highness that he, in reality, simply couldn't be, threw mud on his father's dream. The one wish his father had always had was right in front of him, and River wasn't capable or worthy of seeing it come true. It wasn't possible. To remind himself just how impossible, he clenched his left fist, making the metal creak.

That was why.

It didn't matter how much his father had longed for or dreamed of this because River had screwed up so badly, he wasn't worthy of even touching that legacy. It wasn't what he wanted, but he had to console himself with merely finding a way to help Her Highness while she was here. It didn't matter if some gem kept sending him its dream; he wasn't worthy of that either.

Him meeting the Dragon Kin—River meeting Her Highness— was just a brief intersection in all of their lives and nothing more. It couldn't be anything more, no matter how much he wished it could.

Taking a deep breath, he pushed those thoughts away and focused on the task right in front of him. All at once, he heard the scuff of a foot behind him and immediately ducked out of sight.

A moment later, Will popped up beside him, nearly startling him off the mountainside.

"What is wrong with you?" River hissed. "I thought you followed Thala."

Will shrugged. "She's already done her bit and left, so I went to check on Adonis and the others before heading back. I just happened to bump into you."

"Are you sure checking on them was wise?"

"I figured not taking my regular routes as much as possible would be far more suspicious than disappearing altogether."

River eyed him before shaking his head and continuing on his way. He supposed Will had a point. No one would notice River's absence—especially since the boyar had announced that—but Will and Thala had moved through town much more often than he. Someone would most likely miss them if they were gone for too long.

"So," Will continued, padding along beside him. "If you're heading back already, I take it you learned something."

River nodded.

"As we suspected, you were able to find whatever it was the princess wants without any problem. After all, you were the only one able to find anything during that doll debacle. All those royal investigators hadn't found a thing, but you showed them all up quite handily." Will tucked his thumbs behind the belt around his waist like he didn't have a care in the world. "That said, for someone who goes on and on about being unworthy of your family's legacy, you sure don't act like it."

River shot him a glare.

"Yeah, yeah, give me scuzzy looks all you want, buddy. I ain't scared of you." Will sighed. "I was just saying."

"Whatever," River muttered. It wasn't like there was any point in getting Will to understand anyway; it wasn't something he could understand, even if he wanted to. Besides that, it was River's problem.

All at once, there came the crunch of rock from behind them. A chill raced up River's spine as he peered back over his shoulder, though he kept walking. There was no one on the path behind them, but as he continued on, that uneasy feeling didn't go away.

Chapter Thirteen

Redrinna jerked awake as someone nudged her arm. She sat up straight, wincing at the crick in her spine because of the rock she'd fallen asleep against.

Tak eyed her with an almost concerned expression.

"Sorry. I promise I'm awake."

A bit of a smile curled the corners of his mouth. "It's okay to sleep if you're tired. We had a rough night and a very big day of doing pretty much nothing."

That got her to smile. "Are any of them back yet?"

"No," Astra said, sighing from her place behind them.

"Waiting is never fun," Redrinna said. She glanced over at Leonora, who had Kyvo flopped across her lap while she played with his fur. "I suppose we could figure out something to do."

"You don't want to do anything too loud or it might echo down the mountainside," Leonora said mildly. "These mountains are good at that. Oh, and a lot of the rock is brittle, so sometimes it gives way beneath your feet."

Redrinna and Kyvo sighed at the same time. Until they could make a plan, they were stuck being bored.

She leaned back against the rock she'd accidentally fallen asleep against and spotted something that made her freeze. Near Tak's foot was a little grey-ish brown lizard flecked with off-white spots, its head slightly turned like it considered him. Her heart skipped a beat. She'd never seen a lizard before.

Without giving it a second's thought, she crawled forward, keeping as quiet as possible.

"Um...Redrinna?" Tak asked as she crawled towards him, concern in his voice.

"Shh," she said, her gaze focused on the lizard. She'd read lizards were fast, and if startled, this one would likely take off before she could examine it closer. Fortunately, Tak remained still, and the lizard stayed where it was, its head still turned, throat pulsing.

Somehow, she managed to crawl right up to the lizard, it's head only turning more her way. She hardly breathed as she studied it, every fact she'd ever learned about the little creatures flashing through her mind. If she was careful, maybe she could catch it?

"Wh-what are you doing?" Tak whispered, making her realize that she knelt right next to him.

"Look," she murmured. "It's a lizard. I've never seen a real one before."

He shifted slightly, just enough to startle the lizard. It took off, nearly scaring Redrinna with its suddenness.

"Aww," she said as it scurried out of sight.

"Sorry," Tak said, a bit of a grimace twisting his face.

"It's okay," she said, getting to her feet. She was a little disappointed, but at least she'd been able to see it up close for a few seconds.

"Redrinna, there's another one!" Kyvo squeaked, making Redrinna turn.

On one of the nearby rocks, almost looking like it basked in the sun, was another lizard, almost identical to the first one. She didn't even hesitate before creeping forward with Kyvo sneaking up beside her. They stalked closer to the rock, and then Redrinna just stared.

"I don't get what's so fascinating," Astra said, loud enough it made the lizard twitch.

"What's fascinating?" Will said, making Redrinna jump. She'd been so focused, she hadn't heard the other three's approach.

"Her Highness found a lizard," Leonora said, sounding a bit like she was trying not to laugh.

"A lizard, eh?" Will said, almost from right behind Redrinna, making her jump again. In a flash, he leaned forward and snatched the lizard. It squirmed a little, but somehow, Will managed to get it to kind of relax. When it was calm, he extended his hand towards Redrinna. "There. Now you can get a good look."

"Wow," she breathed. She'd always equated the dragons as lizard-like, and while there were definite similarities, now that she was studying a real lizard for the first time, it was obvious they were different too. She grinned at Will without a thought. "Thanks, Will. How did you catch it? You were so fast!"

He blinked, his cheeks going bright red. That seemed to distract him enough that the lizard launched out of his palm and scurried away. He stared after it. "Oops."

Kyvo bounded a couple steps after it, but then he said, "Aww, it disappeared too."

Redrinna glanced at him. "That's okay. We shouldn't pick on them."

Getting to her feet, she turned to the others. They'd all returned, which meant she didn't have time to get distracted by lizards.

As River came and sat near Leonora, his sister glanced at him and Will. "How'd it go?"

"Well, we didn't die," Will said, sitting on Leonora's other side and pointedly not looking Redrinna's way.

River stared blankly at him. "You weren't even there."

"I still could've died."

River rolled his eyes.

Redrinna glanced between the two of them before she spoke. "So, I guess we should figure out where we stand."

The others nodded and gathered in a bit closer before turning to her. Redrinna froze for a second before she lowered her gaze, trying to collect her thoughts.

When she was ready, she lifted her gaze and turned to River. "Did you learn anything?"

He dipped his head. "I was able to listen in on a meeting between the boyar and some of the nobles—I don't know all who. He's allowed the news that I've escaped to spread, but he's pretending he still has Leonora and that she's deathly ill. I think he's using her as leverage to—" All at once, he stopped.

Not sure what to do with that, Redrinna stared at him before her gaze flicked to the others and back.

"Uh...do you want me to tell you everything I heard or just stuff that's important to us?" he asked.

"Oh," she said, a bit of relief flashing through her chest. She'd thought someone had found them or something. "Anything you heard might end up helping us."

"Okay. He's using her as leverage to keep the nobles calm. He also mentioned he's been giving the nobles gifts of dragon blood in order to keep them pacified."

"So gross," Xandrin muttered.

"More than likely, that means he's got it locked up somewhere, and it might just be your dragon. He didn't say where it is, but I have a good idea."

"You do?" Redrinna asked.

River nodded. "I want to double check, but I'm certain it's hidden in these mountains somewhere."

"Oh, that makes sense," Leonora said. "He hid the dolls here before."

"It might even be in the same place," Will chimed in.

Redrinna took that in, her heart taking courage at the chance the dragon might still be alive. There was a possibility they might be able to save it. "All right, Thala. What about you?"

"The general stationed here is named Cael," the girl answered.

Redrinna frowned.

"Do you know him?" Leonora asked.

"I don't think so," Redrinna said slowly. "Though his name is familiar for some reason."

After a second's pause, Thala continued. "However, he's not here right now. They said he'd taken some of the soldiers and they were going around to the different villages to check the extent of the damage from the quake. He's not supposed to be back for a couple weeks."

"That gives us plenty of time to hunt for any evidence we can find," Astra said, some life returning to her eyes.

"You won't be able to help with that though," Tak murmured.

Her ear frills drooped a little.

"Also, I'm pretty sure the boyar has something over the soldiers or ears in the guard house. The captain I spoke to wouldn't badmouth the boyar." Thala dipped her head a little. "He was a captain I was under when I was a doll, and he's not the type of person to do that."

"All right. The boyar probably has both ears and leverage then," Redrinna said, her mind whirling with all this information.

Even though it would clue the boyar in that something was going on, Redrinna wanted to get the dragon away from him as fast as possible. It would put the boyar in a more precarious situation, and perhaps it would pressure him enough to slip up just enough for them to find something to use against him.

"So what are we going to do?" Xandrin asked, studying her with his big, dark eyes.

She frowned a little. "Well, it would be helpful if we kept someone near the army. Not only would we stay up to date on the movements of this General Cael, but if they were careful, they could possibly figure out what the boyar is using to keep the army afraid of him and under his thumb."

"I'll do it," Thala said immediately.

"No," Will barked. "You've already been in the army once. I'll do it, got it?"

She shook her head. "I already know how the army works, so I can make my way through it much easier than you can. Plus, in order to get this information, I told that captain I was thinking about coming back. It won't be a surprise if I do it."

"Thala, who knows what they might make you do again? You shouldn't have to do this."

"Why not?" she asked, her voice a little forceful, but she didn't seem angry. "Why shouldn't I get to fight too? That man is the reason I'm messed up; he did this to me. If I can help get rid of him, then I want to do this."

"I think you're making a good point, Thala," Redrinna cut in, trying to cull the argument.

Will shot her a glare, but there wasn't any heat in it. On the contrary, he almost seemed...scared.

"If what I've heard about what the dolls were put through is true, then I think Thala is our best bet for having ears in the army. That said," Redrinna paused, her gaze dropping to her hands, "this might be selfish of me to say, but I want you to avoid being put in a dangerous position as much as you can help it. The last thing I want is to force you to be a doll again. So don't do more than you have to while you're there."

Thala nodded.

Will's mouth popped open, whether to protest or from the shock, Redrinna didn't know.

She quickly spoke in case it was the former. "River, you and Will are the best suited for sneaking into the noble houses for information, right?"

"Yes, Your Highness," River said.

"So sending Thala into the army would be more useful than trying to have her spy on the nobles."

"Indubitably."

Will closed his mouth, though he glared now.

"Okay, if the two of you are okay with that, that's what I want to ask you to do. You can work together or alone; I'm sure you'll understand a better way of making this work than I will."

Will cocked his head. "That almost makes it sound like you think we do this a lot."

Leonora elbowed him in the ribs.

"Well, you've done it more than me, I guess?" Redrinna said, not sure if that made it better or worse.

"I seriously doubt you've done something like this ever," Will said.

"I did once. Or tried to."

River and Leonora both looked at her in sync. "You did?" they said.

She nodded. "I tried to sneak into the Imperial City after my parents had thrown me out, but it was destroyed, so I guess it doesn't count."

Will stared at her with a weird expression. "Your parents threw you out?"

She froze, realizing while she'd explained about Osiris and the Dragon Kin, she hadn't explained her own story. However, she didn't want to talk about that.

Even though she was doing better at not letting what had happened drag her down, it didn't mean it'd stopped hurting or that she wanted everybody to know about it.

Attempting a smile though it didn't feel quite right, she said, "It's nothing. Don't worry about it."

Even still, their new companions stared at her with curious or troubled expressions that made her uncomfortable.

Getting to her feet, she said, "I'm going to go find some water," and hurried out of the clearing.

After a minute, she heard little footsteps, and with a hint of a smile, she glanced back at Kyvo trotting after her.

"I'm thirsty too," he said once he caught up. "So we can go together!"

Though she didn't say it out loud, she appreciated his company.

That would help her keep the thoughts that had closed in like vultures at bay long enough they'd pass her by.

The trip to the nearby river wasn't a long one, but it was just long enough to put them out of sight of their makeshift camp and the others. Now that Redrinna wasn't in the moment anymore, she regretted just getting up and leaving, but she couldn't change what she'd done. She just hoped they wouldn't pester her about it when they got back.

As they got a drink, Redrinna studied the frail rock along the riverbank. It seemed to peel back on itself like a leaf when it got wet, with pieces often flaking off and getting lost in the foam. Even the rock that wasn't wet crackled when she stepped on it. It made her miss her northern mountains even more.

Once her and Kyvo's thirst was quenched, they turned to trek back to their camp, Kyvo bounding in excited circles around her as they left the river's banks behind. When they were within sight of the others, a chill shot over Redrinna's skin, unnerving her enough she stopped.

She didn't hear anything, but the uneasy, cold feeling persisted. Kyvo seemed to sense it too, because he stopped, ears perked.

Hesitantly, she glanced over her shoulder, scanning the mountainside behind her. Nothing. So why did she still—

"Boo!" someone said from in front of her.

Redrinna whipped back around, nearly jumping out of her skin at the strange man standing in front of her. He was...peculiar. He had long, unbound, black hair, and was dressed in similar fashion to River—a tunic, breeches, and low boots—except he wore a light, linen cloak with cuts in the sleeves for his arms. However, the strangest thing about his appearance were his eyes. They were like a void threatening to suck her in, pulling her into endless, empty depths. Even though she'd never met this person before, something about those eyes was hauntingly familiar.

He laughed at her reaction, a strange breathy sound that didn't really sound like laughing. "Couldn't resist!"

Redrinna stared, taking a small step back.

"Oh, don't be like that," he said, seeming young but at the same time, there was something about him that seemed...old. Almost ancient. "I did come all the way out here just to meet you."

"Who are you?" she asked, looking askance at him.

"Me?" With a wide, cat-like grin, the man touched a hand to his chest and said, "You can call me Tehl. I wouldn't say I'm a friend, but I'm not exactly your enemy at the moment either."

Redrinna frowned, not sure what he meant by that.

"Tehl," River barked, hurrying towards them. "I should've known you'd follow us."

"Now, now," Tehl said with a laugh as he turned to face River. "I did help you and your sister get away from the boyar, so you should be nice to me, especially since I couldn't care less what you two are up to at this current second. I came here for something else." His weird eyes turned back to Redrinna, and she found herself shrinking a little beneath his gaze.

River crossed his arms, a deep frown on his face. That said, his stance was relaxed, so Redrinna guessed this Tehl person must not be that big of a threat. Or so she hoped.

At that second, Tak and the dragons appeared from amongst the trees, eyeing Tehl with wary expressions.

To Redrinna's surprise, Tehl grinned and clapped his hands a couple times. "Oh, how lucky for me. The entire Dragon Kin has fallen into my lap this time around. I thought my hunch was right, but I am wrong sometimes, so it was better to confirm it with my own eyes."

"What do you want?" Redrinna asked, her heart beating fast.

"Nothing serious, I promise." Tehl spun on his heel, facing Redrinna once more. "No, I find you so much more fascinating. After all this time, I just had to see you for myself."

She took a quick step back, wondering if she should try and run. Kyvo growled from near her feet.

Tehl studied her with his strange eyes. "Are you scared of me?"

"I don't know you," she said defensively.

He hid his mouth behind his hand as he chuckled. Then, without warning, he vanished in a pool of black mist, and Redrinna's eyes went wide. She knew that magic.

All at once, he was behind her, gripping her shoulders with bony fingers. It wasn't in a particularly creepy way, but something about it gave her chills. He leaned over her shoulder, and she turned her head just enough to see his eyes. He smiled, and then, all at once, his eyes turned a familiar, haunting blue. Her heart almost stopped.

"Hello again, Princess." Even though it was Tehl's mouth moving, that was Osiris's voice. She recognized it in a heartbeat. "It has been some time, has it not?"

Abruptly, the air around her went cold—so cold. She could hardly breathe.

"You have traveled far, so allow me to be the first to welcome you to Póli. I hope you enjoy the game I have prepared for you. Consider it my treat, for how the last one turned out."

"G-game?" she managed. "I don't want to play anymore of your games."

That made him laugh, but Tehl's hands tightened on her shoulders, gripping so hard it hurt. She flinched, but he didn't ease his grip. "That is not fair, Princess. I made this game with you in mind."

Redrinna closed her eyes, fighting against the urge to cry as she squirmed in discomfort, making Tehl's hands tighten even more.

"I do not plan on taking you yet if you lose; however, I will leave you with this warning: tread carefully here with whatever you choose to do or you will regret it. In order to be made to suffer, you do not necessarily need to experience physical pain."

Redrinna jerked away, and he let her go. Darkness gathered on the edge of her vision, her heart thudding a thousand miles an hour. It was then she realized she was shaking and breathing hard.

Kyvo leapt between the two of them, snarling with his tail fluffed up.

Tehl's eyes returned to their normal shade as he glanced down at the kitsune before lifting his gaze to her again. "Well, see you around, Princess. I'm sure it'll be fun."

In a swirl of all-too-familiar shadows, Tehl vanished.

Even still, the fear sparking hot in Redrinna's chest didn't go away. She couldn't breathe; it felt like Tehl's bony fingers still dug into her. In an instant, she realized what was happening.

"Not this again," she managed right as her legs lost feeling and she fell to the ground. She managed to keep from falling on her face, rocks biting into her fists when they hit the ground. She just had to wait it out; she knew that. She just wished it wasn't happening with such a massive audience.

Kyvo nudged her arm with a bit of a whine, and Tak arrived a second later.

"Are you okay?" he asked, crouching next to her.

She managed to nod. "Sorry," she managed. "Sorry."

Neither he nor Kyvo said anything, but after a minute, Tak reached out and put his hand over her clenched fist. It was warm, and when she focused on that, there was the slightest easing of pressure in her chest.

No one said anything. Everyone else minded their distance, and eventually, Redrinna's breathing slowed and the intense coils of fear released her.

Even though she knew it wasn't something to be embarrassed about, she couldn't help the shame that blossomed inside her. They'd come to help this city, and already, she'd displayed her deep, unending fear caused by just one man. She hated it so much. She hated being so scared all the time. Why couldn't she get past this?

"What happened?" Kyvo asked, staring at her with big, concerned-filled eyes.

"I'm sorry," she said, the usual exhaustion arriving. "It's just—for some reason, I don't know how—Tehl's eyes were *his* eyes."

Tak's brow furrowed. "His? You...you mean Osiris's?"

"It was his voice too, and I—" A shuddery breath cut her off.

All at once, Xandrin and Astra arrived, both of them giving her a gentle nudge. She put a hand on both of their snouts.

"He said we're going to play another game," Redrinna whispered, choking fear filling her at the idea of what that implied.

A chill settled over them like smoke.

Another game. What did that mean? Was he going to take someone? Was he going to try and kill someone? Who? Which of her friends would be in danger?

What if she couldn't protect them again?

"Hey," Tak said, getting her to meet his gaze. "He's not going to get any of us, okay? We're all going to protect each other, I promise."

Her fists tightened. Maybe it shouldn't have surprised her, but she was startled to find she believed Tak wholeheartedly. She didn't like it, but she couldn't do this alone, and a rush of gratitude for her friends flooded her. At least this time, she didn't have to face this 'game' of Osiris's alone. If she had, she already would've lost.

Chapter Fourteen

River went on the move before the sun had even started to rise the next morning, leaving his sleeping companions tucked into the partial safety of the mountain's shadows. The boyar wasn't fond of mornings, so if River wanted to sneak into where he suspected the dragon was with as little risk as possible, then early in the morning was the best time to do it.

He headed to the river and walked in the direction opposite its flow, making sure to keep away from the weak stone on its banks. He'd been a good swimmer when he'd had both of his arms, but now having a metal limb made it difficult to stay afloat—not to mention the threat of rust that came from it getting wet. It also was difficult to maneuver the limb effectively enough in the water to swim well.

He followed the rushing river to a cliff face, where the water fell in a brilliant icy blue plume from a wide cave some thirty feet above him. The cave where Thala had been turned into a doll. There were easier entrances elsewhere, but this was the hardest to access and the least likely to be watched.

River eyed the pale, moss-slick stone in front of him before taking a deep breath and taking hold of the first rocks that held his weight. Unlike with the boyar's mansion, he went slow, testing his weight on each lip or ledge before he would trust it. Several pieces crumbled with only a part of his weight on them.

The climb was slow and arduous, and by the time River crested the ledge of the cave, he was drenched with sweat, and the shoulder hooked to his prosthesis ached so bad. Both his shoulders ached, but that one was the worst. The one thing his younger self hadn't foreseen about making a prosthesis permanently attached to himself was that when his stump hurt, there wasn't anything he could do about it. There wasn't any kind of reprieve for it. It had turned out to not be one of his finer ideas. On the flip side, it was a helpful tool in every other respect.

He shook those thoughts away as he inspected the cave before him. It was dark inside, the river's water quickly shifting from dark blue to black. Now that he was nearer to the source, the water was calmer and quieter, almost like a whisper, especially when compared to the thunder of the waterfall below.

Nothing moved and there were no sounds beyond the rush of the water, so River straightened and carefully made his way into the dark of the cave, the chill in the air making shivers shoot up his back.

He slowed as he made it to the edge of what his eyes could see. Once they adjusted to the darkness, in the distance, he made out the faint gleam of torchlight. A grim smile almost touched his mouth.

Fire meant life. That meant there was a good chance he was right.

Taking slow, measured steps, River stalked closer to the torchlight, his ears pricked for the faintest sound.

After a couple minutes, he found himself on a ledge peering into a dim but enormous chamber lit by a handful of torches. Held fast to the floor by massive chains—that had to be nearly as thick as River's arms—was a dragon with gigantic fins, its scales a dull, blueish gray. It appeared to be asleep, but even from his vantage point, he could tell the creature was half-dead from starvation. Its ribs were pronounced as it breathed, though its breaths were shallow. Red blood stood out here and there along its body.

River had only the vaguest memories of meeting this dragon

before; when he and Leonora had first been brought here, Will and Thala had taken them to the beach, and this dragon had saved the four of them from a riptide. River didn't remember the details well, but even still, compared to how this dragon had been then, the sight of it like this made tears burn in his eyes.

That horrible, repulsive, and repugnant boyar. All this time, River had been worried about himself and his sister while the dragon who'd taken pity on four stupid children had been trapped here for who knew how long. Anger churned in his chest.

River was on the verge of climbing down to free it right then when he heard humming. He crouched, shuffling a couple steps back. Tehl and the boyar entered the chamber seconds later. Because he'd ducked down, he couldn't see them or the dragon anymore, so he closed his eyes and focused on listening.

Tehl spoke first. "I'm afraid you won't be able to get much more out of this one. Even the strongest dragons succumb within a few years."

"Don't speak to me like I don't know what I'm doing," the boyar shot back, his tone making River's blood boil. "I've cared for this beast well enough it has lasted me longer than any of yours ever did."

Tehl huffed but kept quiet.

"That said, it is too weak for me to bleed it now. Not that those nobles actually want it at the moment. Perhaps I should withhold it again until they decide to remember their place."

Tehl muttered something, but River was far enough away he couldn't catch it. The boyar didn't respond to it though.

There was a long minute of discomforting silence before the boyar spoke again. "Are you going to tell me why you're following me yet?"

"I have a question for you. A couple."

"Fine."

"I'd keep your temper in check if I were you," Tehl said, the threat in his voice as plain as if he'd pressed the blade of a knife against River's neck. "Where did you get this dragon, Athanasios? You've never said, and Father is tired of playing your games."

Another pause, and then the boyar spoke. "Beneath the volcano."

"Is that the only dragon you've found near here?"

The boyar laughed, but a strange kind of hiss that set River on edge slithered through the air. Quickly, the boyar said, "Yes."

"Wonderful," Tehl said as another of those strange hisses slithered through River's ears. "I do love when you remember your manners. After all, it does no good to bite the hands that feed you, does it?"

A chill crept across River's skin, and it took all of his willpower to remain where he was.

"Now, I have one last question, and you'd better be honest with me or your reign here will come to a swift and abrupt end." Tehl paused, and River stiffened. "If the princess were to come this way, could you be trusted to keep your own, misguided grudges out of the way to deal with her however we dictated?"

River's heart stuttered.

There was a longer pause this time before the boyar answered. "O-of course."

Tehl chuckled, but there wasn't any humor in it. "I'm serious, Athanasios. If you put even one toe out of line this time, you'll be out of toes in a heartbeat." All at once, Tehl's voice changed, just like it had when he'd been talking to Her Highness. "Do you submit? Or do I need to remind you what it is like to be broken?"

Even though River was far away and not the object of that man's fury, fear still twisted through his veins, thick as blood, just as it had before. It was as intense as when Tehl's eyes had changed and Osiris had apparently spoken through him earlier. Something about this man, even though he wasn't physically present, was enough to make even River's breathing short and choppy and his hand shake.

River knew evil's many faces. He'd seen several of them firsthand. However, he'd never seen this face before, and it was the first to genuinely spark terror inside him.

"My own desires are second to yours," the boyar simpered in

response, and River got the distinct impression the man was not as afraid as he should have been.

"I do doubt that," Osiris/Tehl continued. "I do believe you are in dire need of reminding who gave you your power."

There was a crack and the boyar screamed, making River jump.

"I will only ask you this one more time: will you obey me?"

"Y-yes," the boyar's voice was weak, barely audible to River's ears.

"Good." Tehl's voice returned to being his own. "It's about time Father did that to you. He gave you your power, and it would do you well to remember just how fast he can take it away."

The boyar's only response was a groan.

"Oh, quit sniveling, you baby. You'll be fine soon enough. At any rate, with this reminder, Father has decided to entrust you with a new task: Her Highness is here, near your city. You leave her be unless she comes to you. In that case, you can catch her and then send for me. But," Tehl's voice dropped dramatically, and River leaned closer in order to hear him, "if you harm so much as one hair on her head, I won't show you the same mercy Father did. Got it?"

The boyar didn't make a sound.

"Good. Now get out. I think we've got a sentient rat in these caves. You don't check them well."

River stiffened. He wasn't sure how, but he knew at that second that somehow, Tehl knew he was here. It was only because of the training he'd received from his father that he didn't bolt out of the tunnel.

Denying the fear urging him to run, he remained where he was until the two of them departed. Then he left as calmly and quietly as possible. Even by the time he was out of the cave and at the base of the waterfall, his hand still shook. For almost a full minute, he stared at it, fascinated. It'd been a long time since something had made him feel like that.

Her Highness was fighting against that man. Even though it was obvious he terrified her, she was going to fight him.

River clenched his fist. He'd had that dream, the gem's dream. It'd not only told him to open his eyes, but it'd called him by name. It was so insistent, but he needed to tell it no. He couldn't do it; he wasn't worthy of that. He hadn't been for a long time.

Even still, the thought of letting Her Highness go against Osiris while he sat and did nothing made his stomach churn. That man was clearly behind the corruption of this city, and beyond that, he'd caused the war that had stolen River and Leonora's parents from them. He'd caused the war that had twisted Thala into a shell of what she'd once been.

Osiris was no longer just some arbitrary being to River; even though they'd never met, already, the connection and animosity between them was personal.

Sighing, River thunked his forehead with his prosthesis hand because he knew that one would hurt. "You can't. That's what you get when you choose to be stupid."

Shaking himself, he glanced at the sky. A thin crescent of sun crested the mountains in the east. In his mind, he'd been gone longer than that, but he supposed not. Chest tight, he left the mountain behind, his troubles clinging to his heels like a shadow.

❦

Thala stared at the eastern sky as the upper lip of the sun peaked over the mountains, a few slender rays streaking out and staining the clouds a pale orange. If she wanted to stick to her usual routine, she needed to head to the farm in case there was work she could do. It was the least she could do to continue helping Aretha and Adonis as best she could with the money from that. Being a soldier made some more money, but every leaf helped.

As she stood, Redrinna squirmed in her sleep. Thala blinked, staring for a moment. All at once, the young woman cried—it was soft, barely audible, but it was the kind of ragged cry that sounded like a part of someone's soul was being ripped away.

Without hesitation, Thala went and shook her shoulder.

Redrinna popped up almost immediately, out of breath and eyes wide. "Wh-what?"

"You were having a nightmare," Thala explained.

"Oh." Redrinna was still panting hard, almost like she'd been running. "Sorry for waking you."

She shook her head. "I was already awake. I just...didn't want to leave you in a dream like that."

Redrinna glanced away, almost like she was embarrassed.

"I used to have those dreams," Thala offered, not entirely sure why she did. "They're awful, but they go away eventually."

"Thank you," Redrinna said, though she still kept her gaze lowered. "But...why are you awake so early?"

"I usually do work on a farm. It's not much, but every leaf helps my friends. Plus, Will said we should try to stick to our usual routines as much as possible to avoid raising suspicion for as long as we can." Thala fingered the end of her braid. "And people will notice if I disappear."

"That's a good idea then."

"When I'm finished there, I'll be going to the guardhouse and joining the army. I doubt I'll learn anything useful today."

Redrinna looked up at that, giving Thala a clear view of her bizarre but interesting red eyes. "Perhaps not, but keep your ears open anyway. Even the smallest detail might prove useful to us."

"Right." Thala turned to go.

"Hey," Redrinna called, pulling her up short. "Be careful, okay?"

That made Thala pause. In her mind's eye, all at once, she remembered how her father used to say the same thing before every one of their missions in the desert, and she was suddenly... Nostalgic wasn't the right word. She didn't miss that time of her life. That said, she missed her dad. Perhaps...homesick was the right word for the sensation resonating inside her? No, that didn't seem right either.

After a minute, Thala glanced back, meeting Redrinna's steady gaze. She'd heard several rumors about how 'demonic' the princess was with those eyes, but in that moment, she couldn't help thinking how regal they made her appear.

"I will be." Then, still reeling from the sensation of a feeling, Thala left.

⁕ ⁕ ⁕

By the time River made it back to their makeshift camp, everyone but Xandrin was awake, and they were already preparing a small breakfast of fish and some berries Tak had scrounged up. He joined without a word, getting a little smile from Her Highness, Kyvo plowing into his knees, and a wave from his sister. Tak met his gaze, but the young man didn't say or do anything. Granted, he didn't seem comfortable speaking much to anyone besides Her Highness, the dragons, and Kyvo.

Thala and Will were both absent, but River supposed he should've suspected that. They'd both been going and helping out on one of the local farms for as long as he could remember, even when times had been tight and they hadn't received any money for doing so.

Once breakfast was ready, they gathered around (Xandrin quickly roused himself) and tucked in. River noticed Her Highness took the smallest fish and every bite she ate made her nose wrinkle. A couple times she shuddered, but she ate until the fish was gone.

"Your Highness?" he began.

Her disgusted expression vanished as she met his gaze. "Yes?"

"Do you not like fish?"

Her cheeks went pink. "No...not really. But it's better than being hungry."

He eyed their meager breakfast. He liked fish, but for some reason, the idea Her Highness was in a position that she had to force herself to eat food she didn't like made him ashamed. She was putting herself at risk to help them, and they couldn't even provide her with something she enjoyed eating. It wasn't his fault—it wasn't any of their faults—but even still, he couldn't help it.

"That's not important though," Her Highness said with a shake of her head. "You went to look for the dragon today, right?"

That got most everyone's attention.

River nodded.

"So?" She leaned forward, fixing him with her intense red gaze.

He could only hold her stare for a second before the shame burned white-hot. He lowered his gaze. "I found it. It's right where I suspected it'd be."

"Is it okay?"

"I...I'm not sure. It seems really weak." He paused, having to steel himself to say the rest because he knew Her Highness wouldn't enjoy hearing it. "Tehl and the boyar came while I was there. They were saying the dragon isn't going to last much longer."

Her Highness sat back, one hand resting on the glowing gem hanging from her neck. "So we need to act before it runs out of time."

Tak dipped his head. "I-if Tehl was there with the boyar, then that means Osiris is working here too, right?"

"Most likely," Leonora said. "You know, I remember when Tehl first came here. It was right before the situation with the dolls."

"So there's a chance that was something Osiris caused or influenced as well," Her Highness said with a sigh, closing her eyes. After a minute, she opened them and returned her attention to River. "Do you know what the boyar and Tehl were doing there?"

His gaze fell to the ground again. "They discussed the dragon for a bit. Tehl mentioned something that sounded like Osiris has done the same to other dragons before. Tehl also stated the boyar is borrowing their power in order to accomplish what he's doing. Then they..." Almost without realizing it, he found himself trailing off again.

"What?" Leonora and Astra asked, almost in sync.

It took River a minute to figure out how to say it. "Well...they—Tehl and Osiris—told the boyar..." He sighed. "The boyar knows you're here, Your Highness."

A chill swept over the group.

Xandrin crept a little closer to Her Highness. "What are we going to do now?"

"Granted, he was ordered to leave you alone unless you happened to fall into his path. I don't know what they threatened him with, but he'll comply for a while. I just don't know how long it'll be until his greed and ambition get the better of him."

"Maybe you should go," Kyvo suggested, pressing himself against her leg. "He can't get you if he can't find you, right?"

Her Highness stared at him, not speaking.

"Redrinna," Xandrin added, lowering his head next to her, "I'm not going to let him get you, I promise."

"That's right," Astra added.

Her Highness squeezed her eyes shut before she took a deep breath and lifted her chin. "If he's supposed to stay away unless I get in his way, then we'll be fine so long as I don't do anything stupid. The dragon is more important at this second."

"It doesn't sound like it's doing well," Leonora said. "We should get it out of there as soon as we can. I'm afraid if it has to stay in that cave for much longer, it'll be too late."

"Exactly," Her Highness said with a nod. "If it's possible, I want to get it out today. What do you think, River?"

Today? That was fast, but...

"It's possible. Of course, it'll depend on whether the dragon is strong enough to get out of the cave on its own. Since the boyar just checked on it, now is the best time to try it."

"Okay, who should go?"

"I'll go," Astra said immediately.

River shook his head. "I appreciate your enthusiasm, but the passages to get there are small enough, I'm not sure you or Xandrin will fit."

"Seriously?"

"Then how did they get the dragon in there in the first place?" Xandrin asked, head cocked to the side.

Her Highness glanced at him. "That should be obvious enough. If the boyar has been working with Osiris and can borrow his power, then he probably used that same shadowy transportation magic to get it there."

"Oh, that makes sense."

"How are you going to get the dragon out then?" Kyvo squeaked, ears back.

Frowning, River thought for a moment before he responded. "Well, I'm not sure, but there is a back passage—it's what I used to get in there in the first place. It's too small for Astra and Xandrin to get through, but with how starved that dragon is, it might be able to make it out that way."

Astra flicked an ear frill. "If it doesn't, we can probably break in."

A concerned expression flicked across Tak's face. "That...should be a last resort."

"The rock here is so brittle, you'll probably bring down the entire mountainside," Leonora observed.

"We'll keep it as a last resort—something we'll only use if we must," Her Highness said. "In the meantime, I think we should only send in a couple people. I don't know if the boyar will have anyone watching it, but we should prepare like he does. So, the less people who go in, the better. Obviously, River will have to go since he knows where the dragon is and the best way to get it out."

River nodded. He'd already been planning on it.

"So who else should go?" Kyvo asked. "Obviously not me. I can't fight."

"Not me either," Leonora said. "I can't fight much or well."

"So either Tak or me," Her Highness said with a frown.

Tak frowned too.

The dragons glanced at each other. Astra began to say, "Well—"

"Don't." Her Highness cut her off with a shake of her head.

Tak slowly said, "Between you and me, I think you should go."

She glanced at him in surprise.

"You're the better fighter out of the two of us. Besides, when it comes to recruiting dragons, that kind of feels more like...it should be your job than mine," he finished quietly.

Her Highness grimaced—it was only for a second, but River noticed. "I'm not the better fighter, Tak. You are."

"With weapons, maybe. But I don't even have one of my own, plus, when you use your magic, you are a better fighter than me."

Open-mouthed, Her Highness stared at him.

River leaned forward. "Your Highness, you have magic?"

"What do you mean?" Kyvo asked, ears flattening. "She used it when those skeletons attacked us."

He frowned. "I was too busy fighting to watch what she did."

For a minute, Her Highness stared at him before lifting a hand and opening her palm. Flames appeared a second later, dancing above her fingers.

He was familiar with magic (he'd performed some before), but for some reason, seeing hers fascinated him. "You can use magic without a circle."

She blinked at him, her fire snuffing out in a whiff of smoke, but she didn't seem to notice. "What?"

He stared. "A magic circle."

"What's a magic circle?"

"You don't know what a magic circle is?" he asked, staring at her in disbelief.

She stared at him then at her hand. "Well, I found out about my powers on accident, and a spirit helped me figure out how to use it without killing myself, and after that I've been...teaching myself?"

River stared, his mind racing and leaving him without a thing to say. He knew people like Her Highness existed—people whose magic was so strong, they could use it well with little formal training—but he'd never thought he'd meet someone like her. That said, if her magical prowess had come by her relying on instinct, how on earth was he going to explain magic to her in a way she'd understand?

Chapter Fifteen

Redrinna stared back at River, not sure how to respond to the blank stare he gave her. She glanced at Leonora, but the girl stared at her with the same expression as her brother, which helped Redrinna very little.

"Your Highness," River began, still looking a little dumbfounded, "don't you know how magic works?"

A bit flustered, she said, "I know how mine works, a-and we're trying to figure out how Tak's works."

River glanced at him, almost seeming surprised. "You have magic too?"

"H-healing magic," Tak said, his cheeks a bit pink.

River stared at the two of them. Then he sighed. "Okay, let me try to explain. The way you do magic, Your Highness, is something only a handful of people can do. We're talking less than five percent."

Redrinna stared at him before her gaze flicked to her hands.

"Healing magic is a bit different, but that's a discussion we can have another time. Magic works in one of three ways: first, there are a select few people who are born like you. You, on a physical level, are so much more in tune with the world, which is why you can create magic without needing a circle. People like you are born on a spectrum—your magic comes in varying degrees of strength and you can only use natural elements, like fire or water. Depending on where you fall on the spectrum will dictate how many of the elements you can use, if you can use more than one."

Redrinna nodded. She hadn't come across anything like this in the books in the Mount, but then again, she'd only studied texts that had discussed how to use her magic rather than how it worked, so perhaps that was why.

"The second group of people are also a small amount, even less than people like you. They are people who aren't compatible with magic in any way—they can't use items with magic in it and strong amounts of magic can even make them sick.

"The third group and the one most people fall into, are the people who can use magic but can't use it naturally. Instead, they can access it through gates, also called magic circles. Granted, all magic is a pain to learn, but gates are infuriating. In order to use it, you have to learn a massive list of magic symbols and how to combine them correctly in order to achieve what you want. If you make even the smallest error, they can go horribly wrong. That's why unless someone is born with natural magic like you, most people don't bother learning it."

Redrinna frowned as she thought about that. Was that why Timothon had said he'd never bothered to learn it? She'd assumed he'd meant magic like hers, but all at once, some of the comments he'd made when she'd first begun trying to study it for herself made sense.

"I'm surprised you didn't know this, Your Highness," Leonora said, "since you seem to know so much."

"Studying magic didn't happen when I was in the palace," Redrinna said, still frowning. "I knew it existed, but my parents never had me study it or anything related to it. That's why I didn't even know I had any until I accidentally set something on fire."

"And nearly killed yourself," Xandrin added in undertone.

Abruptly Tak gasped, making her turn to him in alarm. "Wait. Does that mean those blood circles we keep finding are magic gates?"

Her eyes went wide.

"Blood circles?" River leaned forward, his brow lowering.

Redrinna explained. "They're these massive circles with lines and weird symbols drawn in blood. We've found two so far. Are those these magic gates you talked about?"

"Do you remember what they looked like?"

She paused. Then grimaced. When she saw them, she recognized them for what they were, but because she didn't understand the symbols, they were fuzzy blurs in her mind. "Not...really."

"I'd recognize one if I saw it," Kyvo chirped. Then his ears drooped. "But I can't remember it clearly."

"Yeah," Xandrin said with a sigh, his ear frills lowering too.

River frowned before grabbing a rock, clearing a patch of loose dirt, and drawing. Redrinna rose and came over, watching as he made a circle, drew two lines running parallel to each other, and then four symbols around the edge of the circle.

Glancing at her, he said, "Was it something like this?"

"A bit, but the blood circles are a lot more complicated." She cocked her head. "What does this circle do?"

River obliged her by touching his right hand to the circle. It glowed before the dirt formed a kind of mudball. "Nothing serious." He pushed a finger against the ball, making it crumble to pieces.

She stared at the circle in fascination. The symbols were different, the lines much simpler. There was a strange kind of elegance to it, something that was different from the blood circles.

Either way, this meant those blood circles were magic gates.

"What kind of things could you do with a gate?" Redrinna asked, meeting River's gaze.

He quickly looked down, something he did a lot around her. "Almost anything you can imagine. Granted, there are certain, unbreakable laws that limit things, but you can do anything with a gate, from starting a fire to building an entire castle if you know what you're doing."

Xandrin stared at the little circle on the ground, a distant look in his eyes. "Which means Osiris could be doing anything with those blood circles."

Silence fell over their group, and for a couple minutes, Redrinna's heart fluttered in fear. The possibilities were endless, and even though they now knew it was some kind of magic, they still didn't know what those circles meant.

All at once, Astra cleared her throat, making Redrinna jump. "I'm not trying to be rude because this is all good information, but don't we have a dragon to save?"

"Oh right," Kyvo said, eyes wide.

Redrinna straightened, a bit surprised she'd forgotten. Then again, whenever there was the opportunity to study something new, she seemed to lose track of things.

The question still remained of who should go with River. She would feel safer if they all could go, but they couldn't. Tak had voted for her to go, but inwardly, she cringed. She couldn't help remembering how Timothon had said her friends already viewed her as the leader of their little group, and this was unwanted confirmation.

However, that dragon didn't have time for her to sit here and wrestle with indecisiveness. It wasn't like going to rescue a dragon would make her the leader of the group. It didn't mean anything like that, which meant she could handle it.

"All right, I'll go," she said.

Tak's shoulders relaxed a little.

River got to his feet. "We should get going."

Leonora nodded. "The sooner the better."

"Just be careful," Tak said, that concerned look of his appearing on his face.

"We will," Redrinna said, doing her best to give him a smile. It was small, but it felt genuine at least.

Xandrin's ear frills stayed lowered, but he didn't say anything. Astra nudged his side hard enough to nearly knock him over.

"They're not going to die, red beast."

"I know that!" he snarled, putting more distance between the two of them. Then he glanced at Redrinna. "I'm just worried."

"You could always come sit outside the cave," River suggested. "Then you'll be right there when we come out."

Both dragons perked up at that.

"But only one of you should," Redrinna said with a sympathetic grimace. "It's not a good idea to have everyone sitting outside the cave where the boyar might find us, so one of you needs to stay here and protect the others."

Astra deflated a little.

"Let's go," River said, turning in the direction of the river. "We need to be quick."

Redrinna nodded and, with a goodbye wave to the others, turned and followed him, Xandrin on her heels.

Her nerves sparked with life, but she did her best to stay calm. They had to save that dragon, and if she let her fear convince her to hesitate, they might run out of time.

After they'd walked for a while and the sun had nearly lifted off the mountain peaks, they came to a waterfall pouring out of an opening in the cliff face.

River glanced back at Xandrin, his black eyes stern. "You should wait here, out of sight. This is where we'll come out."

"You're going in a different way?" Xandrin cocked his head to the side.

With a nod, River said, "That cave leads straight to the room where the dragon is being kept, but it opens pretty high up. It's steep, so while it won't be terrible to climb up, it's almost impossible to climb down."

The blood drained from Redrinna's face at the image that created in her mind. "I don't know how to climb."

Even though River didn't meet her eye, a sympathetic look appeared on his face. "Don't worry. Even if you don't know what you're doing, it's simple. It'll appear intimidating, but you'll manage it."

She still wasn't confident, but they left Xandrin at the waterfall and continued around the mountain, the rocky ground sloping down and dipping them into the shade, where the air was cold. Even though it was summer, the chill almost made Redrinna shiver.

A short time later, they came to a ravine running between two mountain peaks. River crouched and cautiously approached the edge, and, after a moment's hesitation, Redrinna did the same. The ravine was rock and the plants were sparse and scraggly, but it was devoid of human life.

"The main entrance to the cave is in here, a bit up the way still," he explained. "We won't go in yet, but as you can see, there's almost no cover or anywhere to hide. If the boyar comes, this is a bad place to get caught."

She nodded her understanding, and they walked along the top of the ravine. Redrinna didn't mind heights, but the steep sides of the ravine made her wary. Falling from here, while survivable, would seriously hurt, and she didn't want to risk that. Even if she had strange healing powers, she wanted to avoid needing them as much as possible.

They walked along the edge of the ravine (and Redrinna had to scurry away from the edge after it nearly crumbled out from beneath her) for a while before River stopped. He pointed out a narrow opening in the wall of the ravine.

"There it is. You ready?"

"As I can be," Redrinna replied, her voice hushed even though there'd been no sign of the boyar.

River nodded and, turning sideways, carefully stepping onto the loose rock and dirt of the ravine wall. Redrinna's heart leapt into her throat as she followed suit, doing her best to step only where he stepped. It was steep, and the rock was brittle and complained every time one of them put their weight on it, little chunks crumbling away. They'd almost reached the bottom when Redrinna put her foot down and the rock beneath her snapped. She instinctively leaned to the side, her hand attempted to grab onto the rock, but she ended up sliding the short distance to the bottom. Her fingers stung and some of her new scrapes bled, but she was fine otherwise.

River hopped the rest of the way down. "Are you all right?"

She nodded, brushing off her dust-smeared leg. "I'm fine."

Narrow, early morning rays shone into the ravine, and even though it was still early, it was already hot and bright. As they stepped up to the cave's narrow entrance, a bit of cool air wafted out, pooling around their legs like mist before the heat of the outside world burned it away.

With nothing more than a hushed, "Stay close, Your Highness," River led the way into the cave.

The immediate chill once they'd left the sun's warmth made Redrinna shiver. The cave was dark but there were occasional torches providing enough light to illuminate the glistening rock walls and allow them to crawl past the boulders and infrequent gaps in the floor. River led her slowly, and he seemed to be constantly on the search for any sign of movement. However, a bit to her relief, Redrinna could hear nothing except their own breathing and the occasional drip of water, and nothing and no one popped out at them.

As they crossed a large cavern, headed towards a narrow opening on the other side, a burning itch flared in her nose, and she sneezed in response. She sneezed into her elbow, muffling it as much as she could. It still echoed through the cavern.

River stopped.

Hesitantly, she peeked at him from behind her arms.

He glanced back, almost meeting her gaze but not. "Bless you, Your Highness," he whispered.

"Thank you," she said, a bit abashed as she lowered her arms. Another sneeze burned at her nose, and she wrinkled it to try and get it to abate. However, a few minutes later, once they'd entered that narrow passage, she sneezed again.

"Bless you," River whispered. Then, almost in an afterthought, he added on, "Your Highness."

"Stop it," she said before she could think about it.

He froze and, while hard to be sure in the weak light between torches, looked back at her with either shock or surprise.

"I'm not a princess anymore, but you and your sister keep calling me 'Your Highness.' Why do you—" She cut herself off with a sigh. River didn't deserve to be scolded because of the way being called 'Your Highness' made her feel. "Sorry. Forget I said anything."

River hesitated before he nodded, and they continued on. Redrinna couldn't help the grimace twisting her face.

After a few minutes, she sneezed again, much to her annoyance.

There was a pause before River quietly, almost demurely said, "Bless you, Your...Highness." The words almost seemed to get caught in his throat, like he'd either said it out of habit, or he just couldn't bring himself not to say it no matter how hard he tried.

"I'm sorry I keep sneezing," she whispered. If the boyar was here, he would find them because her nose had issues.

When River spoke, there was almost a smile in his voice. "You must be allergic to something in the cave. It's not that big of a deal."

She nodded, realizing a moment later he couldn't see it. All at once, her gaze stumbled into a set of thick, massive doors carved from stone that were cracked open enough for her to look inside. There was light inside, some of it managing to touch the darkness of the narrow tunnels, but it wasn't torchlight. It was sunlight.

 Something about it made her stop. River stopped too.

Slowly, she stepped up to the doors, and River hesitantly followed, staying a step behind her as she peered inside.

It was a large cavern, and high up in the walls, almost out of sight, were narrow, window-like slits. The sunlight streamed through them, illuminating a massive statue carved into the wall at the far end, some of its details just visible. The statue was that of a kneeling, robed woman with her hands cupped in front of her, her palms shining upwards like she tried to collect the sun's meager light. The end of her robes and long, unbound hair flowed out like water, melting into the smoothed stone wall. The ground around her glittered with dusty blue tiles, almost like she rose from the ocean itself.

"What is this?" Redrinna breathed, something about the place filling her with an ache she didn't understand.

"Before the Empire came and outlawed religion, this place was a temple—a sacred place, of sorts," River whispered. "It's difficult to find any information about it these days, but I think this statue represents the goddess the people here believed in."

"Goddess?"

"A powerful being. A lot of people believed gods and goddesses were creators of life and that kind of thing. Some cultures believed in many, and some believed in one."

It clicked in her mind. "Like the Torijin and their belief in a man called the Divine?"

"Right," he said. "This goddess was a powerful being they revered as a protector and guardian of all life. They believed she guided and watched over them, and to show their love, they worshipped her."

"Oh," she said, still unable to take her eyes off the statue. Even though it was hard to make out the finer details, it was clear whoever had carved it had loved their goddess. The details were exquisite and gentle, and the woman wasn't posed or dressed in a promiscuous way. Whoever had done this had taken their time to show devotion to someone they respected.

"If I remember right, they called her Pelikyra. However, that's pretty much all we know about her."

Redrinna's heart seized with pain. Pelikyra had been the name of the country that had been here before the Empire had swept in and claimed it. "So they'd even named their country after her, but because of the Empire, now she's been forgotten."

River didn't respond right away. "People have been doing things like this to each other long before the Empire did it here, Your Highness."

Even still, it made her chest tight and heavy to think something so many people had loved and cared for was left to decay.

However, she forced herself to step away. They had to rescue the dragon, not grieve for the lost things of the past.

After a few minutes of walking, they stopped again. Slow, faint breathing echoed to them from up the passageway.

"Do you hear that?" River asked, voice barely audible.

Her gaze was fixed on the semi-darkness ahead. "It's the dragon." They were close.

Staying silent, they continued through the dark, musty passages. As they drew closer, the biting smell of blood touched Redrinna's nose, making her grimace.

A few minutes later, they stepped into a dim cavern, the majority of the space lost in the darkness. The stench of blood was strongest here.

After a moment, her gaze found the dragon, the limp creature half-hidden in darkness. Her eyes went wide. Its scales seemed to be a deep azure blue with flecks of gold on the edges, making the dragon look like it was made of water with the light of the setting sun framing each scale. Its frill, a sea green color, rose high on its neck and back, drooping like wilting plants. The color of its two horns shifted from a deep blue to the same bright sea green as its frill, but they were straight and low, staying close to its neck. One webbed set of claws lay in view. Bright splatters of red blood smeared the ground around it, and patches of blood stained its scales. Its painfully thin chest rose and fell in the rhythms of sleep, but its breathing was shallow, almost weak.

Tears pricked Redrinna's eyes. "How could anyone do this?"

At the sound of her voice, the dragon's dark, green eyes slid open, its gaze locking on the two of them immediately. It stared at them, and they wordlessly stared back. Baring gleaming fangs, it hissed.

Chapter Sixteen

The dragon hissed at them, fangs bared, but in River's ears, it sounded so weak.

Her Highness took a step forward. "I know people have been hurting you, but I'm not here to do that. I'm here to help you."

"Help me?" the dragon said, painstakingly lifting its head, a grimace of pain twisting its features. "You're wearing dragon scales. You killed a dragon to get those, didn't you?"

"I didn't hurt anyone for these scales. They were a gift from a dragon friend of mine."

The dragon hissed again.

"I know it's difficult, and I understand why you don't want to trust me, but please give us the benefit of the doubt. We came to get you out of here."

The dragon shifted one of its thin legs, making its heavy chains rattle and grate across the stone floor. "How?" It asked that like it was a challenge, but also like it didn't believe freedom was even a possibility. The despair in its voice resonated with River's soul, sending ripples of sympathy rushing through him.

Her Highness glanced at her hands for a second before lifting her gaze. "I'm not sure if it'd work, but I have fire magic. If I can get it hot enough to weaken the chain, maybe you'd be able to break it."

The dragon lowered its head to the floor with a weary sigh. "I'm not strong enough to do that."

"Oh," she said, gaze falling.

A touch of sympathy filled River at the crest-fallen expression on her face, tears glimmering in her eyes. While he was angry at the dragon's state and situation, she seemed like she was genuinely in pain—like she felt the dragon's suffering as her own.

He envied her that.

Closing his eyes, River braced himself. He hated his own magic, and he despised using it even more. However, in a situation like this, especially for Her Highness, he had to do something.

So, swallowing his apprehension, he stepped forward. "Your Highness, even if the dragon was strong enough to break out, the heat you would have to generate would burn your hands."

"I wondered if that might happen," she admitted, almost demurely.

He almost couldn't believe his ears. She was so desperate to free this dragon, she'd been okay with the idea of crippling her hands?

For a second, he looked askance at her before remembering his place and shaking the surprise away. A brief flash of jealousy flared through him. How would it be to believe in something so much that you'd be willing to sacrifice your hands for it?

Carefully, River approached the dragon. "Her Highness's magic won't be able to help, but mine will. So allow me?"

The dragon studied him, eyes narrowing. River could only hold its gaze for a couple seconds. There was a good chance the dragon no longer remembered him; that didn't bother him. In fact, it was for the best if it didn't remember. After all, River's grandfather was the reason the dragon was in its current state.

"What do you think you can do?" the dragon asked, once again in a strange mix between a challenge and despair.

"I have the power to use earth, and metal is earth in an altered state." River rested his right hand on the nearest strip of chain and closed his eyes. The awareness of the earth inside the chain flared to life in his mind, and with a surge of power that almost made him cringe, he snapped the bands. They popped before clattering to the floor in a mess around the dragon.

Eyes wide, the dragon stared in disbelief. "You did it."

Her Highness smiled as she padded closer to the dragon, the weak torchlight glittering in her red eyes. "I told you we came to help."

Shaking itself, the dragon got to its feet, one of its wings dragging on the floor at an awkward angle. River grimaced at the sight of it. A broken wing that was trying to set on its own. Hopefully they weren't too late to fix that, otherwise the dragon would never be able to fly again.

All at once, the dragon studied him again. "Wait, I remember you."

River stiffened, a chill settling in his chest.

"Your hair was a little different then, so I couldn't remember right away. But you also...only had one arm."

Eyes going wide, Her Highness stared at him.

Fighting back a sigh, River pulled down the leather sheath he wore over his metal arm, the metal catching the orange flickers of torchlight. "I still only have one arm, technically."

"I've never seen a metal prosthesis before," she said.

River straightened the sheath back out, not relaxing until the metal had once again been hid. "I made it with my magic. My grandfather didn't drag my sister and I here because he loved us, so he didn't care about me or my injury. Left to my own devices, I created this."

Her expression became a mix between pained and thoughtful. Then, she turned back to the dragon. "For now, we need to get you out of here. When we're safe, then we can talk."

The dragon nodded.

"By the way, what's your name?"

He seemed surprised by Her Highness's question for a couple seconds. "Kelvair."

She smiled, almost looking like she was going to say something else.

Before she could, someone else did. "Well, just what do we have here?"

River snagged Her Highness's arm and yanked her behind him. A second later, his grandfather stepped into view.

"Oh, my filthy half-breed grandson and my dragon. What do the two of you think you're doing?"

Her Highness sucked in a breath, but River tightened his grip on her arm. She had to stay hidden or they would be in serious trouble.

Kelvair, weak as he was, took a threatening step forward. Without warning, the boyar flicked a hand and shadow ropes yanked the dragon to the ground. Her Highness stiffened.

"That beast is mine, and you have no right to take it from me." The boyar wiped his fleshy hands against each other like they were dirty. He paused, an eerie smile touching his mouth. "I see you've made a friend since you ran away."

River's heart lurched.

"Hello, Your Highness," he said, sneering as he said her title.

Crap. River stepped back, pushing Her Highness behind him as much as he could. Even still, Her Highness glared at the boyar from around his shoulder, which, while admirable, wasn't helping.

"You think you, of all people, can protect her from me? You seriously think a crippled half-breed like you is capable of reviving our family's cursed history?" The boyar half-laughed, half-snorted. Then his gaze flicked back to Her Highness. "I was told to leave you alone unless you got in my way, and I think you trying to steal my property definitely counts as that. That means I have a bone to pick with you, Your Highness.

"A long time ago, some uppity little princess found the evidence needed to convict one of my own. In fact, you were able to find enough evidence to have him sentenced to death, despite the fact a little recluse like you shouldn't have been able to find so much as a scrap. To add insult to injury, you evaded the assassin I sent to repay you and killed him too."

"If you didn't want to be punished, then you shouldn't have broken the law," she snapped, her voice steady despite the fact her arm shook. "And this dragon isn't your property."

The boyar smirked. "You think that, if it makes you feel better about yourself. I can't kill you like I want, but I can say I've struck against you as best I can. Have you heard about the executions? I'm sure my grandson was quick to tell you about those. Though...I'm sure you want to know what all those people were executed for?"

She stiffened and didn't speak.

"For you. Each person I've sentenced to death refused to deny you as their princess. They chose loyalty to you over loyalty to me. Because of you, I've killed over a hundred people. They died in your name, Your Highness."

She didn't say anything.

Time seemed to freeze as shock rolled through River's system. He didn't want to believe what the boyar said, but it made sense. It was something he would do. The executions had started after the incident with the dolls. Maybe the boyar was telling the truth after all.

The reason Thala and so many others believed the princess would save them was because they knew about how she'd managed to find and ensure just punishment for one of the worst offenders in the creation of the dolls: the man who'd held them captive and beaten Thala and the other kids past the point of feeling.

All those years ago, Her Highness had already saved them. Despite the despair lurking in River's heart, he for one, had never truly been able to forget that.

Without warning, Her Highness burst out from behind him, and with a powerful kick, she sent a massive wave of fire rushing at the boyar. Then she spun around.

"Let's go!" she commanded.

The shadows holding Kelvair fast vanished, and the dragon

scrambled to his feet. They raced for the back of the cave, their escape route high above their heads. There was no way they were going to be able to climb that before the boyar caught up.

Her Highness looked at Kelvair. "This is our only way out. Can you get us up there?"

Kelvair glanced at the opening with wide eyes. "U-up there?!"

The boyar let out a cry of outrage.

River stepped forward but froze. The only way he could help was with his magic.

Her Highness beat him to it. She ran two steps before sliding into a martial arts form, the movements similar to what River's mom used to practice but different. Fire roared around her before she released it in a powerful, snarling stream straight at the boyar. It raced towards him, bringing him up short.

"Okay, I'll try," Kelvair said. He scooped her and River onto his neck and, spreading his wings as far as he could—grunting with pain at the movement in his broken one—vaulted upwards. He leapt three-quarters of the way up the cliff before hitting the wall, stones cracking and rocketing away beneath his claws. They slid a couple inches before he caught himself. It took nearly all of River's strength to hold himself and Her Highness on the dragon's neck as he swarmed up the remaining cliffside.

The boyar let out another shout as they scrambled into the opening.

Kelvair whipped around, a racking hiss burning in his throat, his chest pulsing with bluish-white light.

River's eyes widened. "Cover your ears!" he called.

They both did, and a second later, Kelvair shot a jagged bolt of lightning out of his mouth, the boom making the cave rattle and rocks tumble from the ceiling. Then he raced off through the cavern, having to slow as it narrowed.

Sunlight spilled in through the opening ahead.

"That's the way out," River called to the dragon.

Kelvair raced forward, having to tuck himself in as tight as possible to launch through the opening. His bad wing couldn't pull in far, and it struck the wall as they flashed out into the sun. His cry of pain almost drowned out the roar of the waterfall below.

He didn't soar out of the cave; they mostly fell to the ground.

Xandrin was there in an instant. "What happened?!"

"The boyar!" Redrinna called as she vaulted off Kelvair's neck and onto his. She glanced at the panting Kelvair. "I know you're hurt and tired, but we can't stop yet."

He managed to nod.

River tightened his grip.

They raced away, leaving the cave behind as they sped off, not heading straight for their campsite, just in case. They followed the winding arc of the river for at least a mile, maybe two, until it raced off the side of a cliff, the water roaring as it fell and pounded the distant ground with intense fury.

Xandrin skidded to a stop, his claws sending rocks flying in all directions. He stopped at the cliff's edge, which let out an ominous crackling. As he scrambled back to safety, a large chunk of the cliff tumbled into oblivion.

"I don't like these mountains," he said, panting hard.

"You and me both," Her Highness said, rubbing his head.

She glanced at Kelvair, who panted so hard it sounded like he was hyperventilating. River hopped off his back just in case that might help.

Her Highness vaulted off Xandrin and to Kelvair's side, a hand on his snout as he fought for air. "I'm really sorry to have pushed you like that, but I think we left him behind."

"That's okay," Kelvair managed. "I don't like running, but the fear of getting caught again helped. So long as we don't have to run anymore, I'll be okay."

She nodded towards the river. "You can get a drink if you want."

Kelvair eagerly did, and when he was finished, he kept his head next to the water, letting the spray rush over his scales. Now that he was in the sun's light, it was obvious how frail and dull Kelvair's scales actually were. There was more dried blood smeared across his scales than River had first thought.

His attention was caught by Xandrin nudging Her Highness, his expression filled with concern.

She, though her voice still trembled a bit, almost smiled. "I'm fine, Xandrin. I promise."

"So, the boyar found you?" Xandrin asked. "He attacked you guys?"

She nodded.

River hung his head, shame filling his insides. He couldn't keep her safe. On the contrary, she'd been a big part of the reason they'd gotten out, and that made the shame dig its claws into the tattered remains of his soul.

Her Highness lifted her head. "I don't think the boyar is after us anymore, so we should head back to the others. Kelvair is injured, and we need to get him taken care of right away."

Kelvair lifted his head from the river at that, and River noticed then that his broken wing had broke again, just in a different place.

"Don't worry," Her Highness continued, glancing at the dragon as a bright smile illuminated her face. "We don't have to run this time. We can walk."

Turning, she led the way through the trees, and River followed swiftly on her heels, the guilt from failing to protect her compelling him to be her shadow. The dragons were quick to follow.

Their group walked in silence for a few minutes, but then Her Highness checked her pace, and, all at once, River walked side by side with her. Right as he made to slow down, she said, "I want to ask you a question, River, and I hope you'll be straight with me."

His mouth went dry.

"I appreciate that you tried to protect me from your grandfather. It was brave of you. However...he said something that's strange to me. What did he mean when he said you protecting me was like you were trying to revive your family's curse?"

His gaze hit the ground. It was only right for her to know, but even still, he hated the idea of having to tell her. "Well...it's not a curse; he just hates it. Either way, the simplest answer I can give you, Your Highness, is that...my name...my family's name, that is...is Zamfir."

She stumbled before looking at him with wide eyes. "I know that name."

"I thought you would."

A long time ago—nearly back to the age of the priestess of legend—the royal family and River's had been close friends. Then, for two kids from both the families, their friendship had taken a step beyond that. River and Leonora's ancestor had sworn an oath that starting from them forward, the Zamfir family would protect the royal family. Until River's grandfather had stepped into the picture, they'd faithfully done so.

"According to that oath between our families," River continued, his voice quiet with shame, "the person who should've been sent to you was me, since you and I are closer in age than you and my sister. She's nineteen while I'm seventeen. I'll be eighteen come winter."

She didn't speak.

"My grandfather refused to send my father to yours or me to you. He hates your family, and because of him, the oath was broken." He steeled himself for what he really had to say. "But...even if he wasn't the way he is and things were normal, I...can't honor the oath either."

"Because of your arm?" she asked.

"In a way, but," he paused, "the arm...isn't the issue."

She was silent long enough River glanced at her. There was a thoughtful look on her face, one he wasn't sure how to read. Eventually, she said, "It's fine, River. I wouldn't want to make you do something you don't want to do."

"I do want to do it," he snapped, making her look at him. He dropped his gaze. "I just... I can't. I made a mistake—a big mistake—and I don't have the right to protect you. I'm... I'm so sorry."

"It really is fine," she said, her voice kind. Even still, it still stung to hear the words. "The oath between our families is old; it can't possibly last forever. Besides that, you're already doing so much to help me and my friends, and I couldn't ask you to do more than you already are."

River didn't say it, but he couldn't deny how desperately his heart wished to be able to do something more. His father's greatest wish had been to uphold the family legacy, and he'd died without ever getting the chance. Now, River had the opportunity to do it. He had the chance to see his and his father's deepest wishes realized, and because of his own stupidity, he'd lost it for both of them.

That deep, unending shame that seemed fixed to his soul tightened its grip. Why had he been so stupid before? If he hadn't made that horrible mistake, things would be so different; his and Leonora's lives could've been the complete opposite of what they'd been.

He hated it. He hated constantly having to regret it, too.

Staying silent now, they continued on, walking through the forest. River shook his doldrums away, doing his best to keep an eye out for the boyar as the air became hotter, the sun washing its heat over the rocks and trees. Unfortunately, it couldn't burn away the cold hollow of shame hunkering inside him or undo what was done.

Chapter Seventeen

By the time they returned to their camp, Redrinna managed to shake off most of the shock from the boyar not only finding her, but also what he'd said. So long as Kelvair needed help, deciding if the boyar had made some sick kind of bluff could wait.

The others looked up as they arrived, relief washing over everyone's features (Kyvo entwined himself so tightly around Redrinna's ankles she tripped). Redrinna managed to give Tak and Astra a smile, though it took a bit of effort to put it on her face. Even still, it seemed like a real smile, so that was something, she supposed.

She shook that thought away and turned to Kelvair.

He watched her warily, keeping a bit apart from everyone.

"We need to check your injuries, okay?" she said.

Hesitantly, he nodded.

She approached with Tak and Kyvo on her heels. After a minute, River and Leonora came too. The dragon did not seem the least bit pleased or comfortable with their scrutiny, but he endured it nonetheless.

After a few minutes, Leonora said, "Most of your injuries seem old and healed or minor ones, which is good. I'm sure with time and good food, you'll be okay."

Kelvair relaxed.

"That said, your wing is a problem."

They all eyed the wing with one incorrectly healing break and a brand-new break from their escape.

River frowned at it. "Well, the best chance for it to heal properly would be to break it again and reset it."

Eyes going wide, Kelvair subtly pulled his injured wing away from them.

"However, once a bone is broken and heals, the part that broke is impossible to break again without proper equipment and knowledge, so we shouldn't do that."

Kelvair relaxed.

With a thoughtful expression, Leonora turned to Tak. "You have healing magic, don't you?" She glanced at her brother then. "That could help, right?"

River hesitated before he nodded. "It might. But we'd have to be careful."

A hint of discomfort passed over Tak's face, but he didn't voice any kind of refusal.

Even still, Redrinna's heart leapt into her throat at the idea. What if he used too much? What if it hurt him?

"You don't have to, Tak," she said quickly, almost before she could think about it.

He glanced at her, a complicated emotion in his green eyes. "It's okay, Redrinna. If I can help...then it's okay." A hint of a smile touched his mouth. "Thank you though."

She wasn't sure if she should be scared or afraid, but if he wanted to use his powers, she should let him try. Even if the idea made her mouth go dry.

River glanced Tak's way, brow furrowed with thought. "With healing magic, it is possible for you to reset the bone without us having to break it again. That said, it'll take a lot out of you, so you won't be able to heal any of Kelvair's other injuries without putting yourself in serious trouble."

"Tak, if you hurt yourself," Astra snarled, head lowered and wings flared, "you're going to be so grounded."

That concerned expression of his flashed across Tak's face, but he took a deep breath and squared his shoulders. Turning to Kelvair, he said, "I-if you're okay with it, I'll give it a try."

Kelvair considered him for a moment before nodding. "I can't fly if it stays this way, so please, if you can do anything, I'd be grateful."

Tak hesitantly glanced at River.

The young man immediately stepped over to the wing in question, and Tak followed.

It took all of Redrinna's self-control to remain where she was, her heart pounding in her ears. If they did this wrong, the penalty would be more than she could bear, but at the same time, Kelvair would never be able to fly again if they left his wing the way it was. Kyvo pressed against her leg as her gem pulsed with comforting warmth.

River spoke quietly to Tak over Kelvair's wing, the dragon watching the two of them with a curious expression, however, there was an exhaustion on his face too. He was so thin—unnaturally thin, especially compared to Xandrin and Astra.

Just like when they'd first found the dragon, fire burned in Redrinna's gut at the extent of his injuries. How dare the boyar do this. It made her so angry, she wanted to cry.

All at once, she imagined storming the city, sweeping in as the Imperial Princess and forcing the nobles—and the boyar most of all— off their self-constructed thrones and into a prison cell where they belonged. They'd agreed it was too dangerous for her to do that, but what might happen if she did? What if that could change something here?

Then her mind recalled what the boyar had said in the cave. 'Each person I've sentenced to death refused to deny you as their princess. They chose loyalty to you over loyalty to me. Because of you, I've killed over a hundred people. They died in your name, Your Highness.'

The pain those words created wasn't something she could describe. She wasn't sure he'd been telling the truth; he'd lied before.

However, if it was the truth...then maybe being a princess wouldn't help anyone or make things better.

At that moment, Tak lifted his hands over Kelvair's wing, snagging her attention back to him. He positioned his hands right over the crooked part of the wing, hesitating before taking a deep breath. Almost without realizing it, Redrinna took a couple steps closer.

"Remember," River said, his voice calm and collected, "only focus on this part of the wing. Take it slowly, just to be safe."

Tak nodded, closing his eyes. A second later, clean white light appeared beneath his palms, something about it making Redrinna stare. She'd never seen his magic before. Compared to hers, his was beautiful, almost breathtaking.

Kelvair's wing let out a crack, making the dragon flinch. Tak didn't move, intense concentration written across his face. The wing popped a few more times before the light from Tak's hands went out.

He staggered back a couple steps—she rushed to support him—but he managed to stay upright. With exhaustion in his eyes, he glanced at Kelvair and then at her. "Did it work?"

Redrinna turned to Kelvair.

The part Tak had worked on wasn't completely straight; there was a slight crookedness to it. However, when Kelvair straightened it as best he could considering his other break, his wing could move.

"I-I think it did," Kelvair said, some life returning to his eyes. It was then Redrinna realized his voice wasn't anywhere near as deep as Xandrin's, but it was still quite low and melodious. The dragon shot Tak a genuine smile. "Thank you."

Tak acquired a ghost of a smile.

"We should bind your wing so the new break will heal right, though," Leonora said, stepping up with a long bandage. "Otherwise you're going to be in this exact same situation again."

"O-okay," Kelvair said.

River approached with a couple long, straight branches, and he and his sister quickly set to work binding Kelvair's wing to his side, splinting it firmly so it wouldn't move. Leonora's bandage only wrapped around his narrow ribs twice, but she produced two more rolls out of her sack, and River produced one as well. Between the two of them, they had the dragon sorted in short order.

Kelvair thanked them as well.

Redrinna studied him for a minute before turning to Xandrin and Astra. "Will one or both of you go find something for all of us to eat?" She didn't want to make a big deal of it, but the sooner they got Kelvair eating, the more at ease she'd be regarding his condition.

The two dragons looked at each other.

"I hunted this morning," Astra said.

"Sure, but we have another dragon now. I think we're going to need more food."

She frowned. "Fair point, red beast. Let's go."

They turned and vanished. Redrinna still had no idea what to make of their weird relationship.

Regardless, she turned back to the dragon. As she did, he ventured a couple steps closer and crouched so they were more on level with each other. "Um...I'm grateful for what you've done for me, but who are you guys?"

"I'm Redrinna," she said, almost smiling, "but we're the Dragon Kin."

His eyes widened a little. "The Dragon Kin?"

On a whim, she said, "Have you heard of them before?"

"A long time ago," he said, "but what does your Dragon Kin do?"

With some overly excited interruptions from Kyvo, she explained.

He frowned. "So, the person who abducted me and stole my blood is working for the people you're fighting, and they want to kill us dragons, among other things?"

That pretty much summed it up.

For a few minutes, he seemed to consider it, tapping a webbed claw against his cheek a few times. "I'm not sure how helpful I'll be, especially right now, but okay. I'll join you."

Relief and worry intertwined in Redrinna's chest. Another member meant someone else for her to keep track of, but at the same time, she no longer had to fret about whether or not Osiris had gotten to him yet. Plus, he was no longer in the boyar's clutches, and in time, he'd be okay.

With worry for him no longer bogging down her mind, her thoughts returned to what the boyar had said in the cave once again. It couldn't be true...could it? He had to have been lying, just saying something to get under her skin. He hated her enough she could see him doing that.

Even still, by the time the dragons returned with food for them all, the fear that the boyar might have been telling the truth wouldn't go away. If he had been serious—if what he said was, in fact, the truth—the guilt was so intense, she almost couldn't breathe.

She was so distracted by her thoughts, she didn't realize she hadn't even eaten a bite until Kyvo nudged her leg.

"Hey, are you not hungry?"

"What?" She stared at him, distracted enough it took her a moment to realize what he'd said. She glanced at her untouched fish. "Oh."

Tak stared at her, exhaustion in his eyes still, but there was more color in his face now that he'd eaten. "Are you okay? You're not hurt or anything, are you?"

"No," she said immediately, realizing the entire group was watching her. "No, I'm okay. I was just...thinking."

"What's about?" Xandrin asked, creeping a little closer. She noticed that while he and Astra had brought back plenty of fish, they'd given Kelvair most of it, probably more than he'd be able to eat. Even still, the blue dragon seemed overjoyed, his eyes practically sparkling.

Redrinna almost kept her concerns to herself; she hated thinking about it, and the idea of talking about it made it worse. What if it was true?

"Well, the boyar found us in the cave."

Tak's concerned expression flashed across his face. "And?"

"It's mostly something he said. I..."

River's brow furrowed. "Most of what he says are lies. He likes manipulating people."

She met his gaze—he quickly dropped his, as usual—and said, "River, can you honestly say he was lying this time?"

He opened his mouth but didn't speak, which told her all she needed to know.

Leonora's brow furrowed. "What did he say?"

"He said that through the executions, he's killed over a hundred people," Redrinna began.

"How is that not enough proof?" Astra hissed to no one in particular.

"He also said the reason he killed them was because they refused to choose him over me and my family. He killed them because they were loyal to me. And if he was telling the truth..." The guilt and shame flooding her made it impossible for her to continue.

Kyvo leaned against her leg, chin on her knee, as her gem pulsed with warmth.

Even if he told the truth about what he did, that doesn't make it your fault.

"Hey," Tak said quietly, getting her to meet his gaze. "You're not responsible for the things that guy has done, not even if he says you are. You know that, don't you?"

She couldn't hold his gaze any longer. That made sense; of course it was logical. But that didn't keep her from feeling that what had happened was her fault.

"Why does this guy hate you so much?" Xandrin asked with a hint of disgust.

"That's easy," Redrinna said. Sometimes, she could forget about the assassin who'd come for her life, but that was largely because of Captain Brion. He'd been assigned to her for a couple years by then, and she'd still regarded him warily.

However, when the assassin had burst into her room, throwing shards of glass everywhere, Captain Brion had protected her without a moment's hesitation. He'd ended up getting a nasty gash on his arm, but because of him, she'd walked away from the encounter without a single scratch.

"He hates me because after the dolls were rescued, my parents went through all the evidence and reports, but couldn't find anything to convict any of the boyar's gang. They'd known who was responsible but couldn't find enough evidence to prove it and the case was closed. When things like that happened, they would sometimes give the case to me, just to study it and figure out procedures and what I should do in a similar situation. As I was going through that, I found something that had been overlooked in the investigation. Because of that, my parents secretly reopened it and were able to convict one person. He was sentenced to death for what he'd done."

"I remember," Leonora said with a hint of a smile. "The whole city celebrated when he was caught."

Almost in an embarrassed way, River added, "That was why when the boyar and his crew managed to take back power, the entire city believed if you came here, you could fix it again."

Redrinna hunched her shoulders a little as she stared at the ground. She'd only been able to catch one person out of that ring. It'd been almost nothing in the grand scheme of things.

"Wait," Will said as he unexpectedly joined them, his face shining with sweat. "The one who caught that—"

He called the man a name that made Leonora gasp and say, "Will!"

"—was really you?" Will finished, unperturbed, his gaze fixed on her face.

Cheeks warming, Redrinna said, "Kind of."

He stared at her, mouth hanging open. Then, he noticed their newest dragon. "You were the dragon the boyar had? I remember you."

Kelvair glanced up in surprise and blinked. "Oh, I remember you too. You look the same as before."

Will seemed confused by that last comment, but then his attention turned back to Redrinna. "You're serious that the one who managed to catch that guy was you? A hundred percent?"

She shared a wary glance with Tak. "Yes?"

He frowned, staring at her with... It wasn't quite suspicion, but Redrinna wasn't sure what it was. Slowly, he glanced around the group. "You know, considering you guys rescued the dragon, none of you seem happy about it."

Redrinna blinked, unsure what she was supposed to say in response to that. She glanced at Tak and the dragons, whose expressions mirrored her own confusion.

After a moment more, Will's expression brightened. "You know what this needs?"

"Please don't," River said.

"A party! We should celebrate!"

"Celebrate?" Astra repeated. "But we haven't won yet."

Will crossed his arms. "No, but you scored a massive point against the boyar by stealing the dragon, right? The war's not over, but we've won the first battle, which means we have to celebrate. Wait here, I know what we need!" Without another word, he raced off once again.

Redrinna slowly turned to the others, noting that most everyone seemed confused. For her part, Redrinna didn't think Will had the wrong idea. Rescuing Kelvair was something worth celebrating. The problem—for her, at least—was that she'd never...had a party before. The few celebrations that had taken place at the palace she'd stayed away from; the guests would have been uncomfortable if she'd attended, so it'd been easier to stay away. She'd celebrated her birthdays, of course, but they'd been quiet affairs with just her parents, Reyna, and Captain Brion.

Will returned a couple hours later with Thala in tow and a bundle. He carefully unwrapped it, producing a bottle, a few clay glasses, and a wrapped wedge of cheese.

"It's not much," he said, as Thala greeted Kelvair, "but considering how hard I worked to get this, it's practically a feast."

Redrinna, the taste of the fish still lingering on her tongue, eagerly eyed the pale, crumbly cheese.

Leonora eyed the bottle suspiciously. "Please don't tell me—"

"It's not wine, if that's what you mean," Will said, passing the cups around. "It's just grape juice. Actual wine is too hard to steal, plus the last thing we need while on a mission that could cost us our lives is to get drunk enough to be stupid."

To Redrinna, Tak whispered, "I've seen enough drunk people to never even be tempted."

Redrinna couldn't say the same, but she had heard people were often sick afterwards and had wondered several times what the point of being drunk was when it seemed miserable to deal with.

Will gave them all a little to drink and broke off pieces of the cheese and passed them out too. He even fed a little piece to Kyvo (who experimentally sniffed it, licked it once, then devoured it) and the dragons, though he was hesitant about the later. That said, he even gave them some of the grape juice too.

Leonora eyed her cup. "You didn't steal this, did you?"

Will whipped around, looking mildly offended. "Excuse me?"

She gave him a weary but scolding look.

"It belonged to someone who spends more time drunk than not, but he's got so much, I doubt he's going to notice."

River went from eyeing the drink to drinking it. Redrinna did the same. It'd been a rare occasion when they'd had grape juice at the palace, and she couldn't recall the taste. A cool burst of sweet and tart raced across her tongue, a pleasant enough shock it made her smile a little.

"Your Highness," Leonora protested, eyes wide. "Don't encourage him."

Redrinna looked up in surprise. "But...he stole it from one of the nobles, who basically stole it from your farmers, right?"

Thala's eyes widened slightly. "How did you know that?"

"It's usually obvious when money only flows one way," Redrinna said.

"Okay, but at least tell me you didn't steal the cheese," Leonora said, turning back to Will.

"I did not steal the cheese. I earned it," Will said with a sniff. "So excuse you again for only thinking the worst of me."

"Most of what she thinks is true though," River pointed out without looking up.

The two of them squabbled with Thala occasionally making interjections that were definitely not in Will's favor, and despite how much they still had to do and prepare for, Redrinna found herself grinning.

All at once, as Redrinna fought to smother a laugh, Will glanced her way. She froze. For a second, so did he.

He smirked. "So you do laugh, eh?"

"When I feel like it," she said.

"If you can laugh, then you can dance," he said, putting aside his empty cup and hauling her to her feet. He grabbed Thala's hand too. "No party is complete without a dance. Come on, you guys."

Leonora quickly got to her feet, dragging River with her. Tak sat frozen, the look on his face mirroring the panic sparking in Redrinna's chest. She knew a handful of dances, but not many. As Will and the others all took each other's hands and started making a circle, it was clear she didn't know this one.

Overwhelmed by self-consciousness, Redrinna desperately tried to tug her hand out of Will's grip.

"Nuh-uh, princess," he said.

"But I-I don't know how—"

"I know," he said. "This is a dance native to here; I know you don't know it. But while you're here, you're one of us—so I'm going to teach it to you."

"Wow, Will, that was almost nice," Leonora teased.

Will blushed. "Be quiet already." He glanced over his shoulder.

"You too, Tak. Come on!"

Hesitantly, Tak rose and joined the circle, standing a little closer to Redrinna than usual.

"Now see," Will began, "we all hold our hands like this."

They all held hands, and, keeping their elbows bent and near their sides, raised their fists to about shoulder height.

"Now we dance." Will demonstrated the steps, which Redrinna hesitantly copied. Tak slowly did the same.

They went slow at first, dancing in their circle. Then, as Redrinna and Tak got a grip on the steps, they began to speed up. They went fast enough they occasionally tripped on a rock, but nobody fell. Eventually, Redrinna didn't have to focus on the steps so much, and, all at once, it became fun. She was out of breath like the others, but that didn't stop her from laughing.

All at once, Redrinna tripped, and this time, they'd been going fast enough that she fell, dragging the entire group down with her. Embarrassed, she apologized, but Will, Tak, and Leonora all laughed. River and Thala didn't join in—they didn't even smile—but their features both softened, and it was clear they weren't unhappy either. When Kyvo burst into the group, pouncing on people at random, Redrinna finally laughed again.

The dragons watched the whole affair with amused expressions, and when Redrinna glanced at Xandrin, his ear frills lifted and he grinned. For her, this was a new side of friendship—and she wasn't even sure she could really call Will and the others her friends. However, at that moment, despite the fact they barely knew each other, it didn't seem to matter. Instead, it was like they'd already saved the day and regardless of what lay ahead, everything would work out.

◦ာ☺ ☺ာ◦

By nightfall, the group was so worn out that most everyone went to sleep without a sound. Tak lay on Astra's back, doing his best to stay still since she was keeping watch and he didn't want to disturb her.

Instead, he stared at the stars, admiring the little burst of lights twinkling in the dark expanse above him.

Will's impromptu party reminded Tak of days long gone by, days when he'd used to do things like that with his aunt and uncle. The memories did make him a little sad, but even still, it'd been fun. It'd been a long time since he'd been able to do something like that, and, even though it surprised him a little, he'd actually had a good time.

More than that, Tak couldn't get over the tiny bubble of happiness swelling in his chest. He'd used his magic again and, while it'd drained him, he'd managed to help their newest companion without hurting himself.

Thinking about it made him smile.

All at once, he couldn't help but wonder if this was how it'd been for his mom too. Had she also had this surge of profound gratitude whenever she'd been able to ease someone's suffering or take a weight off their mind? Was that why she'd put up with the utter exhaustion that followed?

He didn't have those answers, and, in truth, he probably never would. However, even without those answers, it was like he'd taken a step closer to his mom and understanding her. He had a slightly clearer picture of what she must've been like. That made him so happy, he didn't know what to do with himself.

Chapter Eighteen

It was a strange thing to be eating in a guardhouse, surrounded by guards in white uniforms while wearing a matching uniform after not being in a guardhouse for several years. Thala wasn't sure what to make of the observation, but it was there all the same. There was, however, the smallest twinge of almost pain at the memory that last time she'd eaten in a guardhouse, her father had been with her.

Shaking that thought away, Thala returned her attention to her lunch, the portions only slightly better than what Aretha and the others had ever been able to scrape together. It had barely any flavor. Compared to the juice and cheese Will had scrounged up last night, it was almost disgusting. Clearly, the boyar was not bribing the soldiers with food.

Around her, a few guards sat in pairs or small groups, their voices low, almost nervous. Thala studied them as best she could out of the corner of her eye while she ate. Some of them discussed her; she'd already heard multiple, strained whispers about the 'Azure Demon' just that morning. However, they would surely become bored with talking about her soon, and their conversations would hopefully turn towards the information she wanted.

She ate slowly, but learned nothing she thought the princess would find interesting. So, when she couldn't reasonably linger any longer, she left, heading for the training courtyard at the house's center. There were more soldiers there, and when she entered, their conversations faltered for a long minute before they continued.

Women weren't a strange sight in the army; just one with blue hair. That said, Thala noted there weren't many female soldiers here. There were a handful, but she thought it'd been like that in the desert too. Even still, they didn't seem more nervous than their male counterparts—just the same amount of nervousness—so she didn't think they were being targeted and used to manipulate their fellow soldiers.

So that was another possibility crossed off the list.

Thala knew it would take time to learn what it was, but even still, a part of her had hoped that since she was a new recruit, the others would warn her quickly, just to be safe. Apparently, she hadn't taken into account the fact most of the soldiers seemed afraid of her. It might take a few days before anyone would be willing to fill her in.

To make it seem like she had a purpose being in the training room, she took one of the lances off the rack and joined the others doing a random assortment of drills. She hated how accustomed she was to the weapon in her hand despite the years she'd gone without it. She hated how the drills were familiar—too familiar. She hated the way doing them reminded her of being trained in the darkness of that cave.

After some time, someone whose voice was vaguely familiar called out, "Private Thala!"

She glanced over her shoulder. The young soldier who she'd nearly run into the other day to talk to the captain stood at the edge of the grounds, watching her warily.

"C-Captain Andor is looking for you," he managed.

She returned her weapon to the rack and followed the soldier out.

With her behind him, his walk was stiff, almost awkward, but Thala paid him little attention as they went to the captain's office. Once there, to her surprise, the young soldier went in with her.

Captain Andor sat at his desk, sorting through a stack of papers.

"Privates," he said without lifting his head.

"Sir," the two of them said in sync, standing at attention.

"Because of the earthquake situation, you two are going to be working as partners. I wanted to pair both of you with more senior soldiers, but that simply can't be. That said," he looked at the two of them, his blue eyes stern, "Thala has enough combat experience for you to be all right, and Indigo has trained with the senior officers. It's not an ideal situation, but you will do all right. Even still, I will be assigning you to the afternoon patrol, middle city sector. It's calm, so you shouldn't encounter much in the way of trouble. That said, be careful."

They both nodded.

"You'll take over for the morning crew in half an hour." His gaze shifted to Indigo. "You know the proper location and the patrol routes, don't you?"

"Yes, sir."

"Then you're both dismissed. Oh, and Privates?" A hardness appeared in his eyes, putting Thala on her guard. "Remember, not one toe out of line. Do nothing that will draw the boyar's attention, is that clear?"

She and Indigo spoke at the same second. "Yes, sir."

He nodded, and they exited the room.

Indigo didn't speak to her, still seeming a bit wary, but Thala barely paid him any mind. That was an interesting warning. There definitely was something going on, something Captain Andor couldn't or wasn't willing to share.

She snuck a glance at Indigo, her dark-haired companion. There wasn't much anxiety on his face, so she couldn't help wondering if he knew. If he did, there was a chance she could get him to tell her. If not, what did the senior soldiers know that they weren't willing to tell them? And why weren't they willing?

∾ღ ღ∾

River remained hidden in the shadow of the fir trees lining the perimeter of the gardens of his target, watching the setting sun as it vanished beneath the waves with a fiery display of oranges and reds. With Kelvair out of the boyar's hands and with Her Highness, he could focus on hunting for all the incriminating evidence they could find. Will had managed to get a general layout of all the houses and routines, so now it was time to begin the next phase of their plan.

He didn't consider himself the spiteful or vengeful sort; however, his first target was the house of the scum who wanted to marry his sister to use her like a broodmare. Of all the nobles in the city, beyond his own grandfather, that was who he wanted to make sure wasn't going to be able to run free.

He'd been hiding in the garden for a while, wanting to give the house a sense of complacent safety before they went to sleep and entrusted themselves to the night. Plus, while the guards patrolled the town, they weren't allowed on noble property, so it was safer to sneak in during the day, when patrols were lighter, and then wait.

River was used to having to wait until inconvenient times to act, so he wasn't terribly bored as he watched the sun sink beneath the watery horizon and the sky go dark, only a sliver of the moon visible in the east, crowning the mountain peaks. There was some beauty to it, but what he enjoyed about the night even more was the way it enveloped him and kept the shame and guilt further away. In the night, it was almost like he could pretend nothing bothered him, that he had nothing to be ashamed of.

There was a freedom that came to him under the quiet glow of the moon he couldn't find in the light of the sun.

He waited a bit longer, until it'd been nearly an hour after the last light in the windows went dark. When the mansion stilled, River moved.

He stayed on the perimeters of the garden, stepping carefully so as not to turn his ankle on the rocks beneath his feet, until he reached the shadow of the house. Remaining as quiet as possible, he slipped in through the kitchen door.

There were a few slaves huddled around the glowing remains in the hearth, but with how relentlessly the house undoubtedly worked them, they didn't stir as he entered and passed through. When he arrived in the main part of the house, River paused, creating a mental map of what he could see of the mansion. There was no sense in checking everywhere—only a handful of places would hold anything of value. Besides, as nice as it would be to find every piece of condemning evidence, all he needed was one thing. That was all it would take to get this batch of bad, noble blood turned out on their ears.

River made his way through the house and past dark, star-illuminated windows to the first place that might hold something: the study. This house's was located in nearly the exact same place as the one in the boyar's mansion, so it was simple to find.

Once inside, he took a minute to take note of the layout of the room and the placement of most the items before he moved in. If he wanted it to appear untouched, he needed to know what it looked like before he touched it.

When he was confident he had a good sense of the room, he went to the desk and eased out the first drawer. He checked through it, double checked for any compartments or false bottoms, and when it resulted in nothing, he moved on. He found a long receipt of gifts of dragon's blood, which, while disgusting, wasn't technically illegal.

When he reached the bottom drawer on the left side, the last drawer he hadn't checked, he found a false bottom, and inside, slave records. A grim smile twisted his mouth as he slipped them out. If he took them all, it would be obvious someone had broken in. Also, he decided against trying to copy it—it would be far too easy to make the argument of a forgery with the intent to frame.

Instead, River counted them (fifty-two, in all) and selected two to take. He picked one of a middle-aged man who was neither too prestigious or low-ranked, someone who'd been with the house for some time and hadn't done anything to get himself sold and therefore—most likely—his record wouldn't be missed. Then River picked one of an older woman, someone whose job was important and more difficult to replace. She was also unlikely to be sold in the next couple weeks.

At the bottom of the certificates were scrawled the names of the owner and the seller, which were what they needed. So long as he had this paper, printed in ink and dated, even if the noble caught on and destroyed the rest, these two could put a severe dent in his reputation, at the very least. Two records, with different dates of sale, would be difficult for any respectable general to ignore.

Tucking the papers away, River returned the rest to the drawer and restored the false bottom. He worked carefully to leave it as he'd found it before vacating the mansion. He didn't allow himself to relax until he was over the back wall and headed into the safety of the mountains. That had gone a bit smoother than he'd expected, but even still he was relieved. One house for sure would be in serious jeopardy. If the general turned out to be honest, then one of the worst offenders (and someone River despised) was done for.

For the first time since Her Highness had come, he allowed a tiny flicker of hope to ignite in his, choosing not to blow it out. Perhaps it was possible for things to change here.

After a while, he heard someone on the trail behind him. He ducked out of sight, tension snuffing out that little flame inside, until the person stepped through a bright patch of starlight. It was just Will.

A bit annoyed, River waited until the young man was even with his hiding place before stepping out of the shadows. Will jumped before glaring at him.

"What the heck was that for?" he hissed.

River turned and continued on his way. "Because you're always following me."

"I'm not following you on purpose," Will shot back as he caught up. "We're just going to the same place, you know."

River responded with a shrug.

"Anyway," Will continued, not sounding at all tired despite the late hour, "did you find anything at your house?"

"Slave papers."

"Aww, that's way better than mine. All I got were smuggling records."

River looked askance at him.

"You'd think they'd hide stuff like that better, you know?"

River sighed. "They were hidden. Just not well."

Will seemed to concede, because he remained silent, not speaking as they continued on to their makeshift camp. When they arrived, Her Highness was the only one awake, keeping an eye on the camp.

"You're back later than I expected," she whispered, sitting on a boulder near a fire that was mere embers. "But I'm glad you made it. Did it go okay?"

"Fine," Will and River said in sync.

"Good," she said, the relief in her voice strong enough River was sure even Will noticed. She indicated a little pot on the fire. "Thala brought us that, and dinner is inside if you're hungry."

Will hesitated before approaching the fire. Her Highness handed him a bowl, which he eagerly filled. Seconds later, and he was already eating before River even had the chance to accept the bowl the princess held out to him.

It seemed to be some kind of fish soup in the pot, and while it was simple, River was hungry enough he copied Will without even thinking a single complaint.

Once Will's bowl was mostly empty, he looked at Her Highness (who'd gone back to scanning the mountainside) and said, "Hey, we both got something from the houses we hit. Now, there's only three of the major houses left, unless we want to hit the boyar's mansion."

Her Highness grimaced. "That seems dangerous."

"Especially since the boyar knows you're here, Your Highness. He might decide that's a good enough reason to justify coming after you,"

River said, setting down his own empty bowl.

Will looked at River in alarm. "What?"

"The boyar knows, but he's supposed to leave her alone."

"Why do you guys never tell me these things?"

Ignoring that, River turned his attention back to Her Highness. "We'll have to be careful, but I'm sure we can avoid drawing his attention."

"If you're sure," Her Highness said, her dislike for this phase of the plan clear.

He expected Will to say something, whether it be a snarky comment or what, but to his surprise, Will didn't speak. Instead, he nudged a rock with his knuckle, making it fall over.

Not sure what to make of that, River found himself staring.

After a few minutes, Will whispered, "I'm such a jerk."

That rendered River speechless.

"I mean, I already know that, but I forget sometimes."

Her Highness stared at him with a startled expression before she said, "What...makes you think you're a jerk?"

"I've been rude to you ever since you got here. I know it's stupid, but I keep doing it, and it just makes me feel...dumb."

"That's 'cuz you are," River said.

Will didn't shoot him a glare like he normally would, making River realize his friend was sincere. "I feel like a stupid kid, being mad and angry for things I know aren't even your fault—but saying those things make me feel better. But after all the things we've been doing together, and the way you reacted when Tehl did that weird thing, I..."

River remembered. Seeing Her Highness react that way, to realize in an instant what she must have been through in order for her to still be suffering had shocked him to the core.

"Thala used to have those," Will whispered. Hesitantly, he risked a glance at Her Highness, who stared back with a startled expression. "I didn't... I didn't make it worse, did I?"

Stunned, River just stared at him.

"No," Her Highness said, a hint of a smile appearing on her face. "You didn't make it worse."

For some reason, that made Will scowl. "Stupid princess."

Both River and Her Highness drew back a little.

"You just let me be rude to you this whole time; do you always do that? You let people bully you all the time? Heck, I think I would've been even meaner to you if it hadn't been for River and them, and you know what? I'm pretty sure you would've let me say a lot worse than I did! I don't think I've even meant most of the garbage I said. I was just repeating all the stuff people used to say before you got that guy arrested."

Her Highness almost looked embarrassed.

River dipped his head. The day he'd learned Her Highness had put away the man who'd made one of his best friends suffer horribly had been the first time since River's stupid mistake that hope had glimmered on the horizon. It'd only been for a moment, a fleeting second like a flash of lightning, but for that second, he'd been able to imagine there might actually have been people out in the big empty world who cared about little people like him.

For the first time, he'd been able to believe there might even be hope for himself.

Will dropped his head into his hands. "I still want to be angry at all that stuff that happened, but now I don't know who to be angry at!"

"Why not trying the people who were responsible?" River suggested.

"I could've been lying about wanting to help here." Will pointed an accusing finger at Her Highness, who stared with wide eyes. "I could've been working for the boyar or something—but you took what we said at face value. If you keep living like that, people are going to scam you out of everything!"

"I figured you were too mean to me to be a spy," Her Highness said, still wearing an embarrassed kind of grimace. "And I'm so used to people being mean or not liking me that it's what I expect. I don't know what to do when people don't hate me, actually."

"So you would've been more mistrusting if I was nice to you?"

"Probably," she admitted.

"What kind of messed up life have you been living that you think better of rude people than nice ones?" Will asked accusingly.

Even still, Her Highness laughed, which made River relax. At least Will wasn't offending her or anything, he supposed.

"I can't say for sure since I haven't met a lot of people," she said, "but I think you're funny, Will."

"Oh yeah?"

"I think I misjudged you."

Will snorted, but River thought there'd been a hint of a smile. "I guess we're more alike than I thought."

"Hey, can I ask you something?" she asked, leaning forward. "It's kind of personal, so you don't have to answer, but is it okay if I ask it?"

"I guess."

"So, River and Leonora want to take down the boyar because he's their abusive relative, and Thala joined the fight because she was a doll, but where do you fit in? Why do you want to?"

Will tucked his hands behind his head. "What makes you think I have some personal vendetta against him? What if I just don't like him?"

"Well, there's that, of course," she continued, undeterred, "but what we're doing here is risky—life ending risky. I've found that few people are willing to risk their life to take down someone they simply 'don't like,' you know?"

River glanced at his friend, wondering what he would say.

After a minute, Will surprised him again. "Fair enough, and I guess there's no reason not to tell you. I'm fighting with you because the boyar killed my dad."

Her Highness leaned forward a little more, eyes wide. "In one of the executions?"

Will shook his head. "Nah, he was too desperate for that. He murdered my dad in cold blood because my dad was the boyar. He was the boyar before the dolls and everything, and he tried to stop the current boyar from doing anything he was planning. So the boyar killed him. I'm going to make sure that pompous prick gets what he deserves in exchange."

Her Highness didn't say anything to that, but her frown deepened.

Will glanced at River and kicked his knee. "What about you?"

River scooted out of Will's reach. "What about me?"

"Don't think I didn't notice you scolding me with your eyes, mister. You don't have much right to lecture me, you know. Does she even know who you are?"

Slowly, he nodded.

Will's eyebrows lifted. "Oh yeah?" He glanced back and forth between the two of them.

Her Highness suddenly seemed to remember she was supposed to be keeping watch and turned away. Then she rose. "What is Kyvo doing?" she muttered before leaving.

River took a minute to answer Will (and he got the impression Her Highness had intentionally left the conversation, regardless of whether or not Kyvo was actually doing something). "She said it was okay for it to end if that's what I wanted."

"Are you okay with that?"

He scowled, turning his head away from Will. "How could I?" he hissed.

"Then do something about it already."

"Like what?" River snapped.

For some, irritating reason, Will smirked, apparently his doldrums in the past. "You know what. Things have changed since you were a kid, River; you've changed. Don't you think you ought to stop beating yourself over the head for what you did then?"

Deep-rooted shame burrowed inside River, and instead of continuing the conversation and letting Will patronize him, he left, finding the furthest corner of the camp he could go to and sitting there.

He needed to sleep, but his thoughts kept going in circles in his mind.

Rest didn't come for a long time.

Chapter Nineteen

The next morning, Redrinna woke up just in time for River, Thala, and Will to leave. She remained frozen for a minute before extracting herself from Kyvo's side and hurrying after them. She had a request to make, and she couldn't bother Thala about it; not only was she unsure how to read the girl but asking her to 'borrow' a weapon for Tak might arouse suspicion. She was pretty sure she could ask River, and he'd do it, but it made her cringe considering the circumstances between them, especially after the awkwardness of last night.

In truth, she'd forgotten there was a promise between her family and the Zamfir family. Around the time River technically would have been sent to her side was when Captain Brion had been assigned to her instead, and she couldn't help but wonder if the reason why the captain had been assigned to her was because of the actions of River's grandfather.

Even still, she hated the idea of someone following her around like a shadow, ready to lay their life down in order to protect her. Honestly, she'd prefer that the promise between their families be laid to rest. Their ancestors couldn't have expected their descendants to carry it on for centuries, could they? Surely, they would understand. Wouldn't they?

Shaking away her doubts, Redrinna focused on her current

problem: finding a weapon for Tak. Since the boyar knew she was here, Tak needed to be able to protect himself, and there was a good chance she wouldn't always be able to give him her sword in time. River and Thala weren't the right people to ask.

That meant—much to her chagrin—Will was the best option.

Steeling herself, she hurried and caught up with him. "Will?"

He spun around, freezing solid when he saw her. His mouth opened, but no sound came out.

For a second, their conversation from last night flashed through her mind, rendering her speechless as well. After a long, awkward minute of them staring at each other, Redrinna decided to get it over with and hope things went well.

"I...have a tiny favor, if I can ask something of you?"

A wary look graced his features. "Of me?"

"Well, I... Tak doesn't have a weapon of his own. Most of the time, he borrows mine, but since the boyar knows I'm here, I think that might be too much of a risk."

"Yeah, it is."

"So do you think you could find him something?"

One dark eyebrow lifted. "You want me to find him a weapon?"

She nodded. "Unless it would be too risky."

After a long, awkward pause, he said, "What kind?"

"Anything's fine. He's pretty good no matter the weapon."

Will paused, adjusting the hem of one of his sleeves. "You know, River's like that too. He can make just about anything into a weapon if he has to."

That made her thoughts go back to what River had said, but she kept quiet.

"He said he told you about his family, and when I brought it up, you left," Will continued slowly, almost cautiously. "You're really okay with letting that die?" She'd expected him to ask that with more of an accusatory tone, but he didn't. Instead, his question seemed genuine, catching her a little off guard.

For a moment, she didn't want to explain it to him. After all, he'd been borderline rude since they'd first met, and her and River's relationship was theirs, not his. However, ever since their impromptu party, he was...amicable. While he'd accused her of some funny things, he hadn't seemed all that angry. He'd even agreed to try and find a weapon for Tak, which he had no real reason to do. It wasn't like it would give him some kind of advantage; on the contrary, she supposed it could get him in trouble or even danger.

Sighing, she relented. "It's just... All my life, there's been someone there to protect me. For as long as I can remember, there have been people willing to get hurt so I don't have to." That soldier from the trial, Captain Brion and the assassin, Tak in the forest, and then Xandrin all flashed through her mind. "I hate it. I hate how people keep getting hurt in my stead. If River were to become my bodyguard because of a promise between our families, more than likely he'd get hurt for me too. He could even die trying to protect me. Maybe it's selfish, but the thought of that happening—" She shuddered.

Will didn't respond, and, while apprehensive, Redrinna peeked at him. He watched her with a seemingly impassive stare, but when she met his gaze, there were complicated emotions flickering there, things she couldn't puzzle out.

With a sigh of his own, he glanced away for a second. "So that's it," he whispered. Then he met her gaze again. "Maybe you and I really are more alike than I thought."

She didn't know how to respond to that.

"Hey, don't worry, Princess. I'll find a weapon for your friend, okay? It won't even be hard or life-threatening. Per se."

Despite her reservations, she let herself smile a little. "Thank you. I'm sorry for asking a lot."

"It's not that big a deal," he said.

"Aww, how cute!" a hauntingly familiar voice cut in with a laugh, making them both jump and turn. To Redrinna's horror, Tehl leaned against a nearby boulder, watching them with an almost mocking smile.

"What do you want, you creep?" Will snapped, planting himself between her and Tehl, which surprised her.

Tehl laughed. "That's not a nice way to greet somebody. I would've thought your parents would've taught you better manners than that. Oh wait, you don't have parents anymore, do you?"

Will's fists clenched.

Tehl's weird, unnerving eyes turned to Redrinna. "So, were you the one who orchestrated the release of the dragon, Princess? If so, I must say, it was a spectacular show. Loved every second."

A chill swept down her spine at the idea Tehl might have been watching. Was he implying Osiris had *let* her free Kelvair?

"Regardless, I came with another message for you."

It was difficult to swallow.

"Father hopes you're having a good time; however, the game's gotten a bit dull, don't you think? Wouldn't you like something more exciting than just raiding noble houses and waiting for information?"

"No," she said immediately, taking a half a step forward. It was a bit boring, but her friends were putting themselves in danger. She didn't want to do anything to put them more at risk.

Tehl erupted with laughter. "Oh that's cute. Did you honestly think I was asking what *you* wanted?"

She grimaced.

"Father is introducing a new piece to our game. Would you like to meet him?"

"What?" Him? Who was him?

Smile dripping with malice, Tehl shrugged a little before pointing coyly behind her and Will. Redrinna hesitantly looked but didn't see anything. When she turned back to Tehl, to her surprise and alarm, he'd already vanished. A chill seeping into her gut, she eyed the trees behind them again.

"Any clue what that was supposed to mean?" Will asked as he studied the trees too.

"No," she said, wondering if Tehl had been messing with them.

Was this just some kind of joke in order to put her on edge?

All at once, a man stepped out from behind one of the nearby trees, something about him seeming familiar but it was hard to tell while he was still in the depth of the early morning shadows. Her mind thought it might be the boyar, but that didn't seem right.

He took a slow, measured step forward, and Redrinna was struck with a distinct feeling of familiarity. She knew this person, but she couldn't place who he was. The height and build were familiar. The way he walked. Even the way he carried himself; she knew this man. But who—

He stepped out of the shadows and into the light of the morning sun. Her eyes went wide, heart stuttering in her chest. That face. She knew the tanned weathered face of the man she'd once seen every day. She knew the graying hair. She knew those green eyes.

"Captain Brion," she breathed.

However, there was something different about him, something off. She recognized him—the relief he was alive so sharp, it was almost overwhelming—but no recognition appeared in his eyes. Instead, he walked towards them, head lowered and gaze fixed on her. He didn't speak a word. There was almost...a darkness clinging to him, a foreignness Redrinna didn't understand. This was her captain, wasn't it?

"Captain?" she called to him, but there was no response.

Will took a step forward, a knife already in his hand.

Redrinna grabbed his wrist, making him glance at her in surprise. "Don't fight him. Please."

"Why the heck not?" Will's gaze flicked to the captain. With a wary expression, he pushed her back, forcing her to retreat a step for every one the captain took forward.

"He's my friend."

"You sure make weird friends!"

"No, there's something wrong with him. I don't know what, but please, don't hurt him."

Will let out an exasperated growl before shooting another glance at the captain. "All right, then you'd better run!"

She managed to take one last look at the captain—just in time to see shadow swords materialize in his hands. Her heart thrummed in her chest. Why was he attacking her? Panic sparking through her chest, she ran back towards their camp, Will hot on her heels.

The captain thundered after them, making her heart leap into her throat.

Redrinna pushed herself faster. After almost five months of having to believe he might be dead only to have him stare at her like she was a total stranger, she wanted to cry. He was there. He was right *there,* yet he'd never seemed further away. What had Osiris done to him for him to be like this? More importantly, how could Redrinna undo it without hurting him or getting her friends hurt in the process?

They nearly made it back to camp—close enough to see it through the trees—when Captain Brion caught up and took his first swing at them. Will tackled Redrinna to the ground, the impact knocking the wind out of her. Will rolled back to his feet, but Redrinna wasn't as athletic. Scrambling to her knees, she glanced back. The captain's gaze was still riveted on her. For a brief second, their gazes met. Now that they were close, only a few feet apart, she noticed the shadow in his eyes, a deadness that had never been there before.

"Captain," she cried, her heart aching when he didn't respond. "What have they done to you?"

Without warning, he swung at her again. She just managed to avoid the blade. As he drew back to swing again, Tak was suddenly there, and he deflected the blade off his arm, the shadow sword hissing as it struck the scales of his shirt. Her heart leapt into her throat. Tak was brave, but he didn't have a weapon.

Mind working fast, Redrinna backed away. Captain Brion was focused on her, so if she led him away, he'd leave Tak alone.

As she'd hoped, the instant she moved away from Tak, the captain's gaze tracked with her. Tak noticed and tried to move between them. The captain knocked him out of the way.

"Tak!" Redrinna cried, heart thrumming in terror.

He quickly pushed himself up, so he was probably okay.

Captain Brion stalked closer as tears burned her eyes. He didn't recognize her, but she couldn't bring herself to hurt him, nor could she run forever. If she tried, her friends would keep planting themselves between the two of them, but that meant they would keep putting themselves in harm's way. They could fight him, but how were they supposed to win if she didn't want the captain to get hurt?

"Redrinna!" Tak called.

"Princess, move!" Will shouted.

Redrinna remained where she was. If Osiris had done something to him, the captain probably wouldn't kill her; maybe hurt her or attempt to abduct her, but not kill. So what could she do? As he closed the distance between them, she searched his face, hunting for any sign of the man she'd once trusted.

"Why don't you recognize me?" she whispered, heart fluttering weakly like a crushed butterfly.

Then she saw it. For the briefest of seconds, when she'd spoken, something flickered in his green eyes. Was her captain still in there somewhere?

Right as she thought that, he swung a sword straight for her. She didn't even have a second to think.

The blow never came. Instead, a harsh crunch rang out.

She blinked, stunned at the sight of River standing between her and the captain, his metal arm raised. Captain Brion's sword had slammed into it instead, leaving a disturbing dent.

Throat clenched, Redrinna snagged his other arm. "River, don't hurt him."

He grimaced.

Captain Brion swung again, this time, going for River's chest. Unlike Tak, he didn't have scales to protect him. Without hesitation, Redrinna jerked him back, putting herself in front of the blade.

For the briefest second, horrified recognition flashed through

Captain Brion's eyes. It was quickly swallowed by darkness. The next second, blinding pain lanced through her side, the force behind the captain's swing slamming her to the ground. Fire erupted in her ribs.

"Redrinna!" Tak cried at the same second River and Will shouted, "Your Highness!"

Wincing at the pain, Redrinna pushed herself partially up, just enough for her to look the captain in the eye. He stood frozen, staring at her with what seemed like shock, something flickering in his eyes. Without warning, he turned and raced off through the trees, quickly vanishing from sight.

As she stared after him, her heart plummeted beneath her toes. After all this time, the captain was alive. However, in that state, it was like he'd been taken away all over again, and she didn't know if it was possible to save him.

Tak was the first one to arrive at her side, pulling her from her thoughts. "Are you okay?"

"Fine," she said, her side burning as she pushed herself onto her knees. "What about you?"

"I-I'm okay," he said. "It didn't hurt."

"Yeah, that guy got you both good," Will said as he approached.

River crouched on her other side. "Are you sure you're okay, Your Highness?"

"I am," she said. "The scales took the brunt of it." She pushed herself to her feet, and while her side still ached, it was starting to ease.

Tak rose with her, studying her with that concerned expression. However, he didn't say anything.

River rose. "Well, if the pain doesn't go away or you notice it bruises badly, your ribs might be cracked. However, with how well you're doing right now, I doubt they're broken."

If they were cracked, they wouldn't stay that way for long, a thought that made a chill trickle down her spine.

Will watched the three of them for a moment before he glanced in the direction Captain Brion had disappeared. "Okay, now that we know everyone is okay, what on earth was that?! And what do you mean that guy is your friend?" That last question was directed at Redrinna, accompanied by a scolding glare.

Redrinna also glanced in the direction Captain Brion had run off. "I don't know what that was. And he is my friend—or at least, he was. He was the knight assigned to protect me when I lived back in the palace, but I thought he was dead after the attack on the city."

"So you knew him?" Tak asked.

She nodded.

"That explains his weird behavior after he hit you," River murmured. "But it doesn't explain why he attacked you out of the blue."

"I guess this is part of that 'game' Tehl was talking about," Will said, arms crossed. "I guess possessing old friends and sending them after you is that Osiris guy's idea of fun?"

Redrinna shrugged, her heart still sagging. "Sending a beast to kill my friend while forcing me to watch is also his idea of a game, so it makes sense."

"Possessed?" River said, turning to Will. "What makes you think he was possessed?"

"He was acting funny but freaked out when he hit the princess. What else could it be?" Will explained that like it should have been obvious.

River frowned.

"Don't give me that. I'm thinking really hard here!"

"No, it's not that. It's just that possessing someone shouldn't be possible..."

"That's what Osiris's magic does," Redrinna cut in. "Things that shouldn't be possible. With his magic, his followers can't be killed. Like, they seem to die, but then they're just magically fixed."

A disturbed, almost confused look appeared on River's face.

All at once, in the distance, Xandrin's voice rang out. "Why are there always so many stupid trees? Every time something happens, I get stopped by something. First it was rocks, now it's trees!"

Astra hissed something, but what she'd said wasn't clear.

Xandrin shot back with a partial retort before Kyvo's high squeak cut them off.

Despite the weight on her chest, Redrinna couldn't help smiling a little.

Will turned to River. "Wait, what are you doing here? I thought you were already gone."

"I'd started, but then I heard you and Her Highness talking and figured I should come back."

"Why?"

"In case someone decided to be a jerk."

Will drew back, looking quite affronted.

Then, serious once more, River turned back to Redrinna. "Your Highness, we should consider moving our camp. Not that it won't keep them from finding us again, but Tehl and the boyar both know where we are. I think, given the last couple days, it's dangerous for us to stay here."

Redrinna nodded. "That's a good idea."

"We'll have to tell Thala somehow," Will pointed out.

"That won't be too difficult," River said.

Quietly, to just Redrinna, Tak said, "We should get back to the others, just in case something else happens."

She nodded, and led the way, getting all three of them to follow her back. They informed the others of the plan, and once they got the camp cleaned up (it wasn't hard considering most of them didn't have anything to clean), they set off, moving to a place further away from the cave where the boyar had had Kelvair hidden. It appeared similar to where they'd been before, but the trees were a bit sparser here and it was further away from Póli. Kyvo tested the ledge, hurriedly leaping to the safety of Xandrin's snout when it crumbled beneath his paws. The view that lay before them now when they stared down the rocky mountainsides was that of the lower slopes sprinkled with hints of green diving into the frothy blue depths of the ocean.

Even still, the change in scenery couldn't lift the weight off Redrinna's shoulders. After months of hoping and refusing to believe her beloved captain had died in Osiris's assault on the Imperial City, he was here. Alive and unharmed. However, something had happened to him, and given that Tehl had said this was part of Osiris's 'game,' she couldn't help but wonder if what had happened to the captain was her fault.

Once they were settled in their new camp, Redrinna perched on Xandrin's shoulders, hoping the familiarity would give her some comfort. However, every time she thought of the captain, any comfort was chased away.

Chapter Twenty

Tak kept an eye on Redrinna as the day wore on, and while she seemed more somber than usual, at least she didn't seem to be slipping back into that destructive mood she'd had a month ago. Even still, between the boyar and the suffering of her old friend, he couldn't help but worry that mood might return. He wished there was something he could say to her, but he didn't know what. It wasn't like when they'd been back in the Torijin forest and the answers had been clearer; here, he didn't know if there was a 'right' answer.

Not for the first time in his life, Tak realized playing the part of support in someone else's life was much harder than it appeared. Wanting to be able to help but not knowing how, not being able to ease them through the suffering they were going through faster, and not being able to do much more than watch from the outside—it just sucked.

You all right?" Leonora unexpectedly asked, making him jump.

Like he was around most people, Tak was abruptly tongue-tied. "I-I'm okay. Just...thinking."

"I see," she said. "Is Her Highness okay?" She shot a worried glance Redrinna's way.

"I think so," he managed.

Leonora remained quiet for a few minutes before her gaze turned to the ocean, and she took a few steps closer to the cliff's edge. She stayed far enough back to be safe, but Tak kept an eye on her anyway.

"You're...lucky, you know?" she said, half looking back at him.

He cocked his head at her.

"To have the friends you do, I mean. Your little Dragon Kin here..." She paused, and for a moment, Tak thought she seemed incredibly sad. "You all care about each other so much. It's enough to make a person jealous."

Tak lowered his head a little. "We're...getting better, but we haven't always been good at it." He still wasn't good at it. If he had been, there would've been something he could've said or done to help Redrinna feel better. Instead, he was stuck on the outside watching his friend struggle with complex emotions he didn't understand or envy, and he hated feeling this way again.

He knew she needed space to deal with the shock of what had happened to her friend, but at the same time, there was a part of him that wanted to shout at her to not forget the rest of them, which made guilt nip at him. If their roles were reversed, would he really have wanted someone to come and bug him?

Then again...

Since Leonora seemed to be through talking to him, he slipped away, making his way to Redrinna, who still perched on Xandrin's shoulders. Kyvo quickly followed him, and even Astra scooted a little closer.

He stared up at Redrinna, who noticed him after a minute.

"What's wrong?" she asked, her voice a bit flat.

"Well, you seem a little down, given everything that's happened, so I wondered if it'd be all right if we sat with you," Tak said.

Kyvo nodded. "Yeah, I know you're sad about your friend, but it makes me sad that you're sitting here by yourself."

"She's not by herself," Xandrin said, a bit indignantly.

From off to the side, Kelvair snorted.

"She's basically by herself," Kyvo argued, stamping one paw. "So play with us instead, okay, Redrinna?"

Collectively, they waited for her to make a move. Her gaze lowered, and Tak could tell how miserable she was. However, to his pleasant surprise, she slid off Xandrin's shoulders.

"You're right," she said, managing a little smile. "Sitting here moping isn't making it better."

"Yay!" Kyvo said, bouncing on his toes. "I know what we can do!" He raced off.

Tak stared after the kitsune for a moment before his gaze flicked back to Redrinna. She caught his gaze, and they both smiled a little. It was plain to him that she was still upset, but at least she wasn't trying to shut them out again. It wasn't much, but it was something.

⌘

Leonora watched the Dragon Kin as Kyvo returned with a stick he insisted Tak and Redrinna guess what kind of tree it came from, her heart aching a little as she watched. She was sure they wouldn't mind if she joined in, but even still, like Kelvair, she kept herself a bit apart. It made more sense for the dragon to get involved with them than it did for her to; after all, she was just hiding out in the mountains.

Even still, she couldn't deny the intense desire burning deep inside her to be a part of that group. She knew they were just a bunch of friends—albeit very skilled, magically inclined humans and enormous, dangerous reptiles—but when they had moments like this, they were almost like a little family. The thought of that made her ache for the family she'd lost and now barely had with River.

It was a poignant reminder of her past mistakes that had cost her the last bit of her family and made it impossible for her to join the Dragon Kin. She had next to no martial prowess, nor did she have any kind of magical ability. Therefore, unlike River or Thala, she would drag the Dragon Kin down—they might even get hurt because of her. As such, it would be better for everyone if she just stayed away, even though it ached.

River spent most of the day fighting to calm himself and not give in to the panic-driven urge to race back up the mountainside in order to check on Her Highness. She had the Dragon Kin and Leonora with her, not to mention she was pretty capable of defending herself. Since they'd changed camps, it would probably be at least a day or two before Tehl and the others found them again.

So, instead of charging up the mountain like an idiot, he contented himself with pushing all that energy into figuring out what kind of magic could make a person act like Her Highness's friend.

So far as he knew, magic couldn't be used to control another person; it simply wasn't possible. So why did that seem to be the explanation for what was going on with that man, and how were they supposed to keep that man from harming Her Highness if she didn't want them to hurt him? How could they free him when they didn't know how he'd been trapped in the first place?

River supposed the logical thing to do was disable whatever was being used to control him, but if that was Osiris, that didn't seem likely to work or be feasible.

Before he knew it, night fell, and he still had no answer to his questions. So, he shoved it aside and ducked into the noble house he was going to investigate that night. The structure was similar to all the other mansions, though with its own flairs here and there. He went to the study first, carefully studying the layout before moving in. Unlike last night's house, this one was much more disheveled, making River's task a bit harder.

He avoided the piles of papers strewn about on the dark, gleaming surface, determined not to rifle through them unless he couldn't find anything in the drawers.

It took him a bit longer to find something: a hidden compartment in the side of the desk. In there, he found slave records, smuggling reports, and even a bill of sale from an auction that had been held up in the northeastern part of the continent for a 'curiosity.' River didn't have to read much to know that this so-called 'curiosity' was a human being.

Anger flared in his chest, but even still, he only snatched a page of the smuggling record and two of the slave records.

As he tucked them away, he suddenly heard voices coming up the hall. Crap. Quickly and carefully, he hurried away from the desk, squeezing himself into a pitch-black corner between two bookshelves. He'd just managed to get himself situated when the door to the study opened and what sounded like two men strode inside.

River's heart thrummed in his chest, but he stayed still and quiet. They only had a candle to see by, so as long as they didn't approach him and his corner—and River didn't give himself away—he'd most likely be safe.

The man holding the candle set it on the desk, and River was mildly alarmed that they so carelessly put a naked flame beside so much paper. The few times their faces caught the light of the meager flame clued him in to the fact this was the noble and what appeared to be his son.

"Couldn't this wait until morning, dad?" Yep, definitely the nobleman's son.

"No. If you want to marry into the boyar's house, we have to get this squared away immediately. Those blasted Gogola's. If an injury from that wild beast was a good enough reason to get that girl's hand, then we should be the one getting it. Your brother's nose was broken. Who cares if that spoiled Gogola boy's arm was broken? It was just an arm. That's nothing compared to a nose."

The son muttered something River didn't catch, but it seemed like some form of protest.

"What was that?" the nobleman snapped, glancing up from his papers.

The son sighed. "He deserved a broken nose by trying to grab that girl against her wishes. Besides, I don't want to marry her. The last thing I want to do is marry someone just so you can feel powerful."

River raised an eyebrow. So there might actually be some goodness among the nobility after all? Or was this just some kind of teenage rebellion?

The nobleman tossed something onto the table, whatever it was letting out a sharp crack. "You listen to me, Gaylon, and you listen well. Your brother's nose was broken—who do you think is going to want to marry him now except some poor peasant girl so decidedly beneath him it would be a disgrace? You're the next oldest, so it is your responsibility to marry and improve our connections. Is that clear?"

The son stopped responding, just bearing everything else his father said. After a little while, the nobleman found whatever it was he wanted and scolded his son some more before quitting the room in a huff.

For a minute, the son remained where he was. "Maybe I should be like the boyar's grandson instead and run away. I'm the only other son you've got, so what would you do without me to bully around, huh?" Then he left, leaving River in the dark.

Even still, River waited for a while before extracting himself from his hiding place and hurrying out of the mansion. He didn't know why, but there was a part of him a little relieved to know he wasn't the only one who despised the people that had raised him. Even more surprising, he found himself pitying that young man. At least, in River's case, the brute that had raised him hadn't been either one of his parents; he couldn't imagine how he'd feel if the boyar had actually been his dad instead.

River was so caught up in his thoughts he didn't realize a patrol was coming until he nearly got caught. He hastily ducked out of sight (smacking his knee against the ground in his haste), but it'd been close enough the guards lingered for a minute longer than usual, their gazes traveling relentlessly over the dark streets.

Once they were gone and he could continue, he palmed his forehead and hurried out of town. Being stupid like that was a sure way to be found.

As he hurried up the mountainside, he spotted two figures waiting on the path ahead and, after a second, recognized them as Thala and Will. When River caught up to them, Will hopped off the rock he'd been perched on like a hawk.

"It's 'bout time," he said. "What kept you?"

"Almost got caught," River explained. "The noble and one of his sons walked in on me, so I had to wait a while."

Thala glanced at him. "I'm glad you didn't get caught."

He appreciated the sentiment.

Will jauntily walked ahead of them, walking backwards so he could see River and Thala.

"You're going to trip," River said, eyeing him disapprovingly.

"I figure you guys will let me know if there's something I'll—" He broke off as he kicked a large rock with his heel and tumbled over it backwards.

"Point and case," River said, stopping.

Will popped up a moment later, staring at the two of them with a pout. "Why didn't you tell me there was a rock?"

They shrugged and said, "Didn't see it."

Sighing, Will got to his feet and they continued on, though River noted he was facing forward now.

After a few minutes of walking, Will said, "Isn't this like old times?"

River studied his moonlit profile. "How so?"

"Oh don't be like that. It's just the three of us again. Granted, it would be more complete if Leonora were here, but still." Will tucked his hands behind his head. "It almost makes me feel like I'm a kid again."

Thala stared at the dark, twinkling sky. "A lot's happened since then."

River nodded, mostly to himself. He and Leonora had been dragged here when they'd been young—him seven, her nine—and Thala and Will had been quick to adopt them into their little friend group. Those first, innocent days had been brief, but Will's parents and Thala's dad had all been the brains and know-how behind River being able to create his own, functioning arm out of the metal scraps from the blacksmith shops. He'd just provided the magic.

Then the war had reached Póli, and that had irreversibly changed everything.

"You're both thinking about the war, aren't you?" Will said with a huff. "I don't want to think about that. I'm talking about before that happened. Remember how we used to go to the farms and help pick the peaches?"

"And they'd always let us eat some?" Thala said, a hint of a smile in her voice.

For a minute, memories of the sun and bright green leaves flooded River's mind. It hadn't been often when he and Leonora could sneak away from their then negligent grandfather, but when they had, their summer days had been filled with fun and peaches.

River hadn't had a peach in such a long time he couldn't even remember their flavor. Because of the last few years of constant droughts, many of the peach trees had died.

"I wish we had some peaches," Will said wistfully.

Thala's gaze was still fixed on the sky. "It hasn't rained enough for the peaches to grow."

"Yeah."

For a few minutes more, they walked in silence, the sparse, flickering lights of Póli vanishing into the darkness behind them. The only light came from the sliver of the moon, the stars, and their sparkling reflections on the dark ocean. A breeze blew, tugging on River's hair and tunic.

"Hey," Will began again, his voice a bit quieter than it'd been before. "Do you guys really think the drought and the food scarcity are a result of Osiris like the princess was saying?"

"Why not?" River said. "It makes sense."

"You think?"

"Well, if she's right and his magic is something that's against nature, then as he gets stronger, it's going to affect the world around it. That happens with a lot of man-made things, like dams and roads and—"

"Oh yeah?"

"Don't 'oh yeah' me," River began before noting Will's mocking tone. He glared at his friend, who smirked at him over Thala's head. "Why do you do that?"

"I think it's funny when you talk like you're an encyclopedia."

"I do not do that."

Will laughed.

"You're a piece of work, you know?"

"Hey, I have to make fun of you while I still can."

Thala glanced at him. "While you can? Are you planning on leaving?"

"No," Will said, pausing for a few seconds before he continued. "But you guys and Leonora...all of you were chosen by those Dragon Gems the princess talked about. You all had the dream; you told me so."

River lowered his head.

"That means all of you were chosen. So, when the princess is through here, you guys...are going with her, aren't you?"

The following silence wasn't a comfortable one.

"Aren't you?" Will asked again, staring at them both incredulously.

"It means going to war again," Thala said, her voice a bit quieter than usual. Something else was implied by her tone, something she wasn't saying, but River couldn't place what it was. It was almost like...fear, but also not.

"If I'm not fit to serve Her Highness," River whispered, "then how could I possibly join the Dragon Kin, Will?"

"You know, River, if that mistake in your past that you hate so much disqualified you, then how come that gem still marked you?"

That made River stiffen.

"You didn't think I knew?" Will asked, staring in the opposite direction. "The second the princess said something big happened right before you were marked, I knew what it was."

Thala dipped her head, almost like she, too, knew the event. Which, truthfully, she probably did.

"I don't want to talk about it," River said.

"Even forgetting the reason why, River. A gem marked *you*," Will pressed. "And one chose all three of you. You're okay throwing that away?"

Wearily, River said, "Why do you even care? If we do go, you're going to get left behind."

"I know that. I don't care about that part. If you go, I'll be able to brag about being friends to *three* members of the Dragon Kin that put an end to one of the worst baddies we've ever seen!"

Thala stared at him. "But we haven't won yet."

"The last Dragon Kin died," River pointed out.

"You guys are such kill joys," Will muttered. Then he glanced at the two of them. "You know, I know why all three of you were chosen, and to be honest, it makes me so proud that all my best friends were singled out like that. I don't care about being the odd one out. I know in our friend group, I'm the dumb one; you three have always been amazing, even when we were kids. Honestly, I don't think the Dragon Kin will lose so long as they have the three of you on their side. I don't care if you guys have to leave me behind. What's more important to you: my feelings or the fact that if you went and fought, you could make sure we win this time?"

River dipped his head, not having a response for that. Saving the world sounded like something some self-important jerk would say; only Will could say something like that and make it not sound dumb or conceited.

Regardless, he couldn't agree with his friend. He'd never done something so great that it warranted him being chosen by some ancient power to save the world. The event that had marked him was terrible—there was nothing magnificent or awe-inspiring about it. All he'd done was lock the one friend he'd been able to save from the Midnight Raid, Will, in his closet so he wouldn't be found. While that had been great for Will, the memory was punctuated by a sharp sting: that night, while River had saved Will's life, he'd been too late to save Thala. Plus, in order to keep the friend he had been able to save safe, he'd had to keep him locked in there while his dad was murdered—he'd had to physically fight his friend to stop him from going out and getting killed too.

How in the world was he supposed to be proud of that?

Chapter Twenty-One

Redrinna stirred the meager remnants of their dinner as it simmered over the embers of their fire. She'd never say it, but it was nice to have a cooking fire instead of having Xandrin roast all their food. Redrinna wasn't pleased their cuisine was still limited to fish—the only reliable thing they'd found to eat—but at least they could boil it and make watery soup. It was still gross, but it was somewhat more palatable.

At least, at the end of the day, she wasn't hungry.

Tak sat nearby, his hands full with entertaining Kyvo (though it honestly looked more like Kyvo was doing that himself and Tak was trying to keep him away from the fire) while Leonora sat on the other side of Redrinna, her hands extended towards the flames, the light making her palms glow. Even though it was summer, once the sun set in the mountains, the air took on a distinct chill that seemed to cut to the bones.

Astra yawned behind them. "It's so late. Weren't they back by this time last night?"

"We were closer to Póli last night," Redrinna said without glancing back.

At that moment, Kyvo grew tired of whatever he'd been doing and flopped across Tak's lap. "I'm so bored and tired of eating fish."

"Sorry," Redrinna said, glancing at him. "Fish is all we've got."

"I'd offer to eat your fish," Kelvair said, "but then you'd be hungry."

Kyvo let out a little sigh.

"Don't worry," Leonora chimed in. "You'll get used to it after a while, and then it won't be so bad."

That was what Redrinna kept telling herself too, but it hadn't worked yet.

"Do you not like fish either?" Xandrin asked, staring at Leonora with wide eyes.

Leonora gave him an apologetic smile. "Not really. But I'm not originally from here, so that might be why."

"You're not?" Redrinna asked, lifting her gaze from the soup.

Shaking her head, the young woman said, "Mine and River's dad got into a fight with the boyar over my mom. Because she was a foreigner, the boyar forbad them from getting married. So, they ran away and eloped, and kept me and River a secret. The boyar didn't know we existed for most of the time we were kids. We lived up north, closer to the Imperial City than to here."

Redrinna stared in surprise.

"Then what are you doing all the way down here?" Astra asked, resting her head on her claws.

"Our parents died in the battle that started the war—they went to the area as doctors and were killed in that raid. That led to the boyar finding out about us. I've grown to love the ocean, but I still don't much care for fish."

Redrinna paused, wondering if she would be able to love the ocean if she lived next to it long enough. She wasn't all that sure she would; the mountains had her heart in thrall, and this part of the Agicae Mountain range just wasn't the same as the part up north. There was great beauty here, but it wasn't the same as home.

"Oh hey," Kyvo said, scrambling out of Tak's lap and hopping onto Leonora's. "Are you joining the Dragon Kin with us?"

"Huh?"

"I mean, you've been chosen too, haven't you? I can tell."

Tak glanced at the kitsune with a skeptical eye. "Can you though?" he whispered.

Leonora glanced to the side, her smile wavering for a second. "Oh, I don't think I'm cut out for that."

Kyvo wasn't deterred. "Aww, but why not? I know it's boring now, but normally it's way more exciting."

"Exciting isn't exactly the word I would use," Xandrin said, but Kyvo paid him no mind.

"Please? It's much more fun when there are more of us. Plus, I like you, so you should come!"

Leonora blinked before she unleashed a furious tickling assault, distracting Kyvo enough he seemed to forget what he'd been asking her. Instead, he squealed and squirmed, his high, infectious laughter filling the air.

"Keep it down, Kyvo!" Astra hissed, though it seemed like she was trying not to smile.

Redrinna found herself smiling too, though she couldn't help noting Leonora never really answered Kyvo's question. Even still, she understood. Not everyone who had the choice to join would want to nor should they have to.

Given what Redrinna had seen up to this point, she understood Leonora's feelings.

"Oh, there they are," Astra said, getting most of the group to glance up as River, Thala, and Will returned. "It took you long enough."

Will made a face. "It's a long walk, all right?"

Redrinna smiled as the they joined them around the little cooking fire.

Will pulled out a thin sheaf of papers, handing them to Leonora. "There you go. More evidence for that general."

River silently handed his findings to his sister as well, who took them and tucked them safely away.

Thala busied herself with getting food. "Nothing happened my way today," was all she said before she began eating. She sat and scarfed the meager meal, but after a moment, she paused and offered a large piece of fish to Kelvair, who slurped it up with an abashed expression.

Grinning a little, Will said, "I'm sure patrols are a drag when the reputation of the Azure Demon precedes you."

As Redrinna watched them, River sat near her with his steaming bowl of dinner. She glanced his way, then did a double take. "River, you're bleeding."

He glanced at her and then himself, immediately finding the gash in his arm. It didn't seem serious, but a trail of blood stained his sleeve.

Leonora half-rose. "What happened?"

"I almost got walked in on, so I had to hide. I guess this happened then." With a shrug, he returned his attention to his dinner.

"River," Leonora began.

"It's fine," he said. "Don't worry about it."

Leonora stared at him, once again, the happy expression she had wavering. Even still, she didn't say anything else. Despite her silence, Redrinna caught on anyway.

"River, may I treat your wound?" Redrinna asked. If she was right, he wouldn't refuse, which would put Leonora at ease.

His gaze shot to hers so fast, it almost made her jump. He went a little ashen then flushed a deep red. Even still, he didn't answer.

"Please?" she asked again.

"I-it's not that bad, Your Highness," he said quickly.

"That doesn't mean you should ignore it." Redrinna turned to Leonora, who already had the necessary cloth, water, and bandages ready. She rose, taking them from Leonora before turning back to River. "So please?"

He couldn't hold her gaze any longer. "If you insist."

"I do," she said before kneeling on the ground next to him.

Obediently, he rolled up his sleeve, giving her a good view of the injury. It wasn't deep, but the gash in his arm still wept fresh blood.

As she tugged the sleeve of his tunic a little out of the way, she said, "How did you get this anyway?"

"I wedged myself between some bookshelves," he said, his voice a bit subdued. "It must've been then."

"A loose nail or something, I guess," Leonora said, chin resting on her knees.

"How didn't you feel that?" Will asked.

"I was focused on getting out without getting caught," River snapped. He winced a little when Redrinna pressed a damp cloth to the cut.

"Sorry," she said.

"It's fine, Your Highness," he said quickly, almost mumbling. "It didn't hurt until then is all."

"Not every injury hurts right away," she said as she worked to clean the cut. "But that doesn't mean you should ignore it, even if it seems small. Most of the time, that just makes it worse."

He glanced at her for a second at that but stayed quiet.

Redrinna wasn't sure what had compelled her to say that, so she pressed her lips together in an effort to avoid letting anything else like it slip out.

"You know," Will began, already earning a bit of a glare from River, "you really are good at that."

Both Redrinna and River glanced at him and said, "Huh?" at the same time.

"I meant you, River. You're good at ignoring your problems. I mean, how many times have you been whipped, ignored the injuries, and then gotten sick?"

River didn't say anything, but Redrinna thought she knew what he was feeling.

"You're not going to be a burden if you have to ask for help, you know," she said, getting him to look at her again, his eyes wide. "Granted, I don't think I'm the one who should be saying that because

I'm still figuring it out, but letting yourself hurt so you don't bother the people who care about you isn't fair. To you or to them."

"Your Highness," River said softly as she finished wrapping a strip of bandage around his arm, "it isn't that big of a deal. A little cut isn't important."

"No, it is." Lifting her eyes, she met his gaze. "Trust me."

He held her gaze for a second before turning away. "You shouldn't bother yourself with me, Your Highness. I can't keep—"

"It's not about that promise," she said softly. "With or without it, we're still friends, aren't we? And that's reason enough for me to bother myself with you."

He didn't say anything to that.

Deciding to leave him be, Redrinna turned her attention to Will, who stared back, slowly raising an eyebrow.

"You don't have an injury too, do you?" she asked.

"I don't think so," he said slowly. He glanced himself over before letting out an "Ah." Then—Redrinna wasn't sure if she should laugh or be annoyed—he held up a dust bunny.

Leonora rolled her eyes, but she was smiling again. "Oh, har har. Very funny."

Redrinna smiled a little. After two stealth missions, River and Will were still relatively all right, which filled her with the kind of relief that made her tired. It was like she was a toy that had been wound too tight and had finally been able to release the straining tension. Granted, she knew that tomorrow, they would hit more houses and all the stress would be back. She'd been unsure about hitting the houses in succession, but River and Will had both insisted on it—the faster they were in and out, the less chance of the nobles catching on and warning the other houses, if they noticed at all.

For the rest of the night though, she didn't have to worry.

༄༅ ༄༅

As Thala and Indigo went out on their usual afternoon patrol, Thala found herself reviewing how their coup was going. Her Highness and the Dragon Kin had found the dragon the boyar had taken hostage. River and Will had already hit half the noble houses and snatched condemning evidence for each one, and the general was due to arrive in the city within the next week or so.

So far, everything seemed to be going well. So well, it left Thala uneasy.

After the boyar's long, oppressive regime and the bloody path he'd carved to make it happen, surely it shouldn't go down this easily, should it?

Then again, maybe that was just how things like this happened: quietly and without some kind of massive consequence. Maybe there were some things that crumbled away in silence.

Indigo glanced around them, something about the jumpy way he did so catching her attention. "There's a lot of people out today, huh? Is there something going on we don't know about?"

Thala eyed the crowds milling around them. There were a significant number of people out, and she noted most of them seemed to be from the richer section of town. "Maybe there's something good at the market today?"

"So good the nobles have to come see it themselves?"

"It happens," she replied. It wasn't good reasoning, but it did happen occasionally.

"Maybe there's a show or something."

"Captain Andor would've told us about that."

Indigo frowned, eyeing the crowd. "Let's go then."

She nodded, and he fell into step behind her. In the couple days since they'd been tossed together, they'd quickly found an efficient system for getting through crowds. Between Thala's distinct, impossible-to-miss hair and her reputation, if she led the way, the crowds around them would part like water, and Indigo would simply follow behind. In truth, Thala wasn't sure whether or not she should be offended by the treatment, but it was what it was, she supposed. On the plus side, they were always able to get where they needed to quickly, so at least there was that.

After a few minutes of walking, Thala stopped, realizing where the crowd was headed. A chill seeped into her gut.

"What is it?" Indigo asked, drawing even with her. Then he also noticed where the bulk of the crowd came to a rest—at the foot of the massive wooden execution stand. "It can't be."

It would explain why the nobles had come out in force; they always seemed to turn up in droves for things like this. Thala couldn't understand. She'd lived through violence worse than this, but even still, the thought of people being killed here—the thought that someone was about to die with an audience cheering for it—made her sick to her stomach.

A hand dropped on her shoulder, making her jump. Glancing back, she was surprised to find a soldier standing behind her and Indigo, his mouth in a tight line. He seemed somewhat familiar from the guardhouse, but she didn't know his name.

"You two shouldn't be here," he hissed as he steered them into the nearest alley, the buildings blocking the execution stand from their eyes. "What are you doing patrolling all the way up here?"

Indigo stared at the senior officer with a touch of annoyance. "We were checking out the reason for the crowd and—"

The officer shook his head. "I understand but leave it and leave here. Got that?"

"But sir," Indigo pressed with indignation, "that's not—"

"I know, but just drop it. If the boyar realizes you're here, he'll make you watch."

"It's illegal!"

The officer shushed him before throwing a glance over his shoulder. Then, bending down so he was a bit more on their level, the man eyed them both in turn. "You're both just kids. You shouldn't have to see stuff like this yet. I know it makes your stomach turn, but you know what's going to happen if the boyar catches wind of you even implying you disagree with him, don't you?"

Thala didn't, but Indigo seemed to have an idea.

"I don't care if he kills me too," the young man spat.

The officer let out a world-weary sigh. "He won't kill you, Indigo, but think about your mom and your little sisters. He'll go after them if you don't shut your mouth and leave, and I don't want you to have to live with that. Why do you think Captain Andor gave you a patrol far away from here?"

That made Indigo hesitate.

The soldier pushed them farther down the alley, and for a second, Thala would've sworn a deep sorrow appeared in his eyes. "Go on. Don't watch." Then he left, disappearing amongst the crowd again.

"Come on," Thala said, jerking on Indigo's sleeve to get him to follow.

Her mind whirled as they left the alley and returned to the upper crust's outskirts, where the crowds were nonexistent. She'd finally found the reason the officers hadn't done anything contrary to the boyar's wishes; she had the answer. The last thing she needed to do now was something stupid that would prevent her from being able to tell Her Highness.

Even still, she could practically smell the agitation bleeding off Indigo, and she shot him several warning glances to keep him quiet. It was one thing for her to be rebellious; the boyar had already seen to the end of her family. However, Indigo still had a family—they were probably the reason why he'd joined the army so young. If he wasn't careful, they would be the ones to pay the price.

The rest of her shift seemed to crawl by at the pace of a snail, but eventually it passed. She returned to the guardhouse with Indigo, where they gave their report. Even though she'd only known Indigo for a few days, she could tell not reporting the illegal execution gnawed at him. Still, he managed to keep his mouth shut.

Captain Andor nodded when they finished, and she was sure from the pained expression on his face he already knew about the execution despite them not saying a word. A bit wearily, he waved them out.

She'd planned to head straight up the mountain to report what she'd learned, but once they reached the main room of the guard house, Indigo collapsed in the nearest chair, panting, elbows resting on his legs and his head bowed.

A couple other soldiers, a man and a woman, happened to be passing through and noticed. Hurrying over, they said, "Indigo, what's wrong?"

Indigo didn't speak.

Thala watched quietly, unable to bring herself to leave even though she had no reason to stay. Indigo's reaction struck her in a way few things did; maybe it was wrong to feel a surge of jealousy, but she wished she could have those reactions. Instead, seeing the execution stand and knowing someone was about to die there did little to disrupt the numbness that cloaked her. It made her sick. But it didn't touch her in any other way.

"Indigo?" the female soldier said again.

"I'm fine," he said. He glanced up, noticing Thala standing off to the side. "I'm a right mess, aren't I?"

She nodded.

He smirked. "You're not supposed to be that honest."

"Oh. Sorry."

"I bet it looks stupid to someone like you, huh? You've seen far worse stuff than me."

She didn't understand his logic. "It's not stupid."

He sighed. "I'll get past it; I knew this happened, but I always thought that if I joined the army, I'd be able to stop it." His voice lowered to a bare whisper. "I've wanted to stop it since I was a kid. I mean, that was how my dad died."

She wasn't entirely sure where Indigo's loyalties lay, but she was fairly certain, as of this moment, he wasn't on the boyar's side. So, allowing herself to take a risk, she approached him and bent to whisper in his ear.

"I know you can't rebel, but don't worry. I can."

He stiffened but didn't look up. The other two soldiers seemed to lean a bit closer too, but she wasn't sure if she'd imagined that or not.

"He's already taken my family away, so there's nothing for him to threaten me with. And I'm going to see this ended."

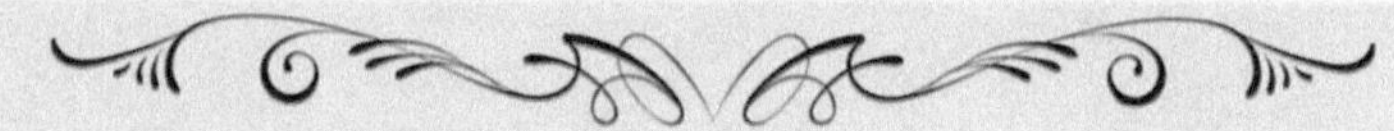

Chapter Twenty-Two

River stalked through the noble house—his third in the last three days—having to move at a slower pace than he liked due to the fact the moon kept slipping behind clouds, plunging him into darkness. After he and Will did this tonight, there would only be one more house to hit, and they would then be prepared for whenever the general returned to Póli.

It wasn't much, but at least they'd been able to do that for Her Highness. Perhaps it was possible her idea would work, and the boyar would vanish for good.

It took River a little longer to find the study in this house than it had in the others. While the layout was similar, the owner had not chosen to employ the same rooms for the same purposes. However, once River found it, he set to work.

In short order, he found the customary smuggling note and two slave papers. As he straightened, something on the desk made him pause. It was a missive from another one of the noble houses—which wasn't of much consequence to River—but as he glanced away, the words 'Imperial Princess' flashed across his sight, making him freeze.

Slowly, heart inching towards his throat, he turned back, picking up the letter so he could put it in better light. As he scanned the note, his chest tightened.

Sofronio,

Tehl just told me. The boyar is lying—the dragon is gone, and so are both his grandchildren. We can't trust him. The Imperial Princess is here. Be on your guard but don't panic. The sudden movement of goods will undoubtedly draw the attention of unfriendly eyes. Sit tight and keep your eyes wide open.

-Vivar

For a long minute, perhaps longer, all River could do was stare, his blood frigid. His mind wanted to say this was some sort of trick; it was convenient for this type of letter to be sitting out in plain sight where River would undoubtedly find it. That said, so far as he knew, none of the nobles had any reason to suspect he would be in here tonight.

More than likely, this was real. Tehl hadn't told just the boyar; he'd made sure all the nobles knew about Her Highness. For what purpose, River didn't know, but he was sure it was bad. After all, Osiris had said they were going to play a game. This was one of his moves.

All at once, there were footsteps in the hall, accompanied by the clack of a dog's claws.

River froze, his muscles already stiff enough from the shock of the letter it almost hurt. Whoever it was went past the study without stopping, though the dog paused to sniff at the door long enough River backed away from the desk, not even realizing he still clutched the letter in his hand.

He waited for an age before the person and the dog returned, not moving until they were long past. Pulse thrumming in his ears, River tossed the letter onto the desk and left the mansion as quickly and quietly as he could manage.

Will waited for him outside of town, but River barely noticed him.

"What's the matter with you?" Will asked, hurrying to catch up with him. "You didn't almost get caught, did you?"

"No," he said immediately, almost without realizing it. Then he stopped, peering at his friend. "What did you say?"

Will eyed him before he frowned, surprisingly stern given his usual demeanor. "What happened?"

"I found a letter from one of the other nobles. They know Her Highness is here."

Will paled. "How?"

"Tehl."

Will swore. "Of course Tehl told them." He paused. "Unless you think it was planted or something?"

"Why? The nobles don't know what we're doing."

"Maybe Tehl planted it."

"But why? Him planting it is even more odd. If this is part of that game Osiris mentioned, then what's the point of a move like this?"

"I guess that makes sense, but we still can't rule out it might be fake." Will resumed walking. "But if we keep standing here like this, someone's going to notice. Let's hurry."

River hesitated for only a second before nodding and hurrying after.

They didn't speak the rest of the way to camp, a nervous tension wafting off of both of them, spurring them on to a faster pace than usual.

Last night, most of the others had waited for the two of them to come back, but tonight, it was only Tak and Her Highness. Once again, Her Highness kept the remains of dinner warm for the two of them while Tak seemed to be the lookout.

Her Highness looked up at their approach—the red of her hair seeming closer to a dark purple when the moon's light was blocked by a passing cloud—and she immediately seemed to sense the tension.

"Did something happen?" she asked, getting Tak to take a couple steps closer, though he kept his gaze on the surrounding mountain slopes.

River told her about what he'd found. "To be fair, it could have been fake to make us panic, but it doesn't seem likely."

She took that in without much of a change in her expression as she ladled out some fish soup for the two of them. "We should content ourselves with what we have. It might be too risky to go after the last one. At least right now."

"Maybe," Will said, accepting his soup but not eating it, the steam coming off the liquid curling around his cheeks. "But as far as we can tell, they still haven't caught on to what River and I are doing—just that you're here and the boyar is lying. For all we know, they might be more concerned with planning some kind of coup, and if we wait, the chance to hit the last house will disappear."

Her Highness's mouth pressed into a line as she held out a small, steaming bowl to River as well. He reached for it, but at that second, a realization struck him like lightning, the intensity of it making him take a leaf from Will's book and curse.

The two of them stared at him with shocked expressions. Even Tak stared at him in alarm.

How could he have been so stupid? It'd just come back to him with alarming clarity—he'd been in such a rush to get out of that mansion he hadn't taken the time to return the letter to where he'd found it. He'd tossed it on the desk and ran. It was very likely the letter had landed far from where it'd been before, which meant, even if it was a fake letter, it would be obvious come morning that someone had been in the study.

"They're going to know about you and me," he said monotonously to Will, the shock of his stupidity rendering him motionless.

"What, how? What did you do?" Will snapped, still staring at him in shock.

"I didn't put the letter back right. I threw it and ran."

Will swore too.

Her Highness glanced at the two of them in turn before she said, "Then we should avoid hitting that last house. If they're going to know you two are coming, you can't go. They'll be waiting for you."

"Actually, it might be best to hit it as fast as possible," Will said.

"It's going to take some time for the houses to realize whether they've been hit or not and even then, they might not be willing to let the others know if they have. Nobles have a lot of pride."

"True," she said with a shake of her head, "but this was how they got away before. They don't like each other, but if one of them falls, they'll all be in danger. They're going to band together and lock up like a wall the instant they realize someone's been breaking in. You can't risk it—not yet."

"We have to," River said, starting to get himself back together. He'd made a stupid mistake, but there was only so much they could do about that now. "If even one house gets away, this whole problem will either start again or just continue once you leave."

"No. River, Will, please, don't go." There was a pleading look in her eyes, something about it making River hesitate. There was something else in her eyes, something he couldn't name, but it fanned his doubts. "If they catch you, who knows what they'll do to you. You can't let that happen, please. I know getting information on every house is important, so you can just wait a few days and then hit it, can't you? The general isn't going to return for a while yet, so you can wait long enough for them to relax before going back."

"If we wait, they'll have time to lay a trap that'll catch us for sure," Will argued. "We have to go now, when they're going to least expect it."

"But—"

"Hey, do you want to change this place or not, Princess? Someone has to do the dangerous jobs, and it can't be you."

"That doesn't mean you have to be stupid," Her Highness said. For a second, River thought her voice shook with anger—then he noticed her hands trembled. It only took him a second to recognize it was from fear. "The boyar held another execution today, Will—"

Both River and Will stiffened.

"—and if you aren't careful, he might try to put you up there next. We have to wait and let the nobles relax before we—"

"Stop it!" Will snapped with enough force that she flinched. He downed his soup in a couple swallows before slamming his bowl down. "You don't know this place or these people like I do. If we want to win, then we have to do this and we have to do it now. We can't wait. Like you said, the nobles know how to respond to this, so if we're too slow, we're going to miss the only chance we've got. Maybe you have the luxury of sitting up here in the mountains where it's safe, and you don't have to think about being hungry, but that town is full of people who can't do that. The longer we wait, the worse things are going to get for them."

"Will," River hissed, alarm bells pealing in his mind.

"People are dying while you sit here and wait. You could stop it, but you're not going to. Instead, you insist you aren't a princess and leave us to fend for ourselves, so don't get upset when we actually do that! If you wanted to boss me around, then maybe you should've been a princess instead of whatever it is you are now. This is what a battle is, Princess—this is what war looks like. If you don't like it and don't want to fight, then why'd you bother to come at all?!" Will stormed out of the circle of light provided by the small fire.

River stared in the direction his friend had gone, his mouth open. Slowly, he managed to turn back to Her Highness. She was kneeling, sitting back on her heels, her clenched fists resting on her knees. Her face seemed expressionless in the near dark, but her eyes were lowered, fixed on the ground.

For a minute, River remained frozen, his soup forgotten in his hand. He didn't agree with what Will had said or how he'd said it, yet at the same time, he couldn't seem to admit his friend was wrong. Even still, it wasn't Her Highness's fault this had happened, and there was merit in her idea of waiting and letting the houses relax.

"Your Highness," he began carefully.

"Don't," she all but snapped, catching him off guard. An irritated sigh—almost a huff— rushed out of her. "I'm not a princess, so please, stop calling me that. Besides, Will is right. I'm overstepping. If you two are that determined to go and get the last bit of information, I have no right to stop you. I'm the outsider here." Without another word, she left as well, heading in Xandrin's direction.

River stared between the two of them before wolfing down his soup and heading after Will. His friend had curled up on a low, squat rock, and after a moment of staring at him, River kicked his foot.

Will grunted in response but didn't move.

River crouched in front of him. "That was uncalled for and you know it. I thought you felt bad for treating her like crap before."

"So what? If we don't see this through, people are going to die—they already have. People I know, and people I care about, have died and suffered because of this. I'm not wasting the one chance I have to change it just to spare her feelings."

"Will—"

Will kicked at him, making him fall back on his metal hand, the impact jarring his shoulder. "Don't lecture me. You're not her knight, and you know as well as I do that we can't make this work without evidence against *all* the houses. If you don't like it, I'll go alone tomorrow."

"You're not going alone," River snapped.

Will rolled over, putting his back to him.

Anger flared inside River's chest. "She's just trying to protect you, Will."

Will glanced over his shoulder, meeting River's gaze with fire in his eyes. "I have people I'm trying to protect too. Should I hide in a cave and wait for someone else to take care of it? Maybe she has that luxury, but I don't. The town doesn't either. I don't care if I get hurt or die so long as this place changes, got it?"

Growling in response, River rose and left, sitting on a boulder that let him stare out at the pitch-black ocean. Cold glints of light on the water appeared at random, at the dictation of the clouds above. Otherwise, the ocean was pitch-black.

⚬⚭⚮ ⚯⚮⚬

By the time morning rolled around, Redrinna was no longer angry, but she was still hurt enough by what Will said that she went out of her way to avoid him. He was correct: she had no right to tell him and River what they could or could not do, but he was wrong for snapping like that. She did want that information; she wanted to change this place for the better. She just didn't want them to have to pay for that with blood or, even worse, their lives.

Even still, regardless of her feelings, arguing with him was futile. After all, what could she say to make him understand she cared? She hadn't even set one foot in Póli. While she had an inkling of what it was like to live there, she had no real idea. She hadn't seen the suffering of these people with her own eyes; she only understood what she'd found in the eyes of River and the others. Not to mention the fact that the longer they sat here waiting, the more the people in Póli suffered— Will had been right about that. Already, at least one person had been executed, and Redrinna hadn't known in time to do anything about it. Because she refused to be a princess—because she feared the idea of attempting something like that—they had to wait for the general to return before they could act. How many more people would the boyar kill in that time?

That said, it wasn't like she would've been able to help, princess or not. That was the one thing Will hadn't gotten right. It was one thing to act as a member of the Dragon Kin, where she had friends who could help her. If she was a princess, she'd have to stand all on her own. The few times she'd done that, she'd failed.

Once breakfast was over and Thala was long gone, Redrinna settled on a rock a bit apart from the others.

Are you all right?

Redrinna shrugged in response to her gem.

Are you mad at him?

"Not anymore," she whispered. "But I was. And I don't want to talk to him anyway."

271

I'm sure Will wasn't trying to hurt you. I think he's as scared as you are.

"Maybe," she said.

Fear was something she understood; she understood the lashing out part. However, if this was what it was like to be on the receiving end of it, it made Redrinna feel all the worse for how she'd treated her friends while they'd been with the Torijin.

The gem stayed quiet, just warming the chain instead.

A short while later, Tak and Kyvo joined her, and Redrinna realized Will and River had already left. Even though it made her chest constrict, there wasn't anything she could do about their choices. She just hoped it would turn out okay and she'd overreacted.

"You look tired," Kyvo observed as he bounded onto the rock next to her.

"Well, I was up pretty late last night," she remarked dryly.

Tak stared at the two of them for a moment before he said, "Hey, are you really okay?"

She blinked at him.

"After what...Will said. Last night, I mean."

Kyvo's ears perked up at that.

Instead of filling the kitsune in, Redrinna scratched his ears, which proved to be a sufficient distraction. "I'm fine. But it's not like he was wrong."

"Even if he wasn't wrong, that doesn't make what he said right," Tak said, resting his weight on his hands, though he wasn't looking at her.

She didn't respond to that, and the three of them lapsed into silence. For a few minutes, Redrinna was distracted from her thoughts by the birds flitting in and out of the trees above. A few brave ones dove to the ground nearby, coming within a couple feet of them in their hunt for seeds and bugs.

After a little while though, Tak slowly straightened and said, "Hey, this is a weird question, but do you think..." He trailed off, getting her to glance his way. "I just mean...i-if something happened and the only way for us to get out of it was for you to be a princess, do you...do you think you could do it?"

That caught her enough off guard that all she could do for a solid minute was stare at him. "What?"

"I was just curious," he said, a sheepish look on his face. "What Will said...made me think. Even if it was just for a few minutes, do you think you could be a princess?"

Discomfort wedged itself between the vertebrae of her spine. "Tak, I can't. The mistakes I've made and all the stupid stuff I've done that has gotten you guys hurt— How am I supposed to redeem myself from any of that? There are people who've lost their lives because of my stupidity, and no matter what I do, they aren't going to come back. Because of me, they're gone. They're hurt and not going to get better. Do you really want a princess who does things like that?"

He sighed, but there was a strange expression on his face, one she'd never seen on him before. It almost looked like...annoyance.

She frowned at him. "Tak, I can't be a princess. I'm not good enough, okay?"

Abruptly, he got to his feet, something about it startling her. "Never mind. Just...forget I said anything." Then, to her surprise, he left, heading back over to Leonora and the dragons.

It was like a door had been slammed in her face, leaving her speechless. Quickly, she lowered her gaze.

Kyvo, ears back, snuggled into her side, putting his head in her lap, but even still, it didn't chase away the heaviness dragging on her heart.

First Will, then River, and now Tak. Nothing she said seemed to get any of them to understand she simply couldn't be a princess—she was barely qualified to lead the Dragon Kin. She couldn't make the calls that mattered, nor could she seem to overcome her fear and reckless stupidity.

How on earth could any of them consider her capable of saving the day if she suddenly donned the hat of a princess? It wouldn't change who she was, and it wouldn't fix anything. Why couldn't they understand she was just trying to keep them safe?

Chapter Twenty-Three

Thala's gaze flicked over the empty streets, the unease from the execution the other day still fresh in her mind. Póli appeared normal on the surface, but for her, it didn't feel normal. There was a threat hanging in the air, almost like a lingering scent that her senses could just pick up on. Even Indigo seemed to notice it.

"We're being followed," he said, his voice a shade darker than usual and his tone grim.

Thala nodded.

She'd noticed the three men tailing them a bit ago. They'd moved in closer now though. It seemed they'd finally gotten brave.

Almost in sync, she and Indigo turned to confront them at the same time.

"Do you need something?" Indigo asked, his normal politeness dried up.

A prickle shot up Thala's spine, and she turned as two more withered men slinked out of a nearby alley.

Five on two wasn't all that fair.

"The boyar killed our brother," one of the men hissed as they pulled out hard wooden canes. "And you lot didn't stop him!"

Immediately, the five men charged in. Thala turned so her back was to Indigo, her lance ready. Even though it'd been years since her days as a doll, somehow, the training she'd endured remained instinctive.

With a couple quick thrusts, she downed the two flankers—but didn't kill—and then she turned to face the other three with Indigo. One of his three assailants aimed a thrust for his ribs, and the other two had him distracted enough he wasn't going to be able to dodge.

Thala dove forward, hitting the cane away and throwing the man off balance. The next second, one of the other two men swiped at her. She twisted out of the way, but he managed to catch her shoulder with enough force to send her down on one knee. Despite the mind-numbing pain, she rammed the butt of her spear into his ribs, knocking him to the ground. Indigo managed to disarm his assailant right as Thala swiped away the last man's cane.

"That's enough of that," Indigo snarled, kicking away a nearby cane.

Despite that, the ringleader—the only one still on his feet—glared at the two of them. "You think you can arrest us?"

Indigo glared back. "I should. But I'm not going to."

Thala glanced at him.

The men seemed surprised, sharing startled looks as they nursed their new bruises.

"You're not the only one who's angry about it," Indigo finished. "Just don't be idiots and make me regret this." Without another word, he turned and stomped away.

Thala hesitated before glancing at the ringleader—who stared back with wide eyes—and following Indigo. They'd been on the way to the guardhouse since their patrol was finished, so they went there without speaking to each other.

A short walk later, Thala trudged into the guardhouse, rolling her now stiff shoulder. It didn't hurt much anymore, but it would be sore for a while.

Indigo, walking side-by-side with her, glanced at her, his eyes still bright from the adrenaline. He seemed calmer now. "It's a good thing you were there," he begrudgingly said. "They would've pummeled me otherwise. Though it's kind of strange they didn't seem to care that you're the Azure Demon."

"It doesn't work on everybody," was all she said in reply.

They went and reported to Captain Andor again before parting ways. The spear Thala borrowed for patrols had chipped, so instead of heading to Adonis's like usual, she took it to the army blacksmith to be repaired. A faulty weapon could mean the difference between life and death.

The blacksmith's apprentice eyed her nervously, but accepted the spear without question, mumbling promises about how it would be finished quickly. Since it wasn't Thala's personal weapon, she wasn't all that worried.

She made her way towards the exit of the guardhouse, her thoughts wandering aimlessly, but not aimlessly enough to not notice the tall, slender soldier beelining straight for her. She attempted to step out of his way, but he stepped back into hers. At the last second, she stopped. He threw out an arm, his palm striking the wall, making it clear he wanted her to stop, a moment too slow.

Without moving her head, she stared at him, gauging his posture. While he wore a pretty nasty sneer, he was relaxed, meaning he wasn't about to try and gut her. Yet.

"You're the little Azure Demon, aren't you?" he began, his voice soft. Captain Andor's door stood open a few feet away, so Thala supposed that whatever this man's intentions, he didn't want to be overheard.

Since Thala thought the question of her identity had an obvious answer, she stayed silent.

"I heard something interesting about you," he continued. "Something you said." Slowly, keeping the action silent, he withdrew a knife from his belt and touched it to Thala's neck.

Thala recognized the threat but stayed relaxed anyway.

"You know what you said, don't you?"

"You'll have to be more specific," she responded, her voice soft but steady.

His grip on the knife tightened. "You threatened the boyar."

"Did I?" Thala knew what he'd overheard, but she hadn't technically threatened the boyar outright. However, she supposed saying she would dismantle the boyar's monopoly on Póli could be taken as a threat.

"I could waste time jogging your memory," he hissed, "but I'm sure the boyar would prefer to hear about it from your own mouth instead. So here's how it's going to go: I'm going to put my knife away, and you're going to walk yourself to the jail where you'll wait for him to come visit you. And if you don't..." The knife pressed a little harder, but not hard enough to make her bleed.

Even still, her training prevented her from flinching. Instead of doing what this guy—who she guessed was one of the soldiers loyal to the boyar—wanted, Thala grabbed his wrist in a swift motion, twisting it away from her neck. She'd been taught that move with the intent to twist until she broke her opponent's wrist, but, almost like her dad still stood there, holding her hand to prevent her from twisting further, she stopped the move at the point where the man would be uncomfortable instead of crippled.

She said nothing, just watching him as his face twisted with pain.

"If you do anything to me," the man hissed through gritted teeth, "I'll make sure the boyar knows."

"If I wanted to do anything to you, you'd already be dead," she said. Then she twisted underneath his other arm and shoved back, making him stumble away. Quickly, she left the guardhouse, her heart beating so hard it was almost the only thing she could hear.

After a few minutes, it calmed enough for her to hear footsteps behind her, and she whipped around, weight on her toes. To her surprise, it was Indigo.

He drew up short, a wary look on his face until she relaxed. "Sorry. I didn't mean to startle you."

"It's fine," she said, taking a few slow breaths to slow her racing heart.

"Are you okay? I don't know what Petty Officer—"

"It's fine, Indigo."

He paused, the wariness leaving his face and being replaced by something else. Something Thala recognized but couldn't ever understand when she came face to face with it. "You're still a doll, aren't you? I forget because you don't... But I saw it just now, back there. And when we fought earlier. All that stuff they did to you doesn't go away?"

She shook her head. As much as she wanted it to, as much as she longed to be normal, she was not, and the training that had broken something inside her remained intact, only ever a moment away.

"I-I'm sorry," he said with a grimace. "I'm sorry I keep calling you by that nickname too."

"I don't mind."

He made a face before shaking his head and stepping closer. Speaking in hushed tones, he said, "So what was that guy doing?"

"He was trying to arrest me because of what I said yesterday. To you."

"He's in the boyar's pocket?" Indigo frowned. "There really are spies in the army."

She nodded.

"I swear I didn't tell anybody what you said. I don't know how it reached his ears."

"The guardhouse is a big place," was all she said in reply. It wouldn't have been hard to be overheard by unfriendly ears.

"But beyond that," Indigo continued, a flicker of determination appearing in his eyes, "I don't know what you're doing, but I want to help. If it means taking *him* out, I'll gladly help you."

Thala studied him. "You have something he can threaten."

"I already talked about it with my mom. She said she doesn't care so long as we win. That'll make anything worth it. So let me help you. Please, Thala."

She stared at him, unsure what to say. That was the first time he'd ever called her by her name, but she didn't know why that had caught her so off-guard. It almost...made her feel something.

If she let him in, it would be a way for Her Highness's secret to get out; it could end bad. However, for what they planned to do, the more people they had on their side, the better things would be. Could she trust Indigo enough to tell him or would she be able to stop him if he proved untrustworthy? At the same time, wouldn't someone whose dad had been murdered by the boyar be the perfect person to convince to support Her Highness and what she was doing?

For some reason, Thala felt she could trust him. An awareness of that spread through her like the sun's light as it rose.

After a moment more, she said, "If you think you can keep a secret that will kill you if it gets out, meet me outside of town in one hour."

"Which gate?"

"East."

⊶⊙◌⊙⊶

Thala waited for Indigo perched up high and out of sight. Letting him know the biggest secret in the world could have disastrous consequences, and she wanted to watch him and what he did before deciding one way or the other if she could really trust him. If worst came to worst, the dragons could keep him locked up until all of this was over, however it was going to end.

After a bit of waiting, she spotted him approaching the gate. Once he was let out, he stepped out carefully, his head lowered but his gaze roaming the mountainside. He didn't speak to anyone, but at least he knew not to appear too nervous.

Even still, she let him wait for a while, just to see what he would do.

He walked slowly, heading up the narrow mountain path with almost enough certainty for her to believe he had a purpose. If someone was watching him, they wouldn't think much of him.

After a couple more minutes of testing him, she decided it would be safe. If it wasn't, they would have to keep him hostage, and she'd have to come up with a believable excuse for his absence. Or she supposed she could feign innocence.

Shaking those thoughts away, she left her hiding place. She caught up with Indigo a few minutes later, noticing the slight jerk of his shoulders when she said his name.

He exhaled in relief. "I was starting to think you'd been messing with me in order to make me feel better."

"Why would I do that?" she asked, confused by his logic.

"Never mind," he said quickly. "Why did you make me wait so long anyway?"

"We've only known each other for a few days," she explained.

"Then why are you going to tell me this secret?"

"I might tell you," she said. "If the boyar killed your dad, then you're not on his side, are you?"

"Ah, so this is the old 'an enemy of my enemy is my friend' tactic, eh? All right, I can follow your logic."

"That said, if I decide you can't be trusted..." She trailed off because she wasn't sure what to threaten him with, but it seemed to be effective at any rate.

"You can trust me. Unless this is completely crazy—in which case I'll pretend I don't know anything. The last thing I'm gonna do is willingly give the boyar any kind of information, especially if you're trying to stop him."

That was good enough for her, but the real person who would be deciding whether or not Indigo was trustworthy wasn't her.

The walk to their campsite was long when she didn't have either Will or River with her to pass the time. Instead, she just had Indigo, and he wasn't talkative, even when they were on patrols together. Though, after a little while, he did make an attempt at conversation, which was new for him. Granted, after the day they'd had, something between them seemed to have shifted.

When they drew near the campsite, Thala made him stop. "You wait here."

Without any other explanation, she left him and went ahead. Everyone but Will and River were there, but Thala bypassed them all and went straight to Her Highness.

The young woman stared at her with slightly widened eyes as she approached. "It's unusual for you to be back here so early. Is something wrong?"

Thala shrugged. "Yes and no. I have information for you, but I also brought someone."

Astra straightened. "Are you sure that was a good idea?"

"He's no friend of the boyar. The boyar executed his dad, and he wants to help stop him."

Leonora frowned. "So he could help us, is what you're saying?"

Thala nodded.

Her Highness frowned as well.

"It could be dangerous," Xandrin said.

Kelvair looked decidedly concerned.

"I'm sure we can handle it," Kyvo said. "If he's bad, we can just tackle him and make sure he never gets away!"

"Sure, but it won't be that easy," Tak hissed at him.

"It won't? Why not?"

Tak sighed.

"Well," Her Highness began, getting everyone's attention in an instant, "if you brought him here, that means you think we can trust him. Granted, we'll have to be extremely sure he isn't trying to smuggle any information to the boyar, which we can only do by watching him. That said, if he isn't with the boyar, he could help us."

"Should I bring him?" Thala asked, watching her carefully.

Her Highness nodded. "Let's see what he says."

With another nod, Thala left and fetched Indigo. He waited on a rock, but quickly joined her when she reappeared. With only the slightest bit of apprehension, Thala led him to the others.

Indigo stepped into the little clearing, taking in the dragons and the others, but his gaze stopped on Her Highness. "No way." He hesitantly glanced at Thala. "This is where you keep going?"

She nodded.

He studied the group again, his mouth hanging open, before he seemed to gather himself and approached Her Highness—whose eyes were a little wide—and bow to her, making her eyebrows shoot upwards.

"Y-Your Highness. It's truly an honor to meet you," Indigo said.

She waved her hands, looking uncomfortable. "You don't have to bow. I'm not a princess anymore, so..."

He slowly raised his head. "You're not?"

A hint of a grimace crossed her face as she seemed to search for an answer. "No, but that's beside the point."

He stared at her with an open mouth before he closed it. Then he straightened, cheeks turning pink. His gaze drifted over to Leonora, and for a second, he stared at her in shock too.

Leonora glanced to the side, clearly embarrassed.

"You're the boyar's granddaughter, aren't you?"

"Unfortunately."

He almost smiled. "Yeah, I don't envy you that." Slowly, he studied the group again before turning back to Thala. "So...now that I'm here, what's the secret?"

Thala took a few steps closer, but she stayed on her feet, just in case.

"That's easy," Leonora answered. "We're going to remove my tyrant grandfather and change Póli for good."

"How?" Indigo asked, brow furrowing.

"We're finding evidence against each of the noble houses, and we're going to give it to the general so he can seize command of the territory and get rid of the boyar," Leonora continued. "When the general comes back, we'll be ready, and then we can get rid of the boyar and all the corrupt nobles that follow him for good."

"Oh, I get it," Indigo said, a spark of life returning to his eyes. "General Cael would go for that in a heartbeat."

"You've met him?" Her Highness asked, watching his face carefully.

Indigo nodded, eyes lighting up. "He's awesome! Besides, don't you remember him, Your Highness?"

"Should I?"

"Of course you should! He was the captain who, when he found out that the boyar was turning those kids into monsters—" Breaking off, he glanced at Thala. "Sorry."

"You're not wrong," she said.

"Anyway, when he found out about that, he opposed the boyar and got thrown in jail, and—"

"I would've thought the boyar would've killed him," Astra said, making Indigo jump.

For a long second, he stared at the three dragons in shock before he found his voice again. "I think he planned on it, he just didn't have time, so putting General Cael in jail was to keep him from getting away."

"Oh, that makes sense," Astra said, her and Kelvair nodding at the same time.

"Anyway, so General Cael was in jail, waiting to be executed, and he broke out and made a mad dash to the Imperial City where he told the Emperor about the dolls. People say he ran so hard he passed out right after delivering his message."

Her Highness's eyes went wide. "That's who the general here is?"

Indigo nodded. "The boyar does all his law breaking when and where General Cael can't prove he's doing anything wrong, otherwise General Cael would've ended him ages ago. If there's anyone the boyar is genuinely afraid of, it's General Cael."

Thala paused, mulling on that thought. So the general here now...was the man responsible for her being saved from the war.

"So the general is gone," Her Highness said, a frown touching her mouth. "That's why the boyar did another execution yesterday. That's how he's been getting away with it."

"But the soldiers are still here," Astra said. "Why isn't that enough to get this guy thrown out already?"

"Because no one will say anything," Indigo said.

Astra groaned. "This is so frustrating!"

Her Highness met Indigo's gaze. "So there is something keeping them quiet."

He dipped his head. "If we say or do anything, the boyar won't punish us—he'll go after our families."

"And he has some people there who are in his pocket. I met one today," Thala added. "He tried to arrest me for saying something that vaguely threatened the boyar."

Kyvo leapt into her arms, making her stumble back a step as he sniffed her face. "You're all right, aren't you?"

For some reason, that almost made her feel something...warm. "I'm fine."

"Yeah, Thala can take care of herself," Indigo said.

"Will it be safe for you to go back though?" Leonora asked, brow furrowed. "They might try and get you again."

Thala frowned. She hadn't considered that. At the same time, it would be bad if she disappeared from the army all together. "If I'm careful, I think I'll be all right."

"Especially if you're not alone. I'll stick with you," Indigo said. "At the very least, I can get one of the higher-ranking officers. Since what they're doing is illegal, they're too afraid to do it in front of the captains."

Thala nodded. He was right about that.

"So that's what it is," Her Highness said, closing her eyes. "That would keep most of the unloyal soldiers from getting brave enough to try something, wouldn't it? Especially since most soldiers bring their families with them wherever they're stationed, so they're easy targets."

Indigo took a tiny step forward. "Don't worry, Your Highness. The boyar executed my dad a few years ago, so I'm going to help you however I can. I promise. If I'm caught, I won't tell him a thing. I don't care if I die—your secret's safe with me."

A strange look crossed her face. "This might be a weird question, but do you know what your dad was executed for? Not some pretend, trumped-up reason he might have told the crowd, but the real one."

Indigo paused.

Thala glanced at the young woman, not sure why she would ask such a question.

"I-I'd rather not say," he said carefully.

"I need to know," Her Highness said, fixing her intense red stare on him.

He swallowed, unable to hold her gaze for more than a few seconds. Then he mumbled, "It was...it was because he refused to deny you as his ruler."

Squeezing her eyes shut, she turned her head away, something about it making a tiny part of Thala's chest ache, catching her off-guard. "So the boyar was telling the truth."

"The truth? About what?" Indigo asked, concern engraved on his face.

"All the people he's executed, he said he did it to get at me, because I managed to catch someone who was part of the operation to create the dolls. He said everyone he's killed have been people who choose me over him."

Thala stared, her mind going blank. She didn't want to believe it, but she did. If Indigo was telling the truth, then that had to mean the boyar was too.

Chapter Twenty-Four

River took a steadying breath as he watched the house they were going to hit, the final house dark against the even darker sky. After tonight, they would have nothing to do but wait until the general returned in a few days, and that was going to be the hardest part. With any luck though, a few days of quiet would lull the houses into letting their guard down again.

Even though the house was dark, River waited. All at once, the soft but deep, almost guttural hooting of an owl brushed his ears, and he almost smiled. Will's ability to make realistic animal noises was so impressive even he could rarely tell the difference between him and the real thing. Fortunately, the owl call Will liked to use in these situations was that of a bird that lived far to the north instead of an owl that lived here.

Fortunately, no one knew the difference.

With the signal given, River moved in, meeting Will at the servant's entrance. They nodded at each other, not saying a word, before creeping inside the dark mansion. The layout was similar yet different from the other houses, but they found the study quickly. This was the first time the room had been on the first floor, but that was a bit of a relief. The bedrooms were almost always on the second floor, so it was far less likely for them to wake someone up down here.

Once inside, River set to searching the desk while Will stayed on watch near the door. It only took him a couple minutes to locate the secret compartment, but once he had it open, he froze. He shifted to the side to allow the faint moonlight coming through the windows to give him better light. The compartment was empty.

For a second, River wondered if the nobleman here just didn't use it, but then he spied the signs of wear and tear. Clearly used, and after a moment longer of inspecting, he could tell the desk wasn't all that old. Which means this drawer had been used often and recently.

That meant if there had been anything in here, it'd been moved or destroyed.

Panic set his heart to beating a touch faster. However, as calmly as possible, he stood and went to Will.

Keeping his voice low, he said, "They moved it."

Will swore. "We have to go."

"On the contrary, I think the two of you should stay," said a bone-chilling voice almost right in front of them. River's heart leapt in his throat. The boyar.

Lamps flashed to life around the room, the sudden rush of light almost blinding. The only explanation for him, the boyar, being able to do that had to be magic.

A voice that was vaguely familiar laughed from the other end of the room, but River's eyes watered enough he couldn't get a good look at the guy. "You were right after all, Athanasios. We did have a rat problem." That said, it was probably the nobleman of the house.

River forced himself to lift his head, his eyes somewhat adjusted now—though still watering—and found himself and Will standing only a few feet away from the smirking boyar. The man was far too smug for River's liking. All at once, Her Highness's fear came back with such clarity, it made him deeply regret coming. They hadn't even managed to find something to try and escape with.

The boyar smirked, staring at River like he was a child caught with their hand in the cookie jar. "Yes. While it was a bit careless of

Sofronio to leave that letter out on his desk, what the pair of you have done was even more so. So. Where are the documents you two have stolen?"

"We don't have them," Will said, sounding more annoyed than anything else. "They're long gone and it's far too late for flabby old men like the lot of you to do anything about it."

Not entirely true, but the boyar didn't need to know that.

"I doubt that." The boyar's gaze traveled up and down the both of them. "The pair of you have been lurking in the mountains, haven't you? The dust on your shoes says as much."

It took all of River's self-control not to react. He'd been hoping the muck of the city would've covered the grime on his shoes more.

"That was where the princess was, so I'm guessing she has all the information you stole. That is all I needed to know."

"She doesn't have them," River said. Leonora did, but he wasn't saying that. "If you touch one hair on her head, I'll—"

"What? Hide her again?" The boyar's smile was mocking. "I'm terrified."

River grit his teeth but kept quiet. Keeping it subtle, he nudged Will. They would have to run the second they got a chance. If River did it right, he could give them that chance.

He hated using his magic; he despised it with every fiber of his being. However, if he had to choose between life and death, he would choose to live. It was one of the things about himself he wasn't proud of.

"What, you have nothing to say? How disappointing, though not wholly unexpected. Your mother was much the same way." The boyar still grinned like a spoiled child.

A spark of anger ricocheted in River's chest, and it was the reason he didn't hesitate. All it took was one second for him to bend and slam his non-metal palm to the floor. The next, the stone floor buckled, sending bookshelves crashing down.

Will threw the door open, and they ran out. Footsteps pounded behind them immediately. The boyar was so close, River would've sworn the man's hot breath struck his neck. They didn't have time for a detour through the servants' quarters. River charged at the massive window straight ahead, Will falling in behind him. He held his metal arm in front of his face and leapt. The glass shattered, glittering pieces cascading around him as he landed on the ground outside. His feet barely touched the ground before he raced off, pieces of glass crunching beneath his boots.

They were bolting for the back garden wall when the first shadowy lance shot past them. River grimaced, pushing himself to run faster. Bushes and trees slapped his face with their branches as they plunged into their depths. The wall was close. If they could get over it, they'd be out.

Another shadow lance zipped past, tearing through the foliage with a harsh ripping noise. The wall loomed in front of them.

Will sped past River and bounded up it with two steps, perching on top with all the ease of a cat. As River prepared to leap, a third spear shot between his legs. As he stepped forward, the spear rammed into both his knees at the same time, sending him sprawling. He was close enough to the wall that his metal arm struck it (the only reason his head did not) and the leather sheath he wore to protect and hide it tore as he scraped down the rough stone. He landed in a heap in the dirt.

"River!" Will shouted.

The lance vanished the instant its job was finished, but for some reason, it left River weak, almost ill. His head swam, and he had just enough strength to push himself upright. Then, his strength failed, and before he fully realized it, he fell against the stone wall, which was the only reason he didn't collapse into the dirt.

River didn't respond to Will's shout, sure the guy could see the situation just fine from wherever he was. If he was smart, he'd leave.

The boyar materialized in front of him, and River resigned himself to his fate. He didn't know why he couldn't move, but under the effects of whatever this was, there was no chance of him getting out.

A second later, there was a scuff and then silence. Will didn't always act like it, but he was smart.

Fortunately, River couldn't say the same for the boyar.

With a triumphant smirk, the boyar glared down at him. "You've always thought you were smarter than you actually are, and yet here you are: at my feet where you belong."

"It must run in the family." River glared up at him. "Thinking you were smart, I mean."

The boyar responded by striking River across the face, hard enough that the iron tang of blood filled his mouth. A part of River was shocked he'd said that out loud. He'd never had the courage to before, but he supposed the last time he'd been at the boyar's mercy, Leonora had still been a hostage.

Now that she wasn't, there was nothing to keep River from saying what he thought, no matter what it cost him. Truth be told, after all these years, it was satisfying to speak his thoughts.

Maybe the others had been bad influences.

With a bit of a smirk, River met the boyar's steely gaze. "For such a tyrant, you have soft hands, you know?"

Mouth white with suppressed fury, the boyar grabbed him under the arm—his metal arm—dragging him to his feet and holding him just high enough for the metal to bite deep in his shoulder. The burning pain was so intense, River could barely think. Without saying a word, the man hauled him out of the garden, through the empty streets, and to the mansion he'd worked so hard to escape. As much as River wanted to resist, between the weird weakness and the pain in his shoulder, he could not. However, he refused to give in to the temptation to pass out—he would need his consciousness in order to escape. He wasn't sure where the determination to break free came from, but he clung to it in order to keep the encroaching darkness at bay.

The man dragged him through the courtyard and to the basement, where he tossed him into a pitch-black cell. River lay crumpled where he landed, waiting for the pain to ease so he could think.

"I've had enough of you," the boyar snarled. He cursed, loud enough it echoed through the cell, though the echo was a bit strange. "I've wished for a long time to be rid of you, and the time has come. Enjoy your final days, you wretched half-breed. When that princess comes to save you, I'm going to kill you."

River scoffed, fighting off the nausea making his head swim as best he could. "She won't come. She's smarter than you."

With a hint of a laugh, the boyar said, "She's human, and she's weak. She'll come. And when she does, you can die knowing she was captured trying to save you."

The door of the cell slammed shut, plunging River into total darkness. The thought of escape struck him in a panicked frenzy, but he forced himself to stop and breathe, an exercise his dad had drilled into him over and over. When he was calm, he could think. And suddenly realize something.

He propped himself on his elbow. This wasn't a normal cell; between the strange way noises echoed inside and the bite of it against his arm, he was certain it wasn't made of stone. He fingered the floor for a minute before it came to him, the realization turning his blood to ice. The cell wasn't made of metal or stone.

It was made of *wood*.

Forcing himself to his feet, River inspected every inch of the cell he could reach, not caring about the couple splinters he got in exchange. It was all wood. The whole thing. Every inch.

River couldn't use his magic on anything but stone. The boyar, knowing this, had made the perfect cell to hold him.

The reality of the situation knocked the wind out of him, and his legs collapsed beneath him. He was trapped. Really trapped. Either the boyar would kill him, or Her Highness would get hurt in an attempt to save him.

She hadn't wanted him and Will to risk another hit, but they'd done it anyway.

River should've listened. His mind reeled with the reality of the situation he'd put them both in. He buried his face in his hands, wanting to cry—feeling the burn in his throat—but no tears came. He'd been denied the right to tears for a long time. The exposed metal of his prosthetic hand against his face was bitingly cold, but he didn't take it away, needing to feel something other than the emptiness welling up inside him, the unending darkness that had never left, no matter how brightly Her Highness had shone.

He wasn't worthy of being a protector, not for Her Highness or for anyone. He'd let her and both of his parents down, but most especially his dad. This was just a final reminder.

⚜ ⚜

Redrinna jerked awake the next morning, her neck stiff from having fallen asleep leaning against the boulder next to their fire. She blinked in confusion, her eyes settling on the remains of last night's soup hanging over a bed of cold, dark coals. For a long moment, she stared at it, unable to puzzle out why she'd slept here. Then she glanced at the sky, noting that the sun was rising. Night had already passed. Her gaze dropped back to the cold soup.

River and Will hadn't come back last night.

The realization dropped into her gut like ice, freezing her core.

Slowly, she glanced around at the camp. Astra was on watch, but her gaze was fixed down the mountainside. Thala stirred, but the others were all asleep. However, Will and River weren't there.

At that second, Will burst out of the trees a short way down the slope, panting like he'd been running for a long time. Redrinna's chest constricted, becoming unbearably tight when River did not appear behind him.

By the time Will reached the camp, Redrinna was on her feet and moving forward.

Will skidded to a stop in front of her, the rocks grating against each other as a small cloud of dust billowed beneath him. "I'm so sorry," he gasped, hands on his knees. "I should've listened to you—we both should've. I'm so sorry."

"What happened?" she managed, her voice nothing more than a whisper.

"It was a trap like you said it might be," he choked out, staring fixedly at her feet. "We didn't even get anything. The boyar was right there waiting for us."

"Will, where's River?" Leonora said, her voice shaking. She was pale, almost deathly pale.

In a voice full of defeat, Will said, "He got him. The boyar got him."

The world halted in its tracks. Redrinna's heart seemed to stop beating.

"It took so long for me to come back because I was trying to figure out what the boyar is planning on doing with him." Finally, Will managed to meet Redrinna's gaze, and the pain written on his face echoed in her heart. "He's gonna kill him. Tomorrow morning. And there's nothing I can do to stop it."

Tears—whether from fear or sorrow, she didn't know—burned at her eyes, but she forced them away. She didn't have time to give in to them now. Fiery resolve burned in her chest, fueled by the gem. She turned to the dragons.

Will grabbed her arm. "No. I know what you're thinking, and we can't go in after him. It's a trap—a trap for you. He's doing it to get you to come to him so he can catch you. That'll be playing by Osiris's rules, and then that Osiris guy is going to get you too. If you go, it's over."

Redrinna paused. All at once, very distinctly, what Will had told her a couple nights ago about being willing to fight to see a place change came back to her, and the irony almost made her smile. That said, it was a grim smile, and she didn't much like it.

"You know, Will, even though you and I don't get along well, you were right the other day. I think we really are more alike than we thought." She turned back and extricated herself from his grip as she met his gaze.

He paled. "Princess, you can't. I know how you feel, but like you said the other night, we shouldn't be stupid."

She silenced him with a look. "Will, I know it's a trap. I figured that out right away. You know what else? I don't care. River's my friend, and I'm not going to let him die."

No matter what it might cost her, she wasn't going to sit here and let River be killed. He was her friend. Their families had once been so close, they were practically cousins. Plus he'd been chosen by a gem. More importantly, regardless of whether he joined the Dragon Kin or not, he was still worth saving, especially after everything he'd done for them.

She didn't care if this was part of Osiris's game or just the boyar venting pent up anger, but she wasn't going to sit idle. It was her turn to make a move, and nothing would stop her from making it.

All she needed was a plan.

Tak was the first one to appear at Redrinna's side, but the others were close behind him. He met her gaze, a comforting kind of determination burning in the dark green depths of his eyes. "So, what are we going to do?"

Chapter Twenty-Five

Redrinna took a deep breath, doing her best to think calmly and carefully. "The boyar is going to execute River tomorrow, which means we have to act fast. That said, this is a trap, and there's going to be something waiting for us no matter when we go."

Leonora nodded. "River is tough, and he will be able to hold on for a while. Plus, trying to storm the mansion in broad daylight is stupid. There are too many unfriendly eyes."

"I never said he was in the mansion," Will said, gawking at her with wide eyes. "How did you know?"

She smirked, but it was humorless. "When the boyar learned about River's powers, the first thing he did was have a wooden room built in the basement. It was to threaten me to stay in line. So, if the boyar is holding him and wants to guarantee River is trapped, that's where he's going to put him."

"Because River is powerless against wood," Redrinna murmured.

"It doesn't matter," Astra said. "Wood is useless against me, and I'm ready to go right now."

"No, you can't go," Redrinna said. "Since we freed Kelvair, the boyar will probably be more than willing to try and capture any of you dragons. Plus, we're going into town and there are a lot of people there. It's too risky."

Astra stared at her for a minute. "All right, next adventure, I vote we avoid towns as much as possible because they make being a dragon boring."

Redrinna almost laughed, but the gravity of the situation kept her in check.

"Okay, but why would a wooden cage keep River trapped?" Xandrin asked, head cocked.

"River's magic is...abnormal," Leonora explained. "In order for him to use it, he has to be touching whatever it is."

"His magic is earth-based, so unless he can touch metal or the ground, he's powerless," Redrinna finished.

Xandrin paled.

"So if he's in a wooden box," Kyvo said, ears flattening against his skull, "then he's really, really stuck, right?"

She nodded.

"We're going to have to go in, smash the box, then escape," Will said.

Kelvair shivered. "It sounds risky."

"It is, but if we stay here, he's going to die," Redrinna said firmly. "So we need to strike fast, with only a couple people. All of us will definitely be enough to attract the wrong kind of attention."

"Leonora isn't allowed to go," Will said. "The boyar wants her nearly as much as he wants you."

Leonora didn't seem happy with that, but she didn't object either. "I'm not a good fighter, so I won't be of any help anyway."

"If I knew how to fight, I could go," Kyvo said, his tail drooping. "But I think I'd be useless."

Guilt settled in Redrinna's chest. Kyvo would've been perfect to send on a mission like this, but she hadn't wanted to teach him to fight. He could do all right in a little tussle, but in an orchestrated fight like this? She didn't want to risk it.

"Sorry, Kyvo," she whispered.

"So that leaves the four of us," Thala said, glancing at her, Tak, and Will in turn. "We should have two people go inside the mansion to get River while the other two stay outside in case someone comes. Or to make sure the others have a way out."

"So they should be good fighters," Redrinna said, glancing Tak's way.

He responded by looking decidedly concerned.

"I'll do it. I don't like it, but I am a good fighter," Thala said. "Plus, if the boyar finds me, he hates me enough it might distract him from the rest of you."

"I'm going with you," Will said, turning to Thala. "That boyar isn't going to get ahold of you on my watch."

Redrinna nodded. "All right. Tak and I will go in and get River."

"Oh, hold on," Will said, heading over to the rock he slept on. He grabbed a sword and came and handed it to Tak. "Don't worry, I didn't steal it or nothin'. But if you're going into that mansion, you're going to need to be prepared."

A touch of relief passed through Redrinna at the idea that, for now, Tak had a weapon of his own to protect himself with.

"The only thing left is to decide when we'll go," Thala said.

Redrinna frowned. She wanted to go now, but by the time they reached town, it would be in broad daylight. She couldn't walk around freely without someone noticing her, which was bad.

"The boyar—twisted pig," Will spat, "is throwing a party. To-night. To celebrate River's impending doom."

"He's going to expect us to go then," Tak said quietly. Even still, he looked ready to fight at the drop of a hat.

"We shouldn't go during the party, but I think we can use it to our advantage anyway," Redrinna said, her mind whirling with ideas, a plan taking shape. "The best times to sneak in are either going to be when the party is being set up or after it's over and everyone's exhausted." She glanced at Leonora.

The young woman frowned in thought. "The boyar doesn't over-see the planning of the parties, and I don't know where he'll be."

"So we need to go late tonight, when he should be exhausted—not just from the party, but from waiting for us, as well," Redrinna said.

"Oh perfect. I can get some sleep before then," Will said, his expression brightening.

Thala glanced at the sky. "I have to go in. If I disappear, it'll look suspicious."

Redrinna nodded. "Go. But be extra careful."

Thala took off.

Redrinna turned to the others. They'd spent many days up here in the solitude of the mountains waiting, but she was sure today was going to be the worst one yet. "All right, we need to make a plan."

⁂

As the day wore on, Leonora wanted to scream. Her worst nightmare was playing out before her, and all she could do was sit and wait. She hated waiting; she hated having nothing to do but agonize over what might be happening to her brother. Why couldn't she ever just protect him?

Once, long enough ago that the memory was out of focus and patchy, Leonora had promised her parents she would protect River. Then they'd gone to help a tense situation and died. Never once had she been able to keep that promise; even now, there wasn't anything she could do but wait.

⁂

The way her heartbeat thrummed in her ears reminded Thala acutely of the desert, of hiding behind sandstone, waiting for the order to strike. The sensation made her uncomfortable, but she couldn't shake the tension, even with Indigo by her side on their patrol. So far, he'd been true to his word about sticking to her side—the only minute she'd gotten to herself was when she'd used the washroom.

The patrol seemed to drag by, and Thala got the impression the news of yesterday's scuffle had spread: people went out of their way to avoid the two of them. However, after a couple hours of the most stifling, but tense boredom, Indigo leaned in and whispered:

"What is with you today?"

Thala stared at him. Could he tell?

"I've never seen you so tense," he hissed. "It's not my fault is it?"

She shook her head.

"Then what is it?" He paused for a second. "You can tell me, right?"

"The boyar abducted a friend of mine," she murmured, keeping an eye on the people that passed. "He's going to execute him. It's a trap to get at *her*, and even though she knows about it, she's going anyway."

Indigo's face paled.

Thala shook her head at him. They shouldn't talk about it in the open like this any further if they could help it.

The rest of the patrol dragged by, and eventually, Thala stood before Captain Andor's desk, listening while Indigo gave the report.

Captain Andor nodded when they finished, eyeing them both with a critical eye that put Thala a bit more on edge. After a long, long moment, he said, "There's nothing else you two have to report...is there?"

Thala swallowed and shook her head.

Indigo did the same.

The look on the captain's face made her wonder if he suspected something; there was a reason he'd survived the war in the desert. Then, almost mercifully, he dismissed them.

As they turned to leave, he called, "Oh, Thala. Wait a second."

Her heart lurched, a sensation she hadn't felt in so long, it startled her. Slowly, she turned back. "Sir?"

"You wanted to know about the general stationed here when you first arrived, so I thought it only fair to let you know that he's been delayed."

Her heart stuttered.

"He'd planned on returning to Póli within the next few days, but they received an urgent message about a town to the north, so they're going to take longer to return."

"How long?" she asked, having to fight with every fiber in her being to keep any sign of distress out of her body language.

"At least three more weeks."

"Three weeks?!" Indigo spluttered, making Captain Andor raise an eyebrow.

"Do you miss the general that much, Indigo?" the captain asked, a hint of a laugh coloring his voice.

"I—well," Indigo stammered. "I've... I've been telling Thala about him—since she's been curious, like...like you said—and I just wanted her to be able to meet him... So..."

"I see," the captain said. "I doubt another three weeks will kill you?"

"Nope," Indigo said, his smile seeming a bit forced. "I'll be okay."

They hurried out of the guardhouse. Indigo didn't speak, but Thala could tell he was dying to say something.

Thala did her best to stay calm as she checked in on Adonis and his crew, some of whom nursed fresh wounds after apparently taking down a violent gang that had been trying to find ground. However, her mind was in a bit of a daze, and she didn't remember most of the visit. She was pretty sure Aretha, at least, noticed something off, but Thala couldn't tell them anything.

Eventually, as the sun dipped low in the western sky, Thala hurried out of town, Indigo quick to meet her on the way.

When they reached camp, Her Highness was still there, pacing. She stopped when they raced up.

"Did something else happen?" she asked, her voice tight.

"It's minor, but it's bad timing," Indigo said.

"Oh no," Kelvair groaned, pulling his unbroken wing tight to his side.

"The general was supposed to be back in a couple days, but apparently they were called elsewhere on urgent business, and he's not supposed to be back for at least three weeks."

"What?" Kyvo squeaked.

Astra's expression morphed into a glare. "I don't know if we can hide from the boyar that long."

"It does seem oddly convenient that General Cael is crucial to our plan and at the last minute he gets called even further away," Indigo pointed out. "If you want, Your..." He awkwardly cleared his throat. "I can figure out where that message came from. I know some people in the army who might tell me."

Her Highness nodded. "All right, just be careful."

Indigo nodded, started to bend like he was going to bow before he nodded again and took off. "I'll be back soon," he called before disappearing.

Thala glanced back at the others, taking in the varying degrees of stress and determination on all their faces. She glanced at the horizon. There was nothing to do now but wait for night to fall.

⁂

Since they were high above the city, they had a good view of the boyar's mansion if they stood in the right spot. As darkness fell, growing thicker as a sliver of moon appeared in the sky, Redrinna watched the brightly lit mansion go dark.

She glanced over her shoulder where the others waited, not a single one of them sleeping. "It's over. Let's go."

The dragons shared nervous glances, but Redrinna ignored them. There wasn't time to panic, otherwise River's fate would prove worse than Chumani's had, and Redrinna still regretted that every day.

Tak, Will, and Thala stepped up to her, and she noted Tak and Will both had determined expressions on their faces.

"The rest of you stay here, and be careful," Redrinna said, glancing at each of the others in turn. "No matter what happens to us, you all keep each other safe. Understand?"

They all nodded, and Redrinna turned and headed down the mountainside with the other three on her heels.

The reality of what she was going to do was setting in, opening the door for the all-too-familiar fear to follow, but she did her best to keep it from overpowering her. If she let herself succumb to that emotion now, River would be the one to pay the price, and that was unacceptable.

It was a long walk down the mountain, but soon the dark and quiet city of Póli was in sight. Redrinna stopped, eyeing the guarded gates. The soldiers were some of the many people who would be able to recognize her on sight.

"Will, is there any other way we can get into the city instead of going through those gates? The soldiers will recognize me."

Will grinned. "You bet there is."

He turned off the main path they'd been following and took them down a thinner path that was harder to see and more steep. It led to a gap in the wall, the hole so low to the ground it was almost impossible to spot in the dark.

Thala knelt in front of it. "It's a bit tight, but nobody will notice us." She crawled through and Redrinna followed after, her heart sitting in her throat. Will came next and Tak came last, and for a couple seconds, he got stuck. His shoulders were broader than the rest of theirs, but with some wiggling, he got through as well.

Then, since they were all safely through, Redrinna was able to take in their surroundings. No wonder why they'd used this hole—it let out onto a street where human refuse gathered in the ditches and fly-infested piles of manure waited beside empty but clearly well-used carts. That was when the smell hit her, and Redrinna fought off the urge to gag.

"See?" Thala said, managing to make it look like infiltrating a city was an everyday occurrence. "On a street like this, we're safe."

Redrinna had to give her that one.

Tak didn't seem disturbed by it, but then again, he'd grown up in a village where this was more than likely the norm.

Shaking that thought away, Redrinna followed as Will led them through back alleys, avoiding every person and set of patrolling soldiers they saw. They passed marbled white houses, the opulence of the upper crust of the city nonexistent in the lower half. Once they reached the upper part, Redrinna was struck by the stark difference between the levels. As they went, lavish walled gardens brimming with blooming, bright plants became more common than the open rock gardens, and the houses grew larger until they reached the point where Redrinna could only think of them as mansions.

They ducked behind one of the first mansion garden walls, and Thala peered around the corner. Then she looked back at the other two. "This is the noble sector of town. That was probably obvious though."

Redrinna nodded.

"The boyar's got River trapped in the biggest one, the one all the way at the end." Will pointed it out, and Redrinna peeked around the corner as much as she dared.

The mansion in question was larger than the others (which was a feat in and of itself), and it seemed littered with pillars and windows and roof decorations and intricate engravings. Two words came to mind as she stared at it: extravagant and gaudy.

She ducked back behind the wall so Tak could take a look as well. The hint of disgust that flashed across his face as he eyed it almost made her smile.

They waited there for a moment longer before continuing on, taking them around the back of the mansion they'd hidden behind. Here, there was a narrow canal separating the noble section with its mansions and the rest of the city. Water rushed by beneath them, but Redrinna found herself eyeing the dark water line that indicated the water's usual level. The water was a lot lower than usual.

They stopped on the backside of the garden wall, next to another hole, though, unlike the one they'd used earlier, this one seemed intentionally made. The sides were too straight and smooth for it to be natural erosion.

"River made it when he and Leonora were kids. They used it to sneak out," Will explained.

Thala nodded. "When we get inside, you two—" she indicated Redrinna and Tak, "—will go to the right."

Redrinna and Tak shared a look.

"On that side of the mansion," Thala continued, "there'll be a little, plain door. That's the servants' entrance. They'll be awake, but even if they see you, they won't say a word—the people inside are people the boyar and the rest of the nobles forced into slavery. There's no affection of any kind between them."

Redrinna's stomach clenched.

"You can get to the basement from there, so don't go through the main house. From there it should be pretty easy to find River." Thala sounded serious, but the look on her face was a calm one. "Will and I will be up front."

"This might not mean much coming from me, Princess," Will said, his expression serious, "but we've got your back. If there's anyone waiting for you outside this mansion, we'll make sure they don't get to you."

They all nodded, and Thala and Will crawled through the hole. Once they'd cleared it, Redrinna and Tak followed suit.

The boyar's garden was filled with large but heavy, drooping plants that perfumed the air with their fragrant scents, making it easy to sneak in and through without feeling like they were about to be caught any second. Before long, Redrinna and Tak arrived at the side of the house, still using the cover of the plants as shelter.

She spotted the door as a slave stumbled from the nearby stables to it. The man's clothes were ragged and worn, but that wasn't what really got her attention as the man vanished inside. His skin gleamed in the moonlight, almost like polished metal.

"Tak," Redrinna breathed. "That man is one of the Hikarijin."

Tak seemed to think for a moment. "One of the races from Takota's story?"

She nodded. "There aren't many of them left after the Empire's creation, but I had no idea they were here." A scowl twisted her face.

They waited a few minutes before approaching the house and cautiously stepping inside. No one was near the door, but there were two, short staircases in front of them, one leading up and one down, both thick with silence.

"Which way?" Tak whispered.

"Well, that one probably leads to the basement." Redrinna indicated the one heading down. Hopefully it wasn't some kind of dead end.

Staying close to each other, they descended the short staircase. It led into a wide, dimly lit room bare of furniture or decoration. The air inside was warm, almost too warm considering the temperature outside. That said, it was not devoid of people.

There was a throng of Hikarijin slaves huddled in little groups around the room, some asleep, and some not. There was a floor hearth in the center of the room, and there was a tiny group settled as close to it as they could be, buried in blankets. The hearth was filled with embers, though there wasn't any wood to rebuild the fire with.

However, all the slaves who were awake stared right at Redrinna and Tak. Unlike the man from earlier, almost none of their skin glowed. A mature pale-haired woman stood, gauging the two of them.

They stared at her, silent.

She stared back, watching the two of them with guarded eyes.

"I'm sorry if we scared you," Redrinna began, taking a couple steps into the room. "We're looking for our friend. The boyar abducted him."

The woman visibly relaxed, but there was still a wariness in her expression. "If it's River you're after, you'll need to go that way." She pointed to an opening in the wall opposite Redrinna and Tak. It was narrow and dark enough Redrinna didn't notice it until the woman pointed it out. "It'll lead you to the cellars. Don't go anywhere near the entrance; there's a beast there."

Redrinna nodded. When she reached the entrance, she paused and looked back at the woman, who still watched them, the light from the embers illuminating part of her tired face.

"I'm sorry, but can I ask you something?"

The woman raised an eyebrow.

"You're really slaves?"

She nodded, her mouth in a hard line.

Her stomach turned. Before Redrinna could think it through, she said, "We're going to get rid of the boyar and the nobles, and when we do, I'm going to make sure you're all freed."

The woman stared at her with a hard gleam in her eye and said nothing.

Redrinna turned and went down the stairs after Tak, descending into near total darkness.

Once they were at the bottom and their eyes had adjusted to the lack of light, Tak whispered, "How are you supposed to free them if you're not a princess?"

That pulled her up short for a second. "When the general takes over, they'll all be freed, won't they?"

He made a noise, and she couldn't decipher its meaning. That made her think back to last night, when he'd left after she'd refused to be a princess. It kind of bugged her the others were so hung up on this idea, but at the same time, it left her...almost embarrassed. Ashamed. The fact that she seemed to keep upsetting her friends accentuated the guilt inside her heart.

She shook her head. She couldn't let herself get distracted. Pushing those thoughts aside, she began making her way down the narrow, dark hallway.

They both stayed quiet as they walked, passing several rooms, but none of them seemed to be made of wood. However, at the end of the hall stood a wooden door with a wooden knob and wooden locks.

"This one?" Tak whispered as they stopped in front of it.

Redrinna nodded.

The locks were complicated and looked hard (and possibly loud) to figure out, so instead, Redrinna lit a sharp little flame and burned through them all, careful to make sure the rest of the wood didn't catch on fire. Before she put it out, she caught Tak watching her with an amused smile.

Then they pushed open the door. They were met with darkness, so Redrinna lit another fire, this one a bit bigger than the last, and held it up. The light fell a little ways into the room, and she thought she spied feet towards the back, but they were just out of the halo of light.

There was a quiet shuffling noise and River stepped into the ring of light, his movements stiff. He winced as he came into the light, but other than that, he seemed all right.

"What have you done?" he hissed, stopping once he was in the light.

That wasn't the reaction she'd expected. "We're here to rescue you."

A grimace twisted his bruised features. "No. I mean, I appreciate it, but you shouldn't have come. He's trying to catch you, Your Highness."

"We know," Tak said softly.

"And you came anyway?" River sighed, the disappointment evident in his voice almost making her annoyed. "Thanks, but no. You guys have to go."

"We're already here, and we're not leaving without you," Redrinna said, setting her free hand on her hip. "Come on. The others are worried about you."

He hesitated.

All at once, a door creaked open above them, light illuminating part of the cellar a short distance away. They all froze. Redrinna snuffed out her fire. For a long, agonizing minute, it was silent. Then footsteps rang out as someone began coming down the stairs.

With stiff, almost jerky movements, River yanked the two of them in his cell and shut the door as quietly as possible. He shoved the two of them into the space behind the door, and they waited in total darkness and silence.

Whoever had come down the stairs made their way to the cell. Once outside, they paused, standing there for a while before pushing the door open. Bright torchlight cut through the darkness, illuminating River where he sat against the far wall once more. Because of where River had shoved Redrinna and Tak, they were hidden by the door.

"Tell me, boy," the boyar drawled, making a shiver race up Redrinna's spine, "how your door was put in that state by a half-beast who can't use his magic in here."

River remained quiet.

Redrinna's heart beat a frantic rhythm against her ribs.

The boyar stepped past the door, gaze fixed on River. Tak grabbed Redrinna's wrist, and she was sure he would try and get out the door. However, without warning, the boyar turned. His gaze locked on to the two of them. And he smiled.

Her heart stopped.

"See, half-breed? I told you she'd come." the boyar called over his shoulder. "Thanks for doing exactly what I wanted, Princess."

Chapter Twenty-Six

For a second, everyone in the room stood frozen. Tak moved first, yanking Redrinna forward. At the same instant, River pounced on the boyar's back, buying them enough time to run out the door. As they rushed out, Redrinna glanced back just in time to see the boyar throw River off, a nasty thud ringing out. She cringed, but Tak forced her to keep running.

"River!" she shouted, not sure whether or not he'd hear her. "We're coming back for you!"

Instead of running through the servants' quarters, Tak raced up the main stairs.

The boyar let out a mad roar as he raced after them, but as they crested the landing and he appeared at the bottom, Redrinna blew a massive stream of fire at him.

They raced into a large, open courtyard, but Tak skidded to a stop. Redrinna glanced forward, her blood going cold. She only now remembered that the slave they'd spoken to had said there was a beast guarding the front entrance. By 'beast', the woman had apparently meant Captain Brion.

"Well, this is bad," Tak hissed, keeping himself between the two of them.

Redrinna bit her lip. There was still no recognition in the

captain's eyes, but if she could get him to snap out of it, they'd be able to get out of here and figure out how to rescue River before tomorrow.

Taking a deep breath, she raced out from behind Tak and planted herself in front of him. "Captain Brion, stop it! It's me!"

He stepped forward, shadow swords materializing in his hands.

"What's wrong with you? Please, stop!"

He continued his advance, the hard darkness remaining fixed in his eyes.

Lifting her hands, she took a step back. "Captain, don't do this. It's not you. Please?"

For a second, there was a flicker in his eyes, but then it was gone. Before Redrinna could even think, he swung his sword. Fire ripped through her fingers, making her cry out. The pain shot up her arm, the intensity making nausea hit her so hard, she nearly puked.

Tak jerked her back as she glanced at her hand. Blood. A lot of blood. Her head swam at the sight of it spilling down her gauntlet. The captain hadn't cut anything off, but he'd managed to nick her fingers right above the gauntlet, and his sword had bit deep enough that Redrinna caught a glimpse of bone. She clenched her fist tight, almost reflexively.

Captain Brion swung at them again, but all at once, Thala was there. She caught both of his shadow swords on a spear.

"Get her out of here!" Will shouted as he landed in the courtyard, a staff in his hands.

Tak dragged Redrinna to the fringes of the courtyard, setting her down behind a partition. His gaze shot to her clenched fist, and from how fast he went ashen, she knew it was bad. She glanced too. Blood streaked across the backs of her fingers. A lot of blood. Then the crack and hum of weapons struck her ears, the sounds making her heart flutter with panic.

"Please," she managed to choke out through the pain, "don't hurt him."

"We're not going to try to," Tak said gently. He grabbed her hand, making the pain spike. Despite herself, she whimpered.

It took all of her willpower not to cry out as he opened her hand so he could check the wound. She knew tears streamed down her cheeks, but she couldn't get them to stop.

"It's deep," Tak hissed as he studied it. Grabbing her fingers, he pressed his palm tight to them. The pain intensified, but when white light shone out from between their hands, the warmth flooding her fingers easing the pain.

It only lasted for a few seconds, but when he pulled his hand back, Redrinna could no longer see any bone and the bleeding was lighter and slower. Even still, the pain was bad enough to make her hand tremble.

"You can't fight with your hand like this, so I used your energy to help your hand. It's not fixed, it's just better." Tak met her gaze, his eyes filled with concern. "I'm sorry, but you have to stay here. They need my help. We're going to protect you, okay? So don't come out."

A fiery determination she'd only seen on his face a couple times appeared, a look that said more than his words had. So she nodded. Concern flickered in his eyes one last time before he raced away, the sword Will had given him already in his hand.

Shrinking behind the partition a little more, Redrinna swiped her uninjured hand against her pants before pressing it to the wound, wincing as she did so. Then, with nothing but the sounds of the others fighting and the boyar's jeering filling her ears, her heart dipped towards her toes.

Even though they'd known it was a trap, they hadn't been able to save River. So far, they hadn't even been able to get themselves out. Instead, she was hiding again while the others fought to protect her, just like with Xandrin. She'd thought this would've been the best way to save River, but perhaps she'd been wrong. Had she just been rash again?

Sighing, she muttered, "I never seem to learn, do I?"

It's not your fault things turned out this way.

"But I'm not blameless either," she whispered back, to which the gem made no response. This had been her idea.

All at once, there was a harsh crack, like wood being split. Redrinna froze before finding the courage to peek over the partition. Captain Brion had shattered the shaft of Thala's spear, leaving the girl with two useless sticks. Will had backed up, nursing a nasty gash running up his arm. Tak swooped in to give Thala the chance to retreat, and though he was skilled and gifted, Captain Brion was the superior fighter. Redrinna's heart leapt in her throat as she watched them, their swords lashing at each other, missing by mere inches. However, Captain Brion had two swords while Tak only had one—and that gave the captain an edge Tak couldn't compensate for.

With a move that missed clipping Tak's wrist by what had to have been centimeters, Captain Brion disarmed him, sending his sword bouncing across the earthen courtyard.

"Bravo, what spectacular fighting," the boyar called as he stepped into the courtyard. "It's been ages since I've encountered someone as skilled as you, especially given how young you are."

Tak didn't seem the least bit flattered. On the contrary, the anger on his face gave Redrinna chills.

Redrinna noted the singe marks on the boyar's clothes and that one of his cheeks was bright red with a hint of satisfaction. Then, she ducked back beneath the partition to avoid catching his attention.

"I thoroughly enjoyed the entertainment. Now, where is that brat you parade as your princess?"

None of the others gave him any sort of answer.

"Oh, how loyal. It's touching, isn't it beast-man?"

Anger coiled in Redrinna's stomach at the awful nickname.

"Very well, we'll have to beat it out of them."

There was a second of silence before Will cried out, making Redrinna's hair stand on end.

"There's nothing I can do about the green-haired boy—not so long as he's a chosen member of the Dragon Kin. I've been told not to touch you either, Azure Demon—at least not yet. You, on the other hand, son of Leander, are free game."

Redrinna's eyes went wide.

"Beast-man?"

"No!" Tak cried, a pained note in his voice.

Redrinna didn't have to look to know what was going on, and her heart seemed to freeze in her chest. Will had said he was willing to die to get the information they needed to take down the houses. They'd all been willing to be punished or worse in order to rip the boyar's grimy hands off this city. However, Redrinna wasn't willing to let anyone be killed for this. No one else would die in her name, not again.

Like lightning, what Timothon had said to her before they'd left the Mount came back: 'I think people who are good leaders are the kind of people who are able to create a world where those kinds of sacrifices would never have to be made—or at least, they would strive to build that kind of world.'

Redrinna wasn't a good leader; she already knew this. If she was, perhaps they could've avoided things getting to this point. A couple months ago, she'd wondered what Osiris would do in order to get her to go back to him, and it was exactly what she'd feared.

Even still, if this was the reason she gave herself over to him, it wasn't a terrible one. She wasn't a good enough leader to prevent things from going bad like this—on the contrary, she'd spent most of her time here avoiding being a leader as best she could. However, if people were going to see her as a princess, then there was one thing she could do to spare her friends.

As Redrinna rose, her gem burned with warmth—not in warning, but with a warmth that gave her strength. It knew what she needed to do too. She lowered her hands, doing her best to ignore the sensation of blood dripping off her fingers.

"Enough," she said, her voice echoing as the scene before her eyes froze.

Will was pinned beneath Captain Brion's foot, shadow swords

near his neck, while the boyar had Tak and Thala trapped—one of Tak's arms pinned behind his back while Thala was held fast by her hair. All of them stared at her (except the captain), but Tak, Will, and Thala stared at her with looks of horror Redrinna fought to ignore.

She kept her gaze focused on the boyar instead. "I'm the one you want, right? So leave them alone, and I'll give you what you want."

"No!" Will cried. "This is okay, Princess! I'm fine with this!"

Redrinna kept her gaze fixed on the boyar, refusing to respond to Will's protest.

With a grin, the boyar shoved both Tak and Thala away, both of them stumbling. In a flicker of shadow, the boyar appeared in front of Redrinna, the grin on his face making her sick.

Before he could speak, Redrinna cut in first. "If you want, I'll go with you. I won't fight."

"Redrinna no," Tak pleaded, pain in his voice.

She didn't look at him, afraid she would lose her resolve if she did. "But I'll only go on the condition you let all of my friends go, including River."

"You're in no condition to be making requests, princess," he said, that smile still hovering on his lips.

Anger churned inside her as she fueled a ring of fire to appear around him, keeping it tight enough he couldn't move without getting burned. It was hot, but Redrinna fed it more, making it grow a bit higher. He lost his smile, uneasiness stealing across his features.

Over the snarl of the flames, she said, "Are you sure about that?"

He studied the flames for a minute before meeting her gaze. "All right," he growled. "Your friends will go free."

She studied him for a minute before pushing the heat away, making the flames dissipate in a whirl of smoke. "Then you win." She hated saying it.

Even more than that, she hated offering him her hand and the sting of discomfort that flooded her as he clamped a massive hand on her wrist. She had one second to glance over at Will, Tak, and Thala, the fear on Tak's face breaking her heart.

Then, a terrifying, familiar darkness rushed around her, little, invisible hands seeming to dig into her skin and drag her away. It swiftly vanished and a coolness settled over her skin, one that reminded her of the mountains.

The boyar hurled her to the stony ground, knocking the wind out of her. "That's a fraction of the pain I owe you, and you will be paid in full before that Osiris can have you," he snarled as he clicked a metal shackle shut on her ankle, pinching her skin despite her boots.

The next second, he struck her side, knocking her back as blinding pain erupted in both her side and ankle. Abruptly, there was a crack followed by the sound of flesh hitting flesh. Hugging her ribs, Redrinna managed to open her eyes.

Tehl stood over the boyar, who was flat on his back on the ground, an angry red mark already appearing on his unburned cheek.

"You dog," the boyar snarled as he pushed himself up. "If you dare—"

"Don't you dare forget your place!" Tehl snarled, voice booming around the cavern. "Without Father, you're just a pathetic, miserable excuse for an old man! You are beneath my boot. I wouldn't give such a loathsome, pathetic creature like you the honor of licking the dust off my shoes. You make one more move, and I'll remind you just how worthless you are. You understand?"

The boyar shrank back.

Redrinna wasn't sure if she was so afraid she was numb to the emotion or if the pain was severe enough to prevent her from really feeling it, but she just watched.

All at once, Tehl's voice changed, Osiris's quiet, menacing tones hissing out instead. "You know your task. If you are no longer up to it, you will be replaced in the amount of time it would take for you to blink. Do not think for one second you are so special that you cannot be exchanged, and do not ever dare to forget who gave you your power in the first place. If you so much as lay a finger on her again, I will repay everything you have done to her tenfold."

"Fine," the boyar snapped, rising and brushing himself off in a brusque manner. "Fine. I have an execution to plan anyway." He vanished in a swirl of dark shadows.

Redrinna's heart froze in her chest. No. He was going to execute River anyway? Closing her eyes, Redrinna took a deep breath as anger flashed through her gut. With the boyar being the way he was, she should've expected this and was more than a little upset she'd thought he'd play fair.

When Tehl turned to her, Osiris was gone from his eyes. Even still, he regarded her with a cold contempt. "I'm not going to break you out or bother fixing your injuries. You're fine where you are."

"I thought you were supposed to take me to Osiris." The pain in her side made it hard to talk evenly.

"I will, but it's an exhausting trip, and there are things I have to finish first. So you'll just have to be patient. That said, we don't need you yet. Father says if you can get out on your own, you're free to go. This time." He scoffed. "Spoiled brat."

She frowned. A chance to get out. The boyar had already broken his end of their bargain, so she saw no reason to uphold hers. However, she wasn't sure she could get out in time. "Tehl, wait," she said as he turned away.

With a long-suffering sigh, he glanced over his shoulder, his bizarre eyes gleaming like broken glass shards in the faint light.

"The boyar is going to kill River."

"I know. And I don't care."

"You should," she snapped.

He raised an eyebrow. "Oh yeah?"

"River was chosen—he's a part of the Dragon Kin. You need him alive, not dead."

He stared for a moment longer, expression impassive, before vanishing in a rush of shadows.

Redrinna's heart thrummed in her chest. She didn't know if he would do anything, but the idea of trusting the enemy to protect her friends made her sick. The urge to cry burned at her throat, but Redrinna scrubbed at her watery eyes, trying to force the emotion away. She didn't have time for that. Not right now.

Instead, she tried to study the chain binding her ankle. Her vision kept blurring over, tears dripping down her cheeks so fast, as soon as she wiped them away, more took their place.

"Stop it already!" she demanded. There wasn't time to cry. Crying wouldn't save River's life—all it did was make it hard to see.

Shaking her head and blinking furiously, Redrinna fixed her attention on the chain.

River had been able to break Kelvair's chains.

'People like you are born on a spectrum—your magic comes in varying degrees of strength and you can only use natural elements, like fire or water. Depending on where you fall on the spectrum will dictate how many of the elements you can use, if you can use more than one,' he'd said.

Redrinna knew she had fire magic, but it'd never occurred to her that perhaps she could use more than just fire before. If what River said was true, there was a chance she could use earth, right?

What are we going to do now? her gem asked, almost sounding curious despite the situation.

"What's the chance I can use more than just fire magic? Do you know?"

Her gem was quiet for a moment. *Pretty good. Your fire magic is quite strong, which is a good sign you can use more than just that element.*

Redrinna smiled, though it was grim. As she'd hoped.

However, if she was going to experiment with magic, she couldn't test it out on the piece of metal attached to her. With her track record, she'd break her ankle.

Instead, she scoured the ground around her, finding a loose rock and picking it up. "If I can use earth magic, I should be able to break this, right?"

Yes. But remember: earth is a stubborn element. It won't work the same way your fire does.

Redrinna stared at the rock for a minute, overwhelmed by how clueless she was before she glanced up. All at once, she realized where she was. She was in the mountain where Kelvair had been trapped, but she was in the room with the statue of the forgotten goddess.

Now that she was close to it, she could admire the intricacy of the carving, the exquisite details some ancient hands had taken the time to render. Religion had long been forbidden in the empire; Redrinna had never known nor understood the concept of a 'god'. But now, while trapped in a cave with a friend's life hours from being ended, felt like the time when a person needed one.

"I don't know if you're real, or if anything like you exists," Redrinna said, staring up into the forgotten goddess' moonlit face, "but if you're there, or if there's a being out there like you can hear me, please help me. People are going to die if I stay here—so please."

She wasn't sure if she expected some kind of answer, but her plea was met with silence. Even still, as she returned her attention to the rock, all the emotions storming inside her went quiet.

Taking a deep breath, Redrinna focused. To be safe, she tried to break the rock with her own, raw strength. If it was more dirt or sand than actual rock, then the test would prove invalid. It didn't give. The rock dug into the cut on her fingers, forcing her to stifle a cry of pain.

That meant, with her own strength, she couldn't break the rock, so, taking another calming breath, Redrinna focused on the earth's spirit.

With the awareness of that spirit filling her mind, Redrinna examined the rock in her hand. She saw it in pieces, in the fragments that had been pressed together to make it. More importantly, she understood where to apply pressure in order to break it. Pushing with the magic in its weakest place, Redrinna snapped the rock in half. Her cut didn't sting at all this time.

She released the awareness the earth's spirit provided her, staring at the rock in her bloody palms. It was snapped perfectly in two, the break so clean, it appeared as though it'd been cut with a knife.

That was amazing, Redrinna. You really do have astounding magical talent.

Before she even realized it, she was grinning. "Perfect. I think we're going to be able to get out of here."

Excellent. I wasn't planning on us staying captured anyway.

That made her smile even more.

Chapter Twenty-Seven

The shock that flooded Tak's system when Redrinna glanced at him—her eyes meeting his for only a second—before vanishing in a wave of shadow left him immobile. Even his thoughts stopped. Their rescue attempt had gone wrong in every possible way. Everything that could've gone wrong pretty much had.

Tak, his gem said, nearly scaring him out of his wits, *there's no time to panic. We have to move.*

"R-right," he said. He shook his head. "Right."

If his and Redrinna's roles had been reversed, she wouldn't have just stood here in dumb shock. Like when Chumani had been captured, Redrinna would've run half the night trying to find him.

As his heartbeat accelerated, his mind whirling to think of what they could do, he glanced at Thala and Will. Redrinna's possessed friend no longer held Will to the ground and now stood in front of the entrance to the house, making it clear they were not allowed back in. Which meant the boyar still planned on executing River, regardless of what he'd just promised Redrinna.

"Snake," Tak hissed as Will got to his feet.

"Somehow," Will said, his voice thick with pain, "I think this just got a whole lot worse."

"Now what?" Thala said.

Tak retrieved his sword, still annoyed Redrinna's friend had bested him so easily. Of all the times he'd needed to be able to make a difference, that had been one of the most important, and he hadn't been able to do it.

He shook that away. "Come on," he said, heading for the gate. "We've got to get to the dragons. Now."

Thala and Will nodded.

When they were out on the street, it took him a second to orient himself before he headed in the direction of the back gate. Thala led the way, but as they neared it, someone called her name, making them all glance back.

It took Tak a second to recognize the young man Thala had brought along with her the other day, though he couldn't remember the kid's name.

"Indigo," Thala said, her voice as calm as ever.

"I was on my way back but..." the kid began, his gaze roving over the three of them before settling on Will and his injury. "What happened?"

"A lot," Will said with a bite. "But we have to go."

"We don't have time to explain." Thala hurried off. Tak and the others quickly followed.

It was still a long way to the hideout, and by the time they made it, all four of them were panting hard.

Xandrin stared at Tak with a horrified expression. "No."

"Yes," Will said before heading to Leonora. "Help."

Tak beelined it for the dragons.

Xandrin stared with wide eyes. "Where is she?"

"The boyar got her," Tak said. "She gave herself up to protect us, so we're going to have to find wherever the boyar put her and get her out."

Determined resolve appeared in Xandrin's eyes.

"Where's River?" Leonora asked, still pale despite the fact she was binding Will's injury without a flicker of hesitation.

It startled Tak when everyone turned to him. However, he swallowed his nerves as best he could; there wasn't time to panic. What would Redrinna do? That was what he needed to do too.

"We couldn't get him out. The boyar found us while we were in his cell. We busted the locks to get in, but River attacked the boyar so we could escape. He didn't follow us out." Tak still remembered the split second where his and River's gazes had met in that cell. Even though they hardly knew each other, he'd known what the guy had wanted him to do.

"So he's either being stubborn," Will began.

"Or he's hurt badly enough he couldn't leave," Leonora finished, growing a little paler.

Tak nodded. "The boyar is still going to try to execute him, and there's no way we can break into the mansion again."

"We need to find the general and get him here as fast as possible," Will said. "He's the only one who can do anything to stop this."

Thala said, "I'll go," without a second's hesitation.

Indigo glanced at the group before joining her, his jaw set. "I will too. I know where he's at."

Thala turned to the dragons.

Astra glanced at Kelvair and Xandrin. "Red beast, you have to find Redrinna. She's your responsibility." For once, her tone wasn't mocking.

"I know," Xandrin said.

"And Kelvair, I don't think you're strong enough yet to carry three people, so I'll go," she finished. She bent down, and Thala and Indigo hopped onto her neck.

"Just in case," Leonora said, grabbing the stack of papers River and Will had stolen out from beneath a rock and handing them to Thala, "take these. They should help you convince him to act."

Thala nodded. Astra spread her wings.

"Be careful," Tak called.

Astra looked back at him and smiled. "I will." Then she grew stern. "*You* be careful, all right?"

He nodded, and she launched into the sky. Then he turned back to the others. Someone needed to search for Redrinna, but he already had a sneaking suspicion where she would be. If the boyar had hid the dolls and later Kelvair in the same cave, he was willing to bet the man had stashed Redrinna there too.

"What else?" Will said, fixing Tak with a serious stare.

Sending all of them into the cave was a bad idea. If it turned out to be the wrong place, then it would be a waste of time. Plus, there was still the issue of River's impending execution. He didn't know how far away the general was, nor how soon Thala and Indigo would be able to convince him to come. They couldn't possibly bank on that to save River's life, not in good conscience. So what else should they do?

All at once, the book Tak had been reading before they'd left the Mount came back to him, the account of the prince who'd turned the city against the king in order to save it weaving through his mind again.

Tak opened his eyes as he put the pieces together. "We have to get everyone in the city to stand with us. If enough people are willing to fight, the boyar might not be able to kill River."

Kyvo cocked his head. "What do you mean?"

Tak's thoughts whirled as the plan took shape in his mind. "Before we came here, Redrinna was convinced she needed to hide because most people would hate her because of the dolls, but it seems people don't hate her; they love her. How many other people feel the same as you guys?"

Will and Leonora glanced at each other. "Most people," Leonora said.

"Especially the poor," Will finished. "The boyar has gone after them the most."

"We now know most everyone who's been executed were killed because of their loyalty to Redrinna and her family." Tak met their gazes. "If we want to kick the boyar out and prevent him from being able to kill River, you guys have to get the town on our side. They have to fight with us. Can you do that?"

Will seemed surprised for a second before a wicked grin twisted his mouth. "That might be all too easy."

Leonora smiled too, some color returning to her face for the first time since River's capture. "Especially when they learn what the boyar's done to her and her friend."

"I'll do that," Will said.

"Me too," Leonora said.

Will looked at her in alarm.

"Don't give me that," she snapped. "I've been stuck in camp while you guys have done everything. I can't fight, but sowing discontent? That I can do, and I'm going to do it. Besides, I know where I can go so the boyar won't be able to find me."

Will held up his hands in surrender.

Kyvo hopped off his rock. "I'll go with you. I can fight a little."

Tak blinked at him in surprise. "You don't want to go after Redrinna?"

"Of course I do," Kyvo said, his tail drooping a little. "But if you and Xandrin go get her, she'll be okay, so I think Leonora needs me more this time. Redrinna will understand, right?"

Tak smiled a little. "She will. But if I'm wrong about where she's at, she might be in town, so keep your ears open."

The three of them nodded.

"Kelvair," Tak turned to the dragon, who stared at him with wide eyes. "I know you're still recovering, but you stay near the town too, in case there's trouble. I think that might be the easiest thing for you to do."

"O-okay, I'll try," Kelvair said.

They all left, leaving Tak and Xandrin alone. That was the best Tak could do, so it was time to go after Redrinna.

He turned to the dragon, who watched him expectantly.

"Now are we going to find Redrinna?"

Tak nodded. "I think she's in that cave where Kelvair was hidden.

It can't hurt to check, at least. Do you remember where it is?"

"Yep," Xandrin said as he lowered himself so Tak could hop onto his neck. "At least, I know where the back entrance is."

"That's close enough."

Then they launched into the sky.

They seemed to fly forever before Xandrin landed again, every minute that passed seeming more urgent than the one before it.

Tak stared at the cliff face in front of them, a chill rushing down his spine. Where the waterfall gushed out and where Redrinna had said there'd been an opening was now filled with rocks. It seemed that part of the cave hadn't survived Kelvair's escape.

Xandrin stared at it too, his ear frills lowering. "Are you sure she's here?"

Lifting his gem to his face, Tak said, "You can sense where Redrinna is, can't you?"

Yes.

"She's in there, right?"

A pause. *Definitely.*

"She's in there, Xandrin. I promise."

"All right." Xandrin approached the collapsed cliffside and sniffed around in a dog-like fashion.

Tak raised an eyebrow, not sure what was happening. Even still, he waited until the dragon finished before he asked the question on his mind. "What are you doing?"

As Xandrin lowered his head to the ground, taking a couple deep sniffs, he said, "Every cave has a unique smell, so if I memorize the smell here, we should be able to find the entrance. River and Redrinna went in that way, but they left me here."

Then Xandrin turned and walked, seeming to follow a path only he could see. Tak stayed quiet, sure that Xandrin needed to concentrate in order to identify the correct cave.

Before long, they came to a steep, dark ravine. Carefully, they made their way down and, before long, came to another entrance, this one much narrower than the one by the waterfall.

Xandrin sniffed it a couple times before nodding. "I'm pretty sure this it." He lowered his head, and Tak climbed off.

"Is this the one?" he murmured to his gem as he stood in the entrance, cool air brushing against his legs.

Yes, I think so.

The entrance was far too narrow for Xandrin, so Tak turned back to him. "You wait here. I'll be back soon with Redrinna."

Xandrin eyed the cavern. "Be careful in there."

Tak nodded and entered the darkness alone. It was damp and—compared to outside—cold. Goosebumps broke out across his skin, but Tak only quickened his pace, hoping that would warm him. His gem intensified its glow, the green light eerie but it did help him avoid stepping into any chasms or fissures. Whenever they came across a place where the path diverged, Tak would pause, waiting for his gem to identify the correct path. Then he would hurry on, his gaze raking over the stalagmites and stalactites gleaming with moisture. Given how dry it was outside, he never would've suspected the inside of the cave would be so wet.

He walked for a while longer before his gem flared with heat. *We're here. This is where Redrinna is.*

Tak stopped. He searched around him and, after a moment, spied a massive set of closed, stone doors. It was hard to make out in the light of his gem, but there was some kind of writing inscribed around the frame, some jagged, ancient language he didn't recognize.

He approached, putting a hand on the stone. "In here? You're sure?"

Positive.

Experimentally, Tak pushed against the doors since they didn't have handles, but they didn't budge. Now what?

All at once, he recalled that back in the forest Redrinna had fought Reyna and grabbed the woman's wrist while glowing red. With a strength unlike any he'd seen, she'd prevented a woman who was taller and stronger than her from being able to even budge her arm. Later, Redrinna had explained the phenomenon to him, and while he wasn't sure he could replicate it, Tak was willing to try.

"I need your help," he said, glancing at his gem. "We can push these doors open together, can't we?"

Yes. If that's what you want to do, I can help you do it.

Tak braced his hands against both doors. He didn't know if this would work or not, but Redrinna was in this room, and he would get her out. The boyar didn't get to keep her so he could do who knew what before letting Osiris take her.

Tak had promised Osiris wouldn't get her, and he was determined to keep that promise.

Abruptly, strength flooded him, filling every fiber of his being, and Tak pushed. The doors were still heavy, and even with addition of the gem's strength, Tak fought with every ounce of his own too. However, the doors moved. It was slow, the heavy stone grating as it was forced to give way.

When they were open wide enough for him to enter, he straightened, the strength leaving him. As it left, the green light that he hadn't noticed coming off his skin vanished until he was himself again. For just a second, he allowed himself a little smile. Then he hurried into the room.

Light filtered down through windows set high above, highlighting a massive statue that emerged from the wall itself. However, more deserving of his attention was the fiery red hair of the young woman kneeling in front of the statue.

Redrinna.

She stared at him, eyes wide, and when their gazes met, a massive grin lit up her face. "Tak!"

He was grinning before he even realized it. He hurried across the massive room, kneeling next to her once he reached her. The chain around her ankle, binding her to the floor, did not escape his notice.

"Are you okay?"

She started to nod but paused, brow furrowing. "I am all right, but everything hurts right now."

That almost made him smile again.

"That aside though, I think I'm on to something." She gestured towards a pile of rocks in front of her, something Tak hadn't noticed until that moment. It wasn't a big pile, but every rock had an unnaturally clean break on one side.

He frowned. "What...have you been doing?"

"Look!" Her eyes sparkled despite the situation. She touched her hands to the ground, and, with a little bit of cracking and rumbling, *made a miniature wall.*

Tak's mouth popped open. "You have earth magic? How...?"

"River broke Kelvair's chain with magic, and he said it was possible I could use more than just fire magic, remember?"

"Yeah."

"Since I'm kind of stuck, I figured I could see if I had earth magic, because then I'd be able to break the chain." She glanced at her ankle. "I haven't been brave enough to try it yet."

The chain did appear too tight. It wouldn't take much to snap her ankle if she did the magic wrong.

"Why don't you try breaking one of the links first?" he suggested.

With a frown, Redrinna studied it for a minute longer. "That could work," she murmured. "At the very least we could leave."

She took hold of one of the lower links, fingering it for a minute before her brow lowered and her eyes narrowed.

"This is a little harder than normal rocks, but," she began before jerking the chain. With a loud snap, the link broke in half like it'd been cut with an invisible blade.

Redrinna's face glowed like the sun. "I did it! I-it worked!"

Tak grinned.

For just a second, Redrinna turned that smile of hers on him, looking so pleased and happy, he was powerless to do anything but smile back. It was a weird time to notice it, but whenever she was like this (which was happening more often these days), whether it was because she got down a hard skill or found something that piqued her interest while they were in the library, the way her smile illuminated her face was pretty. For some reason, it always made him just want to sit and stare.

This was what Redrinna was like when she was genuinely happy, something she hadn't been often before. If Tak was honest, he liked it.

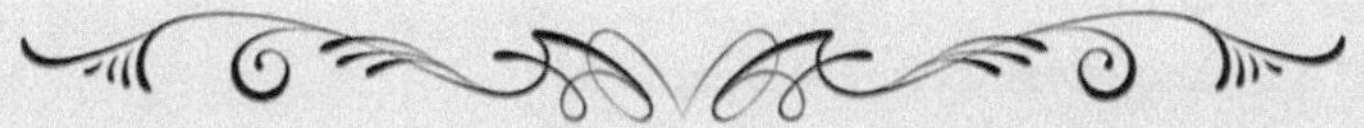

Chapter Twenty-Eight

Redrinna took a deep breath, eyeing the band still on her ankle. She'd been able to snap one of the links without difficulty. Now, she needed to try getting the lock in the band to let go. She could try snapping it if she couldn't get it, but that would be much harder than trying to copy what River had done.

Closing her eyes, she rested her fingers on the bands. Metal was a lot harder than the rocks she'd been practicing on before. She could sense the bits of earth inside, but they were harder to convince to co-operate—more rigid, almost, than their earthen counterparts. Even still, as an awareness of the locking mechanism filled her senses and she worked to shift the gears inside, she knew that metal could be persuaded. After a few seconds, the gears shifted, and the manacle released its biting grip with a click.

Her ankle ached, but in a matter of seconds, it was worlds better.

Tak smiled at her, and she couldn't help the grin on her face.

"You really are amazing, you know?" he said.

She didn't know what to do with his praise, so she shrugged and said, "What time is it?"

"It's late, but there are still a few hours before sunrise."

"The boyar didn't let River go, did he?"

Tak shook his head.

"That's what I thought."

"We need to get going." Tak glanced over his shoulder before turning back to her. "Can you walk?"

"I think so," she said, giving her foot another minute before she tried putting any weight on it. It seemed fine, but the instant she stood and allowed it to take her full weight, her ankle seized with pain, giving out beneath her.

Tak caught her before she could fall.

A bit embarrassed, she glanced at him and said, "Sorry. But thank you."

To her surprise, he didn't say anything. Instead, he stared at her with a funny expression on his face, one she didn't understand and couldn't figure out. After a second, it morphed into something like embarrassment, and he glanced to the side for a second before meeting her gaze again, looking like his usual self.

"I-it's fine," he said. "Anyway, I can carry you most of the way out if you want. Xandrin's waiting for us outside."

"Where's everybody else?" she asked, straightening a little so she didn't lean against him so much.

He held onto her arms to help her stay balanced on her one foot. "Astra, Thala, and Indigo went to try and find the general while the others went back to town. They're going to try and get as much of the town on our side as possible, and with their help, we might be able to stop the boyar from killing River."

That made her pause. "Like the prince of Manon's coup?"

He nodded, a hint of a smile touching his mouth.

That made her grin again. "That's such a clever idea. If we had most of the town and the army on our side, the boyar wouldn't be able to attack well, if at all. Who thought of that?"

He glanced away, but there was the smallest hint of a smile touching his cheeks. "I... Well, I guess I did."

Her eyes went a little wide.

"When you were abducted, everybody turned to me, so I...just tried to think of something you would do, is all. It might not even work."

She smiled at him, gently patting one of his hands. "Hey, it was a good idea. I'm proud of you." If she'd been in the same situation, she didn't know if she would've been able to be that calm or come up with an idea like that.

He still looked a bit embarrassed, but he let go of her arms. Once he seemed sure she had her balance, he turned and squatted down. "Um, i-it's a long way out, so I'll have to carry you like this, okay?"

"Okay." Carefully, she moved her gem out of the way and situated herself on his back, and once she had a good grip, he wrapped his arms around her legs and straightened. It'd been a long time since she'd had a piggyback ride, and it wasn't anywhere near as comfortable as she remembered it being. Though, that might have been because her sides, hand, and ankle all throbbed.

"I'm not too heavy, am I?"

He glanced back, his face close enough to hers she could only see part of it. "You're fine."

As he carried her out of the chamber, Redrinna allowed her head to drop onto his shoulder, her exhaustion making it pound, threatening to beat her into submission. She was already exhausted, but they didn't have time to stop yet. If they did, River would be gone forever.

As Tak walked, her thoughts wandered, and she found herself mulling over the fact Tak had been carrying her for a few minutes now, but he didn't seem all that bothered by her weight. Though, she supposed that the muscles she could feel in his arms and back might've had something to do with that.

Wait, since when had he had muscles like these? Her eyes narrowed while she stewed on that. When they'd first met, he'd been so thin, it'd freaked her out, and then when she and Timothon had talked a little bit about it a week or so ago, all she'd noted was that Tak seemed like he was a much healthier weight and size. She'd had no idea he'd developed this way. Though, to be fair, now that he was happy, eating regularly, and undergoing all the exercise and training Timothon forced them to do, it made sense.

After all, Redrinna had become much more muscular over the last few months too. Granted, not as much as Tak seemed to have, but still, she'd made progress, and the difference between them didn't bug her much. It was easier for men to build muscle than it was for women, so it made sense he'd seemed to develop a bit faster.

Wait, why was she thinking about this?

Shaking her head a little, Redrinna did her best to focus her attention elsewhere. So, her stupid brain decided to bring up the memory of when Tak had walked off after she'd talked about not being able to be a princess, followed promptly by the moment where she'd offered herself to the boyar and the expression that had been on Tak's face. Even though thinking about muscles had been odd, she'd preferred it.

However, the guilt and awkwardness hanging over their relationship nagged her enough she couldn't stay quiet. "Tak?"

"Hmm?" His breathing had gotten a little heavier, but he still seemed to be doing okay.

"The other day...did I...make you mad?"

"Make me mad?" he asked, stopping in his tracks so he could look at her, eyes wide. "What are you talking about?"

"You know," she muttered, her cheeks getting hot with shame, "when I said... When I talked about not wanting...and then you..."

"Oh," he stared ahead again and resumed walking, "when you said you couldn't be a princess, right?"

"Yes," she said weakly.

He stayed quiet, and her heart beat faster from the tension. What was he going to say? Would she be able to take it?

"I wasn't mad," he finally said. "I was more...disappointed."

"D-disappointed?" She stared at the side of his face in shock, not sure how to process that.

"Yeah," Tak began, his voice hushed. "Maybe it's dumb, but I wish—even if it was for only a second—that you could see yourself the way I see you. The way we all see you. I genuinely don't understand why you think so little of yourself. You're amazing, Redrinna. I mean, you were abducted, and what were you doing? Not only were you figuring out you had earth magic, but you were working to get it down so you could break out. This whole plan, everything we've been doing here, were nearly all your ideas. You fought the boyar off and rescued Kelvair. You also rescued Will, Thala, and me from the boyar too by sacrificing yourself for us. I— How can you not see how incredible you are?"

Redrinna's throat clenched so tight, she couldn't speak.

"Even if it was only for one day, I want to see you as a princess because I want you to be able to see yourself as one. I know you hate it, and I understand being a princess is hard, but the things you do, and the things you could do..." He let out a little sigh. "I just wish...you could see them as easily as the rest of us can."

"Tak," she began, eyes downcast, "I understand what you're saying, but I always mess things up. That's a bad thing when you're a princess."

"Everybody makes mistakes, Redrinna. My aunt used to say you'll never learn how to do something right unless you've done it wrong. Making mistakes is part of everything. It's how you learn."

She grimaced. "I-I know that, but messing up making bread, or something like that, and messing up as a leader are on two different scales. You can't just turn around and try again tomorrow if your mistake got people killed."

"Has there ever been a person who became a leader and never messed up? You and I both know for a fact that there are leaders who don't even care if they do something stupid that ends up hurting people. You're not like them," Tak said, a stern tone in his voice. "Trust me."

"How can you be sure?" she all but whispered, her grip on his shoulders tightening. How could he be so sure she would never become something awful or one day realize she'd been a bad ruler?

"Because you *care*; I've seen it. You ran half the night just to save Chumani. You were just willing to hand yourself over to Osiris—the person who scares you more than anything else—just to save mine and Will and Thala's lives. And you fought both Reyna and the Dragon Slayer off in order to protect Xandrin. If you were a selfish or bad leader, I don't think you would've done any of those things."

Discomfort wedged between her vertebrae. "But Tak—"

He sighed. "To me, the things you blame yourself for weren't your fault, but I'll humor you and say that they were. So, okay, you messed up. Then what? You say you're never going to do it again? You decided you had one chance to be perfect at something that's difficult, and because you couldn't do it exactly right you no longer get the chance to learn how to do it better? That's not fair—not to you or anyone, Redrinna."

She didn't know what to say to that. What he was saying seemed right, but it scared her. Fighting to be a princess had always been hard; it'd never come easy. Trying for another chance was opening the door to mess things up again. Trying again meant getting hurt—not just herself, but other people too. How could she take that risk?

"Tak," she whispered, unable to speak any louder, "but what if I did become a princess, and I gave it everything I had—absolutely everything—and it wasn't good enough? Then what?"

Tak seemed to think about that, staying quiet for a few minutes. At length, he said, "I suppose...it might depend on the situation a bit, but maybe also on what 'good enough' means. I mean, like here, in Póli, you were able to catch a member of the boyar's gang."

"It was only one person. I know that wasn't good enough."

"Maybe," he paused for a minute before he stopped walking again. "Redrinna, I know for you, that wasn't enough, and you wanted to do so much more. I get that; that's just who you are. But at the same time, the people here—even though punishing one man was the best you could do—have never forgotten what you did. On the contrary, all these years since then, they've believed you would come and save them again. I think they truly believe in you. We thought they hated you, but I think...I think they love you. They care about you. After they went through something so awful, you gave them hope, and that mattered more than doing it perfectly right."

Redrinna wanted to believe him so bad, but she couldn't quite seem to do it. How could something she'd done—any of those miniscule, insignificant things—ever have accomplished what Tak described? It didn't make sense. However, it wasn't like he would lie to her, plus he was so much better at catching on to these things than she was.

All at once, she nearly startled herself off Tak's back with a violent sneeze.

"Bless you," he said with a hint of a laugh. Then he paused. "Oh look, there's the exit. We're almost out."

She glanced ahead, noticing the slim sliver of moonlight illuminating the rock ahead. "Hey, Tak, put me down, okay?"

He did so, watching as she tested her ankle. "How is it?"

"Better," she said. The pain wasn't as severe as it had been before, but she still limped. That said, she was able to walk on her own for the most part.

They walked in silence (with Tak slowing to match her pace), and all Redrinna could think about was their conversation and the fact it made her chest constrict and her heart pound despite the reassuring warmth coming from her gem in waves.

What if she went for it, charged into Póli as a princess, and it made things worse? What if only some people were like Tak had suggested and most of them genuinely hated her? What if they decided she hadn't done enough, and they came after her and her friends like the rebels used to?

What then?

A few minutes later, Tak helped her make her way over an uneven part of the cavern floor, and then they stepped out into the light of the moon and fresh air carrying a hint of salt as it blew past.

With a squeaky roar, Xandrin all but charged into Redrinna, and it was thanks to Tak she stayed upright.

Xandrin blinked sheepishly. "Sorry."

"You're fine," she said with a hint of a smile. "Thanks for coming to get me." She smiled a little at Tak too, though because it was night and quite dark, she wasn't sure he noticed. However, he did smile a little bit once she did, so maybe he had.

Her friends assisted her to a nearby boulder so she could sit. Xandrin nudged her side in a comforting way, thoughtfully avoiding the side Captain Brion had struck. Unfortunately, the boyar had made sure she didn't have any unsore sides, so she still flinched away from his touch.

Xandrin froze. "Was that where your friend hit you?"

"No, sorry," she said. "The boyar hit me on that side, so they both hurt now."

"He hit you?" Tak asked, his voice soft but angry.

"Right after he brought me here. I think I'm okay though."

"C-can I check? Just in case?" Tak asked, flushing scarlet.

"Check?"

"W-well, when I healed your hand earlier, I could see what was wrong with it." His brow furrowed. "I'm not sure 'see' is the right word, but I...I knew what was wrong."

Her eyebrows shot up. "Maybe that's part of the magic? Not just being able to heal, but being able to fully understand the injury?"

He shrugged.

Since he seemed to be more comfortable with the idea of using his magic, maybe they needed to start studying it in earnest. It seemed it could do more than they'd believed.

"So, do you want me to check?" he offered again, seeming very embarrassed about it.

She nodded. "It couldn't hurt." She moved her arm out of the way.

With the utmost gentleness, he touched his hand to her waist. His magic flickered to life for a couple seconds before he stepped back, his face as red as her hair. "Nothing's broken, and your organs all seem okay. So you're probably fine, just bruised."

Smiling a little, she said, "That's good."

"So..." Xandrin began, glancing at the two of them before turning his snout in Póli's direction. "What are we going to do about River?"

Frowning, Redrinna glanced at her ankle, the swelling intense enough she could see it slightly through her boot—and she could definitely feel it. Her friends could fight if it came to that, but she couldn't. With her sides the way they were, she wasn't sure how well she'd be able to use her magic or even her sword. At the very least, there was no way she could hold her sword with her hand in the condition it was. Timothon had made her practice with both hands, but she was far more proficient with her right.

Even if the others rallied the town and managed to bring the general, there was no guarantee that would be enough to save River's life. Just in case all else failed, they needed to make sure that there wasn't a chance the boyar could even attempt to kill him. Redrinna had told Tehl, but she wasn't sure he'd do anything. While she was sure River was the person his gem had chosen, it wasn't bonded to him, and logically, it could find another if the need arose.

Or perhaps, Tehl and Osiris would wait until the last possible second. Perhaps, to them, this was one more part of that stupid 'game.' Maybe in their twisted minds, they wanted to see if she could figure out how to get River out before they'd deign to act.

Her parents would've been able to figure something out; she was certain. Regardless, Redrinna wasn't sure she'd be able to do the same. She couldn't even imagine what they would've done had they been in her place.

"I don't know," she finally said. "I really don't know. I've never had to do anything like this before."

"Then we've just got to do like Leonora said," Tak said encouragingly. "If we have nothing to base it off of, we make our own."

She met his gaze.

"Well, we already might have most of the town come, and we

might get the general to come," Xandrin offered, though he seemed at a loss as well.

"The nobles will come as well," Redrinna said, frowning as she wracked her brain. "Not because they're going to support us, but because they'll want to watch River be executed."

"Disgusting," Xandrin hissed.

"Yes, but it might work to our advantage." She closed her eyes to help herself focus. "The townsfolk outnumber the nobles, and they work harder too. If they are on our side, they and the army can work to keep the nobles from escaping, and since we have all that evidence, they'll be dealt with. The general can take over once he sees our proof and what the boyar is doing. I'm just afraid the boyar and the nobles will attempt to kill River before we can capture them all."

The other two waited.

An idea took shape in her mind, but it made her squeamish like she'd eaten something rotten. Shaking it away, she offered a modified version. "We need more than one person to confront the boyar so the others can focus on making sure River doesn't get hurt. If we put ourselves there, Xandrin can help keep the nobles from trying anything. Most people do think he's scary."

Xandrin seemed torn between looking forlorn and pleased.

"It could work," Tak said, a thoughtful frown on his face too. "But since the boyar is threatening the army's families, what if the general still won't risk it or the soldiers won't? We don't know who he has that can put that plan in place, so what if they're too hesitant to act?"

She hadn't thought of that, and now that she was, it made her freeze. Again, the full extent of her plan returned to her mind, and she still didn't like it. However, the boyar's threat didn't extend to her and Tak, and even if it did, neither of them had any family he could threaten.

"Or," she began slowly, the words peculiar in her mouth, "instead of forcing the general and the army to seize the city and stop the execution at the same time...I could."

Surprise touched Tak's face, but when he met her gaze, firm, determined resolve burned in his eyes.

"I know I said I wouldn't, and I don't know if it'll change anything, but if I seize the city, the soldiers would be acting on *my* orders. The boyar threatened them for mutiny, but technically they wouldn't be doing that. It's loose, but they might feel like they can obey."

"Instead of having to contest the boyar for control like the general would," Tak added, "you have it the moment you set foot in that town, right? Well, if you go in as the Imperial Princess, that is."

She nodded. "And if he resists—"

"Which he will."

"We can arrest him on the spot. With the square full of witnesses, he'll be gone for good."

Xandrin's ear frills lifted an inch. "That would change everything, wouldn't it?"

"It would," Tak said firmly.

Redrinna lowered her head. What if it didn't work? What if something she hadn't foreseen happened, something out of her control that would end in disaster?

"Hey," Tak said, kneeling in front of her so he could meet her gaze. "If this is the idea you want to go with—if it's the thing you think is going to work best—I'll fight to make sure it happens. I'll be right by your side. I promise."

"Me too," Xandrin said, lowering his head to her level. "We'll be with you no matter what happens."

She stared at the two of them, the fiery determination in their eyes making her throat clench.

"Hey," Tak said, his voice hushed but still strong, "it's okay if it's not perfect. We can adapt, and things will be okay."

I will also be with you, her gem said, its quiet strength seeming to fill her and become her own.

If Redrinna went in as a princess, even if it was just long enough to rip the boyar and corrupt nobles out of this town, then this time, she might be able to save these people from the man who'd been responsible for nearly a decade's worth of suffering. This time, she could make sure he didn't get away.

If she could do that, even if she couldn't do anything else, then being a princess would be worth it.

"All right," she said, lifting her head and taking a deep breath, the gem's warmth seeming to intensify as she did. "I'll do it. Today—just for today—I am Redrinna, the Imperial Princess of the Eridian Empire, representative of the Imperial Crown and its authority, and I will save this city. I will bring the boyar to his knees, and so long as you're both with me, I think it's impossible for us to lose."

Tak and Xandrin grinned, making her heart lift an inch. She didn't know if she could pull this off, but she would fight with every fiber of her being to do so. People counted on her; they believed in her. She wouldn't let them down this time.

Chapter Twenty-Nine

As the faintest ray of light appeared on the eastern horizon, Leonora and Kyvo made their way down the mostly deserted street. A few homeless people slept in doorways or any nook and cranny they could, but beyond them, the streets were empty. It'd been years since Leonora had walked the dirty streets, and a part of her was startled to find it so different than she remembered. When Will's dad had been the boyar, there'd never been so many without a place to go.

After several minutes of walking, Leonora found the building she searched for: the merchant's guild. Any merchants staying in town gathered here, where they were promised at least some form of protection. Taking a deep breath, Leonora entered. She expected to have to fight for permission to enter the back room, but when the guards noticed her, they let her in without a word, their eyes wide.

She hadn't thought they'd recognize her. Or be so sympathetic.

In the back room, the high windows above let in narrow moonbeams that brushing the packed-up stalls, various wares, and the sleeping forms nestled amongst the clutter in muted, blue light. Even in the guild, most merchants couldn't trust their things would be kept safe unless they slept with it in their hands.

"What are we doing here?" Kyvo asked, sniffing at a stray strand of straw on the ground.

"A friend of mine should be here," she whispered. "If we can find her, it'll help a lot."

"Okay," Kyvo chirped, padding quietly after her as she crept around the large room, searching for the right face.

It took several minutes before Leonora found the woman she wanted. The older woman slept amidst her fabrics, and Leonora was certain the fancy ones were in the baskets she slept on, the cheaper ones in the baskets around her.

"This one?" Kyvo asked.

Leonora nodded, creeping up to the woman. Kneeling at her side, Leonora gently shook the woman awake.

The woman glanced around, eyes bleary, almost in a kind of alarm.

Quickly, Leonora whispered, "Cybill, it's me. Leonora."

The woman froze, the sleep vanishing from her eyes as she bolted up, her baskets creaking as she did so. "Oh, Moonbeam, it is you!" she murmured, sweeping Leonora into her arms.

It'd been ages since Leonora had been pulled into a motherly embrace, and for a moment, she stayed there, clinging to the first woman who'd shown her genuine love and kindness after she and River had been dragged from their home. Then she straightened, pulling back. There was something she had to do, so she couldn't linger.

"Moonbeam, I've heard so many troubling rumors," the woman said, stroking her hair. "What happened to you?"

Leonora shook her head with a bit of a smile. "There isn't time for that, but I've been all right. Anyway, I have to ask you a question: are you still connected to those...friends of yours?"

Cybill's mischievous twinkle sparked to life in her eyes. "Always. Why?"

"Because I need you to do me a favor, and we need to get the word out as fast as possible. As in before dawn, fast. But it needs to stay quiet."

Folding her arms, Cybill said, "Does this have something to do with your beast of a grandfather?"

"It does, but there's a different reason it needs to be hushed," Leonora said, dipping her head a little and putting a finger to her lips, doing her best to keep her smile in check. "I need you and your friends to tell everyone *she's* here. She's coming, and she needs our help."

A couple seconds passed before comprehension dawned in the woman's eyes. They widened a fraction. "Her...as in *her*?"

Leonora nodded. "Her. I've seen her with my own eyes."

Cybill grinned. "Just tell me what she needs, and we'll make sure it happens."

⚘ ⚘

The wind ripped through Thala's hair, tugging some of the shorter strands free from her braid, but she barely paid it any attention. They were nearing the village where General Cael was supposed to be, and there wasn't much night left. They had made good time, but Astra would need some time to rest before they could head out again.

"There, that's them," Indigo said, pointing out the military camp to Astra.

With a nod, the dragon dipped down, and a minute later, landed just outside the camp, causing a bit of commotion inside.

As Thala and Indigo hopped off her shoulders she said, "Don't do anything stupid or I'll come in there after you."

They skidded to a stop in front of the guards at the entrance, both of whom already had their weapons drawn. They lowered them when they seemed to realize it was Indigo.

"Indigo," one of the men said, almost sounding annoyed. "What on earth are you doing? And why are you with a dragon?!"

"I'm here on Her Highness's orders," Indigo declared. Motioning towards Astra, he said, "This is one of her friends."

"H-Her Highness?" the other guard stammered, eyes wide.

"Yes. We need to see General Cael. It's an emergency."

The guards glanced at each other before nodding and letting the two of them pass. Thala glanced around at the assortment of tents in many different shapes and sizes. Where were they supposed to go in here?

"Come on," Indigo said, taking the lead. "I know the general's tent."

Thala followed him without hesitation. They weaved past startled soldiers, a lot of whom seemed to be coming to figure out what the commotion had been about. They called out to Indigo, but the boy ignored them, running full tilt towards a large tent in the center.

One of the guards at the entrance tried to grab Indigo while saying, "No, you can't go in, Indigo!"

"Sorry!" Indigo slipped past his grip like a fish, and Thala slid in after, getting the guard to lunge into the tent after them and get tangled in the tent flap. He missed them, but he did make the entire side of the tent ripple.

Inside the massive tent was a table, and a few older men were gathered around it, studying something despite the lateness of the hour (or perhaps it was considered early now, Thala wasn't sure). They looked up when Thala and Indigo burst in. However, while the older officers were impressive and intimidating, the man who captured Thala's attention was the younger man who was the only one seated at the table, his chin resting in his hand. He'd been the first one to react to Indigo and Thala's entrance, but he was the only one who hadn't reacted with some level of alarm.

A wicked scar ran from his left eyebrow to his jaw, but Thala thought the man was still quite striking anyway, and the scar seemed to enhance his features. He seemed oddly young, maybe only in his thirties at the most, with a full head of sun-lightened hair, the color a light brown on the top but darkening to a deep, earthy brown throughout the lower layers. His eyes were dark hazel, and they watched her and Indigo in an expectant way.

"Indigo," a couple of the officers hissed in a disapproving way.

"This is important," Indigo said, glaring in indignation.

The youngest officer lowered his hand. "Oh yeah?"

Indigo took two steps forward, standing at attention. "We were sent here to deliver an urgent message to you, General Cael."

Wait, the youngest officer was the general? All this time, Thala had imagined a much older man than him.

The youngest officer raised an eyebrow before getting to his feet and coming to the front of the table. To Thala's surprise, the deep green sash of the general was secured around his waist, meaning he was, indeed, the general. He propped one fist on his hip, and despite the serious mien about him, a hint of a smile danced at the corners of his mouth.

"A message for me, huh?"

Indigo nodded, opening his mouth.

However, Thala, far more distrusting of the rank and file of the military, cut in, "But it's private."

General Cael's eyes turned her direction, and it was a bit surprising to her that no change in expression appeared on his face. The senior officers behind him shared looks in varying degrees of surprise, but General Cael just considered her for a moment.

"All right." He waved at the officers behind him, and after a second's hesitation, they all went. When the tent flap was securely closed once more, General Cael said, "So what's your message?"

Indigo spoke first. "Her Highness, the Imperial Princess, needs your help."

The general's eyes widened the barest fraction.

"The boyar's going to execute someone in the morning, and she's going to try and stop it, but she needs your help to take the city, so she sent us to get you."

"An execution, eh?" A grim smile twisted his mouth. "That coward always plans those when I'm gone. That said, I'm not sure it's enough—"

Thala pulled free the papers Will and River had spent the last week smuggling out, holding them out to the general.

With nothing more than the lift of an eyebrow, he took them.

"We have these, proof of the nobles' corruption and wrongdoing. If you want testimony of what the boyar's done wrong, I'll do it," she said. "His grandchildren will too. We have the proof, and we're going to stop him for good. But we need your help."

He flicked through the papers one by one before handing them back to her. "You keep those safe. I know there are rats in this place, but I haven't yet found out who. If you leave them with me, they will most likely disappear."

Thala took them back, returning them to her pouch.

The general regarded the two of them with a stern expression. "So, you're telling me Her Highness is alive, here, and requests my aid. She has the proof to rid this city of the filthy vermin that have long infested it?"

Thala and Indigo nodded in sync.

A wicked grin touched his mouth. "Finally."

Relief flickered to life in Thala's chest. Perhaps this General Cael was a good person after all, unlike his predecessor.

"You said the execution is in the morning?"

"That's right," Indigo said. "It's set for dawn."

The general straightened. "There are some things I have to prepare on my end first, so you two get some rest."

"We're going with you, sir," Indigo said, taking a step forward. "And we came here on a dragon, so—"

"I've already heard about the dragon," the general said with the hint of a smile. "But she needs to rest as well. We're a long way from Póll. But if you two expect to be able to do any fighting, you need to rest. You'll be of no help to Her Highness either if you run yourselves ragged."

Thala blinked in surprise. The last general she'd known hadn't cared two figs about the health of his soldiers.

"We'll leave in an hour," the general said. "Not only will it take time to arrive, we'll have to gather the army fast in order to be ready in time. So rest while you can, understood?"

"Yes, sir," she and Indigo intoned.

Thala still wasn't convinced of this general's character, but between this, Indigo's obvious trust and admiration for him, and what Indigo had told them about General Cael's role in saving the dolls, she was willing to give him a chance. He'd changed the course of history before; perhaps he could do it again.

⁕ ⁕ ⁕

The night had nearly past but Will had one last stop to make. He slipped down a narrow alley, dodging out of sight of a patrol. Despite the early hour, there were a few houses with light already flickering behind their shutters. The word was spreading; some of the people who already knew were racing to tell their friends and relations about the princess.

When Tak had suggested this idea, Will honestly hadn't thought it would work all that well, but he'd agreed because it'd given him something to do and helped him forget about the pain in his arm. Plus he'd needed something to stop himself from plunging into the boyar's lair like an idiot in order to get his best friend out.

Lo, and behold, to his great surprise, Tak's plan was *working*.

A bit of a grin nabbed his mouth as he slipped into a narrow opening and into Adonis's hideout. Despite the lateness of the hour, Will knew they'd be awake. So, when he popped into the hideout, he wasn't surprised to find most of the crew there.

Adonis, with his peg leg stretched out onto a nearby chair, studied him with a critical eye. "Don't you know how late it is, Will?"

"I could ask you the same question." He glanced around at the crew, most of whom had gone back to their quiet conversations and their drinks. "You guys just get back from a job?"

"Disrupting the slave trade again," Adonis said, swirling the dark drink in his cup.

"Then you guys haven't heard yet, have you?"

That got most of the conversations to die out again.

"Heard what?" Adonis asked, leaning on the table.

"First of all, the boyar's going to execute River first thing in the morning."

A collective hiss and a few curses went around the room, but Adonis stayed quiet, hawk-like eyes fixed on Will's face.

"And the...Her Highness isn't dead. She's here. Today she's taking the city."

That was greeted with an almost stunned kind of silence.

"Her Highness?" someone murmured, with a good deal more respect than Will would've if he'd been in the man's shoes.

"She's alive?" Adonis asked, his eyes a fraction wider.

Will nodded. "I've seen her with my own eyes. She's been collecting evidence against the nobles, and now that she has it, she's going to take them all out. They're going away for good."

A wicked grin twisted Adonis' mouth, as excited murmurs filled the room. "So that's where you brats have been running off to."

"But she needs everybody who can be in the square before the execution. If the entire city stands behind her, the boyar will lose all of his control. Can you do that?"

Adonis stared at him, almost regarding him. "Will, you seem awfully eager to help a princess I remember you hating."

Will scowled. "River's life is in danger."

Even still, the man continued to stare at him.

He huffed, the memory of when Her Highness's friend had been about to kill him and she'd left safety behind in order to save him flashed through his mind. He also remembered that on the nights he and River had gone to raid the houses, she'd waited up for them. When he recalled those, shame filled him at the things he'd used to say and do.

"She saved my life," he said, almost mumbling. Then he almost glared at Adonis. "So will you help?"

"As sure as the sun rises," Adonis said, getting to his feet. "If that's what she wants, we'll be there. I'm more than ready for the filth that's long polluted and wrecked this beautiful city to disappear."

Will grinned, the expression reckless, but it also...felt good. Things might change. Instead of a far-flung fantasy, it was starting to feel possible, for the first time in his life, to imagine a different way of living.

☙ ❧

River forced his eyes open, the dull, pounding ache in his head recalling the night's earlier events. Well, kind of. They were broken, fuzzy and disjointed, but that was most likely because of the injury and dried blood he'd found on the back of his head. He assumed it was from the boyar, but he wasn't sure; he couldn't remember.

That said, it was just a concussion, so he'd live. He was just glad his cell was dark, otherwise, the pain in his skull would've been worse.

After all, Her Highness was coming for him.

That thought pulled him up short. Never once had he allowed himself to believe anyone would come and save him; he'd long reconciled himself to the idea that anything he wanted—be it freedom, peace, or safety—he would have to fight and claw for.

Yet, even still, while his retention was hazy, the one, distinct memory he had was of Her Highness's distant voice saying: 'We're coming back for you!' Those words kept echoing through his mind, and instead of growing fainter, they grew stronger.

After all the things he'd seen her and her friends do, after the handful of evenings they'd spent around the same fire, and after all the time he'd spent with her, River found that he believed with every inch of his soul she would come.

She would save him.

The realization almost took his breath away. She would come for him.

Hope was frail, so easy to destroy, and in the many years he'd been here, River hadn't dared to allow himself to feel even the tiniest flicker of it. However, now, almost beyond his control, it filled his chest with the force and intensity of a forest fire.

"She's coming," he whispered, ignoring the pain of his dry throat as the words rasped over his tongue. "She's going to come."

For the first time since his capture, instead of despair or fear, River remained calm. He almost felt powerful. When Her Highness and Tak had come before, he hadn't gone with them because he'd been out of fight. He hadn't had anything left. Now he did. Regardless of how things went down today, River refused to die yet.

⁂

Thala was roused by a gentle shake to her shoulder, and she was taken aback to find General Cael the one who'd done it. He was dressed much the same as before, except now he was armed and armored.

"It's time, kid," he said. Then he gave Indigo a hard nudge. "I already woke you up. Don't go back to sleep."

"I'm awake, I'm awake already," Indigo mumbled.

Thala sat up, sweeping off the scratchy wool blanket and extracting herself from the borrowed cot.

General Cael stepped outside the tent, holding the flap open. He glanced back in, a kind of grim excitement in his eyes. "Come on, you two. We need to get back to Póli as fast as your dragon can take us. Dawn approaches."

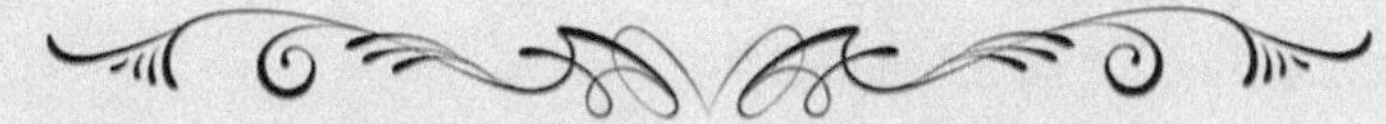

Chapter Thirty

As Thala followed General Cael into the yard behind the guard-house in Póli, a shiver raced down her spine at the power radiating off him. It confused her that she kept feeling that whenever she glanced at him or was near him—he wasn't overly tall or enormous like the last general she'd known. However, there was still something about General Cael that radiated a kind of strength Thala knew meant he could be more dangerous than most of the other people she'd seen. It was quiet, but it was still there.

There was a reason he'd been chosen to be a general despite his youth, she realized. A very good reason.

"Indigo," General Cael said, getting the young man's attention in an instant, "get everyone up. I have something to say."

With a grin Indigo raced for the sleeping quarters.

General Cael stood silent, his hand resting on the hilt of his sword in almost a casual way. He seemed to be relaxed, but there was a storm in his eyes that suggested he was prepared to fight at the drop of a hat.

Thala couldn't take it any longer. "I lied," she said.

He glanced at her, barely moving his head. "About?"

"Why I rejoined the army," she said. She didn't understand what it was about him that made her need to confess, but there was something. Perhaps it was simply that he reminded her so much of her dad—and she'd never been able to lie to her dad. "I said it was because I was lost, but that's not true. I joined it as a spy. For Her Highness."

For a minute, he just stared. Then, with a hint of a grin he dipped his head forward, but since he still looked at her, he stared at her kind of sideways. "Oh I get it. You became a spy—that's a much better reason for you to be here than missing the army."

Thala blinked, unsure what to make of his acceptance. "But...shouldn't I be in trouble?"

"Maybe," he said. "There certainly is some law somewhere about joining the army under false pretenses. However, given the circumstances, I don't see why that ought to apply here."

Stunned, she stared at him. That was something her dad would've done too.

As soldiers hurried into the yard, General Cael turned his attention forward. Once everyone was gathered, he addressed them.

"I've known for a long time there are those among you who are disloyal to not only me, but to the Imperial family. However, today, the tyrant you bent your knee to is about to fall, and those of you who've thrown your lot in with him will tumble as well."

"Sir?" Captain Andor said, an eyebrow raised. "What about...?"

"Boyar Athanasios?" General Cael raised an eyebrow. "What about him? We're not his army, and we never have been. We're the *Imperial* Army—or have you all forgotten that?"

There was a challenge in his voice. No one said a word.

"The boyar believes he owns these lands—he believes he owns us, but he is wrong. We submit to one power, and one power only." A wicked smile twisted the general's mouth. "And today, that power is coming. If you wish to defy me and, by extension, that power, then you'll be removed right alongside the boyar. Is that clear?"

A chill ran through the air, and on a couple faces, Thala spied flickers of fear.

"Now," the general continued. "We've got work to do."

⚜

Leonora could hardly believe her eyes. Dawn was less than an hour away—River's life hung by a rapidly weakening thread—but the city had come to life in a way she'd never imagined. Cybill had spread the word like wildfire, and the merchant's guild was alive like it was midday. Multiple times, she'd heard the words, 'She's coming,' whispered reverently.

Even though Leonora had always believed in the good that might happen if Her Highness would come to Póli, seeing it right in front of her eyes was insane. The reality that she was not the only one the boyar had hurt nor was she the only one who remembered what Her Highness had done for them had been driven home.

Next to her, Kyvo watched the activity with a wicked grin. "This is so cool! I knew other people would realize Redrinna is awesome."

That made her grin. "It is really cool."

All Leonora's life, she'd been the invisible one—even to her grandfather, she was just a possession. River had been the one closest to the princess in age, and therefore, the one her father had trained to be an incredible warrior. River had also been the magical prodigy, comprehending and performing things on the level of a master when he'd only been five. Leonora had always just been his older sister.

That had made her angry once, when she'd been younger and before life had made her realize being special didn't bring happiness. In River's case, it'd only brought him pain.

Leonora had long been reconciled to the reality of being invisible and forgotten. The only role she would get to play in their family's legacy was that of ensuring there was another generation ready to protect any children Redrinna might someday have. She'd hated it once, but her perspective was changing, slowly but surely. Ensuring the safety of the next generation required a great deal of strength—regardless of whether or not that strength was the kind that was visible.

She allowed herself a little smile. Leonora wasn't one of the people who'd be fighting today—she would not hold a weapon in her hand nor would she be the one to claim victory through either cunning or physical prowess. However, because of the little role she'd been able to play, the people who could do that were ready to fight for their city. It wasn't much but she had done something.

Once dawn arrived, Póli would never be the same.

⁂

Dawn bloomed above the mountain peaks when Tak roused Redrinna from the little bit of sleep she'd been able to get.

There was a set determination in his jaw, a bit of fire smoldering in his eyes. "It's almost time."

To her surprise, behind him, Xandrin was already awake. "We don't know when the execution will start, but the sooner we go, the better, right?"

Nodding, she sat up, taking a deep breath before rising, easing her weight onto her ankle. It still burned, but it wasn't as intense as before, and she could handle it.

"Are you sure you don't want me to heal your ankle?" Tak asked, his favorite concerned expression on his face.

"I am. We're both going to need all the strength we have, so I don't think we should risk using your magic." She tried to give him a reassuring smile. "I'm really all right, okay?"

He didn't seem pleased about it, but he relented.

After the day they'd had yesterday, Redrinna was still exhausted. The handful of sleep she'd been able to get hadn't helped at all, but they didn't have any more time to rest.

Dawn had arrived.

Tak helped her over to Xandrin's side as she fought against the pain surging up her leg with every step. As she got ready to mount Xandrin, she found Tak staring at her with slightly narrowed eyes.

"What?" she asked, wondering if she looked disheveled from her brief rest.

"Nothing," he said quickly. Then he grimaced. "A-actually I was thinking that if you are technically a princess today then...y-your hair...doesn't match."

She fingered her ponytail. "It's not fancy, but you know it's the best I can do."

"Yeah," he said slowly, and she knew he had something else to say, so she waited. Eventually, he continued, "It's been a while since I've done someone's hair, so I might be rusty, but I can try if you want."

Redrinna glanced at Xandrin, who shrugged. "We don't have much time," he said.

"It'll be quick," Tak said.

Redrinna hesitated for a second longer before relenting. She supposed if she was going to act the part of a princess, she needed to look it as well, and her simple, messy ponytails weren't up to snuff.

She tugged her ponytail free, and with a bit of an apprehensive deep breath (which made Redrinna smile, though she reined it in until he'd stepped behind her and couldn't see it), Tak got to work. Tak's fingers were quick and gentle, starting what felt like a braid near the crown of her head and wrapping it to the back before tugging the rest of her hair into a low ponytail.

"There," he said.

A chill seeped into her gut as she fingered the braid. "Thank you," she whispered.

"It's nice," Xandrin offered.

Even still, Tak seemed to sense her unease. "Do you not like it?"

"It's fine," she said quickly. "It's just..." She traced the braid with her fingertips. "Reyna wears braids."

"Oh," Tak said, a quiet, sympathetic smile touching his mouth. "I get it. But you know, when my aunt was sick and asked me to do her hair, she always asked for braids because braids are worn by warriors. A-at least, that's what she'd said."

That made Redrinna pause. "Your aunt wanted to wear braids?"

He nodded. "Every day, she had to keep fighting for her life. So she asked me to braid her hair because she said since she was going into battle, she was going to fight dressed like the warrior she was. That's why I gave you one—since today, you're a warrior princess. I-I can change it if you want though."

Slowly, she smiled.

After all, it was true Reyna wasn't the only person in the world who wore her hair in a braid. Redrinna's friends in the Torijin tribe had mentioned they braided their hair when it was long, though she hadn't been able to see it when she'd been there. The people of the Esuni Desert also supposedly favored braids.

The mark of a warrior.

Redrinna fingered the braid one last time. "No. It's fine if that's your reasoning. Actually, now that I think about it like that, it's perfect, Tak."

He smiled a little.

Then they quickly mounted Xandrin and he took off, heading for Póli.

⁂

The faint, early morning sun seemed harsher than usual when River was dragged out into it, his wrists bound in an uncomfortable manacle that forced them enough apart his hands couldn't touch. His head pounded with every step, and once he was loaded and secured onto a prison wagon, every jolt as it rolled out of the boyar's mansion and down the street towards the town's center made the ache in his head spike to near agony. He wanted to puke.

The rumble of the cart became muffled as they neared the center of town, where a large crowd had already gathered. River studied the faces staring at him as the cart passed, but they weren't faces he recognized. There was no anger or scorn in their expressions; rather, there was a strange kind of determination. Their dress indicated there was no way they were part of the nobility, but they weren't slaves either. Were they the common folk? That was strange. They didn't attend executions like this.

It was clear when they had gotten nearer to the front, however, where the nobles had congregated. Unlike the rest of the crowd, they did not stare in silence. They hurled unoriginal insults and jeered as the cart stopped in the shadow of the execution stand.

Even though River's chest seemed to be overflowing with a calm reassurance Her Highness would come for him, he couldn't deny the crushing weight of fear as he eyed the stand.

Within a few minutes, the soldiers had him unloaded and pulled him towards the stand. River didn't resist, but he didn't walk fast either. The longer it took to reach the center of the stand, the more likely Her Highness would be able to come in time.

The boyar already waited for him on the stand, arms folded and a smug expression on his face. Once River had been dragged to the center and forced to his knees (which River fought against out of spite), the boyar turned to the crowd.

"Today is a glorious day! My heathen grandson has been captured and brought to justice at last!"

A cheer rose but, given the size of the crowd gathered in the square, it was a pathetic one.

The boyar noticed. His smile wavering, he called out, "Yes, rejoice! Show me your gratitude!"

That cheer was a little louder, but it was then River noticed that only the nobles cheered; the rest of the crowd, the ones who'd watched River pass in silence, stood silent now as well.

Despite the situation, River couldn't help saying, "It would seem most people here don't think you've done something worthy of their thanks."

The boyar cuffed him, and a racking hiss arose from the crowd like a hoard of furious snakes drew near. Then came the insults—not for River, but for the boyar.

Glancing up in alarm, the boyar said, "Soldiers, corral the rabble."

"I think not," came a new, deep voice River didn't recognize. He glanced over and was more than a little taken aback to find the general himself standing at the bottom of the stairs leading up to the stand. A spear was slung over his shoulder, the way he stood making him seem almost relaxed, but he was like a panther, already prepared to pounce. "What world do you live in that you think my soldiers would willingly obey a tyrannical oaf like you?"

The shadows on the boyar's face seemed to deepen. "General Cael, I would mind your tongue if I were you. It would be a shame if—"

"If what? You threatened to have someone else killed?" With a fiery glower of his own, the general stalked up the steps. "Don't you ever get tired of playing these little games of yours?" A hint of a smirk touched one corner of his mouth. "Or do you really think you're that important? I always knew you were a prig, but that is a level of stupidity I thought beneath even you."

River couldn't deny that the glare twisting the boyar's face was one of the most satisfying things he'd ever seen.

The boyar's gaze zipped to the executioner standing on the back end of the stand.

River heard the heavy footsteps, his heart lurching, but then there was a hum of a weapon.

He glanced at the general. General Cael had swung his spear, the blade in front of the executioner's throat.

"I dare you to take one more step," the general growled. "Just give me permission."

The executioner sent a glance at the boyar before holding up his hands and taking two steps back.

With a snarl, the boyar said, "I don't need him to—"

A shadowy sword materialized in his hand and before the general could react, the boyar swung. River ducked, but the blade never made contact with him. Instead, it cracked against another weapon. River glanced over, his eyes going wide at the sight of Will standing there, the boyar's blade caught on the crossguard of his sword.

"Not on my watch, you pig," Will spat as he tossed the boyar's blade aside.

The boyar staggered two steps back. "How dare you. I'll see you all repaid in full."

General Cael scoffed. "You are a fool."

Will snorted too. "Yep, and I think I bought just enough time."

River frowned at that.

The next second, something large slammed down behind him, making the boards of the stand rattle from the impact. River's eyes went wide; he recognized the deep, heavy breaths. Slowly, he managed to look behind him. Standing there, an intimidating mien bleeding from every scale, was Xandrin, the glower on his face sending a chill down River's spine. It was a poignant reminder that, despite all the dragon's quirks, Xandrin was, in fact, a *dragon*. On either side of him stood Astra and Kelvair, both of them giving River a vivid and powerful reminder that they too, were dragons. Their fins and frills were all flared, making the dragons appear twice their already intimidating size and like real, genuine beasts. Xandrin's wings were flared open, making him seem gigantic.

However, what made River's heart leap in his chest was the fact that, sitting right behind the dragon's gleaming horns was Her Highness herself, her hair done in a simple but stunning braided ponytail that made her appear more regal than he remembered. Then, almost as if the sun had caught onto the idea, as Xandrin lifted his head, the morning light caught Her Highness's vivid red hair just right.

For a glorious second, it was like she wore a crown of bright red flame.

The boyar stared up at her, stiff as a corpse.

"Boyar," she called, her voice ringing through the square. "You and I both know executions of this nature—especially for someone who was never given a trial—are illegal. I'm sure those who came to view this event like it's some kind of sport are also aware of their part in a disgusting and illegal activity. You all stand on dangerous ground, and I would be careful where you choose to take your next step."

"How dare a demon like you question the likes of us," the boyar snarled. "I am the boyar of these lands! They belong to me and what I say is law!"

Her Highness stared at him with cold impassivity before she said something to Xandrin. The dragon lowered his head, and Her Highness dismounted with remarkable ease. "The boyars of the Eridian Empire are not rulers; they are guardians and governors. No true boyar of Eridia would stoop to the oppression and murder you take delight in. You're no boyar. You are nothing more than an arrogant despot who has forgotten his place."

River stared at her, stunned. Maybe he imagined it, but the way she spoke, the way she stood, even the fire in her eyes—she looked like a real princess. He didn't remember this being part of the plan, but if he hadn't known better, he would've thought this had been her plan all along. What had convinced her to change her mind?

At that second, he spotted Tak standing behind her, just off to the side, with a bit of a smile on his face. He thought he got the picture now.

"Besides, you cannot be the ruler of these lands," Her Highness lifted her chin—by no more than an inch—and the effect made her look so regal, it snatched River's breath away, "unless you wish to declare yourself in open defiance to me: Redrinna Ioana Vasilica Luminiţa Ardeleanu, Imperial Princess of the Eridian Empire."

Even though River wasn't the one she'd addressed, his mouth went dry. Between the intensity of her gaze, the glowing gem around her neck, and the way the morning sun suddenly rose over the nearest building and the resulting ray of light reignited that illusionary crown of flames around her head, a shiver of near fear rushed down his spine.

That almost made him smile.

Chapter Thirty-One

Redrinna had never been fond of her full name (it was a mouthful), but the chill that swept through the air after she'd declared her full title was almost palpable.

Plus, the fact that it made the boyar look like he'd swallowed a snail made it worth the effort.

However, she couldn't let that distract her. River was in a better position now, but he was still vulnerable. Will helped him to his feet, but his hands were still bound in an awkward way.

If they wanted to corner the boyar, they had to isolate him.

The shock on the boyar's face didn't last long. Instead, he scoffed. "You're no princess."

"Prove otherwise," she replied, keeping her voice as steady as possible. The last thing she needed was to let her voice tremble or betray the fact she was scared enough her hands shook. However, a good portion of the crowd that'd gathered today had come to stand with her, and she wasn't going to let them down. "Regardless of who I am, unless you can prove River has been convicted and sentenced to death in a legal court of law, you are acting in direct opposition to Imperial Law."

She turned her gaze to General Cael, who was already watching her. She confessed she'd been a bit startled when she'd first seen him; he was a lot younger than she'd expected. However, he'd come with

Thala and Indigo, which meant he must be willing to do what she asked.

"General," she began, getting him to raise an expectant eyebrow. "Will you please have your soldiers arrest all the nobles in attendance today? For the time being, each and every one of them is stripped of their title and status. We'll find out later how many of them are truly guilty and how many were forced to be here."

This was met with a cry of outrage from the noble part of the crowd.

Irritation flashed through her. She stepped forward, having to fight with every fiber of her being not to let any of the pain lancing through her ankle show on her face. "Every action you make has a consequence. If you choose to grab the tail of a snake, you are a fool to blame the snake for biting you in return. Not only is your participation here today a sign that you consent to this illegal activity, but there are other laws you've all broken—and I can prove it. If you didn't want to be punished, you shouldn't have dared to point your blades at me."

Ignoring the continued shouts of protest, Redrinna turned to General Cael.

"As you wish, Your Highness," General Cael said, giving her a slight bow. She dipped her head in his direction, and he hopped off the platform and gave orders to his soldiers. Many of the nobles tried to run for it, but there were soldiers lying in wait, hedging their way. When those nobles turned to try and break through the rest of the crowd, the crowd stood together to form a wall, and not a single noble got through.

With the help of Astra and Kelvair, the nobles were subdued in mere moments.

Redrinna was impressed but turned her attention back to the boyar. "You once told me being punished for lawbreaking was nothing more than a tool to make myself feel good, but I want you to remember this for the rest of your life." She motioned to the city that had completely turned on him. "This is the consequence of your law-breaking, and nothing more. It's not a tool to make me feel good about myself. This is what justice looks like."

His expression darkened, and she sensed something shift between them. Something about the smoldering flame in his eyes reminded her a lot of the trial for the leader of the Esunian rebels. Right before he'd burst free of his bonds, something similar had come over him. It was almost like a resolution to do something they hadn't initially planned on doing.

She took a couple steps to the side, putting herself closer to Tak and Xandrin than to Will and River. As she returned her attention to the boyar, she spied shadows curling in a tight wad around his fist. The next second, he flung them at her. Without thinking, she tossed fire at it, and the two collided in midair and put each other out. Tak reached her side a second later, his sword already in his hand.

"I will not bow to the likes of *you*," the boyar said with a sneer. More shadows gathered around his fist, but when he threw them, he didn't throw them at her. He tossed them on the ground.

It took Redrinna a second to realize what he'd done. The shadows pooled out across the stand, rippling as a person appeared in their depths.

She glanced at Will. "Get him out of here."

"You got it, Princess," he said, escorting River off the stand, though River didn't seem pleased about it.

Redrinna turned back to the pool of shadow as it disappeared, leaving a possessed Captain Brion in its place, his shadow swords already in hand.

A second later, Redrinna realized the boyar was running—or trying to. The soldiers hedged him in. The nobles took that as a sign to renew their fight.

Redrinna forced her attention to Captain Brion. She couldn't fight in her current state—she could barely move.

However, to her alarm, Tak stepped forward.

"Wait," she said, catching hold of his arm.

Tak turned his head towards her, but he kept his gaze on Captain Brion. "I'm all right. He caught me off guard before, but not this time." He glanced at her for a second with the hint of a smile. "I won't hurt him. I promise. So trust me, okay?"

Her breath caught in her throat, but she nodded. Even if she couldn't help him in the fight with her own sword, she still had her magic, and she could at least use that if she needed to.

Tak stepped forward.

⚜

Will tried to pull River into the safety of the crowd, but River squirmed until he was out of his friend's grasp.

Holding out his bound hands, River said, "Get this off me. I have to help."

"You're hurt," Will snapped.

River eyed the bandage on Will's arm. "So are you. I have to fight, so help me get out of this. Then I want you to go find Leonora and make sure she's okay."

"Fine." With a scowl, Will studied the mechanism before giving it a few sharp tugs, making it pop open. River all but threw it on the ground before turning around to take in the scene.

The boyar had dragged Her Highness's friend into this, but Tak was already fighting him, and keeping him distracted. For a second, River stared, eyes wide. Despite how young he was, Tak was *good*. Then he shook his head. Tak would be all right on his own.

A second later, River spied the boyar engaging in a vicious brawl with a squad of soldiers. There was a flash of blue and he knew Thala was there.

Until this morning, River had never truly believed the boyar could be beaten, but now, like there was a bonfire in his chest, he realized that the man could very much be crushed. Even if he acted like a monster, he was still human.

River would have a part in taking him down. For the first time in his life, River realized *he* could beat the boyar. And he would.

⁂

As Thala stepped into the boyar's path, a thousand thoughts—a thousand different tactics and attacks—flashed through her mind. But the second the boyar swung those shadow swords at her, her mind went still as stone.

She ducked, thrusting the shaft of her spear into his path, catching him just enough to make him stumble. The force from his swing knocked him even more off-balance. Thala darted to his other side. Almost like her father stood over her shoulder again, calling out the non-lethal move he'd wanted her to learn in place of the lethal one, she flipped her spear, ramming the butt of it into the boyar's ribs instead of the spearhead. It still did damage, but it didn't require her to kill.

As the boyar staggered back, a wave of shadow flared out from his feet. Thala rolled out of its path. The couple of soldiers it managed to hit didn't die, but they collapsed like they had. She made a note not to let herself get touched by that magic.

Gingerly holding a hand to the ribs Thala had more than likely cracked, the boyar glared at her. "I never should have let you live."

Thala said nothing.

More of that weird magic flared around the boyar's hands, and he kept distance between the two of them, not being stupid enough to get close this time. Thala made to the right, and he shied away. So be it.

She lunged to the left, fast enough he should realize he wouldn't be able to dodge. He braced himself, magic flaring a little more. As he swung, Thala raced past and abruptly turned right. As she flashed by, she slammed the butt of the spear into his ribs again, making him stumble.

He swung out a hand, thick shadows clinging to his skin. Before he could attack, there was a sudden flash of metal. River. He punched with his metal arm, the few bits not covered by the sheath catching the sun's rays. He missed the boyar by only an inch.

River's gaze remained fixed on the boyar. Thala glanced at him, only needing a second to understand his state. It was the River she remembered, the River she'd only seen a handful of times before. This was the River who'd been trained as a warrior by his father. This was the River that didn't hold back and was strong enough, he made even Thala a little uneasy.

This was the River the boyar had spent all these years trying to beat out of him.

A doll's strength came from the ability to fight without the fear of getting hurt or dying, but River's strength had always come from something else, something Thala didn't know or understand. Whatever it was, it made him powerful.

Without needing to speak, she and him lunged forward together, the next couple seconds a flurry of blows and dodging. Thala caught the boyar in the ribs, in the same spot as before, twice. River was everywhere, blocking a shot meant for Thala at the same second he swept the boyar's feet out from under him with a powerful kick.

The boyar hit the ground hard, but before Thala could move, the boyar snatched River's ankle and pulled him to the ground. A second later, there was a shadowy knife at River's throat, and the boyar's knee pressed into River's back, keeping him down.

"Not another step," the boyar said, pointing a finger at Thala. "Or else."

She remained where she was, waiting for her chance to strike. Her doll training would've once pushed her to attack anyway; lives didn't matter so long as the objective was completed. However, her dad had trained that out of her. They'd spent long nighttime hours on the desert sands with him fighting to turn Thala human once more.

No matter what, the boyar wouldn't take that part of her ever again.

Tak watched the way Captain Brion swung his swords, the speed and casualness of the flicks a vivid reminder of this man's skill. They'd fought once before, and Tak had lost. He'd been caught off-guard by such a powerful opponent. Redrinna had mentioned that this man had been assigned as her personal knight, and Tak now knew why.

However, if he wanted to subdue the captain, he couldn't focus on those things. He couldn't allow himself to decide the contest was already lost.

The closest Tak had ever come to fighting someone like this was Timothon, the handful of times the man had sparred with him. Timothon was strong, quick, and clever. Tak had only managed to beat him once, and that was only barely.

While Tak didn't want to beat the captain per se, he did need to figure out how to get those swords out of his hands. Even if Redrinna didn't want him to die, they had to stop him. There was a chance the man could just make new swords or whatever they did with those weapons, but it might give them an edge anyway if they could take away his ability to strike, even if only for a few seconds.

Tak tightened his grip on his sword, admiring the way it felt in his hand while simultaneously hoping Will hadn't stolen it. The guy had claimed not to, but he often danced on a fine line between lies and truth.

Then Captain Brion charged. Tak braced, angling himself to prepare for both swords. The captain didn't use them separately—he worked them together to create a constant, unending barrage of attacks.

The captain swung at his back first. Tak parried that, using the bounce to parry the other sword that came a couple seconds after the first. Then he blocked the attack from above and ducked the side sweep. He parried four attacks in a row before hopping back to avoid the next side sweep. The captain moved so fast, Tak barely had time to think.

A flash of fire burst past Tak, making the captain sidestep. Tak lunged. He struck one of the captain's shadowy swords hard enough to make the captain's arm swing back, leaving the other sword open. Tak struck, their blades hissing as they slid against each other, the crossguards catching. This was how the captain had disarmed him before. Not wasting a second, Tak jerked the sword out of the captain's hand and then ducked and rolled to the side, avoiding the other sword by only an inch.

The other sword, the one Tak had yanked free, struck the ground once with a dull clatter before winking out of existence.

Even still, the captain switched to a different stance, one more suited to fighting with one sword, in the blink of an eye. With the strength of both arms behind his swings, every impact jarred Tak's wrists, but Tak persisted with the stubbornness of a mule, blocking the strokes he could and avoiding the ones he couldn't. He took advantage of Redrinna's well-timed blasts of fire to strike, but the captain parried him just as well with one sword as he had with two.

After a couple minutes, Tak leapt back to give himself a second to catch his breath. Redrinna and her magic ensured he got a couple seconds.

Then the captain came whirling back, moving so fast Tak could barely keep up. Even still, he seemed to sense what the next move would be in just enough time to either avoid it or combat it.

The captain swung hard, their blades slamming together with hand numbing force before the swords hissed, sliding past each other until the crossguards caught. Tak angled his sword to prevent the captain from jerking it out of his hands. The captain tugged anyway, and Tak's stubbornness meant he was dragged forward until they stood chest to chest, swords precariously close to both their necks.

Tak was a little startled by the fact he and the captain were close in heights, with the captain only a few inches taller. All at once, when he met the man's gaze, he caught a glimpse of what Redrinna had insisted she'd seen—there was a human somewhere in there still.

As Tak strained to keep a firm hold on his sword, he hissed, "Redrinna says you're her friend, so what are you doing?"

There it was again—that human flicker.

Tak didn't hesitate; he didn't stop to consider whether this sudden flash of inspiration was his idea or the gem's. Instead, he shoved hard, with all his strength, making the captain stagger back. He took two running steps before jumping and kicking like a move Redrinna had been practicing, slamming his foot into the center of the captain's chest. The man hit the ground, the sword in his hand flying away and disappearing in an instant, just like the first had.

Tak landed next to him and dropped his sword so the tip was at the man's neck. To his relief, the man didn't move.

His breath came in fast, almost desperate gasps, but Tak didn't care. He'd won this time. He wasn't as impressive as the rest of the Dragon Kin, but at least he'd been able to do something.

Redrinna was there a second later. "Is he all right?"

"I think so," Tak said.

She grinned, making his heart lift a little. "Tak, you're amazing, you know that?"

Despite the situation, he blushed. "Not as amazing as you. If you hadn't helped me, I'm not sure I would've made it."

She laughed a little. "On the contrary, there were a couple times I thought I'd gotten in the way. Besides, you're a lot stronger than I think you realize, Tak."

All Tak could do was stare for a second, his mind going a bit fuzzy. He'd never considered himself all that strong; of all the other Dragon Kin members, he paled in comparison. Even still, when Redrinna told him he was impressive, a part of him seemed able to believe her.

Chapter Thirty-Two

River allowed himself to relax a little, his cheek resting against the cobblestone that was just starting to warm. His head throbbed, and the boyar's knee digging into his spine accentuated the pain. Thala kept her distance, but River could tell she was ready to fight the instant she got an opportunity. The soldiers nearby also looked prepared, though they had a more apprehensive air about them.

Even still, the days of training under the shadow of trees with his father whirled through his mind. His father had trained him for situations like this—now River just had to execute with care to avoid the knife. He'd once promised himself to never use his father's teachings—they were supposed to be used to fulfill their family's legacy. However, as those teachings pounded through his mind, he realized that had been a stupid promise.

"Now," the boyar panted, his hot, rank breath cutting across River's face, "with that demon distracted, I can finally finish you and redeem Leon."

River pulled his arms in, situating them right next to his sides. When the boyar drew back the knife, River used the shift in the man's balance to lift himself a hair's breadth above the ground. Then, when the boyar's balance was the most unsteady, River rolled, pitching himself towards the boyar's stabilizing leg.

The boyar flew off his back and landed on the cobblestone hard. River landed on top of him, knee right to the chest, a second later. The boyar let out a funny wheeze as the air was knocked out of him. Then, in a whirl of shadow, he vanished.

River dropped to the ground, hitting his knee hard enough he winced. He popped to his feet, scanning the crowd. The nobles still struggled for escape, but the dragons, the soldiers, and the crowd seemed to have it in control. The boyar didn't appear among them.

Thala was at his side, her gaze scanning the city around them. "Where'd he go?"

"I don't know," he said.

⁕ ⁕ ⁕

Even though it pained Redrinna to see Captain Brion down with a sword being held to his neck by Tak, she stared at him for a moment, searching his eyes for a trace of the man she'd once known.

"Captain," she began, impervious to the roar of the battle to subdue the nobles, "enough of this."

His appearance remained unchanged, though his gaze was fixed on her face. Slowly, he worked himself to his feet, and Tak—after a glance at Redrinna—let him do so. The captain's hand stretched for her in a threatening way.

"Don't," she said, voice low but stern. That was what her father would have done; in truth, emulating him had been more of a reflex than an intention.

His hand stopped, but the muscles in his arms strained as he fought to keep it from going forward.

"This isn't you," she said, meeting his darkened gaze.

The shadows over his eyes flickered like a candle on the verge of going out, but they didn't go away. Instead, he continued to strain to keep his hand from stretching any further, almost like it would grab her if he let it.

Her heart sank a little.

His hand inched forward, making her heart thrum in panic.

"Captain, I know you're still in there. Don't give in, please."

The shadows flickered again, a little stronger than last time, but they still remained.

Without a thought, Redrinna limped closer and took hold of his calloused hand, holding it with both of her own. Instantly, his hand relaxed, like all the fight had gone out of it.

"I'm so sorry, Captain. I don't know what you've been through, and I don't know what's happened to you since we parted, but I want to help you. I missed you. Every day."

She forced herself to meet his eyes again. The shadows still flickered, but the darkness and the distance remained. Her vision blurred. Without hesitation, Redrinna released his hand, stepping past it and hugging him around the middle.

When she'd been at the palace, she'd only been bold enough to do this a handful of times, but Captain Brion had never complained. On the contrary, he'd always comforted her. In that way, he'd almost seemed like a second father.

"I don't want to lose you again," she managed to say. "Please, come back."

She closed her eyes, her grip tightening.

There were a few moments that passed like quiet heartbeats, and then, without warning, one of his big hands gently touched the back of her head.

Surprised, she looked up.

Captain Brion stared down at her with bright, unclouded green eyes, and as their gazes met, one of his rare smiles turned the corners of his mouth upwards. He brushed her long bangs out of her eyes as Tak moved his sword away.

"Is it really you, Your Highness?" Captain Brion croaked, almost like he hadn't used his voice in a long time.

Her throat clenched against the rush of tears, leaving her unable to speak. Instead, she hugged him even tighter.

For a second, he remained frozen. Then, with surprising gentleness, he hugged her back, holding her tight like her dad used to, and if she let herself pretend, it was like she was safe in her dad's arms all over again.

"I thought you were gone forever," he whispered.

Redrinna allowed herself another moment. He was here. Captain Brion was alive, and he was here again. It was something she'd always imagined would happen but had never allowed herself to dream was possible. Yet, here it was. Here he was, and he was real.

Redrinna stepped back. "I'm not gone, but we are a little busy. We'll catch up later."

Captain Brion glanced around, taking in the chaos. "Ah."

Redrinna glanced as well. The soldiers were escorting the nobles away, most of them clad in some kind of handcuff. The crowd and the dragons had helped subdue them, and, to her delight, it didn't seem like anyone had been killed, though she did spy some injuries.

After admiring all their handiwork, she carefully hopped off the stand now that the square was emptier. Fortunately, things seemed to be wrapping up well—maybe coming as a princess had been a good thing after all.

All at once, River shouted, "Your Highness, watch out!"

Redrinna turned. The boyar raced straight for her with Thala dashing after him. Shadows flared off him like he was cloaked in black fire. With a snarl, he slammed a massive wave of shadow right for her. Tak and the captain would get hit with her, as would the townsfolk and the dragons.

Without hesitation, Redrinna leapt forward. Her ankle burned, but she ignored it. Earth would've made a better shield, but the fire sprang to her hands so much quicker. It flared to life in front of her like a flower bursting open and made a massive, crackling shield. She pushed as much life into it as she could, the heat searing as it roared past her.

The shadows struck hard, pushing her back and nearly making

her ankle give out. She bit her lip but hung on as the boyar pushed harder against her shield.

It slid her back another couple inches. The pain she'd been fighting to hide was on her face; she knew it.

The next second, Tak was behind her and he braced against her back with his own. He held her fast, digging his heels in and keeping her from being pushed any further. She took some of the weight off her injured ankle, making it easier to concentrate on her fire. Now that she didn't have to worry about having to fight the pain, she could put more of her strength into pushing against the boyar.

Through the roaring fan of flames and shadows, she spied the boyar—his magic keeping Thala at bay—glaring with concentration. If she could just knock him off balance...

Redrinna wasn't sure it would work, but she focused on the cobblestones beneath her feet and between her and the boyar. Like she possessed a hundred extra hands, she twisted the cobblestones. They shifted in quick succession with a series of little cracks, moving like a line of cards knocking each other down until, at last, the cobblestones beneath the boyar's feet jerked violently. His foot twisted and he stumbled, the shadows disappearing. Redrinna drew most of her fire shield back with her arm before punching forward. The fire launched at him in a stream, almost like a spear, slamming into his chest.

She kept the flames from setting him on fire, but the force of the blow was enough to knock the boyar flat on his back.

Tak stepped out from behind her.

"Thanks, Tak," she said quickly.

He nodded, his gaze on the boyar.

The man sat up, and for the first time, Redrinna spied a small pendant around his neck. He must've been keeping it under his clothes because there was no way it would've escaped her notice. It was a red stone, except when the man used his magic to keep his attackers at bay, it *glowed*.

Her eyes narrowed, but as the man got to his feet, Thala swung at him, making him turn to avoid her. General Cael appeared as well, his gaze so steely it made a shiver race down her spine. River came too, something about him different than it'd been before.

Surrounded by the three of them, the boyar summoned his shadows with a growl. However, as he did, the pendant flared with more light in response.

"River," she called.

River's head swiveled her way though his gaze remained focused on the boyar.

"The boyar has a pendant, and I think it's the source of his magic. If not, it's helping. Get it!"

River glanced her way, wearing the closest thing she'd ever seen to a smile from him. He nodded before turning his attention back to the boyar. With an unnerving and almost unnatural amount of speed and agility, River attacked. He rushed in, zipped past the boyar's attempt at an attack like the boyar held still, and, with his metal fist and a quick twist of his body, punched the man across the face. It was hard enough Redrinna almost flinched. The boyar staggered before falling on one knee. River grabbed the pendant and jerked it off.

The boyar, in a panicky, jerky motion, hit River's hand, making the pendant break out and skitter across the cobblestones. The boyar bolted after it. Redrinna's heart lurched, but before she could say a word, Tak raced forward.

Right as the boyar dove for the pendant—arms outstretched—Tak reached it. He stomped his foot down seconds before the boyar could snatch it. With a fire-fueled glare, he grabbed Tak's ankle like he was determined to snap it. A second later, General Cael's blade glittered against his throat, making the man tense.

"I think that's enough," the man hissed, a clear threat in his voice.

Redrinna steeled herself before she limped forward, unable to hide the pain as the stinging in her ankle intensified to the point she could barely put any weight on it again. Even still, she didn't stop until she stood in front of the boyar.

"Boyar," she said, meeting his gaze and refusing to look away, no matter how dark his glare became. "Taking your crimes today alone into consideration, and the crimes you've committed until now, you are henceforth stripped of your title and position."

A glare twisted the man's face, but Redrinna ignored it.

"You are charged with the abduction and abuse of your own grandchildren, murder, slave dealing and ownership, multiple counts of abduction, and for assaulting me. So long as I get my say, you are going to spend the rest of your days in the deepest pit I can find."

"I can help with that," General Cael said, his expression brightening. "There's a wonderful cell that's had his name on it for a very, very long time."

"Thank you, General. I leave him to you."

With a wicked grin, the general hauled the boyar to his feet and chained his hands together. With assistance from a couple of his soldiers, General Cael escorted him from the square. The townsfolk behind her raised a massive cheer.

The next second, Kyvo bounded onto her shoulders, nearly knocking her off balance. "That was so cool!"

She smiled a little. "Thanks, but where were you?"

"I can't help with fighting without getting hurt, so I kept Leonora company."

Redrinna glanced to the side as Leonora stepped out of the crowd with Will hot on her heels, big smiles on both their faces. Then Redrinna looked at all of her friends. Everyone seemed pretty tired, but even still, they'd saved River and wrestled the city from the boyar's hands.

In truth, she was surprised everything had worked out, but even still, it felt good. Granted, this was just the beginning of a massive list of things that would need to be changed to get this place back on its feet, but even still, Redrinna couldn't help the little fire dancing in her chest. For one of the first times in her life, maybe being a princess had been the right thing to do.

She remembered the boyar's pendant and turned to Tak. "Where's the pendant?"

Tak lifted his foot. The small red stone gleamed against the cobblestone, almost looking demure. However, before any of them could touch it, its red sheen dimmed, turning to an ashy gray. Then it crumbled into dust and blew away in the wind.

"Weird," Will said.

Redrinna frowned. "Yes, but the boyar couldn't seem to use magic once we snatched the pendant away, which means that shadow magic was most likely coming from it."

"Do you think Reyna and all of those guys have a pendant like this one?" Astra asked as she came over, her frills lowered again.

"I don't think so," Redrinna said. "River said that Tehl said that Osiris had given the boyar his power. Maybe the pendant was just a physical embodiment of it or something like that."

"Yeah, if he really was like Reyna and them, I don't think we would've been able to take care of him that fast," Xandrin said.

Redrinna nodded. Then she glanced around, her mind already whirling at how much they would have to do.

"Your Highness," Leonora said, stepping forward. "You should rest."

"But—"

"No buts. It's going to take a bit for the army to get things sorted, so you can rest while you wait."

Redrinna's gaze flicked to the townsfolk. "But the—"

"Don't worry about them. I can explain," Leonora said. "They know me well enough. But you've had a miserable night."

Redrinna studied the setness of Leonora's jaw before she relented.

"River, take her to the mansion. With the boyar gone, it's technically ours now."

River grimaced. "At least you can sleep in decent beds there."

Before Redrinna allowed River to lead her away, she turned to the townsfolk. Because they'd fought against the nobles to prevent them from escaping, some of them nursed wounds. Even still, they seemed all right.

Beyond that, she was still in shock so many of them had come.

Bowing in their direction, she said, "Thank you all for your help. I'll never forget it."

To her surprise, they let out a massive cheer, loud enough it startled a few birds off the nearby buildings, and bowed back to her. Stunned, she stared until Tak gently grabbed her wrist, reminding her of what she was supposed to be doing.

Relenting, she followed River and Tak with Thala and the dragons trailing after, Kyvo still perched on her shoulders.

Redrinna fell in line with Tak.

"Hey," he began, his voice quiet like he didn't want the others to overhear, "I just... What you did, just now? That was amazing."

She almost smiled, but it felt like a grimace too. "Thanks, I think." She held up a hand so he could see how hard it shook. "That was one of the scariest things I've ever done."

"But you did it, and you were incredible." He smiled—a smile that lit up his entire face—as he met her gaze. Something about it warmed her through, but perhaps that was because Tak didn't smile like that often, so when he did, it was special.

"Though, you know," she began, absentmindedly tugging on the end of Kyvo's fluffy tail, "you asked me to be a princess for only today, but you do realize it's going to take a lot longer than that to get this place sorted, right?"

"It is?" His eyes became round as the moon, making Redrinna laugh.

"That said..." She glanced back over her shoulder. "I still can't believe so many people came to help." After a moment, she cast a hesitant glance Tak's way. "But since they did, I think...I'm okay with having to be a princess for longer than just today."

He smiled at that.

"So, we're going to end up being here for a while, just for however long it takes to get this situation cleaned up enough for General Cael to keep the city under control." She hoped that wouldn't take long, but she was sure it would take at least a few days.

Even still, she wasn't going to leave the city in this state. That was asking for even worse trouble to sweep in and fill the gaping hole left behind by the removal of the top officials. So long as she remained in Póli, that hole would be filled, but once she left, the vacancy would cause issues. While she was sure General Cael could do fine, she wanted to leave the city as close to repaired as possible. That meant finding a new boyar.

She would worry about that later, though, and focus on one crisis at a time.

As they arrived at the massive mansion River had been held in earlier just that morning, Redrinna paused and glanced back over the city. It was pretty derelict, but with the shimmering blue of the ocean surrounding it, she could almost see its real beauty, the beauty the boyar had thoughtlessly or purposefully destroyed. Perhaps there was a chance she'd be able to see it at its true potential and understand why, in the history books, it'd often been compared to a pearl.

All at once, her gaze flicked to the mountains, where somewhere in their depths lay the statue of the forgotten goddess. Redrinna didn't know what the power of a god looked like, so she couldn't say for sure whether anyone had heard her plea. However, things had ended well— better than she'd dared to believe they would.

So, quietly, she smiled and whispered, "Thank you."

Chapter Thirty-Three

River leaned against the smooth stone of his balcony, more than a little surprised how much brighter the mansion seemed even though it hadn't yet been a full day since its most odious patronage had been plucked from it. The world itself seemed brighter, though he knew that wasn't possible. Even still, the world was more alive than it'd been for years.

The boyar, his horrible grandfather, was in jail for all the crimes Her Highness had accused him of and more. General Cael had made short work of the noble houses as well, with a significant number of them remaining behind bars. It was crazy to believe that in such a short space of time—not even a day—the city had already changed so much.

Granted, he was certain that was more due to the force of the person behind those changes than anything else.

He almost managed to smile when he remembered yesterday morning. He'd believed Her Highness would rescue him, and she had. She'd come specifically to save him. After so many years of not even daring to beg for table scraps and living from one beating to the next, that was the most surreal part of this.

Leonora arrived, leaning against the railing next to him. "It's kind of crazy, isn't it?"

He nodded, studying the ocean and the sunlight reflecting off its blue waters like light off a gemstone.

"River, we're finally free," she breathed, stretching out a hand like she would grab the sun right out of the sky. "We can do what we want. Go where we want. Be who we want. It's like it's a dream."

Closing his eyes, River relaxed as a refreshing breeze blew over the balcony. It'd been so long since he'd been free that he didn't know what to do. A nagging part of his brain suggested joining the Dragon Kin, but he wasn't sure. Things had turned out well, but it hadn't been because of him; on the contrary, he'd been rescued. Besides, regardless of anything that had taken place here, none of that changed his past mistakes, so he was, in reality, no more qualified for the job than he had been before.

Even still, a strange fire burned inside him, one that made him want to find his way out of the gutter he'd settled in many years ago. Before, that had been unthinkable. Now, almost out of the blue, he could imagine a life without the weight of his burden. He could simply imagine a life.

"Is Her Highness still asleep?" he asked, opening his eyes as he turned to his sister.

She smiled. "Dead to the world. Also, why is she on the floor in my room?"

"Yours was the easiest to get to, and by the time we got here, she was about to fall asleep on her feet. She refused to take your bed, even though I tried to convince her it'd be okay if she at least slept at the foot of it, but she would not be persuaded. Therefore, she's on the floor."

Leonora laughed, a sound he hadn't heard in years. "For a princess, she's pretty strange, huh?"

"Or perhaps we're just used to rubbing elbows with the wrong parts of high society," he suggested.

"Perhaps. Or maybe she's the black sheep of the bunch. Granted, I think her life growing up was only a little better than ours."

He frowned. That might've had something to do with it, but

given her personality, he couldn't help wondering if this was who Her Highness would've been regardless of how her life had played out. Maybe this deep, thoughtful compassion was just a part of who she was.

"So, what do we do now?" Leonora asked, almost as if to herself.

River stared over the town down to the ocean again. That was the question he'd asked himself several times. He had freedom; it seemed like a great, impassable door had finally opened and his entire life lay right at his feet. So what did he do with it?

"Are you going to join the Dragon Kin?"

He glanced at her in surprise.

A slight smile touched her mouth. "Don't give me that face. I know you've had that dream they talked about too."

His gaze flicked away. "I thought about it but..."

"They need you," she whispered. "A lot more than they would need someone like me."

That made him stare.

"Don't make that face," she said, a complicated emotion flickering in her eyes. Then she looked away. "The gem keeps calling to me, and I...I should tell it no. But I can't seem to do it, you know?"

River lowered his gaze. He hadn't even considered saying no; he wanted to believe the gem wanted him. He wanted to believe he might even be needed somewhere. Was that selfish?

Leonora tapped her fingers on the railing and straightened. "Oh well, I guess. Anyway, I've sat here long enough, and there are a thousand things to do. See you."

"Yeah," he replied as she turned and left the room.

His sister wasn't going to admit it out loud, but he was pretty sure he knew why she wanted to tell that gem no. After all, she'd been the one who'd found him after he'd made his idiot mistake. She'd found him bleeding and missing an arm, and it'd been during her struggles afterwards to save him and help him recuperate that the boyar had found them. River had been powerless then, and Leonora had been powerless to keep them out of the boyar's hands.

She blamed herself, but River was really the one who was to blame.

He sighed. When his thoughts went there, it was impossible for him to imagine the gem could truly want him.

⁘

Groggy, Redrinna pushed herself up into a sitting position, rubbing the sleep from her eyes. For a long moment, she stared in alarm at the extravagant opulence around her, baffled as to where she was. Then, the events from the last time she'd been awake replayed through her mind, and she managed to piece things together.

They'd removed the boyar from power. Her friends, and Póli itself, were finally free. For now, they needed to focus on helping Póli get back on its feet. Redrinna wasn't sure how long she'd been asleep, but considering no one had come to wake her up, she supposed things were going okay without her so far.

Now that she wasn't dead-tired, she was able to take in the mansion around her. It was...garish. That was the only word that came to her mind. The floors and walls were made of polished white marble with streaks of gray ribboning through it. Gold leafing seemed to cover every surface, regardless of whether or not it was reasonable, and everything else was draped in lush purple velvet. Not even the Imperial Palace boasted this level of obscene finery. If she was honest, this place kind of hurt her eyes.

It was little wonder why River and Leonora had seemed so content to live out on the mountainside.

Redrinna turned away from it, choosing instead to focus on the one thing that didn't seem determined to stab her eyes out: the massive window. Sunlight streamed through it, and if she ignored the rest of the room, it was beautiful.

That aside, Redrinna had one, very important question: how long had she slept this time?

She shifted, making pain shoot through her ankle. Grimacing, she pulled the thin blanket covering her aside and examined her wound. Because of how tired she'd been, she hadn't given a thought as to whether or not it was a good idea to take off her boots. Her ankle had been swollen before, but since she'd thoughtlessly removed her boots, it'd doubled in size, a nasty, garish bruise darkening her skin. Between the manacle and the fight in the city afterwards, it'd been battered.

She wasn't going to be able to walk on it now, at least not until she was able to get the swelling to go back down. Closing her eyes, she did her best to remember anything from one of the many medical books she'd once studied. Ice was the first and most persistent thing in her mind, but she didn't have any of that here; it was far too hot. She wasn't Timothon either, who always managed to scrounge up whatever they needed when they needed it—regardless of logic, it seemed.

While she thought, the door of the room opened. Opening her eyes, it took Redrinna a second to recognize the slave woman who'd helped her and Tak when they'd broken into the house the other day peeking in. She appeared even more haggard in this light.

Wary, Redrinna nodded in her direction. "Hello again."

"So you do remember me," the woman said, entering the room and setting one hand on her hip. Unlike the other day when she'd been sitting in a dark, windowless room, there was a faint glow coming from the woman's skin.

At that moment, Redrinna recalled reading somewhere that while the Hikarijin tribe could emit light, it was an ability they only had if they were able to spend time in the sun.

"I didn't take what you said seriously the other day, but I didn't realize you were the Imperial Princess."

Redrinna wasn't sure how to respond. "That's okay. I'm just grateful for your help that day."

"We all like River—he's a good kid. But no one could stand that horrible old man." The woman shook her head. "So, what are you doing on the floor?"

"I can't take someone else's bed." Sleeping in someone else's bed without their permission was weird. To Redrinna, it came off as abusing rank.

The woman laughed, a deep warm sound that made Redrinna smile. Her gaze dropped to Redrinna's ankle, and the mirth faded from the woman's face. "That's a nasty one. The boyar do that?"

Redrinna nodded. "I'm fine though. I don't think it's as serious as it looks."

"Oh yeah? You realize you slept through the rest of yesterday and all of last night without stirring even once?"

Wow. She must've been way more tired than she'd thought.

"Anyway, since you're awake, I'll let that green-haired boy in. He's been waiting for a while."

A little smile touched Redrinna's face. Tak was by far the most patient person she'd ever met.

As the woman turned to leave, Redrinna called, "Wait. Please."

The woman glanced back.

"If...if it doesn't bug you, would you tell me your name? Please?"

The woman regarded her for a long minute before she said, "Nadeja." Then she left.

Before the door could shut, Kyvo dashed in, followed by Tak. Redrinna grinned at the two of them.

Kyvo leapt into her arms. "I was worried about you, but you're okay!" His tail wagged a hundred miles per hour, almost swatting her in the face. "And everybody else is okay too! The city is already lots better."

She laughed before looking at Tak. "Really?"

He nodded as he knelt next to her. "Yep. Everything is going well so far."

Relief blossomed in her chest, almost overwhelming in its intensity.

"So, can I take care of your ankle now?" he continued as he eyed it.

Kyvo squirmed so he could see it. "Oh, that doesn't look good."

"It only hurts a little."

Tak touched it with his fingertips, making her hiss in pain. He met her gaze and raised an eyebrow.

"Until you touched it, it only hurt a little."

That seemed to make him smile. "You'll just have to hang tight."

For some reason, all at once, it occurred to Redrinna when it was just her and him, or them and Kyvo, Tak didn't stutter around her much anymore. That made a tiny smile touch her mouth.

"What?" Tak asked, staring at her.

"Nothing," she said. Taking a deep breath, she braced herself for the inevitable pain. "Okay, I'm ready."

Tak tugged the hem of her pants up a little, exposing her swollen and bruised ankle entirely. Dried blood lay crusted in a jagged circle where the manacle had bitten deep. No wonder it ached as much as it did.

"Ready?" Tak asked, shooting a concerned look her way.

She nodded. She was as ready as she'd ever be.

As he placed a warm hand over it, a zing raced over her skin. His dark eyebrows lowered slightly as white light emanated from his palm, the resulting rush of warmth startling her. In a way, it reminded her of the gem and the moment when the spirit had given her that strange mark.

She grimaced at the initial rush, but then she happened to look up, her gaze settling on Tak's face, particularly his eyes. They were lowered, focused on her injury, but even still, she was close enough to spy lighter flecks of almost spring grass green sprinkled amongst the predominant dark forest green. His lashes were a bit long and dark like his hair. She couldn't tell if they were green or black, but they framed his eyes in a way that was extraordinary.

All at once, he looked up, the light streaming through the large balcony window catching on the green and making them shine. His eyes almost seemed to contain an entire forest with sunbeams trickling through the dark branches. As she studied them, the entire world slowed, and the only two people alive were him and her.

The sight of his eyes lit up like that took Redrinna's breath away. In truth, she didn't think she'd ever encountered something more striking or beautiful than his eyes. Somewhere in her mind, it occurred to her she was staring, but for some reason, she couldn't seem to look away.

Neither could he, it seemed. Normally, he would look down or something whenever they spoke; it was what he'd used to do. However, for that moment, he held her gaze, a gentleness softening his expression in a way that made her heart skip a beat. His cheeks reddened a little. Hers did the same.

Abruptly, Tak glanced to the side, shattering the spell and making the world come rushing back into her awareness. "W-what do you think?"

For a second, she didn't know what he was talking about, but then it clicked. Her ankle. Right! That was what they'd been doing.

She studied it, experimentally flexing and pointing her foot. The swelling had been reduced and the cut was gone. There was some slight pain as she moved it—and there was some swelling still—but she was sure she'd be able to walk.

"I-it's a lot better. Thank you."

A blush still clung to Tak's cheeks. "Y-you're welcome."

Doing her utmost to keep from staring at him again, Redrinna stared at her hands. Tak's magic had reminded her of the mark that was there, nestled in her palm. She wasn't wearing her gauntlets (they were uncomfortable to sleep in), so it was easy to see. Since she'd gotten it, she hadn't told anyone about it, and while she and Tak hadn't promised to tell each other everything and anything back in the forest...all at once, she wanted to tell him about this.

"Tak?"

He raised an eyebrow.

"There's something I didn't tell you, back in the forest. I haven't told anybody yet, actually. I-I wasn't trying to hide it or anything, but I just...didn't know what to do about it."

That made him and Kyvo cock their heads in sync.

"While we were there, I met a spirit."

"Like the one that guards the gems?"

"Kind of like that one, yes, but this one was like a guardian of the tribe. After we killed the demon, it came and gave me this." She held out her bare palm, the sun-shaped mark there standing out as clear as day.

Kyvo and Tak both studied it, neither of them speaking. Kyvo sniffed it a couple times before licking it. He cocked his head at it.

"The spirit said it was a gift."

"A gift?" Tak asked, lifting his gaze from it to her.

"Yes, but it didn't tell me what it was or how to use it or anything. So I don't know what it is." She lowered her gaze a bit. "I just...wanted you to know about it."

"Well, if it was a gift from a spirit, it's most likely something good, right? That's kind of who spirits are. However, knowing you, I'm sure you'll figure it out soon." He grinned.

That almost made her embarrassed for not telling anyone sooner, but she didn't know what to make of the spirit's gift still. So far, it hadn't done anything. It was just there.

Maybe we can find something about it in the books at the Mount, her gem suggested.

"Or, we might be able to find something about that weird pendant the boyar had," Redrinna said. Then she had to explain what her gem had said to Tak and Kyvo so they'd stop giving her weird looks.

"If we could figure that thing out," Kyvo said, ears perking up, "do you think we could figure out how to stop their weird magic?"

"Maybe," Tak said. "Depending on how it works, it's always possible."

She nodded, thinking on that. Osiris's magic was a serious problem, but if they could figure out some way to counteract it, that could go a long way towards helping them win.

"Oh, I just remembered," Kyvo began, staring up at her. "Everybody's waiting for you. They're saying they've done almost all they can without you."

With a groan, Redrinna flopped back onto her makeshift bed.

Tak grimaced, but there was a hint of a laugh in his voice as he said, "I'm sorry. I guess asking you to be a princess for a day has backfired spectacularly."

She smiled a little. "It's okay. After yesterday, this feels like nothing." She pushed herself back upright. "Tell everybody I'll be out in a little bit."

He got to his feet. "Come on, Kyvo."

"Don't take long, okay?" Kyvo chirped before padding after Tak. As they left, her gaze lingered on Tak until he shut the door. Her thoughts lingered on him too, which was kind of strange. However, as the image of him leaving the room flashed through her mind again, she paused in the middle of rising. She frowned again. She was pretty sure it hadn't...right? His shoulders hadn't always been as broad as they were now...right?

⚬⊶⊷⚬

Tak's breath rushed out of him once he'd left Redrinna's room, his chest still tight. Once again, even though it'd only happened a few minutes ago, his mind replayed the moment when he'd finished healing Redrinna's ankle and looked up to find her gaze on him. Her eyes had been absolutely striking in the sunlight, the many different shades of red seeming to glow like hot embers.

For the second time in a few days, he found himself thinking about how beautiful Redrinna was, except this time, she hadn't been smiling. It was just...*she* was beautiful, no matter what she did.

Thinking about her made his heart stutter. What was this? His face was hot like he was embarrassed, his stomach in fluttery knots; maybe he was getting sick?

"Come on, Tak," Kyvo chirped from down the gaudy hallway, bouncing on his toes.

"C-coming," Tak managed, trying to push all those thoughts about Redrinna out of his mind. Even still, thoughts of her kept coming back, and Tak was bewildered as to why.

Chapter Thirty-Four

Thala had been lost for many years, but handing in her resignation to Captain Andor was one of the first things she'd done that felt right. She didn't know what she wanted to do with her life, but she knew one thing she didn't want to do.

When the captain took her paper, he'd studied it for several minutes before he looked up. "So, this was all a ruse so you could gather information for Her Highness? The general told the truth?"

She nodded. With the reason brought to light, she hoped he would understand why she wanted to leave.

To her surprise, he smiled. "Thank goodness. You have no idea how much I agonized over the idea of you being in the army again. I'm glad you weren't that lost."

She was as well.

"Well, I'll get this submitted promptly, and you can quit service today."

"Today?" Much faster than she'd expected.

"That was what General Cael said." He set her paper on top of the stack on his desk. "Given everything that's happened, it seems better to let you go without any of that pomp and circumstance, don't you think? Besides, I'm sure you have other things you'd rather be doing."

Thala stared. Other things?

"You've been spending all of your free time with Her Highness and her crew," Captain Andor said, implying something with his tone.

She frowned. "Well...she did ask me to join the Dragon Kin with her."

One of his eyebrows shot up in response.

"It's because of this." She tugged on the end of her braid. "It's a sign I was marked to join, and the gem chose me."

It'd sent her another dream last night. The dream always puzzled her, but last night, for some reason, when she'd woken up, she'd buzzed with something almost like excitement. It'd been so long since she'd felt that, she'd forgotten what it was like. However, ever since the Dragon Kin had landed in her life, Thala had begun to feel things again, and she didn't want to lose that. It might not be a great reason, but she couldn't help wondering if she went with them maybe she'd find her human self again.

"So...I've been thinking about it."

"From what I hear, it means more fighting."

That was true... "But it's for a much better reason than last time."

"And, I suppose, from what I've heard about the situation, that if the Dragon Kin wants you, they couldn't have made a better choice."

Blinking, Thala stared at him.

A hint of a smile tugged on his mouth as he rose, stepped around his desk and approached her. He thunked a fist lightly on her head, and despite herself she ducked her head a little. "Kid, I hate the reason why, but you're a good fighter. And you're strong. If a war of mythical proportions is coming, someone like you is a perfect choice."

That made her smile a little. "Thanks, Captain."

"None of that. I'm not your captain anymore." He made a shooing motion towards the door. "Now scat."

She did, and to her surprise, Indigo waited outside.

With wide eyes, he said, "So it's true you're leaving already?"

"I only came to help Her Highness," she said.

He sighed. "Aww, but I finally had someone the same age as me!

Plus, you made patrols so easy because everyone was freaked out about the Azure Demon."

Thala seemed to remember him having the same response to her at first, so she just stared at him.

"But," he continued, almost sounding like he was pouting, "you're going to help Her Highness, aren't you?"

Thala nodded.

"I guess that's fine too," he said with a bit of a smile.

Thala settled for just staring at him again.

"Well, have fun, I guess," he said, rising from his seat on the front desk. "We'll keep Póli standing once you leave."

"Sure," Thala said, trying to decide if he was saying goodbye even though the Dragon Kin wasn't leaving yet. When he said nothing else, she turned to leave the garrison, her shoulders a bit lighter than they'd been for a while.

"Hey, Thala!" Indigo called, making her turn. He stared at her for a second before he waved.

A hint of a smile touching her mouth, Thala waved back.

Then she went to find Her Highness, who was in the sun parlor of the boyar's mansion, mountains of paper surrounding her and the others.

Thala eased past the precarious piles and approached her.

Her Highness glanced up. "Hey, Thala."

"I'll do it," Thala said, almost cutting Her Highness off.

Brow furrowing, Her Highness stared at her. "Do what?"

"I'll join the Dragon Kin. The gem asked me to, so I'll do it."

"Are you sure?"

She nodded. It'd been a long time since she'd been this sure of anything.

The barest hint of a smile touched Her Highness's mouth. "All right. Welcome."

Despite what it would mean, Thala couldn't help the hint of a smile that touched her mouth.

Even with everyone pitching in to help Her Highness in some way, it was nearly three weeks before Póli started feeling like a real city again. River helped where he could, finding himself just as busy as the rest of them as a result.

Once they'd managed to sift all the corrupt and twisted nobles out from the meager few decent ones, they uncovered the matter of the lately arrested nobles having ripped power away from Adonis and his crew before stealing their lands and homes after the Imperial Family had cleaned things up before. Her Highness had seemed hesitant about what to do until Will had told her about the part Adonis and his crew played the day of River's attempted execution and what they'd been doing behind the scenes before then. To River's surprise, Her Highness immediately went and found them.

Adonis, more stern and serious than River had ever seen him, had been prompt to rise from his chair the second she'd walked into their hideout. Even still, regarded Her Highness with a searching gaze.

She eyed him too. "So, you were one of the nobles before the boyar took over the city?"

River understood her skepticism. Adonis and his crew may have been nobles once, but their rough, street-worthy appearance screamed otherwise. They'd been scraping by like everyone else for a long time.

However, Adonis tugged out a collection of worn but cared for certificates that showed proof of their status and land ownership. "I don't look it, but I am. I apologize for my appearance, but this is what a few years on the streets does to you."

"I know how that feels," she said with a hint of a smile. "How did the boyar and his crew take everything from you again?"

"We," Adonis motioned towards the abashed looking men behind him, "went to fulfill our duties as nobles by joining the Esunian War. We remained there until it was well and truly finished, which was long after the doll incident."

Her eyes widened.

"That is a nobleman's duty," he said, his jaw set. "We fight hard so the common folk can stay safe. However, while we did, the boyar and his thugs swept in and stole everything from us once again."

"So that's how he did it," Her Highness murmured. She stared around at the lot of them before she said, "Are you interested in having the chance to perform those duties again?"

Adonis gave a start. "A-are you sure? I'm not sure we'd be up to the task. We've been roughing it for a long time. Besides that, we failed you not just once but twice already."

Some of the other men nodded, conflicted expressions on their faces.

"If you were given noble status by the Imperial Family, it's your duty to return now that you can," she said. "People might not fully understand, but the nobility in our society plays a crucial role, and without that here in Póli, the town might fall right back apart. It needs strong leadership, and you were all able to weather the boyar's storm. Moreover, you came at my first call that day in the square. If you want the role of a noble again, it's yours."

Despite Adonis' gruff nature and intimidating size, he stared at Her Highness for a moment before tears glittered in his eyes. Kneeling in front of her, he pressed a fist to his chest, right over his heart, the sign soldiers and nobility gave in salute to the Imperial Family alone. "Your wish is my command, Your Highness."

The other nobles also bent the knee, pressed their fists to their chests, and swore the same.

Her Highness looked uncomfortable with that, but she accepted it and said nothing. It was a sharp reminder to River she wasn't acting in this role because she wanted to; it was because she had such a strong sense of duty that she couldn't possibly *not* take on this role in order to save all of them.

That made River feel all the more guilty for sitting on the fence about joining the Dragon Kin.

They then found hoards of gold leaves the boyar and his lackies had stashed away. After the three days it'd taken to count it all, Her Highness set about redistributing it based on need. She tackled the issue with the slaves, ensuring their freedom and ways to help them integrate and sustain themselves in everyday life. Dozens of jobs were opened in order to complete the various construction and refurbishing projects needed in order to make the city properly livable.

"They're not great jobs," she'd said, "but they will help the economy here get back on its feet, and, of course, the citizens will reap the benefits afterwards."

To River's delight, one of the many projects she set in motion was the building of a school. There'd never been a formal school, open to anyone, in Póli.

She set such momentous things in order in such a short span of time that River's mind spun. He hadn't even been able to even dream about her coming here and changing the city, so seeing her do it before his eyes was astounding. When and if things were carried out the way she intended, the city would never be the same again.

All too soon, the night before Her Highness and the rest of the Dragon Kin's departure arrived. River intended to relax in his room, but when he arrived, Will was there, which meant any chance for relaxation was gone.

He was able to tolerate Will, but then, to his complete surprise, Her Highness came to visit him.

"I hope I'm not bugging you, but I wanted to talk to you, if that's okay?" she said as he gaped at her, unable to think of a single thing to say.

"I promise you're not bugging him," Will called from where he sat on River's table. "All he does at this time of night is mope."

River shot him a glare.

With an apologetic smile, she entered, raising a scolding eyebrow at Will before turning to River. "I've been meaning to come and talk with you for a while, but I've been struggling to find the time. I'm sorry about that."

River folded his arms, leaning against the wall to hide his discomfort. "Do you want me to kick Will out?"

"Hey."

Her Highness glanced the guy's way before shrugging. "Only if you don't want him here, I suppose. What I wanted to talk to you about isn't anything serious or deeply personal."

River glanced at the young man in question. "Stay quiet or you have to leave."

Will stuck his tongue out, but he remained where he was.

After a moment, Her Highness turned back to River.

He fought hard not to drop his gaze. He wasn't her servant, so he didn't have to, but it was weird not to.

"I..." She sighed, shifting her gaze. "You've had the gem dream Tak mentioned, haven't you?"

The muscles in River's back stiffened, making him acutely uncomfortable. "I...I have."

"I thought as much," she said, melancholy appearing on her face.

That gave him pause.

"I hate asking people to come to war with me, but I... Do you want to come with us?"

River hesitated, the same debate he'd been having almost since the Dragon Kin had arrived playing through his head again. "I...I don't know."

"I'm not going to force you. If you want to come, it has to be your choice," she explained, meeting his gaze again. "But we are leaving soon, and we won't be able to come back."

"I know," he said, unable to hold her gaze this time. "But...a long time ago, I messed up. Big."

"You mentioned that once. It's the same reason why you can't uphold your family's promise, right?"

He hesitantly nodded. "After what I've done...I can't join the Dragon Kin. I don't think it would be right."

She was quiet for a few seconds before she said, "Can I ask you a question? When did the gem mark you?"

"What?"

"I mean, was it before or after the big mistake you made?"

"After." River remembered clearly the event that had turned his hair and eyes to this jet-black shade like it'd happened yesterday.

Will glanced down.

"You know the gems only mark the people they feel are the right ones, don't you? If you made this big mistake of yours before you were even marked, that means the gem chose you despite that mistake."

Startled enough he couldn't think of anything to say once more, he just stared at her with wide eyes.

"If that's the case," she continued, "you shouldn't beat yourself up over it anymore. Maybe I'm not the person who should be able to say that, but still. That one mistake doesn't define who you are for the rest of your life. So, if you want to come with us, you can. Okay? And if you don't, that's okay too."

He continued to stare, his jaw slack.

She glanced somewhat awkwardly between him and Will before bowing a little and saying, "That's all I had to say, so good night." Then she left.

River stared at the place where she'd been standing, his brain replaying what she'd said.

"So." Will hopped off the table and stalked over to him. "What are you going to do?"

River shut his mouth, but he didn't have a clue what to say. If he was honest, he did want to join the Dragon Kin. If they could do in other places what they'd done here, that alone would be worth it, but even more than that, he'd been chosen. Someone/something believed in him. They wanted him. How could he say no?

Especially when he knew that if he agreed, his parents would've been proud of him. Granted, they would've been proud of him either way, but even still, after how much he'd let them down with his mistake, maybe joining the Dragon Kin would equal things out.

"Mate, you wanna hear my honest opinion?" Will huffed, folding his arms.

River begrudgingly met his gaze.

"Just go. You know you want to." Will turned and flopped onto River's bed. "All right, I'm going to bed now."

"Get out of my bed, weirdo," River snapped.

"But I don't have one, and yours is massive. Just let me borrow this corner."

River rolled his eyes but said nothing. However, instead of going to bed, River went out onto his balcony. The sun dipped into the ocean, and tonight, it lit up the sky with beautiful pinks and reds. As he watched the sun fade away and the dark blueness of night sweep into its place, River still mulled over the Dragon Kin issue.

Once the sun vanished and the sky burst with hundreds of little stars, he finally decided: if the gem sent him its dream one more time, he would go. Otherwise, he wouldn't do it.

෨෩ ෨෨

Leonora didn't know what to think when she opened her door to find the princess standing there, biting her lip (though Her Highness immediately stopped as the door opened). "Did you...forget something?" she ventured, glancing back into the depths of her room.

"I didn't have anything to forget," Her Highness said. "So no. I wanted to talk with you for a minute if I could."

"Oh, of course." Leonora opened the door to let her in.

Almost in an embarrassed way, Her Highness entered, pausing before turning back to her. "I just have to ask you a question."

Leonora knew what the question would be before it was asked. "Is it about the Dragon Kin?"

Her Highness nodded, an apologetic look appearing on her face. "We're leaving, so I have to know for sure whether or not you want to come."

A smile touched Leonora's mouth, but it wasn't a happy one.

"Thank you for asking, Your Highness, but I can't."

She stayed quiet, watching Leonora with those unnerving red eyes.

"I can't fight—and even if I could, I hate doing it. I'm glad you have Thala and River, but you won't need me."

Her Highness didn't respond right away. "Is that really the reason?"

That made Leonora pause. Deep inside lay the regret and guilt from all those years ago, the pain that festered and never left, and she still didn't want to feel them. Going with the Dragon Kin might drag all of them to the surface.

Her Highness seemed to wait, not saying anything.

"Well," Leonora managed, "I...I can't. I couldn't save my brother, so...how could I..."

"I understand," Her Highness said softly. "Trust me, Leonora, I do. But when were you marked?"

"I don't remember," Leonora admitted with an apologetic smile and a shrug. "I think it was while I was trying to save River, but I was so busy and concerned about him that I didn't take care of myself—let alone have a mirror. I realized afterwards that at some point, my appearance had changed."

"So the gem chose you after that."

Her Highness hadn't asked a question, but Leonora turned away. "It doesn't matter when it happened—the point is I can't. I'm going to tell the gem to choose someone else."

After a moment's hesitation, Her Highness nodded. "Okay. If that's what you want, then it's okay. Just...can I say one more thing?"

Leonora relented.

"I don't have room to talk; you and I are similar, I think. Even still, I think if you're going to go through the rest of your life thinking of yourself as that little girl who failed her little brother, you're never going to be able to be anything but that." With a bit of a sheepish smile, Her Highness turned to the door. "Have a good night."

Leonora nodded, and then the princess was gone.

Sighing, Leonora rested her head against the door. It didn't matter if she wanted to be more than what she was; after what had happened with River and not being able to protect him for years, Leonora didn't deserve to be anything else. How could she?

At the same time, if she remained here and River left, she wouldn't be able to protect him. On the contrary, it'd be exactly like when their parents had left for the war. If he went alone, knowing him, there was a good chance he'd never come back.

Shaking those thoughts away, she went to bed—utterly exhausted—and the gem's dream came the second she shut her eyes. It seemed so earnest. The sensation and desire to accept was so powerful, Leonora couldn't imagine saying no.

As the dream lingered with Leonora standing on that mysterious beach and staring out at the endless stretch of water, she couldn't deny the pull inside her. Even though she felt like the most worthless person to walk the earth, she wanted to matter. She wanted to protect the people she cared about. Desperately, she wanted to believe she could be a member of the Dragon Kin.

Chapter Thirty-Five

Redrinna leaned against the balcony railing, still feeling a lot better now that she wasn't imposing on Leonora any longer. They'd been here long enough they'd found rooms for everyone, so there'd been no need to camp on the young woman's floor for long. At the very least, Redrinna was relieved they'd stripped a lot of the gold and velvet from the mansion to give what could be salvaged better uses, so it didn't hurt her eyes to look around anymore.

A part of her mind reeled from everything that had happened in Póli—specifically everything she'd somehow been able to do. For some reason, no matter what had cropped up in front of her, she'd been able to figure out what to do, the memories of things her parents had taught her and made her study guiding her. After she'd turned her back on that part of herself, she hadn't expected it to stay with her so well.

Even still, after tomorrow, she was more than a little relieved to be able to step out of the princess spotlight and return to being herself, a regular member of the Dragon Kin. The expectations and attention were exhausting. Plus...despite how well things seemed to be going, she couldn't help thinking...

Can't sleep? her gem asked.

Redrinna rested her chin in her hand. "Kind of. I was just thinking."

Ah, one of your favorite past times.

That almost made her laugh. Then her last thought returned. "Do you think any of this is going to make a difference here?"

I do.

"But...is it the right difference? I mean, am I doing it right?"

That's hard to say, her gem said slowly, almost like it was thinking. *It's often difficult to tell whether something is the 'right way' until after you've chosen it, but...the town is better. That counts for something.*

Redrinna frowned. The people seemed happy, at least. Her gaze traveled back into her room, where, on the small bedside table sat a little sprig of dried, light purple flowers. As she'd been traveling around the city the other day, a little girl had hesitantly approached and given it to her, saying they were a bunch of thyme she'd dried so Redrinna could keep it forever. The girl's mom hadn't seemed pleased her daughter had given Redrinna an herb as a gift, but the little girl had fiercely defended her present, claiming if she didn't give a gift unique to the mountains around Póli, then how would Redrinna remember where she'd gotten it?

Nobody had given Redrinna such a gift before. She'd done her best to keep her emotions in check at the time, but once she'd had a minute alone, she'd examined the minute flowers more closely and found herself crying.

She didn't know if she'd done the right things here or even the best things, but she had done the best she could. And that did seem to be making a difference to someone.

"You know what's weird?"

Hmm?

"No matter what situation I've had to deal with here, I've always known what I needed to do. I never had to think; I just knew."

Her gem was quiet for a minute. *Your parents must've taught you well.*

That made Redrinna's eyes go wide.

I mean, the only reason you haven't struggled was because they prepared you so well you would be able to fall back on their teachings without hesitation. Perhaps you don't want to hear that, but that's probably why.

"I..."

They must've loved you a lot.

Redrinna's vision blurred. That familiar painful ache that had dwelled in her chest since she'd learned of her mother's death made itself known again. Her feelings about her dad were still conflicted, but even still, in that moment, she realized that deep in her heart, almost deep enough she hadn't noticed, was nestled the wish—even though neither of them were with her anymore—that if they knew what she'd done here, they would be proud. She'd never wanted to be a princess—she still didn't—but she hoped they would've been pleased with her efforts anyway.

She buried her face in her hands.

෯෨ ෨෯

It took a long time for River to fall asleep after he'd shoved Will to the far corner of his bed and curled up to go to sleep in the opposite corner. He lay there for seemingly hours, watching the moonlight filter more into the room while his thoughts went in circles and loops, but eventually, he must've passed out, because all at once, he was dreaming.

He knew he was dreaming, but even still, he stared at the beach beneath his feet and the ocean stretching out before him. This was not the ocean he'd spent the last several years seeing every day, but at the same time, standing there on that beach, it was like he was home. He couldn't explain the sensation, but it was there nonetheless.

A familiar voice came to him on the wind, his heart burning with warmth the instant it touched his ears. *It's time. Open your eyes. I'm still waiting for you.*

River jerked awake, winded like he'd been running. He was still surrounded by the deepness of night, the dark objects of his room highlighted by the pale moonlight. It took him a minute to realize his cheeks were drenched with tears. He scrubbed them away, that burning sensation that'd been in his chest during the dream still pounding through him even though he was awake now.

Before he'd gone to sleep, River remembered thinking that if the gem gave him its dream one more time, he would join the Dragon Kin. He'd only thought it; he'd never said it out loud.

"How did you know?" he whispered.

Only silence greeted him, but even still, the fire in his chest burned on.

"All right, already," he whispered. "I'll do it."

⚬⚬ ⚬⚬

The next morning, the day the Dragon Kin was leaving, Redrinna struggled to sit still while Captain Brion wound her hair into one of his intricate creations. As one of her final acts as a princess here in Póli, she was going to address the town. She had no one but herself to blame for the idea, but she was still so nervous.

Even still, during the weeks they'd been here and after all she'd done, she couldn't just up and leave this place; not after all the kindness the townspeople had shown her.

Her gaze shot back to the dried bunch of flowers. That wasn't the only gift she'd received; she had a small collection of pebbles, shells, and tiles painted in bright colors to go with it. Plus, people had shown her kindness in other ways. She wasn't sure who'd been responsible for organizing it, but since her and her friends had been busy organizing documents and money and making all kinds of arrangements, the townsfolk had made them dinner every night. Now that the food wasn't being hoarded, there was a lot more to go around, and she and her friends hadn't had to cook a thing. The townsfolk had even been willing to give feeding the dragons a try, though Redrinna wasn't sure how well that had worked. Kelvair had recovered some, so he was eating more, and the dragons ate a lot to begin with. Even still, the dragons hadn't complained. On the contrary, they'd seemed to enjoy the attention and testing out most of the creations people had made for them.

Somehow, word had spread that Redrinna harbored a strong aversion to fish, and the meals they'd been brought had subsequently been fishless. Or there had been a portion set aside for her that had remained fishless.

She wasn't sure how that had gotten around, but she'd appreciated the gesture all the same. It'd been a relief to not have to constantly force herself to eat something she hated.

When Captain Brion finished with her hair, Redrinna jerked to her feet, unable to sit still a second longer.

The captain seemed like he was trying hard not to laugh. "There's no need for you to be nervous, Your Highness. Your parents taught you how to do this."

"I know," she said, distinctly remembering the hours they'd spent practicing how to project and annunciate. "But I've never had to do it in front of actual people before."

A smile touched his mouth, making her pause before she smiled too.

"You'll do all right," he said. "I know it."

That boosted her spirits enough to make her feel like she walked on air.

All at once, there came a sharp knock at the door, and before Redrinna could say a word, Captain Brion went and opened it, acutely reminding her of how things had once been before her life had been turned on its head. However, as General Cael entered the room, she shook those thoughts away.

"Forgive me for coming unannounced," he said, giving her a bow. "But there was something I wanted to say to you without so many ears around."

"You're fine," she said, unsure what else to say.

"I wanted to tell you this before, but it's been so busy, I haven't had the chance. Your Highness, I wanted you to know it's been an honor to work with you to save this place. You were able to do what I'd always wanted but couldn't."

Redrinna was too embarrassed to respond.

"I'm in your debt for that," he continued. "But I'm okay with it. Regardless, you and your Dragon Kin are preparing for war, aren't you?"

She nodded.

"That's what I'd heard. Now, I don't yet understand fully what you're up against or what's really going on, but I wanted you to know that regardless of what happens out there, when you need me, I'll be there, Your Highness."

"Wh-what?"

"You can't fight a war on your own and expect to win," General Cael said with a hint of a smile. "So when the time comes, you can count on me to be there with you."

"But I... After today, I won't be a princess anymore."

"I'd heard that. But, even if you ultimately don't want the throne, you'll have to take it long enough to pass it on to someone else— otherwise there'll just be more war. So even if it's only for a little while, you will be my princess. And if one day you truly do cease to be a princess in name, you will forever be one in my heart."

Her eyes burned at the corners, and Redrinna did her best to hold the tears back.

"I confess I had doubts about you taking over the empire."

"It's only natural to be wary of new leadership," she said quickly.

"Yes, but the rumors surrounding you were far-reaching, and since we'd never met, it was easy to surmise there was truth in them. However, after what you've done here and what I've seen you do with my own eyes, I can now say I believe those rumors to be founded on falsehood." With an actual smile, General Cael turned towards the door, one fist on his hip. "I grew up hearing the legends of the old Dragon Kin, you know. What you and your friends have done have brought them all to mind. So, for as long as you're a princess—and maybe even afterwards—wherever you go, I'll follow."

Redrinna lost that battle against her tears.

"Good luck," the general said as he opened the door. "And know that all of our strength will go with you."

Once he was gone, Redrinna swiped at her tears, but they kept coming.

"Are you all right, Your Highness?" Captain Brion asked, holding out a handkerchief.

Even though Redrinna smiled—a real, genuine smile—she couldn't seem to get the tears to stop. "I'm fine."

He smiled a little too.

Eventually, Redrinna managed to get herself back under control, and then it was time. For the last time, Redrinna left River and Leonora's mansion.

When Redrinna joined the others outside, Leonora's face lit up a little. "Oh, your hair is so pretty like that, Your Highness."

Redrinna blushed, unsure what to do with that kind of praise. Out of the corner of her eye, she caught Tak eyeing her, his cheeks going a bit pink. It hit her that this was the closest any of them had ever seen her to being a princess, and that made her palms itch with sweat.

General Cael, more formal now, stepped up, glancing around at their little group before turning to her—the sharp intensity of his gaze softening with the hint of a smile—and said, "It's time, Your Highness. Everyone's waiting."

"Right," she said, following him to the square, her friends falling in behind her.

A few minutes later, they arrived in the square, and the moment they did, a cheer went up, making Redrinna jump a little. When she glanced at the people who'd gathered to hear her speak (it was like the ocean itself stood before her, there were so many people), she was met with smiles and bright countenances, a complete turnaround from the last time she'd been in this square.

When she reached the stairs to the boyar's old execution stand, she paused, taking a deep breath.

"You can do it, Redrinna!" Kyvo squeaked.

"Y-yeah," Xandrin said, his wings tight to his sides and his movements a little jerky. "You can do it."

She smiled. "Thanks." Taking another deep breath, she mounted the stairs, thinking through everything she needed to remember to say and what she had to do in order to make sure everyone could hear her. She spied a few familiar faces, but the ones that drew her attention the most were Adonis and the other, reestablished nobles.

When they noticed her gaze on them, they drew themselves up straighter. In truth, when she'd decided to reinstate them, she'd been wary, but so far, those men and their families had been true to their word—and the stories she'd heard about their exploits as a gang corroborated their behavior. The city's successful change had been as smooth as it had because of them.

They were true noblemen.

Once Redrinna reached the center of the stand, a hush fell over the assembly, the buzz vanishing so fast, it was almost like Redrinna had suddenly gone deaf. All at once, her mind went blank, and she couldn't recall any of the things her parents had taught her about this.

Even still, she took another deep breath and spoke.

"Good morning, everyone," she said, her voice echoing and almost scaring her.

A few people called greetings back, making her smile.

"I'm glad all of you could come, because as you already know, I'm leaving today. So this is the last time I will get to see you for a while."

Redrinna was startled by the disappointed expressions on some people's faces.

"Before I go, there are some things I need to say. First and foremost, on behalf of the Imperial Family, I have to apologize. When your children were taken and forced to become dolls, there was so little we could do in order to stop and punish the people who were responsible for your suffering, and even then, in the years since, you have still been suffering. I am so sorry." Redrinna bowed deeply to the crowd, pausing long enough to get her emotions back under control as best she could. Then she straightened.

"There have been many changes put into place here," she continued, "and it will take all of you cooperating for them to work and change Póli for the better. That said, there's one more thing I need to do before I can leave. For the last three weeks, you have no longer had a boyar. I've been here, so it's been okay, but since I'm leaving, it isn't. Therefore, it is high time I appoint someone to take over as your boyar, someone I trust will take care of and protect you as a boyar should."

A few murmurs swept through the crowd, and Redrinna waited until they'd gone silent before she continued.

"The person I've chosen is someone I believe to be a good man. He's noble, and he's faithful. With him at the helm, I believe your city of Póli will change for the better." She turned her gaze to Adonis, whose eyes went wide. "Adonis, can I entrust you with the mantle of the boyar?"

He stared at her, seeming stunned, his mouth open with no words coming out.

"It's a big responsibility; I know. But after what you've shown me during the last few weeks, I believe you can do it," she whispered to him. Not only that, but General Cael—who had surprised her with his own, intense loyalty—had recommended him.

After a second more, Adonis seemed to shake himself out of his daze and joined her on the stand. When he reached her, he knelt on one knee, and for the second time since she'd met him, put a clenched fist to his heart. "If you believe in me, then I accept. I will act as the boyar here to the best of my abilities."

Steeling herself, Redrinna drew her sword. She'd only seen her parents do this a couple times, and while they'd made her practice it, it took all her effort not to let her sword tremble as she touched it to both of Adonis' shoulders, the crown of his head, and then his heart.

"I, Imperial Princess Redrinna Ioana Vasilica Luminiţa Ardeleanu, bestow on you, Adonis Lykaios, the rights and powers of the boyarship of these lands. Do you swear to uphold your duty, protect this land and its people, and to defend your charges with your life?"

"I so swear," Adonis choked out, tears gleaming in his eyes when he lifted his head and met her gaze.

"Then rise," she said before turning to the crowd. "I am pleased to present to all of you your new boyar, Boyar Adonis."

A massive cheer rose, making her smile a little. Adonis was a little overcome with emotion, but he managed to bow to the crowd.

Redrinna shooed him back off the stand. Turning to General Cael, who watched her with a faint smile on his scarred face, she said, "If you would, general."

He gave her a salute and turned to his soldiers, issuing a few commands. The soldiers backed the crowd away from the stand, earning her several confused looks. While Redrinna waited, she glanced at Xandrin, who looked determined. He nodded when she met his gaze, and she nodded back.

Her gaze slipped to the dark stain at the front of the stand, the vivid reminder of the lives that were taken here. Lives taken in order to strike at her. That stain would haunt her, but even still, she refused to let fear be what made her look away. She didn't know if she'd done anything of lasting worth here, but at the very least, no one would ever be killed here again.

Once everyone stopped moving and the crowd quieted back down, Redrinna put her hands on her hips. "With your new boyar in charge, I believe you're all going to be fine. That said, there's one last thing I want to do before I go." She tapped her foot against the stage making a hollow, haunting sound echo through the square, the chill that passed over the crowd almost palpable. "I remember some questioning my decision to not have this dismantled, but I had a good reason for it. This is the last standing testament to what the previous boyar did and the pain and suffering he put all of you through. But now, you're all truly free. So there's something I need you to see." She turned to Xandrin. "Are you ready?"

He nodded, and Redrinna left the stage, joining her friends. Xandrin took a long slow breath, his chest glowing a bright red. The next second, a plume of flame engulfed the stage. The fire swarmed over the dry wood, eagerly biting into every inch of it.

Silence fell over the crowd, not a sound to be heard except the roar of the flames and creaking and popping of the wood. Sparks spluttered through the air as the wood groaned under the fire's bite.

All at once, a burning sensation ignited on the palm the spirit had marked—not painful but not pleasant either—but given the crowd around her, Redrinna clamped her fist shut and did her best to ignore it.

To distract herself, Redrinna noted the expressions on the faces of her new friends. Thala looked calm, almost peaceful, a sharp contrast to her usual voidness of expression. The light of the flames reflected off Will's glistening eyes, and a couple tears made tracks down Leonora's cheeks. River, however, seemed somewhat puzzled.

Inching closer to him, she whispered, "Do you know why I did this?"

"How did you...?" He trailed off, his attention fixed on the flames.

She almost smiled but turned her attention to the fire as well.

"For so long, the boyar used that platform to control you. If you spoke out or did anything to upset him, this was what he used. But fire purges. This is the last physical thing of his that still has its hooks in you, but the fire will burn it all away. From this moment forward, he no longer has a place in your life. You're free, River."

He didn't speak, but his eyes became bright.

Even though Redrinna's time in Póli had been brief and her interactions with the boyar limited, there was something cathartic about watching something of his—something he'd lorded over her—be destroyed. He'd killed so many in her name there, and now, no matter what, he would never be able to do it again.

The stand let out a final groan before it collapsed. Sparks shot high in the air, bright orange against the gray clouds covering the sky.

No one moved, the crowd staying silent as they watched the platform until it'd burnt itself out, becoming nothing more than a pile of ash and ember. Then, almost as one, they turned to Redrinna, catching her off guard.

Slowly, they trickled forward, and General Cael moved closer, his eyes roving over the crowd. They gave her hesitant little bows, and some brave people even reached out with shaking hands just to touch hers. However they responded, the one thing she kept hearing over and over again was two simple words: 'Thank you.'

Her eyes misted over too.

When the last person departed, Redrinna swiped at her eyes and turned to her friends. Kyvo hopped onto her shoulders, and she smiled at him before turning to Thala. "Do you have everything you need?"

Thala nodded. "I don't have anything, so I'm good to go."

Redrinna glanced at River and Leonora.

Before she could say anything, River took a tiny step forward. "Don't worry, Your Highness. I'm coming with you."

She smiled a little at that.

Leonora glanced at River, a complicated emotion in her eyes, before she stared at the ground. Hard.

Redrinna waited.

Slowly, the young woman raised her head. "I'll go too, though I don't know how much use I'll be."

That caught her by surprise. Given what Leonora had said last night, this wasn't what she'd expected. However, she nodded and said, "I'm glad you'll be with us."

Kyvo rose on her shoulder, and she braced herself. The next second, he vaulted to Leonora, who scrambled to catch him. "Yay! I don't have to leave my friend behind!"

Will laughed. "Don't worry about me. I'll make sure this place changes for good."

Redrinna smiled at that.

"Don't be a pest," River said, a disapproving tone in his voice.

"When am I a pest?" Will demanded.

Thala and Leonora both looked at him at the same time.

Redrinna couldn't help it; she laughed. For some reason, that made all the others relax as well.

Someone cleared their throat, making her glance to the side. Adonis stood there with the dark-haired, almost severe looking woman she'd been told was his wife. Aretha, she thought.

"I'll do my best to live up to your expectations, Your Highness," he said.

Redrinna thought it strange—almost funny—that such a massive, overbearing man with a pegleg could be so meek. Then again, she was realizing people were often more complicated than their appearances suggested.

"I'll keep an eye on him," Aretha said with the hint of a smile. Venturing closer, she hesitantly took one of Redrinna's hands in her own. "Your Highness, we'll never forget your kindness. Before you go, is there any way we can repay you? I realize nothing will do, but at least let us try."

All at once, Redrinna was reminded of how, just a few weeks ago, she'd been obsessed with the same question. However, now that she was on the other side—now that she had Tak and Kyvo's perspectives—she understood why they'd answered the way they had.

There were some debts that simply didn't need to be repaid.

With a bit of a smile, she said, "Thank you, but as long as you and the rest of the people here can be happy, then I don't need anything."

Aretha opened her mouth to protest, but Adonis touched her arm. They stared at each other for a moment before turning and dipping in deep bows. Then they left.

Redrinna turned to the dragons. Before she could move in their direction, Captain Brion approached. A part of her was still sad that he'd said he would not be going with her. He hadn't explained why, but she had her guesses.

"So," he began as the others prepared to leave, "now that that's over, you're going back to not being a princess."

She nodded.

"Then...I suppose I can be a little informal for a minute," he said, almost looking uncomfortable. "I've never been able to tell you this before, but I was married once."

Redrinna's eyes widened.

"Long before the war. My wife was pregnant with our first child, but my duties as a soldier called me away. I wasn't there when she gave birth, but neither she nor the baby made it." A sigh slipped out of him, and the melancholy expression she was used to seeing on his face returned. "But, sometime after, I was assigned to you. In a way, after all the things we went through together, there were times when I could almost imagine you were my child. I know that's silly, but even still, I felt it often."

"That makes me happy, Captain," she managed to say, her throat tight with emotion.

"But while you were on that stage, you were so much like your mother it was like she was here again. So I know I'm not your father, and I have no wish to overstep. However, if you had been my daughter, then I would be the proudest father in the world."

Her mouth popped open, and her vision blurred.

"This body of mine is getting old and it doesn't work like I want it to," he said, carefully stroking her hair. "I'm afraid the only help I can give you now is support from afar, but no matter what lies ahead, I'll be right behind you, Your...Redrinna." He stepped back.

Redrinna vaulted forward, hugging him around the waist. Captain Brion hugged her back, and, for a moment, that was all she could think about.

While she'd had a father of her own and he'd been present in her life, Captain Brion had filled in some of the gaps he'd left behind. Once he'd been taken from her life, that was when she'd realized how much a part of her he had been.

At least she didn't have to worry and agonize over him so much anymore, and inside her heart, it was no longer quite so hollow.

All at once, something wet struck her cheek, confusing her for a second. She glanced at Captain Brion—he wasn't crying—before she glanced at the sky. Another drop of rain fell, nearly hitting her eye. Smiling, she held a palm up, catching a couple drops as rain began to fall.

"Hey!" Will cried. "Rain!"

Leonora laughed a little as Kelvair fanned out his one working wing, almost like he was trying to catch the water.

Then Redrinna turned to the others, all of them smiling.

Kyvo returned to her arms, and once she was settled on Xandrin's neck, the others followed suit. With a final wave to Will, Captain Brion, and General Cael, Redrinna turned her attention forward, and Xandrin launched into the sky. Astra followed close behind while Kelvair raced along beneath them and dove into the ocean. With his wing still broken, he couldn't fly, but he could swim most of the way back. It would take a little longer, but Tak could only use so much of his magic a day to help the wing heal faster.

However, as the first rain Redrinna had felt in months struck her face, she found she didn't mind so much.

Chapter Thirty-Six

As Póli shrank behind them, Thala found herself glancing back one last time. One of the last things her father had said to her before he'd died had been to 'be happy.' For several years, she hadn't been able to puzzle out what he had meant.

How could she be happy when she'd been so alone and lost?

How could she be happy without some kind of purpose?

How could she be happy when all she knew was fear?

She still didn't have the answers to those questions, but for the first time in her life, it almost felt like it was okay not to know yet. Joining the Dragon Kin was one of the first things she'd ever done of her own volition since her time as a broken doll, and maybe it would be the catalyst that helped her finally find those answers. Perhaps even one day, she'd be able to live her life as her father had wished.

Closing her eyes, Thala tightened her hold on River's waist a little more so she wouldn't fall off, and fortunately, he didn't seem to care much. Then again, the two of them had always been like siblings. Ever since the war, River had been one of the few things that had made sense, and he'd been able to help her find sense too.

With her eyes closed, she could sense the distant pull of her Dragon Gem, its call becoming stronger and clearer the longer they flew. It wasn't going to last, but for now, this was her purpose. Helping

Her Highness and the rest of the Dragon Kin stop Osiris was her mission. There was a chance she might even find herself—the self the boyar and his demons had worked tirelessly to destroy—somewhere along the way.

They flew most the rest of the day and settled near a forest far past the Diablo's Maw to sleep. The next morning, they headed out again, arriving at the beach Thala had seen in her dreams within a couple hours.

Soon, she had her hands on her gem, its color a perfect match to her hair, the warmth that spread through her every time she touched it, shivers racing across her skin. It was surreal to think this thing had not only chosen her but been waiting for her to come.

River obtained his gem as well, though he seemed a bit more...sullen about the whole thing. He frowned, but it wasn't his usual thoughtful frown. Even still, he allowed himself to be chosen, his real hand holding the gem like it was one of the most precious things he'd ever held.

Leonora was more hesitant than either of them, but even she acquired a little smile once she had the gem. Thala glanced between the two siblings—the two, very stubborn siblings—and for the first time since she'd met them, she relaxed. Things were different now. Their hesitancy wasn't the same as it'd been that day they'd first arrived in Póli, both pale with their heads bowed. But perhaps it would someday become a good different.

⁂

As the Mount came into view, Redrinna's heart rose in her chest. Finally. They were almost home. After an entire month, they were back in a place where they could rest and where she didn't have to be a princess. For just a moment, they could pretend Osiris wasn't a threat.

Xandrin landed on the ledge of the Mount a few minutes later, pushing the doors open and slipping inside. Astra shot in seconds later, and Kelvair tentatively followed after. Redrinna was still impressed Tak had managed to help his wing heal enough that the dragon could fly again. Kelvair hesitated for another couple seconds, Thala and River slipping off his shoulders, before he turned and fought to close the doors with Astra's help.

Redrinna hopped to the ground and helped Leonora down. Kyvo bounced out of Tak's arms before he could dismount, and, with a squeal of delight, shot off down the center passage, more than likely on the hunt for food, Timothon, or perhaps both. Either way, she couldn't help smiling after him before she turned to the others.

Tak dismounted, rolling his shoulders. Their four new additions all stared around the Mount with a sense of wonder, which made Redrinna smile a little. When she'd first arrived, she'd done the same thing.

She gave them a few minutes, admiring the gems hanging from their necks while she waited. The gems suited them.

When they seemed to have their fill, Redrinna said, "Welcome to the Mount."

Thala shivered. "Compared to Póli, it's kind of cold."

"I like it better though," River said.

"Speak for yourself," Kelvair said, pulling his wings and tail in tight as he curled into a ball. "I already miss the sun."

Leonora smiled a little but stayed quiet.

"Well, we're pretty far north now," Redrinna said, doing her best to keep from laughing. "Summers are a lot cooler, especially in the mountains."

"So, how was the Diablo?" Timothon suddenly said, almost scaring Redrinna out of her skin. She whirled, her heart leaping at the sight of her red-haired uncle with Kyvo hopping around his ankles like a rabbit. Kyvo was chomping on a piece of what looked suspiciously like bread.

"I was lied to," Astra said with a sniff.

Timothon raised an eyebrow at her. "Were you?"

"Yeah," Xandrin said, ear frills flaring out. "You guys all said the volcano was dormant, but it exploded!"

"It...it did?" Timothon said, eyebrows vanishing beneath his bangs.

Redrinna nodded. "I'll tell you about it later." Then she made all the introductions.

Once she was finished, River eyed Timothon for a long minute, which made Timothon stare back at him in the same manner. "He's your uncle?"

"Would've been," Timothon corrected. One of those sad smiles Redrinna was starting to hate appeared on his face. "I am dead."

Kelvair looked him up and down, eyes wide and scales paling a shade. "Y-you are? But you don't seem dead! Oh, n-no offense."

"None taken," her uncle said, a hint of a real smile touching his mouth. "I'm glad I don't look like a walking corpse."

"Don't worry," Redrinna said quickly. "I'll explain everything later. For now, I'll show you to your rooms, okay?"

She busied herself with getting their new members settled and making sure everybody else was all right too. As she did, she couldn't help the little pang in her heart. Whether she liked it or not, she was the official leader of the Dragon Kin. No one had said it; there hadn't been a vote. But how everyone felt about it was in their eyes.

She'd been able to pull some things off in Póli, but she couldn't stop thinking about them and thinking about the things she could've done better. Had they been enough? Had she appointed the right people? Was the city going to recover, or had this all just been a bandage, a temporary solution covering up a massive problem?

Kyvo's request still lurked in her mind as well. It'd been quiet in Póli, but now that her mind and hours weren't so occupied, it kept coming back. She still hated the idea of him fighting, but at the same time, the fight with the mysterious skeleton creatures had put him in danger. The fact he'd had to run to one of them for protection had put the rest of them in danger too. Plus, if he'd been able to fight, he might've been able to help break River out. It frightened her out of her skin to think about it, but he needed to be able to protect himself, and she needed to make peace with that.

Beyond that, they nearly had half of the Dragon Kin now. They were all counting on her, and the fear that she might let them down—that any one of them could die on her watch—became more pronounced than ever.

Once Redrinna had everyone settled and had stashed her gifts in her room, she tried to escape her thoughts in the Hall of the Dragon Kin. Sunlight slanted in through the windows, painting the room with color. Once she was on the dais, she studied the three statues of the people who'd born the same colors Thala, Leonora, and River now did.

One was a stern-looking woman with long, braided turquoise hair. Like Thala, she had the build of a warrior. The second was a man with black hair who, despite not having any trace of foreign blood, bore a striking resemblance to River and Leonora. The third was a tall man with amber hair and eyes, his dress simple but his bearing noble. He didn't stand out in the same way many of the others did, but there was something about him that made Redrinna pause on his face.

Once again, the fear that their Dragon Kin would meet the same fate as Timothon's sharpened in her chest, making it difficult to breathe. Wrapping her arms around herself, she instinctively reached for her gem's warmth.

"What brings you here this time?" Timothon said from behind her, making her turn.

For a moment, she stared at him before turning back to the statues. "I don't know. I just..."

"Looking for some kind of answer?" he said as he strode onto the dais. "That's usually what brings you here."

"Maybe that's it," she said, meeting his gaze. She glanced at the statues again, her gaze flicking to the one of a woman with curly, green hair. Then to the golden-haired Mato, a proud gleam in his eyes. "When you and the rest of the Dragon Kin fought, were you the leader?"

He nodded, the sunlight making the red of his eyes seem to glow. "Yeah. That's what they wanted, so it's what I did."

"And towards the end, you became the King of Eridia too. How did you...how'd you deal with that?"

"I honestly don't know." He stared up at the statues around them. "I guess it's one of those things that you just...handle when it happens."

"You know, I ended up having to be a princess this time," she said after a minute of silence. "A real princess. I didn't want to, but it was the only way to keep some terrible things from happening. In the end, people seemed happy about it, but I can't help feeling..."

Timothon didn't say anything, but there was something in his eyes that told her he understood.

"Did I do the right things? Is it going to help? What if there was something better I could have done?" She sighed.

"Hey, did you do your best?"

"What?"

The corner of Timothon's mouth quirked upwards. "Did you do your best?"

"Of course, but—"

He held up a hand to get her to stop. "If you went out there and did the absolute best you could, then you did the right thing. The right thing is doing what's best for the people who are relying on you and by doing what you believe in. Never compromise your beliefs. After all, you're only going to learn how to be a good leader by making choices you're not going to regret and making changes when you do. It's not about being perfect, you know."

All at once, that called to mind something similar her father had once said. Redrinna eyed Timothon with a quizzical stare. "My dad said something like that to me once. Did you tell it to him?"

Timothon snorted. "Hardly. If anything, we both had it drilled into us by our big sister."

That almost made her smile. Even still, Redrinna's doubts didn't leave, and once everything was said and done, she was simply exhausted.

Almost without thinking about it, she turned and dropped her forehead on his shoulder. If he was surprised, he didn't show it. Instead, he stayed quiet, wrapping an arm around her shoulders.

⁗

Leonora stared at the amber gem she'd agreed to take, still questioning her decision. That said, despite her doubts, she was pretty sure she was well and truly stuck in this mess. She'd agreed to it because it meant she'd be able to stay near River and do better to honor that promise to her parents, but now that it had happened, she regretted it. She was the only member of the Dragon Kin that couldn't fight; how in the world was she supposed to help them?

She looked away before facing the gem where it sat on the little bedside table next to her. When she was around the others, she wore it, but in quiet moments like this where she was alone, she couldn't bear to.

"I'm so sorry," she whispered to it. "I shouldn't have accepted you so that you could choose a better person."

You think so? the gem responded, catching her off guard. It'd never spoken to her before, though Her Highness had said it would. That said, she hadn't thought it would talk to her when she wasn't wearing it.

Even still, she huffed a little. "Don't be like that. I can't fight or anything; you know that."

No one is born knowing how to fight, are they? So why should that matter?

She stared, speechless. What was that supposed to mean?

I chose you for a good reason, her gem continued in a stern tone. *Just because you can't see it doesn't mean there isn't a reason for you to be here. So quit apologizing.*

Leonora drew back, a scowl twisting her mouth. "You're not very polite."

The gem made a tinkling sound she supposed was laughter.

Politeness isn't what I'm famous for, now is it? Fret not, Leonora, you'll get used to it in time.

Skeptical, she turned away from it. How on earth was she ever going to survive this?

⚬⚬ ⚬⚬

The Mount...was a lot to handle. The dragons constantly made a ruckus, though River was never sure whether he ought to be amused or annoyed by their antics. Kelvair was pretty quiet, but Xandrin and Astra always bickered and played some kind of game that seemed like tag. Except whenever one of them 'tagged' the other, the one who would've been 'it' became furious. Her Highness even snapped at them a few times, after which they would become sheepish and demure. For a few hours, anyway.

As Xandrin streaked past with Astra only seconds behind as they played another one of their games he did not understand, River sighed, his hand drifting to the gem that now hung around his neck. They'd only left Póli a couple days ago, and while he didn't regret his choice, he was still...conflicted about the whole thing. He studied the black gem hanging from his neck, taking note once again of the way it lit up and the way light caught on the sleek surface. For some reason, this gem had been waiting for him and chosen him despite his mistakes.

He couldn't comprehend that.

Doing his best to set those thoughts aside, River looked up right as Her Highness slipped out of the Mount's front doors. Where was she going? Granted, she seemed to go off on her own a lot, a fact that surprised him.

After a minute, he hesitantly followed. There was something he wanted to talk to her about, and if he didn't want others listening in, now seemed to be the best time.

Outside, Her Highness stood near the edge of the Mount, arms folded and not moving. He stayed quiet, not wanting to bother her thoughts, but somehow, she realized he was there and glanced back.

"Oh, hi River," she said, a hint of surprise in her voice. "What brings you out here?"

He shrugged, losing his resolve. Maybe now wasn't the best time for the thoughts in his head after all.

After a moment though, she relaxed, almost smiling. "Since you're here, you might as well stay." She beckoned him over, and, since he thought it would be rude to do otherwise, he obeyed. "I haven't thanked you yet, have I?"

"For what?"

"For all your help in Póli. Without you, we might never have found Kelvair." Her gaze was fixed on the mountains towering around them. "Also, I wanted to thank you for telling me about your arm."

A bit elf-conscious, he laid a hand on the arm in question. He wasn't embarrassed about his arm, per se, but staring at it dredged up a lot of feelings and memories he didn't want to give space to. Her Highness didn't need to thank him for telling her about it.

"Can I ask you something?" Her voice was quiet. "You don't have to answer if you don't want to...but is it okay if I ask how you lost your arm?" She regarded him with a hesitant look in her eyes.

River debated keeping it to himself; it wasn't pleasant. However, his father had once mentioned that the bond between their families was unique, one of complete trust, even for the members not fulfilling the promise. Even though they would let that promise dissolve with them, now that he'd come this far, he couldn't seem to justify keeping it to himself.

"You already know about how my parents were killed in the onset of the Esunian War, don't you?"

She nodded. "Leonora mentioned it."

"That happened when I was about six."

A darkness he was all too familiar with clouded Her Highness's face.

"To put it mildly," he continued, gaze on the ground, "I didn't handle it well. Unfortunately, I was always a bit too clever for my own good, so I figured that if the rest of my family was dead, I'd just use magic to bring them back and that would fix everything."

"Is...that possible?"

"No, it isn't. It's a theory among those who study magic, though, that it might be possible to create human beings with magic, under the right circumstances. I was desperate enough I latched on to that idea—willing it to be true, I think. I decided the reason so many others had failed with disastrous consequences wasn't going to happen to me, almost like I believed that because I wanted it more or maybe for a better reason, it would work. It never even crossed my mind that the reason others failed was because it isn't possible. See...have you ever heard of the laws of magic?"

"The what?"

"The natural laws that govern the use of magic."

"It sounds familiar..." Her brow furrowed. "Some books might have mentioned it, but they were never explicit. I also might have just been reading the wrong books. Or just not paying attention."

"Simply put, there are natural laws that prevent certain magic acts from being performed and govern how magic works in general. They define the limitations of magic."

Her eyes lit up. "Oh, like with Tak's magic? How he has to pull energy from somewhere in order to heal a wound, and it only works on certain kinds of injuries. Or with mine, how in order to make fire, I have to either make heat or transfer energy?"

"Exactly," he said. She was smart enough he'd figured she'd catch on without much prompting.

"But what does that have to do with your arm?"

He lifted it, making the metal creak. "This is what happens when you mess with laws that aren't supposed to be broken."

She frowned, eyeing his arm.

"When you break a magical law—or attempt to, at any rate—there's always a consequence. With Tak's magic, it would be death. With your fire, it could be freezing yourself or burning something you didn't intend to, but with other things—things you have to use gates for—when you try it, you meet this...gatekeeper. That's what it calls itself, at least."

"And it...took your arm?"

He nodded. "Because I lost my parents, I figured I would do whatever it took to bring them back to life. I think it was a miracle I didn't end up killing myself with that magic, but because of that, it meant I met the gatekeeper." For a moment, it played through his mind again, and his gaze drifted to his metal arm. He shuddered. "Either way, it didn't even work."

"I'm so sorry," she murmured.

River glanced to the side. The person he was truly sorry for had been and always would be Leonora. She'd been the unfortunate soul who'd found him bleeding out and half-dead.

"So, the gatekeeper's idea of a punishment was mutilation?" Her Highness continued, a hint of disgust on her face.

"It said that was the required payment for what I'd done. Then it crammed my head with more knowledge than I know what to do with and gave me the ability to use magic, though it's a bit broken compared to yours."

"It gave you something? That's odd."

"I thought that way too at first, but now that I've had more time with it, I don't think of it as a 'gift' anymore." He sighed. "There's a lot I know and can do with it—like building this arm, for instance—but at the same time, despite all of that, no matter how smart or powerful I am, there's nothing that's going to bring my parents back. If anything, it just makes it even clearer how stupid and arrogant I was."

"I wouldn't say you were arrogant," Her Highness said slowly. "More like...desperate. Being desperate makes you do things that border on the unthinkable. Trust me; I know."

Silence fell between them for a few minutes, and River couldn't help but squirm with discomfort. Now, she knew. Would she think less of him now?

"Though, you know," Her Highness continued, getting him to glance in her direction. "I just remembered something else I needed to thank you for."

He couldn't recall anything else he'd done that required gratitude.

"Because you talked to me about magic and that kind of thing, I found out I can use more than just fire magic. I can use earth magic."

"Really?" While he knew it was possible for people to be able to use multiple types of elemental magic, it still wasn't all that common. The fact that Her Highness could spoke volumes about how powerful her magic was.

"How many different kinds of elements are there? Do you know?"

"Five: fire, earth, water, air, and spirit. But there are lots of subsets under those five—like ice or weather or wood."

"Spirit magic. What's that?"

"It's what stuff like healing magic falls into."

She stared at him for a second before she gasped, making him jump. Her eyes went wide. Without warning, she hissed, "I have to go to the library!" Without another word, she raced back inside the Mount, leaving him confused.

River stared for a long minute before he followed.

⊶⦿⦿⊷

Redrinna dashed through the Mount, narrowly avoiding a collision with Kyvo and Tak in her haste to get to the library.

"But, Redrinna," Kyvo called, "it's dinnertime!"

With a wave of acknowledgement, Redrinna raced into the library. Because of what River had said, there was something she needed to investigate.

There were five elements that could be used without the aid of a magic circle—shadow, or even light, wasn't one of them.

She burst into the library, staring around at the shelves for a minute before orienting herself enough to move. Studying magic circles and such wouldn't help them much. However, she'd been told several times there was something wrong with Osiris's magic, and she didn't yet know what. Therefore, if she studied the laws of magic, maybe that would help her find the answer.

Heading towards where she thought most of the magic books were, she rapidly scanned the shelves, hoping she'd be able to find what she wanted.

A few minutes later, she found something promising: *The Unbreakable Laws of Magic.* She'd come across it before but hadn't studied it. At the time, she'd been much more interested in finding out what she could do with her magic, not what she couldn't. Tugging it from the shelf, she turned towards her favorite table. Right as she did, Kyvo bounded onto her shoulders, knocking the book out of her hands.

"Whatcha doing?" he asked.

She scowled. "I was about to do some research." Bending down, she retrieved her book.

"Research?" Tak asked, making her glance back. He and River had both followed her, it seemed. "What about?"

Redrinna held up her book and then paused. This was important enough she should tell everyone at once. "Wait. This way first." She hurried to the dining room where everyone else was already waiting.

"What are you doing?" Timothon asked, one eyebrow raised.

"Research." Redrinna set her book on the table. "River said there were five kinds of elemental magic, and Osiris's doesn't fit into any of them. There's also the thing with magic circles, so I figured this was what we need to study in order to get a better grip on things: the laws of magic."

"Okay?" Kelvair said, head cocked to the side.

"We need to do that now?" Astra asked.

"Maybe it'll help us figure out that weird pendant the boyar had," Tak added. "It seemed to give him magic like Osiris's and Reyna's, but neither of them have one."

"It might help with this too." Removing the gauntlet from her right hand, Redrinna lifted her palm for everyone to see. It'd changed after she'd shown it to Tak and Kyvo before. The weird sensation during her farewell speech in Póli had been the mark changing. Now, a crescent moon nestled against the curve of the sun, a similar shade but dark enough it stood out. "This was given to me by a spirit back in the forest."

Tak frowned. "It's different."

"It happened the day we left Póli."

"What is it?" Xandrin asked, head cocked.

"I don't know, and I don't know why it changed the way it looks, either." She slipped her gauntlet back on. "So maybe we'll find some kind of answer here. When the spirit gave it to me, it said we would need it, but I haven't been able to figure out what it is."

"Shouldn't we eat though?" Kelvair said.

Leonora didn't speak, but she stared forlornly at the food.

"Eat while you read, Redrinna," Timothon ordered.

Redrinna relented, and as everyone sat and began eating, she flipped through the thin, leather-bound book. She skimmed the pages—promising she'd give it a more in depth read later—until she found something that made her pause.

"This is something," she murmured as she scanned it.

"What?" Tak asked, moving closer.

"One of the big laws of magic. See here?" She flipped the book around. "Magic requires exchange. In order to get something, you have to give something." She met Tak's gaze. "We already knew this. It's like with your magic."

"Right," Kyvo chirped, the tip of his tail wagging. "Tak and me have to sacrifice energy in order to give it to someone else."

"And with my fire, the heat has to be taken from somewhere else or a reaction has to occur that creates it." Redrinna turned the book back to herself. "But this is part of what's wrong with Osiris's magic. As far as I can tell, they give up nothing. Even if shadows were an element, pulling the dark in would arguably make things brighter, right?"

"Most likely," River chimed in, arms folded and resting on the table.

"But when they use it, it seems to get darker. Plus those swords they can make—if it was just light magic of some kind, they shouldn't be as solid as they are, should they? Hot or cold maybe, but not solid. So what in the world are they using?"

River seemed to consider that. "Those are valid points."

Tak frowned too.

"Don't you know something?" Astra asked, eyeing Timothon.

He shrugged. "They used that kind of magic with us, but we didn't have a chance to figure it out. And I've never seen anything like that mark on Redrinna's hand before. Therefore, I am as good as useless in this regard."

"It also says that in order for something to be moved with magic, you have to use two, paired magic circles, like you were saying." She nodded in River's direction. "But when I went to the Imperial City, Reyna sent me to Osiris without one. And in the forest, she constantly came and went without them there either."

"Tehl did too," Leonora chimed in. "All the time."

Thala nodded. "When the boyar snatched you, Your Highness, he didn't use one."

Kyvo's eyes lit up. "Wait, you're saying that they *should* need circles, but somehow they're doing magic without them?"

"Exactly," she said, a grim smile touching her mouth. River broke a law and was punished for it. But... "Osiris and his crew are able to break magic laws, use magic contrary to its natural course, and create magic that doesn't even exist. That's why it's messing everything up. However, that pendant the boyar had," she closed her eyes, bitterly wishing it hadn't been destroyed, "might be the key to figuring out why."

Epilogue

As Will waited in thick, heavy darkness, he mulled over the past three days that had somehow landed him here—wherever that was. Three days ago, the Dragon Kin had left, taking his three best friends with them. They'd continued fixing Póli. That was the least they could do after all the crap Her Highness had gone through to set it right.

Then, just yesterday (or at least, what he remembered as being yesterday. It occurred to him it might have been longer than that), Tehl reappeared. The last time Will had seen the guy, Tehl had been watching the proceedings of River's execution from a nearby rooftop, almost like he hadn't wanted to be noticed. However, once Her Highness had arrived, Tehl had vanished.

However, yesterday, when Will had spied Tehl again, something had been off. There'd just been something about Tehl that persuaded Will to follow. Now, he was here in the dark with a killer headache. The few things he could smell weren't familiar; he couldn't smell the ocean or the fish or the thyme blooming on the mountainsides. He smelled nothing here.

So, he only had three questions. Where had he been taken? Why? And what did he need to do in order to get out?

Firelight flared to life near his face, making him wince from both the heat and the light that sharpened the ache in his skull.

"Tehl was right," said a woman whose voice he didn't recognize. "You are handsome, aren't you?"

"You said it, not me," he managed, eyes still stinging. He couldn't see much of this stranger, between his eyes struggling to adjust and the darkness in general, but it appeared as though she had dark hair and eyes and bronze-toned skin.

"Not that anyone here cares," she continued. "Father is ready for you, so let's go." Grabbing him under the shoulder in a steely, almost painful grip, she yanked him to his feet and hauled him forward.

Will staggered, struggling to get oriented. Even still, the hairs on the back of his neck stood on end like he was seconds from getting struck by lightning. There was something he wasn't getting, something important.

They walked for some time, with the lady refusing to slow or relax her grip, meaning Will struggled the entire way. The lady led him at a rapid pace, everything dark beyond the meager circle of light the torch in her hand created. They seemed to go up multiple staircases and through many long passages, but no matter how long they walked, it didn't get any brighter. Were there no windows? Was it night? But then he'd be able to see the stars...right?

Then again...after all the weird things that had happened while the Dragon Kin had been around, maybe...the world was dark only to his eyes. His captor seemed to know where she was going well enough, after all. Was it even possible to pull that kind of magic out? River had never talked about anything like it, and it would've been helpful in some of their situations.

Eventually, they came to a massive set of double doors and the lady's torch went out. Abruptly, the doors opened. Bright, searing sunlight slapped Will across the face, so intense it made his eyes burn and water. Even still, like her eyes worked fine, the lady dragged him forward, apparently determined to make him flounder no matter what. Their footsteps echoed throughout the space, and a stale, musty scent hung in the air like the room hadn't been aired out in some time.

The woman shook him as they stopped, making his shoulder burn. "I'd be on my best behavior if I were you. Father doesn't take kindly to your ilk."

"That's not my fault." Will managed to open his eyes enough to glare at her. "I didn't ask to come here, so if you hate me that much, just let me go home."

Snorting, almost in derision but not quite, she shoved him forward. "Here's the one you wanted, Father."

Will scrambled to keep from falling, catching himself on the short staircase that led up to some kind of dais. His eyes still struggled to adapt, so he couldn't see much past his feet.

There came a chuckle from somewhere in front of him.

Fighting through the pain, Will managed to lift his head. His blood went cold.

Two thrones stood before him, one broken and gathering dust while the other stood intact with a man lounging in it. Snow white skin and hair, but the eeriest and most unforgettable blue eyes he'd ever seen. He'd seen them once before when Osiris had used Tehl to threaten and terrify Her Highness. At the time, he'd thought her reaction had been a bit extreme but justified from someone who'd been so sheltered and tormented.

However, now that he was sprawled at the guy's feet, he knew her reaction had been no overreaction. Something about this man—Will didn't know what—made fear like he'd never felt dig deep into his bones.

That made him angry.

"Oh, I believe you have selected a most worthy candidate, Tehl. He has got a wonderful meanness in those eyes, does he not?"

Tehl himself stepped out from behind Osiris's throne, looking far too pleased for Will's liking. "Thank you. And it's not like you doubted me, of all people. Right?"

What the crap had happened to Will that he'd been dragged all the way to the Imperial Palace? And why?!

"It is so pleasant to be able to put a face to the name. Will. It takes a strong character to live up to such a name, you know."

Terror cinched even tighter in his chest; Will was pretty sure he wasn't breathing. He wanted to go home. He didn't have a clue what was going on, but he wanted to get out of here right now.

"It is regrettable to say so, but your going home is out of the question." Osiris grinned, the expression making Will feel smaller than an ant. "Regardless, glaring at your generous host with your mouth gaping open is quite boorish."

Will snapped his mouth shut, which hadn't even been open that far. For a second, the fear's grip on him lessened, anger taking its place. There was no way Osiris would let him go like he had with the princess, which meant—

"So you were with Redrinna after all? I had suspected as much, but I confess I was unsure."

Will stopped, that fear coming back against his will. He hadn't said that out loud.

Tehl doubled over with laughter, clutching his ribs. "That's a face!"

The woman to the side of him snorted again. "Stupid kid. If you don't want him to read your thoughts, stop thinking them."

Will's heart stopped. Her Highness hadn't mentioned anything about Osiris being able to read minds.

"Yes, magnificent, is it not?" Osiris said, lifting a hand. His freakishly pale skin caught the light streaming through the windows, almost making his skin glow. But it was a cold glow, like stone or metal.

Will fought hard, trying his absolute best to stop thinking, but he was unable to keep the flood of thoughts gushing through his mind quiet. Dozens of images—his friends, possibilities of escape, the things he needed to do, the things he still wanted to do—flashed through his head. He didn't want to die. Not here. Not like this.

"Oh, I do not plan on killing you. Not intentionally, at any rate.

On the contrary, I believe you are in for a pleasant surprise: I have need of you. You should be honored."

Will vehemently shook his head. "I don't want to die, but I will before I get mixed up with scum like you."

"Wow. Rude," Tehl said, flicking a strand of hair off his shoulder.

"Quite," Osiris said curtly. "Reyna?"

The woman who'd dragged Will here moved forward.

Will sensed malevolent intent and scrambled to get out of her reach, but in a second, she was behind him. She grabbed his arm—his left, he had time to think—and twisted it behind his back. A bone—maybe two—snapped, fiery pain searing through his arm and shoulder. Reyna did not release him, the pain and the angle bending him double. Will wanted to scream but he couldn't breathe.

"Mind your manners, boy," Osiris said, a hiss in his voice. "Or I will make you suffer far worse before we are finished."

Will puked in response, the pain well beyond the point he could bear. He couldn't breathe; he couldn't process a thought. Rage built in his chest like water piling behind a dam. For a second, he had just enough clarity of thought and strength to look up, glaring at Osiris with all the anger and hate he could muster.

To his horror, Osiris *laughed.*

"Release him," the man said.

Reyna obeyed.

Will crumpled, the pain not lessening at all.

"Now then. I am actively recruiting, and Tehl chose you. After this little display of yours, I find that I am in complete agreement."

"I won't!" Will spat, managing to push himself onto his knees and one hand. "You can't make me."

Osiris's grin widened like a cat's. "Oh, you have greatly misunderstood; I am not giving you the luxury of *choice.* Your friends have joined the Dragon Kin, have they not?"

No. Will thought that with all the energy he had.

"I commend your effort, but your mind betrayed you long ago."

All at once, the man pushed himself to his feet, slowly but surely standing upright.

Will's heart stuttered, the fear being consumed and leaving nothing but despair—a feeling he detested—in its wake. Her Highness had said Osiris lacked the strength to stand, but that was no longer the case. He really was about to die here.

Stepping carefully, Osiris made his way down the stairs, speaking as he went. "They have, which means they are my enemies, and all my enemies will suffer before they meet their ends. However, Her Highness seems to have acquired a soft spot for you. But...you have softened in regard to her as well."

As Osiris came closer, Will drew back. Reyna stopped him with a foot on his back, the hard sole of her boot slamming against his spine.

"She and I are playing a game, you see. She made her move; a good one, if I am honest. So, it is time for me to make one of my own." Osiris stopped in front of him, so close, Will's breath stirred the ends of his robes. "Redrinna owes me reparations for her repeated insults. Your friends...River, Thala, and Leonora, I believe?"

"That's right," Tehl said.

Osiris crouched, staying remarkably balanced. He grabbed Will's chin, hard, bitingly cold fingers digging into his jaw as he forced Will to meet the unrelenting gaze of those blue eyes.

Will just about puked again, but this time out of sheer terror.

"Now they owe me as well. And while Tak does not hold you in high esteem, seeing you like this would still hurt him. But most especially, do you know how much it would pain Redrinna to know this happened to you?"

Ice clogged Will's veins, his mind spinning. This wasn't even about him—it was about the Dragon Kin. This twisted, disgusting psycho—he emphasized that, since the man was undoubtedly listening—was going to use him to hurt them?!

Yanking his chin out of the man's grasp, he chomped down on his hand with all the strength he had. Osiris's smile vanished. The next second, he struck Will upside the head, hard enough to knock him to the ground, stars dancing in front of his eyes.

When Will's vision stopped spinning, Osiris stood over him, staring down at him with a cold, impassive expression.

Will glared at him. If this was how he was going to die, he wasn't going to just roll over. "I won't do it. I won't hurt them, no matter what you do to me. I'll do everything I can to stop you. Just watch."

A low, menacing laugh slithered out of the man. "I will not be the one who hurts them. That will be you."

Burning cold shadows hit Will's chest, forcing him onto his back and pinning him to the ground. His entire body abruptly went weak. Was he dying already? That was lame. His arm flared in pure agony, but because of everything else going on, he couldn't really feel it. Whatever was wrong with it, he knew it was bad. His gaze flicked to it almost compulsively. A flash of white bone. He looked away. Better not to know how bad it was if this was it. It would be easier to die if he didn't know how seriously he was hurt.

Osiris crouched over him once more, staring down his nose at him in a way that made his anger rear its head. "Do not ever, *ever,* threaten me again. Do I make myself clear?"

Will glared in response. He'd threaten Osiris until the second he took his final breath.

"Your stubbornness might be the only thing that saves you." Osiris raised a hand. For a second, it was normal, but then it pulsed with a disturbing red light that concentrated in his fingertips.

Will didn't even have the strength to squirm.

"Let's see how strong you really are, boy."

Don't miss the next book...

STORM

Book Four in the Rise of the Empress Series

Coming Soon

Thanks for Reading!

No, seriously. I mean that!

If you enjoyed this book, then I have a tiny request for you (I promise it's small. It'll take maybe five minutes of your time). You may not be able to tell, but I am an indie author (indie stands for independent). That means I published this book alone, without the help of a publishing house and the team that would go with that. I spent the money from my own pocket in order to put this book in your hands.

Since I chose not to enlist the services of a publishing house (there are several reasons why), then I need your help to keep making books like this one. How? Please, if you liked this book, leave a review! That's it. You don't even have to be on social media or anything like that, nor do you have to think of something to say. Even just giving it a star rating helps too! Please leave it wherever you bought it, or on Goodreads, if you're familiar with that. And if you liked it, just tell people about it. That helps me so much.

And, of course, if you liked it enough, buying the next book helps too.

Once again, thank you! Enjoy some artwork as a treat.

LY Doruga

Acknowledgements

Every book takes a village to make, and once again, I'm deeply grateful for everyone who helped to bring *Ignite* into the world. The first big round of thanks goes to all my family and friends who're so supportive of me on this author journey. The next bit goes to my beta readers, Rachel and Shaylee, both of whom were essential in helping shape this book. I'm also grateful for my proofreader, Janae, who always manages to catch the typos I never seem to be able to see.

The next person who greatly deserves thanks and a round of applause is, as always, the incomparable Lexi for once again gracing this book with her talents. She always manages to take my half-baked ideas and turn them into true works of art that make me smile every time I see them. Thanks also goes to FontMonkey for the use of the Belligerent Madness font.

I would, of course, be remiss if I didn't mention my deep gratitude for God and His encouragement that helps me to forge ahead on a difficult career path. There's no other way to say it: I simply could not do this without Him.

And lastly, but certainly not least, my thanks to all my readers, whose love and support keeps me coming back and writing. This book never would've come into being without all of you.

About the Author

C. S. Doraga is the author of the *Rise of the Empress* series. She grew up in the shadows of the Rocky Mountains with her nose stuck in any book within reach and imagination constantly running wild (to her parents' chagrin, at times). Her favorite author is the amazing Mangaka, Hiromu Arakawa, the author of *Fullmetal Alchemist* and *Silver Spoon*. What little free time she has, she spends playing the *Fire Emblem* video game series and a few, choice others. She has a deep love for the fantastic but also loves mystery and those characters that sit with you long after the story is over.

She has a bachelor's degree in creative writing from Weber State University and lives in beautiful Northern Utah with her family and two, crazy cats.

Join C.S. Doraga's newsletter for all the latest news, writing updates, and the interlogues (special, in-between stories)! Just go to her facebook page (C. S. Doraga) or her Instagram page (@bookdragons.nest) to sign up!